THE
BEACON

For Miriam

THE
BEACON
P. A. THOMAS

echo

PUBLISHING

echo
PUBLISHING

An imprint of Bonnier Books UK
Level 45, World Square,
680 George Street
Sydney NSW 2000
www.echopublishing.com.au

Bonnier Books UK
4th Floor, Victoria House,
Bloomsbury Square
London WC1B 4DA
www.bonnierbooks.co.uk

Echo Publishing acknowledges the traditional custodians of Country
throughout Australia. We recognise their continuing connection to land,
sea and waters. We pay our respects to Elders past and present.

This is a work of fiction. Names, characters, businesses, places, events,
locales and incidents are either the products of the author's imagination
or used in a fictitious manner. Any resemblance to actual persons,
living or dead, or actual events is purely coincidental.

First published 2024

Printed and bound in Australia by Griffin Press

The paper this book is printed on is certified against
the Forest Stewardship Council® Standards.
Griffin Press holds FSC® chain of custody certification
SGS-COC-001185. FSC® promotes environmentally
responsible, socially beneficial and economically viable
management of the world's forests.

FSC
MIX
Paper | Supporting responsible forestry
FSC® C018684
www.fsc.org

Page design and typesetting: Shaun Jury
Editor: Lauren Finger
Cover design: Lisa White
Cover image: Lighthouse at sunset, by Mauro Grigollo/Stocksy

NATIONAL
LIBRARY
OF AUSTRALIA

A catalogue entry for this book is available from the
National Library of Australia

ISBN: 9781760688622 (paperback)
ISBN: 9781760688639 (ebook)

echo_publishing
echopublishingaustralia
echopublishing

About the Author

P. A. Thomas studied medicine in Newcastle, New South Wales, undertook specialist training in nuclear medicine at the Mayo Clinic in the USA, and now works as a specialist at a public hospital in Brisbane. He is also a wilderness landscape photographer: he has had many joint and solo exhibitions, and his images have appeared in *Australian Geographic* publications. He lives in the Byron Bay region, the setting for his first novel, *The Beacon*.

Chapter One
Monday, 4th November 2019

Patrick O'Shaughnessy killed the lights and let his eyes adjust to the inky darkness. The moon had already dipped below the horizon. He climbed out of the car, stared up into the black void and waited. And there it was, high over his head, the beam of the lighthouse sweeping silently through the darkness. And then again, fifteen seconds later, unwavering, as it had done every night for more than a hundred years. It was Byron Bay's beating pulse and Patrick felt that as long as that beacon shone, everything would ultimately be right in the world.

He was always the first surfer here, preferring to be in the sea alone, his only company the lapping water and the pinpricks of a million stars overhead as he eagerly awaited that first precious glimmer of light marking the new day, and its promise of renewal. Some people said he was crazy for paddling out when it was so dark, which was surprising. After all, this was Byron Bay, where normal was abnormal, and strange and eccentric often went unnoticed.

This morning the breaking waves sounded subdued, so he slid out the mal, a board he'd had for such a long time it was almost an extension of his body. His routine was so familiar it was automatic, and yet today he struggled into his wetsuit, an unusual stiffness straining at his muscles.

Something metallic clattered to the ground on the other side of the carpark, an unnatural sound disrupting the tranquillity. Patrick was surprised, and then irritated, to make out the dim shape of a van. The park ranger must have skipped his rounds last night – it was only his banging on doors all hours of the night that prevented the carpark filling up with illegal campers; vans of backpackers keenly embracing the prospect of both a free campsite and waking up beside such a glorious beach.

But Patrick's irritation was soon replaced by pleasurable anticipation as he ran along the forest path and out onto the beach. At the water's edge he stooped and fastened the leg-rope firmly to his ankle. Today there would be few waves to catch, but that wasn't the point. He watched the great beam from the lighthouse trace lap after lap then, breaking the trance, launched himself into the water and began the strong rhythmic strokes that would carry him far out into the deep, beyond the rocks and beyond the reach of the waves crashing along the cliffs of the cape.

When he reached the take-off zone, he sat upright and savoured the smell of the salt, the bobbing of the waves, and the refreshing caress of the water. For Patrick, this was euphoric and addictive, and yet he knew surfers who were afraid this early in the morning, afraid to sit astride their boards with their legs dangling in the deep, their gaze unable to penetrate the black void below. There were sharks near here, many sharks. A few years earlier, a tourist was snatched as he swam across the bay. Newspapers, including Patrick's own, feasted on such shark attacks, but he knew the odds were minuscule. Besides, he felt safer here in the water, even with the sharks, than he did on dry land, where lately he found himself having to fight the constant urge to look over his shoulder.

The first glimmer of daylight approached over the north-eastern horizon and the water beneath him began to take form. The tension in his muscles started to ease, and a soothing sense of joy began washing through him. With enough moments like these, he knew he would find sufficient strength to cope with the difficulties looming before him. He closed his eyes and breathed deeply, trying to clear his mind. Less than a week to go.

A sudden splash disturbed him. His eyes shot open. A ripple was spreading through the water nearby. Something arced through his peripheral vision, perhaps a fin, but by the time he jerked his head around, it was gone. When he felt his heart pounding wildly in his chest, he laughed out loud at his foolishness. Too much thinking about sharks. It was a dolphin, he was sure.

He lay down on the board, closed his eyes again, and began to relax, his mind drifting to his daughter, Caitlin. Today was her birthday and he smiled – he was so looking forward to seeing her.

Then pain smashed into his brain. Unimaginable agony. His leg. His left leg. Below the knee. Before he knew what had happened, Patrick was yanked off his board into the water. Adrenaline surged. His heart thumped. Shark. His leg was being dragged down to the depths, pulling him with it. He gripped his board hard, trying to hang on. Thoughts of his darling Caitlin broke through the agony that was consuming his consciousness – there was no way he was leaving her. He gathered all his strength, wrenched his leg upwards and felt something give, but the overwhelming pain was beyond bearing and Patrick slid helplessly into the cold, dark depths.

Chapter Two

Jack Harris's ascent from sleep was a slow one. Whenever he teetered on the verge of waking, a wispy tendril of thought drifted into his awareness with a stern advisory to stay asleep. That and a throbbing pain somewhere, trying to attract his attention. Where was it? In his head. And what was that horrible pounding? No, better to descend back to the comfort of his oblivion, buried under a warm doona.

Throb, throb, throb.

Pound, pound, pound.

Throb, throb, throb.

The throbbing was in his head. The pounding in his ears.

Pound, pound, pound, pound, pound. Faster and more insistent now.

'Mr Harris, are you all right in there?'

Jack forced his eyes open. The first thing he noticed was that the room was still. He had a vague recollection it wasn't so still last night when he was helped to bed. And then he saw the ceiling, big enough to play tennis on. And those walls meeting the ceiling in perfect straight lines that ran on forever, the kind of thing minimalist architects wet themselves over.

Jack lifted his head, and the room started spinning again. In front of him was a wall of glass, presumably with a view, but all he could see was hostile sunlight frying his retinas as it reflected off shimmering water and white walls. White everything. No cornices. Fuck. He remembered. He was in his father's house. He sat bolt upright.

Jack was possibly the only person who disliked this house, as he considered it a bricks-and-mortar extension of his father's enormous ego. Everyone else thought the house was extraordinary – a mid-century modern, Palm Springs style mansion surrounded by rainforest, and with sweeping views of the coast extending all the way to Cape Byron Lighthouse in the distance. Walls of glass looked out on an azure swimming pool. To be complete, the scene only needed some celebrity photographer like Slim Aarons snapping scantily clad, big-haired models lazing beside a pool they would never jump into. Indeed, being here was like living inside a work of art – but it was the last place Jack wanted to be. Still, there was one consolation for being in his father's house – it was highly unlikely his father would also be in it.

Someone called again from beyond the closed door, presumably the same sadist who kept pounding so loudly on it. 'Mr Harris, are you okay?'

It was Don Hargreaves, the resident manager of the house.

'No,' said Jack.

He heard quiet laughter.

'You're late. Very late. Breakfast is served.'

At the mention of food, another wave of nausea crashed over him. Oh God. Jack threw off the covers and scrambled frantically over the bed towards the bathroom. Fuck, this bed was big. And what was the point of having an en suite if it was twenty metres away? The contents of his stomach at least reached the en-suite door even if, at the time of eruption, Jack had only made it halfway there. The accompanying groan reverberated around the walls and floor. What was Don doing last night, plying him with so much whisky? And from Jack's father's hidden stash of museum single malts, whisky so good it wasn't taking no for an answer?

He sagged to the floor and placed his cheek on the cool polished concrete. He'd never liked it. Hard. Cold. Industrial. At least he'd now found the one reason to recommend it – it was going to be easy to clean up.

Thirty minutes later, Jack eased himself downstairs and into the kitchen, cradling his head in one hand to keep it still as he moved. Don was watching him, and failing to suppress a wry smile. He hardly seemed to have aged – his sixtieth birthday had long gone and yet his hair was still naturally black, he'd barely a wrinkle and he stood with that same upright, ex-military bearing.

Jack slumped onto a stool at the kitchen bench.

'Big night, Mr Harris?'

Jack grunted. 'I blame you.'

Don seemed to be enjoying Jack's discomfort a little too much. 'You'd do better blaming the whisky, Mr Harris. Now you know why I keep those under lock and key.' He slid a plate towards him, covered with a polished-silver dome. 'Bacon, eggs, three sausages, onion – just the way you used to like it.'

Jack's nausea was back again – even more insistent now. There was no way he was going to lift that lid.

'Don, what did you call me when I was three years old?'

'Jack.'

'So lose the "Mr Harris" thing. I'm not my father.'

'If you say so, Jack. Should I send someone up with the mop?'

'I've taken care of it.'

How could Don have known? Then again, an ant wouldn't find its way into this house without Don knowing about it and, even then, it would have to apply in advance for permission.

Jack looked around the kitchen, re-familiarising himself. 'It's been a long time since I've slept in this house,' he said.

'Yes, I'm sorry you couldn't use the old house. There are some guests staying.'

Jack had spent the first ten years of his life in the old house down the bottom of the hill, closer to the beach. When his father's empire started to grow, the new trophy house was built on the hill. It looked spectacular in glossy magazine spreads, and cleaned up all the architecture awards, but Jack still considered the old house home – with its wrap-around verandas, breezeways, timber floors, and windows that actually opened to allow in the cooling sea breezes. His old bedroom door still had the marks where his height had been pencilled on each of his birthdays, and his tiny footprints could be seen in the concrete floor of the old garden shed, alongside the date those tiny impressions were made. After his parents separated, his mother moved back into the old house, taking a delighted Jack with her. Later, much later, Jack would return to spend the last few months with his mother as she faded away.

Don was saying something. 'So, first day in the new job? What time were you supposed to be there?'

Jack checked his watch. 'Oh, shit. An hour ago. Is there a car I can borrow?'

'Of course, Jack. I'll fetch the keys.' Don tapped the silver plate cover with his fingernail and it resonated with a hum that faded slowly. 'I put a lot of effort into that breakfast, don't waste it.'

Jack had never known Don to cook anything. 'Is Sophie still

here?' She had been the chef and housekeeper since Jack had been a boy.

'Her mum's not well. She'll be back next week.'

After Don left, Jack took a deep breath and wrinkled his nose in anticipation before lifting the plate cover. No nauseating eggs, just a tumbler of iced water and a blister pack of paracetamol. Don had nailed it, as always.

A few minutes later, as they both walked across the crushed white quartzite towards the garage, Jack noticed a massive new building among the trees five hundred metres further along the ridge. 'What's that?'

'Another of the movie stars.' Don rolled his eyes. 'Tiffani Swanson's place.'

'It's the size of a shopping centre,' said Jack.

'Your father is furious. Says he came here for peace and quiet. Her chopper almost collided with his on the first day she moved in.'

The garage door slid up silently and revealed one car sitting in a garage large enough to hold a dozen or more.

'Oh, you can't be serious,' said Jack. 'I'm not driving that in Byron Bay.'

Not only was the car a Ferrari, it was a shouty red Ferrari. His father had cars like this scattered around his various houses, most gathering dust. The car looked lonely, staring back at him, pleading with him to take it – like a dog wanting to go for a walk.

'Actually,' said Don, 'you're probably still over the limit. Tony can take you. Can't have you arrested on day one.'

'Does Tony still work here?'

Don didn't elaborate, offering just a brief nod before setting off towards the house.

Jack, on the other hand, couldn't help but smile at the mention of Tony. The lanky Italian had been part of the household, in charge of maintenance, since the big house was finished. He could fix anything and, as a child, Jack had become inseparable from him. Tony had adopted an eager Jack as a mini-apprentice and, from then on, whenever Tony was covered in paint or grease, Jack was also spattered from head to toe. Once, when a sewer pipe blocked during a wild New Year's Eve party, they'd both been liberally decorated with shit. And it wasn't just any shit they'd shared; it had been the Prime Minister perched on the bog when it all backed up.

Tony's car drove up a few minutes later, and Jack couldn't believe it was the same old seventies Holden Kingswood. And still the same outrageous purple.

The driver's door flung open, and Tony jumped out, beaming. He gave Jack an effusive handshake and then, overcoming his embarrassment, a big hug. 'Jack, welcome back.'

The car might still have been in showroom condition, but Tony had packed on a little weight, and that wasn't white paint in his hair. The glint in his eye was still there though, and the perennial smile.

'Tony, you've still got Millie.'

'Sure do. I'm going to be buried in her, sitting in the driver's seat, with Nick Cave and the Bad Seeds playing on the stereo.'

Inside, the car looked and smelled just as Jack remembered, even the furry dice still dangled from the mirror. Tony started the engine and drove down the curving driveway, the V8 engine burbling. Like he'd done hundreds of times before, Jack pressed the play button on the cassette, not expecting anything to happen after all these years, but Hoodoo Gurus' 'What's My Scene' began blasting from the speakers.

Tony smiled at him. 'I hear you have a new job. I hope that means you'll be here for a while.'

'Only if they don't fire my arse for being late on my first day.'

Chapter Three

Jack was irritated, his hangover still goading him. How hard could it be to find a door in Byron Bay? Tony had dropped him a hundred metres away and gestured vaguely in the direction he needed to go. For a town too small for traffic lights, driving could be diabolical, and today the cars were almost at a standstill. Tony had rightly pointed out it was faster to walk.

Since Jack was last here, *The Beacon*'s office had relocated to Jonson Street. According to his phone, he had arrived, but all he could see was a very dodgy-looking kebab shop, and food was the last thing he wanted to think about.

He forced himself to take some deep breaths. What the hell was he doing here? A week ago, he'd been in Melbourne helping his father, Malcolm Harris, run his business conglomerate from the fifty-seventh-floor boardroom. The Harris interests were diverse: freight, hotels, agricultural machinery and windfarms. Jack's stepbrother ran most of the subsidiaries but it was Jack who was in charge of the crown jewel, Harris Media, with its newspaper and television empire stretching from coast to coast. That all ended five days ago when Jack's father had called him into his office and told him he was being stood down as executive director of the Harris board. Instead, Jack was being sent to learn the business, and journalism, from the ground up as the lowest-ranking hack in a regional newspaper,

The Beacon. Jack had been caught by surprise. Had he done something wrong?

Malcolm Harris was a man to be obeyed. Always. A man who demanded total family loyalty. So, Jack had joined his father's business straight after graduating from university and now, at the age of thirty-five, still worked there. Just. Jack was getting very close to telling his father to shove it, but, so far, his courage had failed him. Which meant he had to keep to himself his troubling thoughts about the unethical and unconscionable behaviour of some of Harris Media's newspapers and TV channels, behaviour which was probably encouraged by his father. The best Jack had been able to manage was making a few noises about Harris Media having a social contract with its readers to do the right thing. Noises his father ignored.

Jack had always had a love–hate relationship with his father, but more recently it seemed the needle was moving towards the latter. Maybe some time in Byron Bay would be a good thing. Indeed, the more Jack dwelled on it, and as his anger subsided, the more he realised it actually wasn't such a foolish idea. *The Beacon* was his father's first newspaper, where he'd taught himself journalism. And where the fledgling Harris Media exploded out of the blocks in the race to become one of the country's most dominant and influential media companies. Besides, Jack grew up in Byron Bay. There were beaches and bars. How bad could it be? As long as it was short term. And his father left him alone, which was doubtful.

And so, here he was, in Byron, unable to even find the office on his first day. His phone continued to insist he'd arrived at *The Beacon.* Perhaps he'd walked past it. He turned and took a step just as a someone on a skateboard shot out from a narrow alleyway behind the kebab shop. Jack fleetingly registered denim shorts, a green tank top and a large shoulder tattoo before she collided with him and they both tumbled heavily to the footpath.

Jack lay there for a few seconds in shock. Gravel rash stung the palms of his hands. A graze on his left elbow complained loudly, but not as insistently as his ribs, which had collided with something hard. He tentatively climbed to his feet. The skateboarder was brushing away gravel from her hands and knees. She was only a few years younger than Jack. His eyes would have held her furious gaze if they hadn't been drawn to her freckles. Hundreds of them – there were more freckles than face. And impressive ginger dreadlocks. Jack stretched out a hand to help her up.

'Don't fucking touch me. And, next time, watch where you're walking.' She jumped up, righted the skateboard, and she and her Betty Boop tattoo vanished into the crowd.

Jack tried his luck down the newly discovered alley, and there it was. A door. The door. White lettering on frosted glass announced: *The Beacon. Serving our community for 40 years. Office hours: 9–5 M–F.* Underneath, a yellow Post-it note added: *Back in 5 minutes.*

Jack leaned against the rear door of the kebab shop to wait, but the strong aromas threatened to rekindle his nausea and he was forced to move more upwind of the sea breeze. A stream of ripped and tanned people walked past him wearing nothing on their feet, next to nothing on their torsos and speaking anything but English. A boy ambled past with a large carpet python coiled around his arm, attracting no attention from those nearby.

Ten minutes later, Betty Boop was back, balancing a takeaway cup of coffee as she skated along the alleyway. Jack hadn't notice before how small she was and when she dismounted her skateboard outside *The Beacon,* she lost a further four inches of height. She was tiny. She removed a key from her pocket and inserted it in the door.

Jack ran to catch her before she disappeared inside. 'Hi.'

She spun around in surprise at the sound behind her, and coffee splashed down her front as the cup fell to the ground. She looked warily at Jack. 'What do you want?'

There was no time to answer.

'Shit.' She scrabbled at the front of her top, pulling it away from her skin as the scalding coffee soaked into the material. 'You scared the life out of me.' Green eyes blazed at Jack.

'I'm sorry,' said Jack. 'I didn't mean to frighten you. I've been waiting for *The Beacon* to open. Do you work here?'

The reply was vehement. 'No.'

'But you have a key?' When she didn't respond, he said, 'I'm looking for Patrick O'Shaughnessy.'

'Well don't think you're special. The phone hasn't stopped ringing all morning, everyone wants him. And today, of all days, he decides not to turn up.'

'Where is he?'

'Who the fuck knows?'

'What's so special about today?'

'Nothing.' Then, when Jack didn't say anything, she conceded. 'It's my birthday.'

Jack smiled. 'Happy birthday.'

She said nothing.

'Have you any idea where he is?'

'Really? If you are just going to stand there parroting the same question over and over, I'm done. No, I don't know where he is and, no, he is not answering his mobile.' She stomped on the back of her skateboard, grabbed its nose, and turned towards the door.

'I'm supposed to be starting a new job here today,' said Jack.

She stopped in the doorway with her back to him and said, 'What job? There is no job.'

'I'm supposed to be working with Patrick.'

She still hadn't moved from the doorway. A phone started ringing inside the office.

Jack asked, 'Perhaps we could go and replace your coffee?'

She still didn't move.

'Or, then again, you could just tell me to piss off and you could go back in there and listen to the phone ringing all day.'

In a way, Jack hoped she would tell him to piss off. With her foul mood and his hangover refusing to budge, he was already regretting the invitation.

Chapter Four

Caitlin was annoyed with herself for accepting the offer of coffee. Especially from some jerk who had just scared the bejesus out of her, twice. And why had he lied about starting a job at *The Beacon*? She was seriously contemplating walking away when a waitress appeared and corralled them to a table.

As soon as they'd both ordered, she studied him. He was starting to look vaguely familiar. When he examined his palms, Caitlin could see dirt in the red grazes. She'd certainly done a number on him.

He stood up. 'Would you mind if I just quickly wash my hands?' He went up to the counter and, after speaking with a waitress, headed in the direction she pointed.

Almost every pair of eyes in the café was glued to him as he walked. Jesus, he must be close on six feet five. Caitlin couldn't imagine what it would be like to be that tall. People gawked at her because she was so short. Or maybe it was her red dreads.

She watched him closely when he returned to the table. He'd lost his usual beard but, up close, she was pretty sure it was him. Nobody else in the café seemed to recognise him – he was renowned for being very private, with no presence on social media, but she remembered seeing some photos that had found their way into a magazine. The short-cropped blond hair looked the same, and the hazel eyes. She had to admit he was even hotter in real life – if his nose didn't have that big bump he might have been cast as Thor.

He smiled at her.

Huh, you can smile all you like, she thought. Other women might melt on the spot when one of Australia's most eligible bachelors smiled at them, but there was no way she was letting the poncy prick get through her well-honed defences.

'Do you have a name?' he asked.

'Yes. Several. In fact, five.'

'Five?'

'I may be short, but I have a long name. Siobhán Caitlin Clodagh Maeve O'Shaughnessy. Five names no Australian can spell. Clodagh came from my mother and my grandmothers were Siobhán and Maeve. No idea where Caitlin came from, but it's my favourite, so I've always gone by that.'

She stopped herself. Jesus. She must have delivered that answer a million times, but what was she doing giving such personal information to this prick?

He said, 'O'Shaughnessy. You're Patrick's daughter?'

She nodded. 'So, five names, which makes you look pretty pathetic with a measly three.'

'Three?'

'Yes, three.' He gave nothing away, so she continued. 'I'm good with faces.'

'But we've never met.'

Caitlin stared at him. Either he was being a dick, or he seriously thought she wouldn't recognise him without the beard. Probably he was just being a dick.

She said, 'I don't play games, so don't give me any more

bullshit about being here for a job that doesn't exist. What are you really doing here, Jack William Harris? That's William after your grandfather, of course, and Jack presumably was a drunken stab in the baby-name book when it fell open at "J".'

His smile faded.

'Are you here to close down *The Beacon*?' Caitlin asked. She watched him intently. She'd spent long enough in criminal courts to be a very good judge of when someone was lying.

His reply was emphatic. 'No.'

Jesus, she thought, he was good. 'I don't believe you.'

'My father would never close *The Beacon*.'

Although it had been nearly two months since she'd last been allowed to work, she felt as though she was back there, in court, interrogating a witness in the stand. 'Then why did Harris Media send a letter to my father two weeks ago stating his employment was to be terminated? Twenty years he's worked for the company, and you give him four weeks' notice.'

He looked genuinely surprised. 'Why would my father sack Patrick? I was sent here to work alongside him, to learn as much as I could about journalism, from one of our best.'

'You claim to have no knowledge of any such letter?'

'Correct.'

'I put it to you, Mr Harris, that you are lying.'

His lips had tightened into a firm slit, and furrows appeared on his brow for the first time.

Caitlin didn't care that she was riling him. 'Dad showed me the letter. It was signed by one Jack William Harris. Three names. Your names. You, Mr Harris, are full of shit.'

She rose to leave, but her way was blocked by their waitress bringing a large slice of pecan pie, topped with a burning candle.

The chef had written 'Happy Birthday' in berry coulis on the white porcelain plate. Another waiter arrived with their coffee.

Caitlin sank back into her chair, trapped, and torn. Why did the prick have to be nice when she was so pissed off at him? He was the first person to acknowledge her birthday – her own father hadn't even phoned. Her irritation retreated from the red zone to a slightly less volatile orange.

'Happy birthday,' said Jack.

She sat, fuming, watching the candle burn down before extinguishing it with a quick gust.

He said, 'I didn't write that letter. I don't know who sent it, or why.'

'Why would I believe you? Harris Media has closed pretty much every other regional paper it owns. Or flipped them to digital.'

'Because this was my father's first paper. It was his launchpad to a massive business empire. So, unless he sells out, *The Beacon* is likely to be the last newspaper still in print come the apocalypse.'

'Then why are you really here? Dad doesn't need you. With all due respect – no let me retract that – with no respect at all, you might be an executive director of a media company, but you have no qualifications or experience as a journalist. Perhaps you could make the tea?'

Jack didn't answer.

She persisted. 'Suit yourself, but Dad will tell me anyway.'

Jack looked around, then leaned forward, speaking quietly, 'I've been sent here by my father. I think I've upset him.'

'Derr, obviously.'

He grinned. 'It could be a lot worse than here. We still own *The Broken Hill Chronicle*.'

She suppressed a smile. 'And what about Dad? Does he still have his job? You're not sending him to some shit-hole in the desert?'

'Hell no. I need him here, because, as you so gleefully pointed out, I have no idea what I'm doing. Besides ...' He leaned forward and whispered, 'I'm a bit dyslexic. But don't tell anyone that.'

She laughed. 'A dyslexic wannabe journalist, this is going to be good. Dad will have you on toast.'

Caitlin reached for her water glass but bumped it off the table, sending it smashing to the floor. The shattered glass scattered everywhere. Shit. That was the second time this week. It was probably nothing, she thought – but her hands started shaking and she felt the pinprick of tears in her eyes. All heads had turned in their direction and she heard a titter of laughter.

'Are you okay?' asked Jack

'What?'

'Are you all right?'

Her response was curt. 'Fine.' She snatched at her phone and checked the messages. Nothing from her father. She apologised when the waitress materialised with a brush and pan.

Jack pointed to her untouched pie. 'Don't you want that?'

'No.' She folded her arms across her chest. 'I'm allergic to nuts.'

Jack commandeered her plate and helped himself. Between mouthfuls, he said, 'Is it unusual for your father not to answer his phone?'

'He's a journalist, what do you think?'

'Should we see if he's back at *The Beacon*? If he's not there, maybe we could call around to his house, just to check on him?'

She *was* becoming increasingly concerned about her father.

Where the hell was he? She needed a plan beyond repeatedly calling his mobile, and here was someone offering to help, someone who might have wheels bigger than her skateboard's. Someone being nice.

She hurriedly rose from the table. 'Let's go.'

Chapter Five

The lady looked to her left. All she could see of her first ever Tinder date was a black Greenpeace T-shirt, a pair of binoculars and a mouth constantly in motion spraying out facts about whales. Tedious facts. It was like being in a David Attenborough documentary, but worse, as it featured a whiny Australian narrator who had nothing interesting to say. At least she was out of the house.

Her daughter had encouraged her to sign up for Tinder, probably hoping it would stop her repeated phone calls on some flimsy pretence or other. And it was worth it to see the whales, who were providing all the entertainment as they migrated back towards the cold southern waters. Up here, on the brow of Cape Byron, the lighthouse usually grabbed most of the attention, the Instafamous backdrop to incessant selfies, but today all eyes faced the other direction, out to sea. Conditions were perfect for whale watching, the ocean a mirror of blue and not a wisp of wind to disperse the plumes as they shot skywards.

She knew Mr Tinder had been coming here for years with his folding chairs and his Thermos flask and the pastries from the quaint patisserie in Bangalow. She also knew there had been a succession of women sitting in this chair before her, but she was happy to play along. Whether he would end up with the sex he presumably wanted she wasn't sure, but she doubted it. She hadn't been intimate since her husband died almost five years ago. Would she even remember what to do?

Her attention returned to the monotonous soundtrack. '... you can tell them apart because the southern right whale has two plumes, whereas the—'

A whale exploded into view right in front of them, arcing out of the water in what seemed like slow motion. It was so close to shore she could see the barnacles stuck to its white belly. The whale twisted and crashed down on its back with a splash that sent water flying high into the air. The crowd gasped and pointed in unison. Even motormouth stopped talking.

She lifted the binoculars and tried to focus on where the whale had been. Another whale breached but she missed it entirely – the binoculars seemed to point anywhere but where she wanted to look. Instead, she saw something red floating in the water. She tried to find it with her naked eyes, but could see nothing other than the wash of the whales. She lifted the binoculars again, but it was just blue everywhere she looked. Did she imagine it?

She tapped Mr Tinder on the shoulder, but he didn't notice.

'Humpback whales can weigh up to thirty tonnes ...'

She tapped him again, harder. 'Could you just shut up for a minute? I saw something red floating near the whales. A surfboard, maybe.'

He trained his binoculars to where she pointed. 'There's nothing there. Binoculars can be tricky if you're not used to them. Did I tell you individual humpbacks can be recognised by the markings on their tails ...'

Exasperated, she fiddled with the binoculars again, and a red blob came into focus. It *was* a surfboard. 'There,' she said, pointing. 'It's just floating in the middle of nowhere. There's nobody on it.'

'So what?' he said. 'It's just a surfboard.'

A short time later she was striding down the road away from the lighthouse. She'd had her first and, as far as she was concerned, last argument with Mr Tinder. He didn't think it was worth reporting a drifting surfboard, but she had an uneasy feeling. Why would anybody leave their surfboard to float away? He did at least point out, albeit with bad grace, where she would find the Marine Rescue office. This Tinder thing was rubbish. His condoms would be remaining in their wrappers. And she'd tasted far better Portuguese tarts.

The office was easy to find once you knew where it was, tucked behind one of the old lighthouse keeper's cottages down the hill. The door was ajar, and she heard voices crackling from radios. Inside she saw a small desk on which rested a pair of callused feet in thongs. The feet were connected to a pair of knobbly knees and the knees to a heavily overweight man whose navy singlet was under serious tension as it stretched over his large belly. He and the chair looked to have been moulded in one piece.

The man saw her and took his feet off the desk. 'The toilets are around the back past the café, love.'

'It's you I want, I think, although perhaps I'm just being a worry wart.'

Moments later, Harry had grabbed his portable radios and was hobbling up the hill with his walking stick, trying to keep up with her as they headed towards the lighthouse.

When they arrived, Mr Tinder had packed away the catering and was obviously still sore from the argument. Harry scanned the water with his binoculars.

'Sorry,' said Mr Tinder to Harry. 'I'm sure you've more important things to do than to look for some lost surfboard.'

Harry put down his binoculars and sized up Mr Tinder. 'Next time you come off your surfboard I'll be sure to finish doing the crossword and scratching my arse before I look for you.' He resumed gazing through the binoculars. 'If I look for you at all.'

Mr Tinder, muttering something inaudible, packed up the chairs, collected the rest of his gear and walked off without saying goodbye. She didn't mind. It was a lovely day, and he was a dick. She should have swiped left. Or was it right?

'Oh, bloody hell,' said Harry when he spotted the board. 'There aren't many red mals like that. I think it might be Patrick O'Shaughnessy's. I'll give him a call.'

He made the phone call, but there was no answer. He took a few steps away from her and reached for his radio. 'Hey, this is Harry, could you send a couple of your fellas on jet skis to check something out for me?'

Chapter Six

Jack and Caitlin zigzagged among alfresco diners, past bustling surf shops, and trendy boutiques selling plain white T-shirts for hundreds of dollars. A young busker was playing 'Isn't She Lovely' on a baritone saxophone almost as tall as she was. Jack dropped five dollars into her case.

'How long have you lived in Byron?' he asked Caitlin.

'Are you always this nosey?'

'I'm practising being a journalist.'

'Well get used to being told to fuck off and mind your own business,' said Caitlin, without malice. 'I've been back about six weeks. But I grew up here.'

At *The Beacon*, she unlocked the front door and pushed her way inside. Jack followed her, then stopped abruptly. He'd spent his life in and out of newspaper offices big and small, but none had ever looked like this.

'What's up?' asked Caitlin.

'Where's all the shit?'

There was no lino, no cluttered pin boards, no teetering piles of coffee-stained paper, no overflowing waste bins. The walls weren't beige and there were no overstuffed gun-metal grey filing cabinets. Instead, sunlight poured in through a bank of high windows running the length of the room, casting warm light over white walls, timber floorboards, minimalist white desks and leather chairs. White bookcases lined one wall, their shelves holding folios of back issues, each in perfect alignment. A small kitchenette at the rear boasted a gleaming espresso machine. In the centre of the room, two cantilevered desks appeared to float, their impossibly thin writing surfaces devoid of pens, takeaway cartons and Post-it notes. Journalist chic was out and Scandi design was in. Perhaps Patrick was running an interior design consultancy on the side. There were even indoor plants.

Caitlin smiled at him. 'Dad likes uncluttered. It helps him think.'

'Two desks,' Jack said. 'Who else works here?'

'Margot the office manager, but she moved interstate a few weeks ago. All the freelancers work from home. There's nobody else. At least not officially, although I've been helping him out.' Jack saw some of the anger return to her eyes. 'He's really stressed at the moment. That letter from you, that you say wasn't from you, almost finished him off. He thinks he's going to lose his job in a few weeks. He's been trying to get your paper out during the day and working all night on some massive story he's rushing to publish before he finishes up.'

Jack could feel rising anger himself. Who would have written that letter and put Jack's signature on it? Did someone inside Harris Media really want Patrick fired?

Caitlin pulled out her phone and dialled, but there was still no answer. 'I want to go out to the house, see if he's there. It's at Ewingsdale.'

'Do you have wheels?'

Caitlin pointed to her skateboard. 'I don't drive.' She rifled through drawers behind the reception counter. 'The Beacon has a beaten-up old car, but the keys aren't here.'

'What sort of car?'

She shrugged her shoulders. 'A white one.'

'How old is it?'

'Seriously, do I look like a used-car dealer? Why don't you take a look?'

A cupboard stood at the end of the row of bookcases. Jack opened the door and found a couple of Patrick's sports coats hanging inside. This will be fun, thought Jack. He took one of the hangers and followed Caitlin outside.

The lane ended on a large carpark. Old bombs with fading paint stood side by side with colourfully resprayed Kombis, half-million-dollar Porsches, beaten-up utes and, most numerous of all, superannuated delivery vans reincarnated as campervans. One was disgorging enough backpackers to make up an entire football team.

Caitlin led the way to a tired-looking white Toyota. Perfect, thought Jack. He glanced around and, seeing they weren't being observed, bent the coat hanger into shape and inserted it between the window and the sill. It had been a long time since he'd felt this simultaneous frisson of fear and excitement. Within seconds he had the door open and was sliding into the driver's seat.

Caitlin was speechless.

'You'll find it easier to give me directions from inside the car,' he shouted, before his head disappeared under the steering wheel.

She hesitated, then walked around and stepped into the car. Before she'd even sat down, the engine was running.

'I'm a lawyer,' she said. 'Do you know what happens if I have a criminal record? And don't even think about saying I don't look like a lawyer, like every other misogynist prick.'

He looked at her, bemused, until a Mercedes pulled up

and repeatedly honked its horn, impatient for their park.

'You can't be charged with hot wiring your own car,' he said. 'Besides, nobody saw us.'

They drove for a few minutes in silence before she said, 'That was some trick for the director of a Top Five Hundred company.'

'Ex-director, as of last week. And I've done a lot worse.'

She raised an eyebrow.

'My father packed me off to a very exclusive boarding school when I was twelve years old. And by exclusive, I mean financially exclusive, not academically exclusive. It proved to be a big mistake for my father, but I loved it. My best friend at school was Ricky Martinelli.' He glanced at her and grinned, waiting for the usual response.

'Holy shit, not *the* Ricky Martinelli?'

'The very one.'

The Martinellis had been in and out of newspaper headlines for years, more recently occupying the obituary columns. The gangland wars in Melbourne had accounted for many of them. During a particularly violent string of reprisal killings, hardly a month seemed to go by without another Martinelli being shot in front of their family or found bleeding out in bullet-riddled Lamborghinis.

'Ricky and I had very wild childhoods. It was only our fathers that kept us out of the juvenile courts; my father because he knew secrets, Ricky's by straight out threatening people.'

'Do you still keep in touch?'

Jack looked across at her and smiled. 'Besties.'

The road wound through forest and over low hills with views to the distant range, but Jack had no time to admire it. He was too focused on avoiding the endless potholes threatening to destroy the car's suspension. One large pothole had even been incorporated into an artwork painted on the bitumen: a fisherman with his line cast into the hole.

Jack asked over the rattles, 'If you are a lawyer, who do you work for?'

Now Caitlin looked at him and smiled. 'Bernstein.'

'Oh shit . . .' Jack took his eyes off the road and stared at her in shock. The car collided with a large pothole and the sickening thud sounded like a wheel coming up through the floor.

Bernstein was the only one of the 'big five' law firms that Harris Media didn't have on retainer, and were the first choice for anyone wanting to take on Harris. And Bernstein were very good at it. They'd won a slew of high-profile cases, the most recent being that of an A-list English actress whose revealing photographs were lifted from her stolen laptop. Harris Media paid out millions. Bernstein was still running cases against Harris, including a big defamation case for a Queensland judge that Harris would probably lose.

'I can't be seen talking with you,' said Jack. He waited for a few metres of pothole-free tarmac and then stole another glance at her. 'Tell me you're in accounts, not really a lawyer.'

'Senior Associate in the Sydney office.' She seemed to be enjoying his discomfort. 'Corporate law, with a special interest in media.'

Jack forced his eyes to return to the road. 'Then I definitely can't be seen with you.'

She let him stew for a while before responding. 'Your coronary can wait. I'm not on the Clarkson case, and you seem to have forgotten you've had your sorry arse fired from head office. Anyway, nobody knows I'm a lawyer when I'm not in my power suit. Turn left at the top of the rise.'

Jack turned the car towards Ewingsdale. 'Are you any good? As a lawyer?'

'I'm five foot one. I'm a woman. I have dreadlocks. People underestimate me, which is a big mistake.'

'And does Betty Boop go to court?'

She laughed. 'Only under cover. And her hourly charge-out rate is higher than mine.'

A lightly forested area of eucalypts gave way to houses scattered on acreages. Caitlin pointed to a loose gravel drive.

'Turn in here.'

The car wheels spun, and rocks pummelled the underfloor. After a hundred metres, a large timber house with a wrap-around veranda came into view. It was situated on the top of a small rise with views over rolling hills to the rugged volcanic plugs jutting up among the mountains in the hinterland.

Caitlin jumped out of the car even before Jack had brought it to a stop, and she ran to the front door and knocked. Jack checked out the garage – there was no car inside. He walked around the back of the house and found a well-kept lawn stretching between grevilleas and other native trees planted around the boundary. Water lilies drifted on a small pond nestled among flowerbeds. A pair of squawking galahs flew down to a stone birdbath outside the back door.

When he returned to the front, Caitlin had her phone to her ear, but it went unanswered. She caught his eye. 'I want to go in, just in case something's happened and he's in there.'

'Wouldn't his car be here?'

'I just want to be sure.'

'Have you got a key?'

'Not the new one.'

'You're not staying with your father?'

She hesitated, and looked away. 'He thought it would be better if I stayed somewhere else this time.'

Jack waited for her to elaborate, but she didn't. He examined the lock on the front door and felt a tiny prickle of unease. This was no ordinary lock. It was an Abloy high-security lock with rotating discs, not pins. It required a special restricted key that couldn't be duplicated by your average locksmith. Definitely not the kind of lock normally found on the front door of a house, never mind one in the middle of nowhere.

Caitlin interrupted his thoughts. 'Don't tell me you not only hot wire cars, but you pick locks?'

'Normally, but not even Ricky Martinelli is opening that lock without the key.' Jack took a step back and looked again at the windows on the front of the house. 'Caitlin, why would your father have a high-security lock on his door, and stainless-steel security mesh on his windows?'

'He just upgraded everything. He's been worried about the story he's investigating.'

'It's *The Beacon*. The last headline was about a Mrs Buckley rustling her neighbour's chickens.'

'You made that up.'

'Yes, but you know what I mean.'

'Then perhaps it's to keep criminals like you out.'

Jack just shrugged.

She smiled at him. 'Well Mr I-can-break-into-anything, is that all you've got?'

He smiled back, accepting the challenge. He retrieved the tyre lever from the boot of the car then inserted it between the front door and the jamb. He shoved all his weight against it until the jamb gave with a loud cracking sound. A large chunk of wood fell off to reveal the timber was only decorative and covered a solid metal door frame. Jack's unease grew. He leaned the tyre lever against the wall. There was no way he was getting in through the front door. Or any of the windows. He couldn't remember the last time he'd been beaten. In frustration, he pushed the door handle. The door opened.

They looked at each other, sharing the same thought. Why spend all that money on security and then go out and leave the front door unlocked?

Caitlin rushed inside. 'Dad?'

Chapter Seven

Inspector Ken Begley wished he could araldite himself to his position as station commander of Byron Bay Police Station. He loved this job, the job loved him and he wanted to keep it that way. Byron was one of the best gigs a policeman could hope for, plus his police pension was only a year away and he and Veronica planned to retire right here, in paradise.

In the eight years he'd been head of the station, the crime rate had fallen by thirty-eight per cent, which meant those further up the food chain in Police HQ left him pretty much alone. What he'd never told HQ was that his predecessor was wrestling some serious demons. He'd liked people to obey the law – every law, at all times. The prisoner dock had to be full every night, even if it meant a late-night dash down to the main drag to hoover up half-pissed backpackers for jaywalking.

Begley took the opposite approach. He looked the other way, preferring a tolerant attitude to minor misdemeanours. What harm was there if the locals cycled on the wrong side of the road without helmets or lights after having had a skinful at the pub?

Thanks to his overzealous predecessor, and through minimal effort on his part, Begley looked good to cruise comfortably into retirement. But he couldn't completely drop his guard.

There was a disorderly queue of restless colleagues itching for his Byron gig, watching his every move, and Begley knew he was only one minor fuck-up away from being transferred back to some vomit-filled inner-city police station bulging with crackheads and gangland thugs. So, Begley spent much of his time trying to stay under the radar. It wasn't always easy; he had his own demons.

The shrill ring of the telephone on his desk interrupted his thoughts. 'Begley.'

'Ken, it's Harry up at Marine Rescue. We've found a surfboard floating offshore.'

'Harry, Harry, Harry. Why are you calling me? I've got staff for minor stuff like this; bored constables sitting on their spotty arses doing fuck-all. Some tourist probably forgot to put on his leg-rope and floaties. I'll put you through to Anderson.'

'Ken, I'm pretty sure it's Pat O'Shaughnessy's board.'

Begley was silent as it sank in. O'Shaughnessy. A bloody journalist. That's not good. The reporters will be knee-deep if it's one of their own missing. No room for fuck ups with this one. His radar switched on, loud and insistent. *Ping, ping, ping.*

'Ken, are you still there?'

'You've tried his phone?'

'Nothing.'

'Right, I'll send Sergeant Kowalski out to his house to see if he's there.' He ended the call and swivelled in his chair to look out the window. It was wall-to-wall blue sky. Being the station commander, and buried under bureaucracy, he rarely left his office, especially if an incident meant visiting some hellhole of a commune in the hills, or shutting down a doof-doof party in the forest. But, on a glorious day like today, and with the promise of lots of standing around staring at the ocean, Begley figured it was time for some hands-on policing. More importantly, if it really was Pat O'Shaughnessy's surfboard and the shit hit the fan, he needed to make sure the fan was pointing at someone else.

He phoned Sergeant Kowalski in the office next door and instructed him to drive out to Patrick O'Shaughnessy's house to see if there was any sign of the missing man. Begley then hollered Constable Anderson's name down the corridor and soon both men were walking out of the building towards the carpark. Begley climbed into one of the four-wheel drives and, just because he still got a buzz out of it after all these years, flicked on the siren and the flashing lights, and started the car.

Five minutes later, they reached the summit of Cape Byron. The National Parks ranger waved them through, and they drove up onto the wide, paved apron surrounding the lighthouse. Begley was first out of the car, breathing the salt air deep into his lungs. He loved this spot, with its views across the vast horseshoe-shaped bay to the mountain range beyond. He wondered whether he would see turtles rising to the surface for air then disappearing back into the depths. Or a pod of dolphins. He checked himself – today he wasn't here for the wildlife.

A white timber fence circled the clifftop. Begley found Harry leaning against it, his binoculars scanning the ocean. They shook hands.

'Well,' said Harry, 'if it's not the big cheese himself, finally out from behind the desk.'

'Have you found him?'

Harry shook his head.

'What are the chances?'

Harry shrugged.

Begley knew nobody was as familiar with these waters as Harry, and he didn't look confident.

Chapter Eight

Caitlin almost knocked Jack over as she rushed to get inside the house, calling out for her father as she went.

Jack could hear music inside, classical music he didn't recognise – King Gizzard & the Lizard Wizard was more his jam. He followed the sound into the lounge. The room was light and airy, with white sofas arranged to take in the panoramic view through the picture window to the mountains beyond. Large pen and ink drawings of birds hung from white VJ walls, and a radio sat on an Art Deco sideboard, kept company by a row of framed photographs. Jack studied them. Patrick with Cate Blanchett, drinks in hand, lost in conversation. Patrick and Steve Waugh arm in arm, their heads thrown back in laughter. Caitlin at her graduation, flanked by her proud mother and father. Patrick, in a wide-lapelled, white suit over a blue ruffled shirt, looking like the happiest man in the world, standing beside his beaming bride. Jack knew of Patrick's reputation for not only being a good journalist, but for being fun, and he was looking forward to meeting him.

Jack slid open one of the two drawers in the sideboard, revealing wooden chess pieces and a board. The other drawer held a small sheaf of papers. He picked them up. *The last will and testament of Patrick Liam O'Shaughnessy. Twenty-sixth October, 2019.* He frowned. That was only ten days ago.

He fanned the pages and stopped at a second document, a life insurance policy. Two weeks old. Jack felt even more uneasy. It seemed a strange place to leave such personal documents, unless he wanted to ensure they were found. Jack heard approaching footsteps, replaced the papers, and quietly closed the drawer.

Caitlin reappeared. 'He's not here.'

'What's with the music then?'

She looked puzzled. 'Elgar?'

'The radio is on, but nobody's home.'

'Oh, it's always on. Ever since Mum died. Mum loved music, and always had the radio on. So Dad leaves it on now. It's like her presence is still in the house. I like it.'

'How long has she been gone?'

Caitlin pointed at her graduation photograph. 'Eight years. That's the last photograph of her. She died two days later.'

Her mother looked perfectly healthy in the photograph, piquing Jack's curiosity, but now wasn't the time to ask how she died. Instead, he said, 'I'm sorry.'

She shrugged, but he could see the hurt she still felt in her eyes.

'Your father never remarried?' he asked.

Caitlin briefly looked confused. 'Oh, no. He still considers himself married. He and Mum were the ultimate fusion couple. They were never apart; it was as though there was an umbilical cord between them.'

Jack picked up another photograph, a more recent one of Patrick with his arm around a woman who looked vaguely familiar. 'Who's this?'

'Zoe Lonergan. They're friends, not partners. He spends a lot of time with her.'

Jack nodded, he recognised her now, although she'd put on

a few years since her heyday when her image was everywhere.

'It's kind of hush-hush,' said Caitlin. 'When Zoe retired from pro tennis, she moved back home and now runs a quiet little salon in town. I've already phoned her – she hasn't seen Dad this morning either.'

Jack replaced the photo. His eyes were drawn back to the bucolic view through the large picture window, filtered through a security screen. Was Patrick trying to protect himself, or something else valuable inside the house?

'Do you mind if I look around?'

Caitlin led the way. A tidy kitchen, with neatly stacked recipe books, not a dirty dish in sight. The master bedroom, its bed made without a wrinkle, and George Eliot's *Silas Marner* placed square on the bedside table. The bathroom, and the claw-foot bath in particular, enjoyed a tranquil view through louvre windows to the garden. A large unlit candle stood on a shelf, and the room smelled of sandalwood. The next bedroom had floral wallpaper, a single bed and a student desk in the corner.

'This is my room,' said Caitlin. 'I normally stay here.'

'But your father wanted you to stay somewhere else this time?'

She nodded. 'He said it was safer, and that he'd cost me enough already – whatever that meant. I decided not to push him about it, he's pretty stressed, so I'm staying with Zoe. She's always been very kind to me.'

'Did he tell you anything about what he's working on?'

'Normally you can't shut him up. But not about this one – total radio silence.'

'There's no office here. Does he keep documents somewhere?'

'As you've seen, he likes clean surfaces. He keeps everything on his laptop.'

'And the laptop?

'Goes with him everywhere.'

Jack thought of the unlocked front door. 'Has anything been moved, or taken?'

She glanced around the room. 'I'm not sure. I think so. Something seems different.' She did another circuit of the house, but was none the wiser. 'Jack, I'm worried. Where the hell is he?' She tried his phone again. 'Voicemail.'

Elgar had just given way to something else classical, but more sombre, when they were interrupted by a loud, insistent knocking.

Jack followed Caitlin to the front door. There was a man standing there. A policeman. He didn't look friendly.

Chapter Nine

The policeman stood ten paces away, a hand resting on his gun holster. He had a long thin face and his head was topped with hair shaved to within a few millimetres of his skull, making no attempt to cover over a hairline that, for a man who seemed to be in his late thirties, was prematurely receding. An ID badge on his chest said: Sergeant Steve Kowalski.

The officer exuded calm as he ordered Jack and Caitlin to slowly step outside and move away from the door. He nodded towards the tyre lever leaning against the wall. 'Is that yours?'

'Yes,' replied Jack.

'Is this your house?'

Caitlin answered nervously, 'This is my father's house.'

The policeman appeared unconvinced as he took in her dreadlocks, tattoos and coffee-stained shirt. 'You're breaking in to your father's house? With a tyre lever? Do you have any ID?'

'Why would I have ID?' Caitlin said. 'I wasn't planning to be accused of breaking and entering.'

The policeman shifted his gaze to Jack. 'Are you related to the owner of the house, or to this lady?'

'No.'

There was a long silence before the policeman continued. 'You can see my problem. Signs of forced entry and neither of you are the homeowner.'

Caitlin looked alarmed. 'You're not seriously going to arrest me?'

The policeman ran his eyes over them again before coming to a decision. 'Why don't we sort all this out at the police station?' He ushered them into the prisoner pod on the back of the paddy wagon and locked the door after them. Jack felt almost nostalgic at being bundled into a police car again after all these years, but Caitlin wasn't sharing any of Jack's amusement – she was restless, wild eyes darting backwards and forwards.

Jack watched through the grille as the policeman returned to the house, took photographs of the front door and placed the tyre lever in an evidence bag. Sergeant Kowalski walked a circuit of the house, then disappeared inside for a few minutes before re-emerging and locking the door. He spoke into his radio before returning to the car, but he was too far away for Jack to hear the conversation. The engine started and the police car skidded down the gravel drive.

Caitlin was like a caged animal, constantly changing position, hands fidgeting. She closed her eyes. 'Shit, shit, shit, shit, shit.'

'Caitlin, you don't have to worry. It's your father's house. It'll be sorted in no time.' She didn't answer, so he tried a different angle. 'Why are you really here?'

'What do you mean?'

'What are you doing in Byron Bay? No lawyer working for one of the big five is allowed six weeks' leave. They're lucky if they get any and, if they do, they're still checking emails and taking calls.'

Her shoulders slumped and she stared at her feet. There was a long silence before she answered. 'This is a really bad time for me to be dragged off to a police station.' She looked back at him with those vivid green eyes. 'I'm on bail.'

Jack smiled, impressed.

'And take that grin off your face. This is serious. Two months ago, I arrived home from work to find four police officers with a search warrant waiting outside my apartment door in Sydney. They turned the place upside down, of course, made as much mess as they could, but one of them went straight to my freezer and pulled out a large bag of white powder.'

Jack's lips pursed involuntarily. 'Not yours, I assume?'

'Ha, fucking ha. Cocaine it turns out, nearly half a kilo. Well, more baby powder than cocaine – whoever it was didn't want to waste too much of the expensive stuff.'

'Was it one of your flatmates?'

'I live alone.'

'And no security cameras?'

She shook her head. 'One day life was normal, an awesome career ahead of me, the next day the Legal Services Commissioner suspended my licence to practise pending the court case. My prints weren't on the bag, but it's probably not enough. Bernstein, of course, had to stand me down.'

Jack had a horrible feeling about this. The story sounded vaguely familiar, which could only mean one thing. 'Did it make the papers?'

'Your crappy papers were the worst. Page three. "Top Lawyer Arrested for Drug Offences". Even included a photo – you bastards. I came here to hide from it all. And to help Dad, although that didn't work out too well. He was apoplectic when he heard what had happened, especially when it was Harris Media doing the dirty. He works for Harris for Christ's sake.'

The police car slowed down as it joined the inevitable queue of traffic crawling into the town.

'I'm sorry,' said Jack, 'about our papers. We don't seem to care too much about the people behind our stories.'

'Yes, well, you don't need to tell me about that.'

'Who set you up?'

'If I knew that I wouldn't be shit-scared right now. Dad blamed himself. He thought I was collateral damage from whatever exposé he's working on. But it's more likely revenge for an old case, or someone trying to take me out of a current one. It's a long list. There was someone hanging around outside my apartment for a few days beforehand, but I didn't recognise him.'

The car came to a halt and Jack peered through the grille – still quite a way to go. A siren suddenly pierced the air, startling them both, and the car lurched forward. Sergeant Kowalski had run out of patience.

Chapter Ten

At the lighthouse, the large crowd lost interest in the pirouetting whales when two lifesavers raced around the cape on roaring jet skis. They were moving at such speed they were hurling themselves airborne off the back of waves, only to crash down to the water with a bone-wrenching thud just in time to take off again. Inspector Begley and Constable Anderson watched on as Harry, speaking into his radio, directed the lifesavers to the lost board.

The radio came back to life when one of the jet skis responded. 'Harry, I think you're right. It is Pat O'Shaughnessy's board. Can you call it in? Over.'

Harry confirmed, then turned to Begley. 'They'll tow the board to Main Beach. I'll get our boat stood up at Brunswick so she's ready to go as soon as we get the word. Then, its over to you – missing persons is your turf.'

Begley had seen many false alarms like this – surfers being separated from their boards, only to be found at the pub a few hours later with their mates. He said, 'I've sent Sergeant Kowalski to O'Shaughnessy's house. I'm sure we'll track him down soon. In the meantime, I'll leave Anderson here for liaison.'

As Begley drove down Lighthouse Road, he lowered the car window and lit up – the real reason he'd left Anderson behind.

Smoking was banned in the cars, and Anderson, a right little do-gooder, would be whining for the entire length of the cigarette.

Begley loved this drive. Panoramic views of the beaches came and went as the road wound its way down from high on the cape. Best of all, interposed between him and the view were women of all ages power walking or running along the elevated walkway. Some wore figure-hugging lycra, others wore less. There were men too, the younger ones often shirtless, their tanned skin canvases for eagles, serpents and skulls, but Begley barely noticed them.

The traffic queued to get back into town would be at a standstill, so Begley switched on the red and blues, hurled his cigarette butt out the window and turned towards the boat ramp at The Pass. He drove along the beach, slowly weaving his way between scantily clad sunbathers and toddlers chasing seagulls.

When he arrived at Main Beach the surfboard had already been pulled onto the sand and a crowd had gathered. Begley didn't like crowds. You always had to assume someone had a camera on, which meant being nice to all of the people all of the time, even when they were lunging at you with a meat cleaver. Why did everything have to be uploaded these days? He was sure some of these idiots would even take selfies sitting on the shitter.

The lifesaver patrol captain introduced himself. Begley had trouble taking anybody seriously when they were wearing budgie smugglers, the silhouette of his little penis clear for all to see.

'It is Patrick's board,' said the lifesaver, 'and it's bad news, very bad.'

'Did you find his body?'

'No, but I'm not sure we will.'

They pushed their way through the seething biomass of

47

rubberneckers. The surfboard was laid out on the sand. It wasn't the large shield-shaped Mark Richards logo that caught Begley's eye, nor the bright-red colour of the board, instead his gaze was captured by a serrated chunk gouged out of the left side of the board towards the tail. A large, semi-circular, bite-shaped chunk. Fuck, thought Begley, a shark. This was going to be a bloody circus. He thought of all the photos that had already been taken. There was no way he was going to be able to keep this in the can.

Begley asked the lifesavers to disperse the crowd, then kneeled to examine the board. The outline of the missing section was roughened by teeth marks. Big teeth. He could only hope the shark attacked the board and missed O'Shaughnessy's leg, and that the man had miraculously found his way to shore. But Begley wasn't confident, shivering at the thought of the gruesome alternative.

The press were going to be all over this. And he was going to be in the firing line if they didn't find O'Shaughnessy fast. He phoned Harry.

'Harry, the board has been attacked by a shark.' There was silence at the other end. 'Are you there, Harry?'

'Sorry, yes. Poor Patrick.'

'We'll set up the search command post up there with you. Can you get the Marine Rescue boat activated?'

'I'm on it.'

Begley called Anderson and ordered him to get his arse down to the beach yesterday. He then made calls to get the search started, and to authorise both the Search and Rescue chopper out of Lismore and the Water Police out of Ballina. He re-joined the patrol captain, who was telling his crew to close the beach. Several lifesavers dispersed with megaphones and whistles, calling everybody out of the water. Buggies roared off along the sand, and the jet skis set off to round up the surfers.

Constable Anderson arrived quicker than Begley expected, he must have commandeered a car. He ran down the beach towards Begley, eager as always. He was like a Labrador pup – excitable, but not very bright. Begley had the constable load the surfboard into the back of the police truck. There was no way Begley was going to be seen carrying that shark-bitten surfboard – a photo like that in the press was no way to keep out of the limelight.

Begley's mobile rang. It was Kowalski.

'Have you got him?' Begley asked.

'No. He's not at *The Beacon* and he wasn't at home. I've sent units to look for his car at the usual surfing spots. You're not going to believe this – I caught two people breaking into his house.'

'You're bullshitting me?'

'I'm afraid not.'

'Are they frequent flyers?'

'They say they're related to Patrick, at least the woman does. But they always say that, don't they? Neither had ID so I've brought them in for questioning.'

'That's a pretty weird coincidence – his house being robbed the day he goes missing.'

'I'll see what I can get out of them.'

Begley cut the call and took a last look out to sea. Those in the water hadn't needed to be told twice to get out, and a wave of people was headed shoreward. With the surfboard safely out of sight, Begley climbed into the police car and Anderson carefully drove between the throng towards the ramp.

Begley lowered his window and lit a cigarette.

Anderson shot him a glance and said, 'Sir—'

Begley cut him off. 'One word, Anderson, one more bloody word and you're walking.' He took a long drag. 'And turn on the lights.'

Chapter Eleven

Jack knew the routine. He and Caitlin were separated, and he was placed in a standard-issue police interview room. Pale public-service blue walls. Plastic chairs. Table screwed down. No clock. The air conditioning deliberately set too cold, to unsettle the 'client'. Jack guessed they would let him literally chill for quite some time, but fifteen minutes later the same buzz-cut policeman entered carrying a document folder and sat opposite him.

'My name is Sergeant Kowalski. Could you confirm your name is Jack William Harris?'

Jack nodded, then pointed at the recorder on the table. 'Have you forgotten to turn that thing on?'

'That won't be necessary. Date of birth?'

'Fourth of April, 1984.'

Kowalski leaned back in his chair and smiled. 'You are that Jack Harris. I'd like to apologise in advance.'

Jack was wary. He'd never received a police apology, never mind in advance. 'Why?'

'Because the station commander, Inspector Begley, is going to hate your guts. Nothing personal, just the press in general and Harris Media in particular. Rumour has it one of your papers mentioned him in dispatches, but I've never had the courage to ask.' Kowalski turned his attention to a document he'd removed from his folder. 'It's quite a record you have, Mr Harris. Eleven cautions and not a single conviction. All before you were eighteen, including break and enter, but you didn't steal anything.'

'We were just kids having fun.'

'Is that why you were breaking into the house today?'

'We were trying to find Caitlin's father. He's gone missing. What were you doing there?'

'Also trying to find him. Is she really Patrick O'Shaughnessy's daughter?'

Jack nodded. He had thought it too much of a coincidence when the police turned up when they were in the house. That was worrying – the police don't go knocking on people's doors just to say hello.

'Why are you looking for Patrick?' he asked.

Kowalski chose not to answer. 'Does Ms O'Shaughnessy have other family in town?'

'I'm not sure. I don't think so.'

Kowalski rose from the table. 'Then please come with me.' Kowalski led Jack to a second interview room and knocked.

Caitlin stopped pacing the room when they entered, launching a red-faced attack on Kowalski. 'That was my father's house. How dare you lock me up in a police station. I'm a lawyer, I'll sue for wrongful imprisonment.'

Kowalski remained calm. 'Are you Caitlin O'Shaughnessy?'

'Of course I am.'

Kowalski pointed to the chair. 'Please, take a seat, Ms O'Shaughnessy.'

She threw herself into a chair, and Jack sat on another beside her.

Kowalski asked her to confirm her date of birth and then

opened his file to check his papers. 'I understand you are on bail, but please be reassured none of today's events will go on your record. However, I do need to ask you some questions. I understand from your colleague that you were looking for your father today. I assume therefore that you don't currently know his whereabouts.'

Caitlin nodded.

He continued. 'When did you last see your father?'

'When we finished up work yesterday. I left about five, but he still had things to do. We were to meet for breakfast this morning, but he didn't show up. He wasn't answering his phone, so I went to the house to check if he was okay.'

'When did your father last go surfing?'

'He would have gone this morning. He goes every morning.'

'Where does he surf?'

'It depends. Usually Tallows, or The Pass. Why are you asking all these questions?'

'Is your father's surfboard a red mal?'

She nodded slowly.

'A red surfboard was spotted floating off Cape Byron today. I'm told it has been retrieved and is a mal. Your father wasn't with the board.'

Her eyes widened and she took a deep breath. 'He's a very good swimmer, are you looking for him?'

'A full-scale search is underway. If he's still out there, I'm sure we'll find him.'

The colour drained from Caitlin's face. 'What do you mean, *if* he's still out there?'

Chapter Twelve

Kowalski had just returned to his desk when he heard Begley and Anderson come in. He sipped from a cup of tepid brown liquid alleged to be coffee by the machine that had dispensed it. It was lying. He wondered why he even bothered.

His mind drifted back to Patrick, yet again. He was upset the man was missing. He liked him. Kowalski thought back to the many times he'd been called to the front desk expecting a tourist reporting a lost phone, a drunken assault or some ice addict halfway to Mars in his head, only to be pleasantly surprised to find Patrick wanting some information on or off the record. There was usually a laugh to be had when O'Shaughnessy was involved. Kowalski shuddered at the thought of Patrick floating around out there, waiting to be rescued. Hopefully he'd be found quickly, as daylight was running out.

Through the door of his office, Kowalski saw the front of the red surfboard appear as Anderson lugged it down the corridor towards the evidence room. The board's horrid gash panned into view and a deep apprehension took hold of him. He stood up and yelled, 'Anderson!'

The ravaged board reappeared, and Anderson propped it up against the wall. Kowalski stared at the sickening sight, suddenly feeling bilious. He felt a phantom pain in his leg, as if the shark had attacked him, not Patrick.

'Anderson, why the hell didn't you didn't call me? I've been in there talking to his daughter.'

Rather than answer, Anderson stared blankly at the floor.

'Any sign of him?'

Anderson shook his head.

'Get that thing out of here before she sees it.'

Anderson collected the board and disappeared down the corridor just as Begley strode into Kowalski's office. Before Begley had a chance to speak, a scream filled the station, reverberating around the walls. They both ran for the corridor.

Caitlin had collapsed on the floor and was howling, 'Noooooooo.'

Jack emerged into the corridor and ran to Caitlin. He bent down and placed a hand on her shoulder.

She shrieked at Jack, 'Get your hands off me!'

Jack kneeled beside her.

'I said get your hands off me, now.'

Begley reflexively reached for his holster, unfastened the retaining strap, grabbed the handle of his pistol and yelled at Jack, 'Move away from her, now!'

Jack turned towards them, saw Begley's hand on his pistol, and put his hands up.

Kowalski called to Begley, 'Sir, I've got this.' He moved in front of Begley so Caitlin couldn't see the gun. 'It's okay,' he said to her gently.

Caitlin resumed sobbing. 'No, please, no.'

Anderson stood transfixed with the surfboard still under his arm.

Kowalski called to him, 'I told you to get that thing out of here.'

Anderson didn't move.

Kowalski yelled again, 'Anderson!'

It was loud enough this time to attract the constable's attention, and he scurried away with the board.

Kowalski turned to Begley and saw the confusion on his face. 'I don't think you'll need the gun, sir.'

'Who the hell are these people?' asked Begley, releasing his grip on his weapon. 'Are these the two you arrested at Patrick's house?'

Caitlin spat, 'I'm not under arrest.'

Begley turned to Kowalski. 'You found them breaking into a house and you didn't arrest them? What were you thinking? Is it okay to burgle houses now?'

Caitlin asked, 'Where is my father? Why aren't you out looking for him?'

Kowalski said, 'This is Caitlin O'Shaughnessy, sir. Patrick's daughter. She was looking for her father up at the house.'

There was a brief silence as Begley processed the news. 'Then why did you tell me they were robbing it? And what were you thinking, bringing her here for questioning?'

Kowalski prided himself on always keeping his cool, but he could feel himself slowly turning red. He took a few deep breaths.

Begley nodded in Jack's direction. 'And who the hell is this? Was *he* stealing from the house, or is this a total balls-up?'

Kowalski tried to suppress his anger. Screw you, Begley, he thought. But he kept his voice steady as he said, 'This is Jack Harris, son of Malcolm Harris. *The* Malcolm Harris.' Then, to push Begley's buttons even more he added, 'He's a journalist at *The Beacon*.'

Kowalski watched with satisfaction as his superior fought to stop himself going thermonuclear in front of civilians. Kowalski knew what was coming, but it had been worth it. He turned his attention to Caitlin and Jack. Caitlin was still sniffling on the floor. Jack looked pissed off. Kowalski said to them both, 'This is Inspector Begley, the station commander.'

'Kowalski,' growled Begley, 'my office. Now.' He spun around and strode down the corridor.

Caitlin called after him, 'You should be out looking for my father, not sitting on your arse.'

Kowalski smiled, but made sure the smile was gone when he turned back to her. 'Please, if you could go back into the interview room. I wasn't aware of the situation with the surfboard. I'll come and talk to you as soon as I find out what's happening.'

Caitlin stood up and wiped her nose on the back of her arm as she and Jack moved off.

Kowalski turned and strode towards the bollocking that awaited him in Begley's office.

Chapter Thirteen

Jack felt helpless as he sat next to Caitlin in the austere interview room. She was slumped over the table, her head resting on her arms, sobbing. He'd only met her a few hours before – how was he supposed to comfort her? His attempts at reassuring words had made no inroads.

There was a knock at the door and a female officer entered. She took a seat next to Caitlin and put an arm gently around her. 'Can I get you anything, love?'

Caitlin shook her head.

'I'm Constable Lucy Swift. Please, call me Lucy.'

Jack quietly let himself out of the room, there was nothing he could do to help. Besides, his curiosity was getting the better of him. He'd only managed a glance at the damaged surfboard during all the chaos a few minutes earlier, and he wanted a closer look.

The corridor was deserted, so he followed it to the far end and around the corner until he found the door he was looking for: 'Evidence Room. To be kept locked'. He retrieved his key ring and its picks from his pocket and, after sixty nervous seconds, let himself inside the room.

Jack flicked the light switch, then closed and relocked the door. Banks of fluorescent tubes flickered to life, casting a cold, blue wash over a narrow, windowless room lined with shelves.

Plastic tubs with handwritten case numbers took up most of one side of the room. The shelves on the other side were stacked with office supplies, biscuits, toilet rolls, jars of instant coffee and cartons of soft drink. The room seemed to double as the staff locker room, with some of the shelves stuffed with sports bags, toiletries and lunch boxes. Two bicycles looked lightweight and expensive, probably ridden in by staff rather than stolen property, although it wouldn't be the first time that the latter had preceded the former.

Patrick's surfboard leaned against the far wall. It looked like an ordinary, well-used surfboard with scratches and dings here and there, and its deck lumpy with old wax. Ordinary apart from the bright-red colour. And the shark bite. Sharp teeth had sliced right through both the board's fibreglass outer and the internal blank, just in front of the fins.

Jack photographed the board from all angles with his phone. There was something wrong, and it was niggling at him. He was standing deep in thought, trying to identify what it was, when the lights suddenly went out and the room became completely black.

Jack considered feeling his way along the shelves back to the door in the dark, then remembered his phone. He tapped the screen to wake it and held up the dim light. He was startled by a face a few inches in front of his and jumped backwards, striking the back of his head hard on a shelf.

'Jesus,' said Jack. 'You scared the shit out of me.'

'Good,' replied Begley. 'It saves me having to beat it out of you.'

In spite of the darkness, Begley walked unfalteringly to the light switch and all the fluorescent tubes came back to flickering life. He returned, standing threateningly close to Jack.

'Why the hell are you in here?'

Jack briefly contemplated the default line, that he was busting for a pee and had got lost looking for the bathroom, but he knew he wouldn't get away with it, so he opted for the truth. 'Because I'm nosey. And, as of today, I'm a journalist.'

A long silence followed, during which Begley's face slowly traversed the Pantone colour chart to settle on a deep purple, his eyes narrowing dangerously. He took a big breath and said, 'I wouldn't want you to go to your grave not knowing how much I fucking hate journalists. Cockroaches, the lot of you. Do you want to know why?'

Jack shook his head, but it made no difference.

'When I was a constable, some scumbag with a rap sheet as long as your arm jumped me while swinging a big fuck-off knife. Just before he slit my throat, my partner shot him. He died at the scene.' Begley stopped speaking. His right hand twitched, followed by his shoulder. He refocused on Jack's eyes. 'The next day, what was on the front page of your Sydney paper? A photo of that little prick's mother and sister with sad faces. And the headline? *"Our Angel Shot In Cold Blood".*' There was another involuntary twitch of the shoulders. 'My partner killed himself three months later, leaving a wife and six-month-old baby. Did you put that on the front page of any of your shit-sheets? Huh, did you? No, you fucking well didn't.'

Even though the policeman looked as if he was about to bite Jack's head off, Jack felt deep sympathy for the man. Instances of gutter journalism like this were all too common at Harris Media, some even more appalling. It was the very reason Jack found himself increasingly struggling with the moral dilemma of working for his father.

'I'm sorry,' said Jack.

'Sorry?' Begley grabbed Jack's shirt with both hands and slammed him up against the shelves. Packets of biscuits showered to the ground. Pain stabbed at Jack's back, the metal shelves digging deep into his flesh. 'Don't you tell me you're fucking sorry, tell his widow and his daughter.'

Begley was crushing him against the shelf so hard Jack could hardly breathe. He knew he could fight back and take out Begley, but he also knew that wouldn't end well.

Begley tightened his grip. 'I've been in charge of this police station for eight years. If a fly farts in here, I know about it. If you ever step back inside this building, I'll make sure you won't be stepping out of it. Even your father won't be able to save your bony arse.'

Jack heard a key in the lock. Anderson opened the door. His mouth dropped open when he saw Begley.

'Sir, I don't think—'

Begley cut him off. 'Fuck off, and that's an order.'

Anderson backed out of the room and closed the door.

Begley hadn't taken his eyes off Jack. 'If you or your newspaper bring this police station or any of my officers into disrepute, you'll discover the true meaning of police harassment. Now get out of here before I lock you up for break and enter, and assaulting a police officer.'

He dropped Jack, turned, and walked out.

Chapter Fourteen

Jack returned to the interview room, where Lucy was now holding Caitlin's hand. The policewoman was older than usual for a constable. She had a kindly face and gentle brown eyes, and a softer appearance than usually seen among police.

Caitlin looked up at Jack when he stepped in. She'd stopped crying, but her eyes were swollen and red. Steam rose from an untouched cup of coffee in front of her.

Lucy asked, 'Would you like a coffee too, love?'

Before Jack could respond, Kowalski knocked and entered the room. 'Ms O'Shaughnessy, they've found your father's car at Tallows Beach. I'm heading out there and I'd like you to come.'

Caitlin looked hopefully at the policeman, but he shook his head.

'No sign of your father, I'm afraid.' They all stood to leave, but Kowalski said, with an apologetic tone, 'Not you, Mr Harris, Inspector Begley's orders.'

'Don't be ridiculous,' said Caitlin, 'C'mon, Jack.'

The police car, with Caitlin, Jack and Lucy on board, made its way through the roundabouts and past the boutiques on Lawson Street. The designer markets sprawled through the beachside reserve, the footpaths teeming with people fondling linen, examining crystals or just ogling each other.

Kowalski turned down Tallows Beach Road where they were

waved through a police road block. After a few hundred metres through the forest, they reached the carpark. State Emergency Service volunteers in fluoro jackets studied a map, ignoring their chattering radios.

Kowalski stopped the car and they all climbed out. A young policeman was standing guard by Patrick's car, an old silver Subaru Forester. It was parked near the walking track to the beach.

Kowalski asked, 'Do you have a key?'

Caitlin shook her head. 'He keeps the spare key back at the house.' She stopped briefly, frowning. Then she walked to the back of the car. 'But he has a lock box.' A metal box with a combination lock hung from the tow bar. She kneeled as she dialled in the code and removed the key. She unlocked the door and they looked inside. Everything appeared in order. A change of clothes sat on the passenger seat – Patrick must have planned to go straight into the office rather than home to shower and change.

Jack left Caitlin and Lucy discussing the progress of the search, and walked down the track through the casuarina trees and out onto the vast expanse of Tallows Beach. To his left he could see the lighthouse perched atop sheer cliffs that plunged a hundred metres to the ocean. People with binoculars searched from the clifftops; lifesavers zipped along on jet skis; small boats scoured the water offshore; a drone hovered at the foot of the cliffs. To the south, the beach made a giant curve through the sea mist to Broken Head seven kilometres away. Normally only a few people would be scattered along the beach, but today there were many volunteers searching along the sand and among the dunes.

Dozens of surfers had joined the search, paddling in formation up the beach. A large wave appeared and one of them couldn't resist – she jumped to her feet on the crest only to be wiped out by a wall of foam. Her board shot out the rear of the wave and then recoiled into the water as her leg-rope snapped taut. All of a sudden Jack realised what was bothering him about Patrick's board. He rushed back to the carpark.

Caitlin and Lucy were in a huddle with the SES volunteers and Kowalski. A white van with a folded satellite dish on the roof pulled into the carpark. ABC News. The whole area would be crawling with journalists soon. Jack was half expecting a call from the Harris newsroom, but then realised they wouldn't know who was missing, and would be trying to call Patrick to update them.

Jack pushed his way into the group. 'Caitlin, does your father always wear a leg-rope?'

'Are you kidding? He wrote editorials savaging those he called irresponsible idiots who didn't wear leg-ropes. He was on a crusade.'

Jack took out his phone and checked the photos he'd taken of Patrick's board. The leg-rope was still attached. At the other end of it, the two ends of the velcro strap had been tightly wound and joined back together, which didn't make sense. Sharks don't untie leg-ropes before attacking surfers. Did Patrick decide to abandon his board? Who would do that with a shark in the water? Maybe he panicked and undid his leg-rope to swim to shore. Then why take the time to do the straps back up? Sure, Patrick might normally be a tidy person, but who thinks about being tidy when a shark is pursuing them? Unless it was done after the board was found – by the lifesavers or the police. Jack searched social media for photographs taken when the board was first found. All the photographs showed the velcro straps already closed. Jack could think of no explanation.

Kowalski said, 'The car can't stay here overnight. I can organise for it to be moved.'

Jack volunteered. 'I can take it if you like, Caitlin. Back to *The Beacon* for the time being.'

Caitlin nodded, passing him the key. As soon as he had driven far enough to be out of sight, he pulled over and killed the engine. He opened the glove compartment, but there was no laptop in there. However, after a quick rummage, he found the keys to *The Beacon*'s Toyota. Next he slid a hand under the passenger seat and felt relief – there it was, safely tucked out of view. Jack's curiosity for finding out what big story Patrick was investigating made it tempting to try to guess his password and log on right then but, out of respect for Patrick and Caitlin, he resisted. Hopefully they would find him soon and Jack would never need to access the man's laptop.

Chapter Fifteen

Jack parked Patrick's car behind the newspaper office, collected the laptop and headed along the lane, pursued all the way by the pungent aroma of kebab. He took a few seconds at the door of *The Beacon* before letting himself in. It was an ingrained habit to inspect locks – on a strictly sporting basis, of course – estimating how long it might take him to open them without a key. This one was a standard-issue Lockwood – under two minutes – but he used Patrick's key.

A large carton was sitting by the front door. He rested the laptop on top of it and carried both inside. He placed the box on the reception counter and opened it; it was packed full of printed copies of this week's edition of *The Beacon*.

Jack placed the laptop on a desk and sat in one of the white leather chairs. He really wanted to know what Patrick was investigating, a story so big the man was worried enough to install high-end security at his house. Although Jack felt it disrespectful to try to log on to the missing man's laptop, searching the office was fair game. He swivelled slowly in the chair, surveying the space. Patrick seemed too security conscious to have left any traces of his investigation in the office, like paper copies of source documents, scribbled notes, or even a scribbled password hidden somewhere, but Jack felt compelled to look, just to be sure. Patrick's minimalist aesthetic meant it shouldn't be too difficult a task.

He started with the bench that ran along the wall below the high windows. There was nothing on the bench, not even dust. Underneath, a sliding panel kept a scanner and a printer out of sight. There were no forgotten papers in either machine. A modem blinked away incessantly.

The shelves on the opposite side of the room took longer. Closest to the back wall was a cupboard. Clothes hung from a rail – spare shirts, a sports jacket, a suit and tie. Jack searched the pockets. He checked inside the shoes. He took out and returned folded clothes on shelves. Nothing.

At the other end of the wall was a bookshelf that was more decorative than functional. A collection of antique typewriters and cameras were scattered tastefully over its shelves, and there were more photographs of Patrick with the rich and famous taken over the years, including Carlos Santana and Lionel Richie, presumably from when the artists had been in Byron Bay for Bluesfest. But there was nothing concealed in any of the photo frames, no pencilled password, no clues.

A phone rang, a startling intrusion into the silence. He followed the sound to a cordless handset discretely stored in a drawer below the reception counter.

He took the call. *'The Beacon.'*

A raspy male voice screamed from the other end, 'O'Shaughnessy, you're a piece of shit!' There was a click as the call ended.

Jack put down the phone, unnerved. He wondered how much abuse Patrick received. Byron was a magnet for fringe-dwellers and it was easy to get on the wrong side of some people. Discussion over dinner with friends or neighbours could unexpectedly spiral wildly out of control. He remembered being turfed out of an ex-friend's house when Jack tried to convince the host that Bill Gates hadn't put microchips in the measles vaccine.

The long expanse of shelves between the cupboard and the bookshelf were stacked with archival storage boxes containing back editions of *The Beacon*. Jack rifled through the issues in every box to check for hidden documents. When he'd finished, all he had to show for his work were black, inky fingers.

The phone broke the silence again and Jack answered, this time more hesitantly. '*The Beacon.*'

The same voice yelled, 'You're a bastard, O'Shaughnessy. Your father was a bastard. Your mother was a bastard. You're a complete bastard.'

'Who's this?'

The line went dead. The caller obviously hadn't heard Patrick was missing. Jack wondered whether the caller was a harmless crank. Or was it more than that? Was he the reason Patrick had upgraded the security at his house?

Jack resumed his search. There was nothing unexpected in the bathroom cabinet and nothing taped under the sink or cistern lid. In the kitchen, everything seemed in order, apart from the dodgy choice of biscuits. Short of climbing into the ceiling void and prising up the floorboards, Jack had searched everywhere and found nothing. No folders of documents, no piles of papers, no scribbled notes. It seemed Patrick really did run a paperless office. If so, he was the first journalist on the planet to achieve the impossible.

If paperless, then presumably Patrick kept everything on his laptop. Harris employees were expected to back up everything they were working on to the Harris Media servers, so Jack might be able to log on himself and check. It was only then that he remembered he'd rushed out of the house that morning in such a hurry, and with such a hangover, he'd forgotten his laptop. He turned on the only computer left in the office, the one at the reception desk, but it refused his logon. His search of the servers would have to wait.

Perhaps, Jack thought, there may be another way of finding out what Patrick was up to. The story was likely a local one, in which case Patrick would have been asking a lot of questions around town. It wasn't too hard for Jack to convince himself he should try talking to some of the locals himself. He'd start in a pub. That's where the locals were. And the beer. Especially the beer – it had been a long day.

Jack strolled the couple of blocks to the Jetty Hotel. With its prime position fronting the beachside park, this was one of the most spectacularly located pubs in the country. A large beer garden offered views filtered through towering Norfolk pines to the ocean beyond and the outdoor areas were buzzing, the patrons enjoying the last rays of sunshine with their drinks while a musician, perched on a raised central stage, vandalised 'Dance Monkey'. Jack settled onto a stool at the end of the bar. The barman looked to be in his early fifties and seemed vaguely familiar, but Jack couldn't place him. He ordered a pacific ale.

'No problemo,' said the barman, but instead of fetching the drink he stared at Jack. 'Did you go to school here?'

Jack nodded.

The barman reached across to shake his hand. 'Mark Smits. I think you went to school with one of my boys.'

'Jack Harris. And yeah I did – with Craig.'

'Of course. Have you kept in touch with him?'

Jack shook his head, but smiled as he remembered how he and Craig had spent a lot of time together in primary school, much of it ending up in the headmaster's office. They'd let down the principal's tyres together. They'd been on detention together.

Mark pulled Jack's beer. 'He got married last year and moved to Sydney.' The beer was placed on the bar but at the next place along. 'I'll have to get you to change seats.'

Jack realised the stool he was sitting on was different to the others. It had arm rests, a padded back support, and a comfortable cushion. A battered 'RESERVED' sign sat on the varnished bar in front of him. Jack raised an eyebrow.

'It's a long story, and I'm not telling it,' said Mark.

'VIP, obviously.'

'He'd like to think so. His name is Frank Cameron, and so this is un-affectionately known as Cameron's Corner. I never know when he's coming in, but if Frankie finds anyone sitting in his seat, he goes apeshit.'

Jack changed stools.

Mark nodded towards the TV behind the bar. 'Terrible thing, isn't it?'

It was Harris Media's news channel, covering Patrick's disappearance. The reporter's face carried an impressively concerned expression, as if she knew Patrick and cared. Jack knew this particular reporter cared a whole lot more about having thirty minutes to blow dry her hair before the video lights came on.

She spoke directly to camera. 'Police and locals became concerned when a surfboard was found earlier this morning.' The vision crossed to a photograph, lifted from social media, of the red surfboard. 'So far, the man hasn't been found. Grave fears are held for his safety, as the board has obvious signs of a shark attack. Inspector Begley of the Byron Bay Police would not reveal the name of the missing surfer, but said the man was a prominent local who was well known in the town.' The vision switched back to the reporter. 'With darkness approaching, time is rapidly running out to find the man. Police say a full-scale search will continue at first light in an attempt to locate him and to bring the family some sort of closure.'

The feed crossed to a shark biologist, sitting in his office. A shark's jawbone, complete with row upon row of razor-sharp teeth, hung on the wall behind him. The scientist confidently said, 'I've only seen photographs of the board, but the pattern of the teeth marks and radius of the bite suggests a mature, female, great white shark.'

Jack could guess the journalist's next question and she disappointed him by asking it. Then again, she did work for Harris.

'This is obviously a terrifying attack. Do you think the government should undertake a culling program to protect swimmers and surfers this summer? Or do you think the occasional death is an acceptable price to pay for allowing these predators to roam free?'

Jack doubted the shark biologist would answer the phone next time she rang.

The hotel was now heaving with people. Some laughed over their drinks, life continuing as usual – the tourists. Other were glued to the TV with worried looks on their faces – the locals.

Mark Smits returned. 'Do you know who's missing?'

Jack nodded.

'Patrick is a top bloke,' Mark said. 'I hope he's okay.' He wiped down the bar with a towel. 'I haven't seen you around, Jack.'

'I've just come back to join Patrick on the paper.'

'Patrick has turned that thing around since he's been here. *The Beacon* was a politicians' bootlicker when he took over from ...' There was some hesitation before he said, 'Your father.'

Jack became aware of someone standing beside him, and Mark moved over to serve them. 'What can I get you?'

'Gin and tonic, sir, if you would be so awfully kind.'

Jack shuddered. The man had only said a few words, but there was no mistaking that crappy faux-posh English accent. Jack turned his head away, hoping he hadn't been noticed. If alien abductions existed, now would be the perfect time.

The voice belonged to Angus Bain. He was Jack's father's go-to investigative hack when he needed dirt on someone. A journalist assassin. Groomed in the sleaze-pits of the London tabloids, Bain had no moral boundaries. Having progressively pissed off all his sources and pretty much everyone who mattered in England, he had transported himself to Australia to sift through virgin shit in a new country. Jack's father hired him straight away. Jack couldn't remember how many times he'd had to drag Bain into his office to reprimand him for serious code-of-conduct violations and yet Bain carried on regardless. In a desperate last attempt to curb his excesses, Jack had even reported Bain to the Australian Press Council and Bain had become incendiary with rage. In the end, Jack's father always backed Bain, no matter how bad the misdemeanours. He was untouchable.

'Jack, old boy, how are you?'

Jack turned to look at Bain, who wore, as always, his trademark tweed jacket. He looked ridiculously out of place in Byron Bay. Hopefully his core temperature was climbing into the forties. His greasy hair looked as if it might start dripping at any moment.

'Angus, what are you doing here?'

Bain was also wearing his trademark stupid grin.

'When the newsroom heard about the little dental incident with the surfboard, they asked if I'd have a poke around.'

'You got here fast; did they send you on a fucking rocket?'

'I was on holidays in the area. Nothing like a shark mauling to sell papers, eh? Hopefully they'll find his body and we'll sell even more.'

'Is that right?'

Bain lent in. 'Say, you couldn't tell me where his daughter is, could you? I'm hoping to get plenty of sobbing-damsel-in-distress coverage.' He winked at Jack.

'I wouldn't know.' Jack took a sip of his beer to help quench his insatiable thirst for decking the pretentious prick. 'So, are Janine and the kids here with you?'

Bain frowned.

'On holidays. Is your family here with you?' asked Jack.

'Oh, no. The children are mid-exams.'

Jack saw hesitation and knew Bain was bullshitting.

'I just needed a break,' he continued, perching himself on the stool next to Jack. The grin was back. 'Your father fucked you over big time in sending you here. What are you planning, old boy? Revenge?'

'Angus, you can shit-stir all you like but I'm just here to learn about the business, hands on.'

'Yeah, right. Were you shagging his new flame? She's about your age.'

Before Jack could return fire, Mark arrived and placed the gin and tonic in front of Bain, then said, 'Sorry to interrupt, Jack. There's a call for you on the landline in the back bar.'

Jack excused himself. By the time he'd walked around to the

other bar, Mark was waiting for him.

'There is no phone call. I just thought I'd save you from that annoying little prick. Let's hope they find Patrick soon, or this place will be crawling with coffin-chasing journos like him.'

Jack smiled. 'Thanks.'

'I couldn't help overhearing the conversation. Sorry. People like that make my blood boil.' Mark lowered his voice. 'Would you like my boys to give him a little welcome to Byron Bay?' He gave a knowing glance towards one of the bouncers.

As much as Jack knew he should say no, he couldn't bring himself to. Shortly after, Jack watched Bain being marched towards the rear exit, half carried by a bouncer who had a fistful of his collar. Jack tried to conjure up guilt and failed completely.

Chapter Sixteen

Later that night, back at his father's house, Jack pushed harder than usual as he stroked up and down the pool. Normally he took a metronomic eighteen strokes each lap but tonight he couldn't find his rhythm, sometimes turning on his left arm, sometimes the right. There were nineteens, twenties and even a twenty-one.

He had always swum, to clear his mind and for the sheer joy of it. But there would be no mind clearing or joy tonight. Thoughts of Patrick, still missing, filled his attention and soon he was imagining a shark pursuing him down the pool as his stroke accelerated. Twenty-two. Shit.

The search for Patrick had been suspended at nightfall. The chopper had stayed up another hour with its all-seeing infra-red eye, finding nothing but dolphins. Unless Patrick had deliberately wanted to go into hiding and been whisked away in a boat or driven off in a different car, the chances of him surviving were slim. But why would Patrick want to run away? And how then to explain the shark attacking his board? Perhaps he was clinging to a marker buoy somewhere, or had drifted over to the offshore Julian Rocks.

There were other factors contributing to Jack's unease, like the security at Patrick's house. Jack didn't know anybody with such a high-level security lock on the front door of their house

– especially in this area. And yet Patrick had gone surfing and left the front door open. It made no sense. Perhaps any threat Patrick felt had passed. Or he'd sold the valuables or drugs or whatever else he was hiding inside.

And the leg-rope made no sense either. If a shark had taken Patrick, the leg-rope would probably have snapped. Instead, it had been undone from Patrick's ankle and re-closed.

Jack's calls to Caitlin had gone unanswered. He wasn't surprised. He had little to offer to comfort her. Jack hoped she was okay. He couldn't imagine the turmoil she must be feeling – all the waiting and not knowing. He wondered whether he would feel the same way if his father went missing.

Jack forced his thoughts back to the swimming, to settle his breathing and get the timing right. With concentration he managed two laps of eighteen strokes and then he thought of Angus Bain, and it all fell apart again. There must be something big going on for him to be sniffing around in town. Bigger than a local journo having a surfing accident.

Jack abandoned his laps, dried himself, then headed into the house through the side door off the terrace in order to avoid Don and that treacherous whisky cabinet. He didn't want another hangover – tomorrow would be a big day.

Chapter Seventeen
Tuesday, 5th November

Early next morning, before sunrise, Caitlin waded through waves, then stepped onto the stone shelf and climbed the stairs to the viewing platform perched on the rocky outcrop fifty metres above the water. From the top, there was just enough light to make out the sandy beaches stretching all the way to Brunswick Heads, some twenty kilometres or so to the north.

The Pass was one of her father's favourite places. How often had he started his day here, floating among the waves below, on his board, waiting for the sun? Was her father still out there somewhere, watching this sunrise?

When her mother died, her entire family had been reduced from three to two. She had no brothers and no sisters, just her father. And now, she shivered, he might be gone as well. One person doesn't make a family, she thought. And because she would never allow herself to marry, she would never be part of a family again; she would be alone in the world. Of course, she had friends, good friends, but they had less time to spend with her as one by one they had become engaged, or married, some were even pre-occupied with children.

She looked, through the dim light, towards Julian Rocks, the huddle of small islands breaking out of the water three kilometres offshore. Waves crashed into their jagged cliffs, sending spray high into the air. Could her father have made it safely out there, to the rocks?

She didn't normally believe in a God that answered prayers, but today she was going to ask God to return her father to her. And she'd ask the ocean too. And anybody else who would listen. Please, Julian Rocks, she thought, return my father to me.

A feeling of warmth on her face brought her back to the present and she saw the first rays of a blood-red sun. Other early risers now shared the lookout, breathing in the new day; some of them smiling and even laughing. Surfers carved down the sides of waves; gannets dived for fish like cannon shells being fired into the water; a white sea eagle soared effortlessly overhead. Business as usual, except for her, her world had been torn apart, her happiness savagely rent to pieces. She wanted to scream into the gaping void before her, but the only things that came were tears.

She wiped her cheeks and looked, through moist eyes, to the heavens. Please return my father to me. Please.

Her pleas were interrupted by the loud chuff-chuff of helicopter blades approaching from the south. From her elevated vantage point, she saw the first searchers fanning out along the beach at Wategos. Volunteers were also gathering at coordination points on Clarkes Beach to the north, and below her at The Pass. They hadn't given up. And neither would she.

Her tears started flowing again. She turned, head bowed low to hide her puffy red eyes, and walked down the stairs.

Chapter Eighteen

The sun glistened off the metallic purple bonnet of the Kingswood as Tony drove Jack towards Ewingsdale to collect *The Beacon*'s Toyota, which was still stranded at Patrick's house after he and Caitlin's free ride to the police station the day before. He and Tony chatted most of the way; there was a lot to catch up on. When there was a natural lull in the conversation, Tony pressed play on the car's cassette. The Angels burst into raucous song. 'Am I Ever Gonna See Your Face Again?' As good as the song was, it wasn't the most appropriate music to be listening to when a man was lost at sea. Jack turned off the stereo.

Byron Bay was still stirring as Jack drove into town half an hour later. The shops were yet to open, the streets quiet, and most of the backpackers still horizontal in their beds. Jack parked the car. The air was dead still, and already hot – it would be a glorious seaside day for the visitors, and one with ominous portent for Caitlin and the locals.

Outside *The Beacon*, Jack was about to insert Patrick's key in the door when he stopped. There were scratches on the lock – tell-tale marks that hadn't been there the day before. Jack felt a trickle of unease. Should he go in?

He quietly unlocked the door, opened it slowly, and peered in. Once inside, he removed the laptop satchel from his shoulder and lowered it silently to the floor. He crept to the bathroom door, threw it open and stepped back.

There was, of course, no big bad bastard with a balaclava behind the door. He laughed at his foolishness.

But he was sure someone had been in here, even though everything looked as it did the day before – Patrick's laptop still sat on the desk exactly where Jack had left it. He fleetingly considered calling the police. Then discarded the idea. It would be a waste of time. His only proof of something untoward was a few scratches on a lock – and he was hardly teacher's pet at the police station.

Jack turned on his laptop, logged in with his Harris Media credentials, found the wi-fi password on the modem and typed it in just before the battery went flat and his screen went black. He plugged one end of the charger into the laptop and then crawled under the desk to connect the other end into the power point. He was just about to back out when he heard a shout.

'Don't move!'

Startled, Jack straightened up, and pain stabbed at his skull as he cracked his head on the table in the same bruised part Begley had smashed into a shelf the previous afternoon. For a moment Jack thought the bastard with the balaclava was back. Before he could back out, a boot was planted firmly against his arse, trapping him. He spun his head and saw a single Doc Martens, over the top of which a tattoo of a woman in thick, black-rimmed glasses stared at him. The tattoo wore a black gown with a white ruff at the neck and on her head sat a crown inscribed with the words 'I dissent'. Jack relaxed and lowered his head. He could only think of one person who would have a Ruth Bader Ginsburg tattoo.

'Who are you? I'm calling the police.'

'Caitlin, Jesus, it's me, Jack.'

He felt the boot lift and he crawled backwards from under the table.

'What the hell are you doing in here, and under the table? The door was open. I thought you'd broken in.'

Jack felt another sharp stab of pain in his head as he yet again whacked the same bruise on the corner of the table as he straightened out. 'I work here, or had you forgotten?'

A hint of a smile forced its way onto Caitlin's face. 'I didn't recognise you by your fat arse.'

'Ha, ha.' Jack stood up and ran a hand over his throbbing head.

Caitlin looked exhausted, eyes red and puffy, her slight smile a thin veneer over the train wreck.

'Did you manage to get any sleep?' he asked.

'Zoe and I took turns crying most of the night. Eventually I walked to The Pass to watch the sun come up. I was half hoping it wouldn't.' She looked to Jack with pleading eyes. 'If he isn't found today …'

Jack wished he could help her, wished he could deliver her father to her, and felt helpless that he couldn't. He couldn't even give her a consoling hug; he was carrying enough bruises already. He could only offer up a clichéd, 'There's still a chance, Caitlin, still hope.'

She rubbed at her eyes. 'At least the search has started again.'

'No news then?'

She shook her head. 'I didn't know what to do with myself. I thought I might find something to keep my mind busy here.'

'I found your father's laptop in his car. Maybe we could log on to see what your father was so secretive about. If you know the password.'

He saw a flash of anger cross her face. 'He's missing, Jack, not dead. Have some respect.'

Jack's better judgement told him not to argue, even though he was busting to see what was on the laptop. But then his better judgement abandoned him.

'Caitlin, when we were at your father's house, I looked in a drawer in the lounge room. There was a new life insurance policy.'

She was suddenly alert. 'And?'

'Do you think he might have staged his disappearance? Faked the shark attack on the board? All that security at the house – perhaps he really did fear for his life. Perhaps he needed to disappear.'

'No way in the world. He's not a runner. And, besides, he would have told me.'

Jack hesitated, uncertain which way the next question would go, but it needed to be asked. 'Then do you think your father might have, you know, been finding it all too diffi—'

Caitlin cut him off. 'Oh, for fuck's sake, Jack. I came here looking for distraction. My father would be the last person to take his own life.'

'But can you be sure? People in that state aren't themselves. They're not thinking logically.'

Jack immediately regretted what he'd said; she looked as if she was about to launch at him – her eyes were wide, her breaths rapid, her mouth a taut line.

'So, you just waltz in here, the wise sage, and think you know everything about my family, about my father. Well, you know fuck-all, Jack Harris. My father would never do that to me.'

Jack wanted to be swallowed up. 'Caitlin, I'm sorry.'

'Well, you'll make a good journalist. A good Harris journalist.

Never letting the absence of knowledge stop you from opening your mouth. Or get in the way of compassion.'

'Caitlin …'

They were interrupted by a loud knock and Sergeant Kowalski appeared in the doorway. Caitlin's expression switched from anger to concern and she rushed towards him.

Kowalski shook his head. 'Nothing yet,' he said. 'You weren't answering your phone, so I thought I'd try here. How are you doing?'

She shrugged and said nothing.

The policeman continued. 'I've never seen so many volunteers, Caitlin, all for your father.'

Caitlin walked to the kitchenette and leaned against the counter with her back to them. She placed her head into her hands and sobbed. Jack moved to her, then hesitated, before extending a comforting arm towards her.

'Don't,' she said, before his arm even came to rest on her shoulder.

Kowalski cleared his throat. 'I wondered whether you might want to go up to the command centre at the lighthouse. That's where the report will come in when we find your father.'

She didn't answer.

Kowalski persisted. 'Caitlin?'

Caitlin turned to him, then nodded. She wiped away tears with the back of her hands and walked slowly to the door, collecting her skateboard on the way out. She didn't look back at Jack as they left.

Jack sank heavily into one of the leather office chairs. He was cranky at himself for being so stupid, so insensitive. She really didn't need him upsetting her now of all times. He'd have to try harder to keep his curiosity in check.

But his curiosity had a backup plan – the Harris cloud servers. Jack opened his laptop, called the Harris IT department and was soon given access to *The Beacon*'s network drive. He was in.

Patrick's desire for organisation extended online. Each past edition of the paper was in a chronological directory and individual sub folders held editorial content, advertising and the like. There were also separate directories for active stories such as coastal erosion, 5G and the plan to introduce street-parking fees in Brunswick Heads. None of those stories looked anywhere near worthy of a Walkley Award, although one of them, the West Byron Housing Development was proving highly controversial and polarising.

Jack settled in to explore more deeply, to search out things that might not be what they seemed. Just for a moment he felt like a keyboard warrior. He searched for directories with suspicious or misleading names. There were none. He looked for file sizes that were much larger than expected, perhaps with their name or file type changed to conceal something else. All of them opened without problems, none with unexpected contents. He opened every file created in the last month, and found nothing untoward. Jack was disappointed. And frustrated.

But he was sure now, more than ever, that what Caitlin had said was true, her father's story was a big one. A story serious and sensitive enough for Patrick to keep it off the network servers where it might be seen by prying eyes. And Jack was also now certain the security at Patrick's house had to be related. It must be some story.

Everything had to be on Patrick's laptop, the laptop sitting on the desk within arm's reach, teasing and taunting Jack. He reached for it and booted to the logon screen. Jack googled the ten most common passwords. None worked. Then the top one hundred. Same result – no result. He closed the laptop.

He knew Ricky Martinelli would split his sides laughing at Jack's feeble attempts – Ricky was a rock-star at this kind of thing. His friend had decided not to follow his father into crime, at least not the family business, when he realised there was just as much money in white collar crime as there was in white powder crime. Hacking was less messy, and nobody died. Jack once watched Ricky successfully hack into a big consulting firm, one that specialised in providing IT security advice. Ricky handed over the exploit for free, but the company paid him a fortune to keep quiet.

When the time was right, he'd again ask Caitlin if she knew her father's password. If he could keep his curiosity in check that long. If not, he'd ask Ricky.

Chapter Nineteen

After leaving *The Beacon*, Jack walked along Jonson Street, pushing in the opposite direction to all the tinted and tanned people in swimwear and thongs heading towards the beach, all apparently undaunted by the previous day's shark attack. Jack only had a few hundred metres to cover and it wasn't long before he found the door he was looking for – this time in the precise location indicated by the map on his phone. The small shop had no sign, just lettering affixed to the glass – *Zoe's. By appointment only.* – and a mobile number. He pushed the door, but it stayed closed. The frosted glass obscured from view whatever was happening inside. The mobile number went straight to voicemail.

He was about to knock again when the door opened slightly, and a pair of eyes peered through the gap.

She said, 'I'm busy, you need an appointment.'

'You're not answering your phone.'

A finger extended through the gap and pointed next door. 'Wait there, and come back in twenty minutes.' The eyes and the finger disappeared.

The place beside Zoe's was a tiny hole-in-the-wall coffee shop. The barista looked up from behind the machine. He was sporting the biggest bushy beard Jack had ever seen. He looked about thirty-five years old, the beard not much younger.

The beard spoke. 'Hey, man, what can I get you?'

A blackboard offered a bewildering choice of roasts and Jack was soon immersed in a conversation about coffee with his new-found friend, Eddie, and trying samples. He settled for a blend called Byron Breeze, asked what Zoe liked, and took both coffees next door.

The door was now open, and he entered to find Zoe checking her phone. She was immediately recognisable, even though many years had passed since she was a household name and today her eyes were swollen and bloodshot. At five foot five she was an unlikely tennis player, but had miraculously won the US Open one year when all the top seeds seemed to knock themselves out. It was the only professional tournament she ever won, but that didn't matter – she was, for a few years, the golden girl of Australian tennis, a brief moment of fame during which her image was everywhere.

The hairdressing salon was tiny. There was just enough room for the chair and, squeezed to the side, a basin. A mirror ran along the back wall above a bench cluttered with the tools of the trade. A large white candle burned in a glass jar, emitting a strong scent of sandalwood. What leftover space there was on the walls and the shelves was crowded with tennis memorabilia. Fading posters showed Zoe at full stretch striking a ball, holding up the US Open trophy, or modelling tennis apparel. One of her old tennis rackets was on display in a glass cabinet.

'You do want a haircut? I'm in no mood for rubberneckers just now.'

Jack smiled. 'Do you get a lot of those?'

'I used to. It was a long time ago. These days they don't hang around when they see the wrinkles – just long enough to get a photo.'

'Well, I'm not a rubbernecker.' He handed her the coffee. 'I'm Jack. Jack Harris. I've come to work at *The Beacon* with Patrick. I thought I'd come and introduce myself and see if I could do anything. Caitlin said you both had a rough night.'

Zoe nodded.

'Are you okay?'

Her puffy eyes stared at him, worried eyes. 'Do I look okay?'

He shook his head.

She sat down in the only chair. 'I feel so useless. I want to be doing something, but there's nothing to do but wait. Just wait. Even though I know what's coming.' She stood up and started pacing restlessly. There wasn't much room to pace, she could only manage tight circles.

'It must be hard,' said Jack. 'Caitlin said you and Patrick spend a lot of time together.'

'It's hard doing it on my own. Apart from Caitlin, nobody else knows about us.' Zoe started crying, gently at first, but then she lost control of it. She flopped back into the chair and lowered her head into her hands.

Jack offered her a towel and kneeled beside her. When she recovered enough to speak, she wiped her tears and tried to smile, 'I'm sorry.'

'You're very close then?'

She hesitated, her hands fidgeting, then without looking up said, 'He was the first man I ever really trusted. The first who didn't want to jump into bed with me, as a trophy. And we both love surfing.' She dabbed the towel to her eyes. 'Sorry, I'm oversharing.'

'Why all the secrecy?'

She looked up at him, at first not appearing to understand the question. 'Oh, I'm a hairdresser. People tell me things,

things they probably shouldn't. It's like a therapy session, or a confessional. In this small room, just them and me. And that is all based around trust.'

'And they wouldn't talk if they knew you were so close to a journalist who runs a small-town newspaper?'

'Exactly. I never told Patrick anything I heard in here, although we did have a kind of shorthand – he would tell me if he intended to publish anything controversial, anything potentially defamatory. If he was making a mistake, I would shake my head. That's all he got.'

There was a knock at the door. Zoe walked over and spoke briefly to whoever it was and then re-closed the door. 'It's my two o'clock.'

Jack got to his feet. 'Caitlin said Patrick was onto some big story. Do you know what it was?'

'No. It was the only time he wouldn't tell me. He was excited by it, but terrified at the same time. He said it was safer for me not to know.'

Jack nodded. 'Do the police know to call you?'

She shook her head. 'But Caitlin will.'

'Let me know if you need anything, a chat, or company.'

She nodded.

He walked away from the salon more uneasy than when he walked in, wondering what the odds were of a journalist working on a big story, scared for his safety and hypervigilant when it came to security, being killed by a shark. Something didn't seem right.

Chapter Twenty

Building was booming in Byron Bay and Josh knew how lucky he was. When he finished his apprenticeship as a chippie, he walked straight into a job. His mates had decided to stay in Sydney and were still looking for work, but here he was, three weeks in, working on what had to be one of the best building sites in the country. Only a narrow road separated the house from Wategos Beach and the huge windows meant they had views of chicks in bikinis all day. Even better, some of them were topless. But he also saw all the lucky dudes out there on their boards, and today the surf was pumping.

When his boss sent him for supplies, Josh floored it to the hardware store, figuring he could sneak in a very quick surf on the way back. He'd tell the boss the traffic back into town from the industrial estate was a nightmare. Who wouldn't believe that?

He flew over the speed humps and parked at Tallows. He swapped his fluoro-orange work gear for his bright-pink boardies, grabbed his board and sprinted down the track to the beach. There was hardly a surfer to be seen and Josh figured a lot of them would be looking for that missing dude. Shark attack, apparently, but what were the chances? Sure, his mates jokingly called them 'men in grey suits' rather than say the word 'shark', but they'd surfed among them heaps of times without a problem.

As he paddled out, he wondered how he would explain his wet hair to the boss. Before he could think of an answer, he was paddling flat chat as a huge wave bore down on him. He sprang to his feet and sliced his way down the wave, one hand tracing through the sheer liquid wall to his right. The mountain of water started to curl over his head, and it was line ball whether he would squirt out the tube just in time or have a massive wipe-out. He crouched low under the arching wave and, just when he thought it was over, shot out through the foam into clear, dry air. Fuck yeah. He only had a few seconds of exhilaration before the break closed out and he bailed off the back of the wave at such speed he was catapulted high through the air. He kept a wary eye on his board as he flew, making sure it was safely clear, then closed his eyes and braced himself for the impact. The landing knocked the breath out of him – it was unexpectedly hard – but his momentum still carried him deep under. He swam back to the surface and emerged gasping for air, with a stabbing pain in his ribs every time he sucked in a breath. He turned to see what he hit. A man bobbed in the water. His face was horrible, grey and bloated. A dead eye stared straight at Josh. One leg was missing below the knee and strips of muscle floated from a jagged wound. Josh turned away and vomited, struggling to stay afloat as great heaves emptied his stomach into the water around him.

Josh looked around in panic, not sure what to do. He thought about leaving the body – he was going to be in so much shit with his boss. He might even lose his job. But he couldn't bring himself to do it. The dead dude was a fellow surfer.

The waves buffeted him as, with shaky hands, he attached his leg-rope to the man's remaining leg before climbing onto his board and paddling to shore. He pulled the body onto the sand above the reach of the waves, unable to avoid looking at the bloated face and the missing leg. The acid rose to his throat again and he just had time to turn his head before his insides emptied themselves onto the sand.

Chapter Twenty-one

At any other time it would have been a perfect day in paradise, with the air so still and only the occasional breaching whale causing momentary perturbations of the shimmering ocean. But the beauty of the day just riled Caitlin even more. She wished mother nature would show some more respect for her missing father and satisfy her dark mood's desire for savage lightning, growling thunder and howling gales.

Caitlin wouldn't have agreed to come with Kowalski if Jack hadn't upset her with crazy conspiracy theories about her father, but when she arrived at the search headquarters at the lighthouse she found some measure of the comfort and distraction she needed in a search operation which appeared highly organised, and she was glad she came. A spotter plane flew in a grid pattern; a flotilla of boats fanned out in all directions; two lifesavers used drones to search the rocky coastline around the foot of the cape while four-wheel drives combed the beaches north and south. It was touching there were so many people who cared, so many volunteers, all looking for her father.

A marquee had been erected beside the Marine Rescue office, providing a rest area with tables and chairs, manned by volunteers handing out drinks and tending to a barbecue on constant simmer. Caitlin smelled fried onions, normally irresistible, but today nauseating.

Kowalski left to help with the search and Lucy replaced him at Caitlin's side. Through unfocused, soggy eyes, Caitlin noticed a woman shimmer into view and soon they were in a tight embrace. Caitlin drank in the smell of her perfume, the same one Angelina always wore, and her thoughts spiralled back to a time when her mother was still alive, Caitlin playing at her ankles as the two best friends laughed away hours on their back deck.

When they relaxed their embrace, Angelina said, 'Oh, Caitlin. It's just so upsetting for you. And for everyone. How are you?'

'Frightened.'

Angelina wiped tears from Caitlin's cheeks. 'I'd be worried if you weren't.'

They hugged again.

There were other kind wishes, from people she knew and many she didn't. Her father's neighbour, Lynette, gave her a quick hug before offering her a swig of something strong from a hip flask.

It seemed to Caitlin she was the first to hear it – a change in the rhythm around her. She turned her eyes to the ocean. The plane had abandoned its grid pattern and was heading south, the drones were returning, and even the flotilla of boats had turned towards shore. The volunteers had sensed it too, and the chatter died away.

Caitlin saw Lucy talking to someone, then stealing a glance in her direction before averting her gaze. The policewoman started walking slowly towards her, and at that moment Caitlin knew. Her father was dead.

Lucy wrapped her arms around Caitlin, who melted into the embrace, burying herself into the policewoman's shoulder, and the sobbing began.

Eventually the wracking of her body eased, and her thoughts surfaced to the present. She couldn't recall moving to the marquee with Lucy, nor who gave her the steaming cup of tea sitting beside her. Caitlin looked at the policewoman. 'Where is he?'

'Tallows.'

Caitlin wiped her tears on the back of her hand. 'I need to see him.'

'I'm not sure that's a good idea. It might be best to let them move him. He's ...' There was a long hesitation before she said, 'He's been in the water for a long time.'

Caitlin stood up, suddenly energised. 'Do you have your car?'

Lucy nodded. 'Are you sure you want to remember him this way?'

Caitlin didn't answer, just ran towards the police car. Once inside, she took out her phone and called Zoe.

Chapter Twenty-two

Jack was walking back from Zoe's salon and had almost reached *The Beacon* when a screaming siren shattered the seaside sounds of laughter and buskers. Then a second siren joined in. Given the normally relaxed pace of the Byron Bay police, Jack realised this could only mean one thing. He sprinted down the alleyway and slid into *The Beacon*'s Toyota. At the carpark exit, he came within inches of colliding with another police car as it flew past, lights flashing. Jack flattened the accelerator and followed, revelling in the irony of pursuing a police car at high speed.

After the convoy reached the busy carpark at Tallows Beach, Inspector Begley hauled himself from one of the cars, but instead of following his colleagues to the beach, the policeman headed straight towards Jack. Jack only had time to get one foot out the car when Begley leaned on the door, trapping Jack's leg against the sill.

'Tell me you're not here in any official capacity with Harris fucking Media.'

'I just want to be here for Caitlin.'

A hostile glare from Begley filled a long silence before the policeman said, 'If you so much as take one photo, or if you quote any of my officers, I will charge you with speeding, dangerous driving and nicking the car you're sitting in. Comprendez?'

Jack hesitated a millisecond too long, and Begley applied more of his ample weight to the door. Pain shot up Jack's leg.

'I said, comprendez?'

Jack nodded and Begley stepped back and let him out. When Jack put weight on his leg, it almost buckled in agony.

Begley set off towards the beach. 'They've found a body. Follow me, I want you to be here if Miss O'Shaughnessy arrives – I can't stand howling relatives.'

'Is it him?'

Begley stopped and turned. 'I bloody well hope so, he's got half a leg missing. Or do you think there's a shark out there with a fetish for left legs?' Begley walked off. 'Do try and keep up.'

The police, including Kowalski, were already busy on the beach. A tent had been erected to cover the body. Two officers pushed back onlookers, another was speaking with a young surfer wearing lipstick-pink board shorts.

Begley joined Kowalski next to the tent, and said, 'I want the gawkers off the beach, now. And delete any photos of the body off their phones. Get the road closed – the media cockroaches can come through to the carpark, but not onto the beach. And no cameras when we move the body.'

Kowalski nodded. 'Should I call forensics?'

'Forensics? What are they going to do, fingerprint the fucking shark? It's not a crime scene, Kowalski, unless you're thinking of charging the shark with murder.' Begley pulled back the tent flap and disappeared inside.

Kowalski barked out the orders over his radio. The police pushed the growing crowd back to the carpark.

When Begley emerged from the tent, the policeman's normally steely exterior was replaced with a pale, grim face and when he spoke his voice was tremulous. 'It is Patrick

O'Shaughnessy, and it's not pretty. Better his daughter doesn't see him like this.' Begley shook his head quickly as though trying to clear it of what he'd seen. When he turned to Kowalski, his voice had regained normal transmission. 'Check if the coroner wants to come here, otherwise we'll move him.'

Kowalski went to make the call and Begley joined the officer interviewing the young surfer. Jack furtively checked over his shoulder and, when he was sure he wasn't being watched, parted the canvas and, bracing himself, went inside. The only other time Jack had seen a dead body was when he was a child; his grandmother lying in an open coffin, dressed in a navy pleated dress, and made-up to look as if she was peacefully sleeping. There was no peace in death for Patrick. His body lay on a surfboard, his blue face bloated and blotchy, his grey eyes staring vacantly. His wetsuit was in shreds below the left knee. Shattered white bone protruded from the jagged stump of the leg. A leg-rope was attached to the remaining ankle, secured to the board Patrick lay on.

After Jack emerged into the light, he took deep breaths to steady himself, but couldn't clear the rancid stench of Patrick's body from his nose. He felt perilously close to vomiting.

The young surfer was now sitting alone on the sand, staring vacantly. Jack sat next to him.

'How are you doing?'

'Shithouse, man. Total gross out. I can't stop seeing his face. And his leg.' He put his head in his hands. 'And I think I'm going to lose my job.'

'Do you want me to call someone?'

He shook his head.

They sat together on the sand for a few minutes until Jack asked, 'So, you found him then?'

'Yeah.'

'Is that your leg-rope?'

The surfer thought for a moment. 'Yep. I had to tow him in.' He shivered, then looked around and whispered to Jack, 'Do you think I can go in and get my board?'

Before Jack could answer, he heard shouting. Caitlin was screaming at a policeman, 'Get out of my way.' The policeman was attempting to grab at her as she tried to dodge past, but Caitlin shoved the officer, who lost his balance and fell, then she sprinted towards the tent, easily outrunning a policewoman in hopeless pursuit. It was Lucy Swift. Jack ran towards Caitlin, but she disappeared inside the tent before he could reach her.

A hand landed on Jack's shoulder. 'Stay out here,' said Lucy, before she followed Caitlin.

Jack was expecting to hear crying or wailing from the tent, but there was only an ominous silence, a silence soon broken by other raised voices from the foot of the track. The same policeman was trying to stop someone else coming onto the beach. Kowalski jogged over and intervened, and soon Zoe was walking briskly down the sand. When she spotted Jack, she walked over to him.

He gave her a quick hug. 'I'm sorry,' said Jack.

'Is it bad?'

He nodded.

She put both hands to her face and rubbed, as though trying to wipe away the pain. 'I don't think I'll go in then.' She took a series of deep shuddering breaths. When they eventually settled, she asked, 'Will you walk with me?'

They slowly made their way south along the water's edge. Neither spoke.

Eventually Zoe said, 'Patrick loved the sea. The surf. Surfing.

Strange when you think about it, him growing up in Ireland. There aren't many waves around Dublin. Patrick always said the only foam they have in Ireland is on the top of a pint of Guinness.' Her smile was fleeting, and she shuddered again. 'I don't know what I'll do now.' She stopped and took off her shoes, then walked with her feet in the water as the waves came and went.

Jack followed, and said, 'Harris has thousands of journalists, most of whom I've never heard of. But I'd heard of Patrick. Everyone wondered why such a good journalist was tucked away here in Byron Bay. He was known to be honourable. And funny. I was looking forward to spending a lot of time with him in the next year or so.'

'Me too,' she said. 'Keeping our friendship a secret seems so foolish now.'

They stopped and stared out to sea. A gannet hovered briefly, then pulled in its wings, turned its head down and fired into the water. After what seemed an impossibly long time, it bobbed back up to the surface like a cork, empty-beaked, and took flight.

As they returned, Patrick's body was being stretchered up the beach beneath a white sheet as Caitlin watched on.

Jack approached her and said, 'Caitlin, I'm sorry.'

She looked at him with blurry eyes and flushed, wet cheeks, and barely nodded in acknowledgement. Zoe reached for her, and they collapsed into a long hug as they sobbed quietly together.

Jack followed the stretcher party towards the carpark, catching up with them as they emerged from the vehicle access track where an ambulance waited, its open rear doors beckoning.

At the other end of the carpark, Begley was running a slick operation with the media scrum. As soon as the body was clear, he released the TV crews to the beach so the reporters could bag the compulsory location shots and put their heavily made-up faces in front of the cameras. Once all the media were down on the beach, Kowalski drove up from the sand, with Caitlin and Zoe on board, and headed towards town.

As Jack pulled the car keys from his pocket, a familiar voice called his name, and he groaned inwardly.

'Jack, old boy, how are you?'

Angus Bain was not looking quite as dapper as he had the previous day. He should have asked one of the news crews to put some make-up on what was developing into an impressive black eye.

Jack said, 'I came back to talk with you yesterday at the pub, but you'd disappeared. Looks like you got yourself into a brawl.'

'A little misunderstanding with some bouncer chaps. Mistaken identity they tell me.'

'Oh, there was no mistake, Angus. Some people around here don't like journalists very much, especially Harris journalists.'

'I don't see you with any shiners.'

Jack shrugged. 'I grew up here.'

'Listen, that officious policeman wouldn't let us onto the beach earlier, you didn't happen to get a few gory snaps of the body, or that spectacular daughter of his bawling her eyes out?'

'Spoken like a true Harris reporter.'

'C'mon, Jack, we're old buddies, batting on the same team and all that.'

'Angus, on my team you definitely wouldn't get a bat. You'd be lucky to be carrying the oranges.'

Bain's stupid grin didn't budge, but his eyes were alert. 'I hear Patrick was onto something big. Any idea what it was?'

'Who told you that?'

Bain said nothing.

'Who, Angus? And don't give me any bullshit about confidential sources.'

'Just the general grapevine.'

'And none of the grapes told you what the story might be?'

Bain smirked and stayed silent.

The uneasy feeling gnawing away at Jack started taking larger, bite-sized chunks. How did Bain know that Patrick, in a tiny town thousands of kilometres from head office, was working on something momentous? What was Bain doing 'on holidays' in Byron Bay, and without his family?

'You might want to put a bag of frozen peas on that eye, Angus,' said Jack, as he turned and walked away. 'Wouldn't want you getting any uglier.'

Chapter Twenty-three
Wednesday, 6th November

The following morning, the gaudy purple bonnet stretched out before Jack and Tony as the Kingswood's V8 growled through the winding curves into town, accompanied by a Jimmy Barnes' cassette not sounding its best after too many plays. Jack was enjoying his daily rides with Tony so much that he hadn't bothered sorting out wheels for himself – besides, it was easy enough to use *The Beacon's* battered old car around town. Nor would Tony have had it any other way – he was also revelling in their rekindled friendship and the trips had the added bonus, according to Tony, of getting away from Don, who had recently began giving him the irrits.

Although it was only twenty minutes into town, before they were even halfway Jack felt the weight of his eyelids and started drifting into sleep. He'd had a very restless night. Though Caitlin's night would have been much worse. He shook himself awake.

Jack was still humming 'Working Class Man' as he checked the door lock at *The Beacon* – no new scratches. Inside, nothing looked out of place and Patrick's laptop sat in the same place on the desk.

Although Jack's father had sidelined him to Byron under the pretext of 'learning journalism from the ground up', his

apprenticeship appeared finished before it had even started –
he was going to have to take over as editor, journalist, executive
support officer, layout designer, coffee gofer and anything
else it took to get this paper out. Fortunately, Patrick being so
highly organised meant Jack was confident, at least for the next
edition, that everything would be pretty much ready to go to
the printers.

Jack logged his laptop into the Harris network and navigated
to *The Beacon*'s directory. Each past newspaper had a
subdirectory, as did the forthcoming editions. He opened the
directory for next week's paper and was surprised to find it
completely empty. There was not a single file. And yet the
following week's had some stories already filed for what was to
be a special edition featuring 'holistic healing'. Jack opened a
few files at random. There was an article on an aromatherapy
practice in Byron written by Genevieve Goodhart, *The Beacon*'s
wellness reporter. She'd been busy, also authoring stories on
reiki, pellowah, holistic nutrition and an advance notice for
the Welcome the Sun yoga festival to be held at the lighthouse
at the end of the month. Sheila Monaghan, the sustainability
reporter had written the cover story, accusing Northern Rivers
Shire Council of 'wilful disregard' for the endangered Mitchell's
rainforest snail in constructing a road bypass through the snails'
habitat. And there were a number of other stories ready to go.
But not a single one for this week.

He searched for a contact in his phone, then hesitated before
making the call. Irina Markov, the Chief Information Officer
for Harris, had a prickly relationship with the Harris board and
therefore also with Jack. She was the right person in the wrong
job, her moral compass unwaveringly pointing true north. Jack
was never sure which would come first, Irina's resignation or her

dismissal by the board, both had always seemed imminent, and yet she'd been at Harris for five years.

Irina answered after two rings. 'Well, if it's not the prodigal son. How are the colonies, Jack? Any sunburn yet? Or even the clap?'

'I'm very well, Irina, thanks for asking. How are you?'

'Oh, I'm enjoying myself immensely. It's not every day you see the heir apparent put to the sword.'

'Is that why you answered so quickly? To gloat?'

'Of course.' She laughed. 'But I'm also curious to know why you're calling me. It's obviously not a social call, God forbid, so you must want something.'

'I need access to someone's email account.'

'Jack, you know I can't do that. Even for you.'

'It's Patrick O'Shaughnessy's.'

'I presume he's one of ours.'

'Irina, seriously? Haven't you seen the news?'

'I spend all day working for newspapers, Jack; you expect me to read them as well?'

'Patrick O'Shaughnessy runs, or ran, *The Beacon* here. He was taken by a shark a couple of days ago. I was supposed to be working with him. Now I am him and I have a newspaper to get out with nothing to go on.'

'Jack, that's awful.' There was a long silence before she continued. 'I'm not supposed to do this, there are rules. I don't need to tell you to be discreet and respect the man's privacy. I'll put you through to one of the admins and they can arrange it for you.'

'Thanks, Irina.'

'And, Jack, call next time you're back in civilisation. You can take me to lunch.'

A few minutes later Jack was reading the dead man's emails and feeling increasingly uncomfortable – it felt like a desecration. He promised himself not to open anything personal and to confine himself to finding what he needed to get the next newspaper out. And to picking up any clues to Patrick's secretive scoop.

Searching through the emails was addictive, and after the first few hundred he almost fell into a trance – just one more, then another, and another. Jack cross-checked the stories emailed by the freelancers with those stored in the Harris directories. All had been assigned to future editions, but Patrick hadn't allocated a single one to the strangely vacant upcoming issue.

The sound of the front door opening broke his hypnotic trance. A skateboard entered, followed by Caitlin who jumped at the sight of Jack, one hand clutched her chest.

'Oh shit, for a moment I thought you were Dad.'

He stood and thought about going to her, but she cut him off. 'Don't say anything, I've cried enough already.'

'Caitlin.'

She slumped into a chair and, with a flick of her head, tossed a few errant red dreadlocks over her shoulders. 'If you even think about offering me another cup of tea I'll break your fingers.'

Jack stretched out a comforting hand, but she snapped hers out of reach.

'Caitlin, you don't need to be here.'

'I thought I'd distract myself from the shitty situation that is currently my life by trying to find out what story Dad was working on. He said it would win him a Walkley Award. I want to make sure the Walkley is his.' She sat upright in her chair. 'By the way, your father phoned.'

'Really?'

She nodded. 'Malcolm seems lovely. Not at all like some of the press make out. He said some very kind things about Dad. That he was one of their best employees and a world-class journalist and that he, Malcolm, would sorely miss him. He said to let him know if there was anything at all he could do.'

'My father? He's never been so considerate with me.'

'Well, your father hasn't just died.'

'No, but my mother did.'

'Oh, I'm sorry.'

He shrugged it away. 'It's okay. It was a few years ago.' But it wasn't really okay. He had never been able to push from his mind the images of his emaciated mother and the sound of her rattling last breaths as the cancer ate through her lungs.

Caitlin gave him a sympathetic look and appeared to be about to say something, but clearly changed her mind. She pointed to Jack's open laptop. 'Have you turned up anything?'

'There's nothing stored online at Harris.'

She reached for her father's laptop. 'Then we need to get into this thing.' She powered it up, then examined it carefully, turning it in her hands. 'Jack, where did you get this?'

'What do you mean?'

'This isn't Dad's.'

'It was under the seat in your father's car.'

'It looks like his, same model and everything, but Dad used his fingerprint to log on because it's more secure – this is going straight to password. And his had a ding on the corner where I dropped it.'

'You think someone has swapped it?' Jack thought she must be mistaken. Perhaps Patrick had bought a new one and hadn't finished setting it up. But his uneasy feeling was back, stronger than ever.

She shrugged. 'It's definitely not his. And if you ask me if I'm sure, I'll throw it at you.'

Something else had been poking away in Jack's subconscious and the talk about logging on brought it into focus. Patrick had been very security conscious – surely he would use two-factor authentication. 'Caitlin, where's your father's phone?'

'He's a journalist. It was glued to him at all times, except when he was surfing, of course.'

'When he didn't turn up for breakfast on your birthday, you phoned him?'

She nodded.

'Can you remember if it went to voicemail then?'

'Yep. And every time I rang.'

'It must be in the car.' Jack grabbed the keys and headed for the door.

He forensically searched the car, reaching into every crevice his hand would slide into, and using his phone camera to peer into those it wouldn't. He checked the engine bay, removed the spare tyre and crawled under the car. Nothing. He returned to find an ashen Caitlin lost in thought.

'It wasn't there,' he said.

Caitlin continued staring straight ahead as he walked to the sink to wash the grime from his hands. He hoped she hadn't worked it out.

'Jack, why did you ask me if his phone went through to voicemail?'

'No reason, I was just wondering.'

'Jack, I'm a lawyer, and you're shit at lying. Don't try to protect my feelings, it will just piss me off.'

'I'm probably jumping at shadows.'

'And there you go again. You were thinking a journalist would never let his phone battery go flat. So, Dad, or somebody else, turned his phone off. The phone is missing.' She held up the laptop. 'And the laptop is different. So, you think somebody broke into the car when he was out surfing and stole the phone and swapped the laptop.'

'It's easy to break into a car.'

'Not Dad's, it has an alarm, a fuck-off-loud alarm with flashing lights. And warning stickers on the windows. Even so, if someone wanted the laptop, why not just smash the window and take it. Why swap it?'

'Because they didn't want anyone to know they'd taken it.'

'But they'd have to know the number of the lock box to get the key.' Caitlin suddenly looked up at him. 'Shit, Jack. That was what was missing from the house. There's a hook in the kitchen. The spare car keys.' There was a long silence as she considered this. 'Someone did steal his phone and laptop.'

Jack watched the colour drain from her face, leaving the freckles standing out even more. She looked at him, intense focus in her eyes, and Jack felt as if he was standing in the witness box.

'You don't think it was a shark attack, do you?'

'Caitlin, it's probably just a coincidence – the laptop being stolen on that last day your father went surfing.'

'Stop bullshitting me, Jack.'

He couldn't hold her gaze.

'You think he was murdered.'

Jack shrugged.

'But his leg was mauled by a shark.'

'Maybe,' said Jack.

Her gaze was still on him, unwavering.

'I'm just saying otherwise it makes no sense for someone to

swap the laptop rather than just take it. As soon as your father tried to log on, he'd know it wasn't his. Unless it wasn't Patrick they were trying to fool, but us. And something else worries me – your father's leg-rope was still attached to his board. It wasn't snapped off; it had been unfastened from his ankle and done back up again.'

She was standing now, her speech hurried. 'You really think there was no shark?'

Jack didn't answer. He was having trouble keeping up with his racing thoughts, and the doubts about his reasoning – doubts that existed largely because he wanted to be wrong. If it was murder, whoever it was got through Patrick's security, without signs of forced entry, to take the spare car key from the kitchen. They must have opened Patrick's front door with a key, a security-controlled key not to be duplicated. They had also known his movements, and the exact make of his laptop. This wasn't some meth-head wanting to pawn valuables – it was serious, high-level, organised-criminal type shit. Unless it wasn't. Unless it was an inside job. He looked up at Caitlin. That beautiful face. Could she be a killer? She'd said she didn't have the new key to her father's door. Was she lying? She'd seemed so genuine in her grief, and in her love for her father. He mentally crossed her off the list – in pencil. Who else had a key? Zoe?

Caitlin sniffed then wiped her nose with the back of her hand.

Jack said, 'I'm sorry, it seems pretty wild, I find it hard to believe myself. I shouldn't have upset you.'

She didn't respond, and he wasn't sure whether she'd heard.

'Whoever swapped the laptop,' said Jack, 'wanted whatever was on it, either to read it or destroy it. Did your father keep backups?'

She nodded slowly.

'Where?'

Caitlin seemed to draw herself back into the present. 'I don't know. But he told me over and over when I was at uni to always keep multiple copies of everything.'

'Did he use cloud storage?'

'That was rule number two. Never use cloud storage. Too easy for people to access, and you have to be connected to the internet yourself.'

'So, your father would have kept a backup at the house. Caitlin, is it okay if I go back to see if I can find it?'

She nodded. 'If you don't mind, I won't go with you. I couldn't face being there at the moment.' Tears began welling in her eyes. 'But if you find anything, I want to be there when you look at it.'

There was a knock and the door opened enough to admit a head. Shoulder-length locks of dark curly hair were wrapped in a gold-embroidered, crimson scarf, set off by matching red lipstick and gold hoop earrings.

'Hi,' the woman said as she entered, 'I'm Cassandra. Horoscopes and spiritual advice reporter. And this is Justine, court and council.'

A solemn-looking girl in a flowing white linen dress and brown sandals entered. She carried a bottle of something in a brown paper bag, and some glasses.

Cassandra continued. 'We heard the news, and didn't know what to do. We decided to meet here – so we could all cry together. And think about Patrick.'

Soon, all fifteen of *The Beacon*'s freelancers were jammed into the office between lamingtons, home-made shortbread, cups of tea and glasses of wine. The mood started subdued. For Caitlin there were condolences aplenty, but Jack could see she was struggling to hold it together. Before he could ask if she was okay, Zena, the vegan cooking contributor, squeezed Caitlin into what must have been an overly long bony hug, and rubbed her back in big circles. All Jack could smell was basil. Soon after, Caitlin made a surreptitious exit.

Jack followed her outside, wanting to provide some sort of solace. 'Caitlin.'

She called over her shoulder as she walked away, 'I want to be alone.'

He watched her walk down the laneway, then returned inside where the impromptu wake was heating up. He stayed only because he needed to meet *The Beacon*'s freelancers, given they had to produce a newspaper together, but all the while he felt a pull out the door – he wanted to search Patrick's house.

He started working his way around the room. Cassandra and Justine were refilling their glasses.

Justine said, 'Patrick gave me my first job out of uni. I started with the lost-dog stories then graduated to court reporter, and later council. I can remember Patrick laughing as he told me all my years of experience reporting on criminals would be good background for reporting council meetings.' Tears pooled in her eyes and Cassandra placed an arm around her shoulders.

The conversations got louder as the number of empties increased and the number of Iced VoVo's decreased.

An exuberant man shook Jack's hand vigorously. 'Warren Parks. Conspiracy theories reporter.' He winked at Jack. 'I'm the only one in the country.'

'Really?'

'There's plenty of work here, though. It's the anti-vax capital of Australia, and now the 5G crowd are chaining themselves to anything that moves or doesn't move whenever they try to build a new tower.'

Jack smiled. 'You must be Mr Unpopularity around here then.'

'You can laugh, but actually it's a tough gig. I try to debunk the wilder claims, while at the same time trying not to piss off a significant number of the paper's readers. Patrick, on the other hand, rarely took any prisoners when it came to what he called the lunatic fringe. Did you read his editorial last week about 5G? It was a cracker.'

Jack shook his head and they both fell quiet as they realised Patrick had written his last editorial.

Jack asked, 'What story have you filed for this week's edition?'

'I had a week off.' Warren looked around the room. 'We all did. Patrick said he had this edition covered. It's all a big mystery but, hey, he said he'd still pay us, so nobody argued.'

That could only mean one thing, thought Jack. Whatever story Patrick was working on, and worried about, had been finished and was ready to be published. All the more reason Jack had to find out what that was.

Several trips were made to the bottle shop over the road to replenish supplies and, by late afternoon, Patrick's pristine office with all its uncluttered surfaces had been redecorated with empty bottles and pizza boxes. Even Cassandra's red scarf and lipstick had come off.

It took Jack much longer to get away than he hoped – these journalists weren't short of words, especially with so much alcohol coursing through their veins. The last freelancer he spoke with was the most verbose of all and Jack hoped he hid his impatience well as Sheila Monaghan, between bites of a pizza topped with what looked like spinach and tofu, expounded for forty minutes about the critically endangered Byron Bay donkey orchid. Jack was only half listening, his thoughts drifting to his imminent search of Patrick's house for the laptop backup that he hoped would reveal all and explain what happened to Patrick. Shark my arse, thought Jack as Sheila rattled away, and he plotted his escape.

Chapter Twenty-four

Jack made his excuses and stepped out into the lane, relieved to be away from the sombre mood inside. He inhaled deeply, the air smelling of salt and kebabs. When he turned towards the carpark he saw Angus Bain leaning against the wall down the lane, smoking. Jack reflexively spun around to escape the other way, but Bain spotted him and bounded in his direction.

'Jack, the very man I was looking for.'

'Why are you stalking me, Angus?'

'I'm not stalking you, old boy, I'm stalking the story. *Shark eats man.* But you've been holding out on me.' Bain took a long, languorous drag on his cigarette. 'What I want to know is why? You haven't filed a story, but I know you have photos. Are you fucking his daughter?'

Jack pushed past him. 'Piss off, Angus.'

'I *will* stalk you if that's what it takes. Or lean hard on your hot little girlfriend.'

Jack stopped and slowly turned. 'Angus, you have always been such a pain in the arse.'

Bain smiled. 'Thank you.' He dropped his cigarette and ground it to pulp with a tan brogue. 'So, have you found out what big story Patrick was working on?'

'I thought you were interested in man-eating sharks.'

'That too.'

But Jack didn't believe him. Any second-rate trainee journalist could cover a shark attack, the story would write itself. And yet here was his father's right-hand man, the shit-stirring muckmeister himself, conveniently holidaying in Byron Bay.

'Can I trust you, Angus?'

Bain's stupid grin became even more offensive, and he nodded.

Jack pretended to look furtively each way down the lane, then leaned in close to Bain and whispered, '*Diuris byronensis.*'

'What?'

'*Diuris byronensis.* Look it up.' Jack turned and set off towards the Toyota. 'And keep that to yourself, Angus. It's a seriously big story.'

As Jack slalomed around the potholes along Ewingsdale Road, he couldn't help smiling at the thought of Angus Bain trying to look up *Diuris byronensis* and, if he could work out the spelling, what he might make of the Byron Bay donkey orchid.

Jack pulled into Patrick's drive just on sunset. God-beams from the setting sun radiated from the distant mountain range across a darkening sky. Black cockatoos screeched overhead as their undulating flight carried them in search of a safe place to roost.

Patrick's door lock had no new scratches, but who would even bother trying? Inside, the house seemed uncannily quiet, so he turned on the radio and classical music filled the room. Brahms or Liszt or Rachmaninoff, who knew? But it seemed right.

Where to start? Patrick would have backed up his laptop to a plug-in hard drive or, in the worst case, a memory stick – Jack could be searching an entire house for something smaller than a Tim Tam. It was going to be a long evening. As if on cue, his stomach growled. He'd foolishly declined the vegan pizzas, wall-to-wall meat was more his line.

In the lounge room, he sifted through every drawer in the Art Deco cabinet before turning them over to check for anything taped underneath. He'd never seen so many cushions – they must have cost more than the lounges they sat on. He removed and replaced each of their covers. Lounge crevices were probed, lamps disassembled, vases emptied and skirting boards tapped. He fanned through every book. Lastly, he picked up Caitlin's graduation photo, in which she beamed with joy, oblivious to the separate tragedies awaiting the proud parents smiling by her side. The photo disturbed Jack – it was such a stark counterpoint to the present, to Caitlin's grief. He slowly lowered the frame, then picked it up again and pulled it apart. There was nothing concealed inside.

In the kitchen, he checked every packet and jar, sifted through flour, looked inside the kettle, at the underside of all the drawers, in and behind the fridge and microwave. More books to fan, some with pages coagulated together by the same food featured in the photos.

By nine o'clock, all he had to show for his efforts was a ravenous hunger. The kitchen could only offer up two large Anzac biscuits in a jar on the kitchen table. He was reaching in for the first one, savouring the delicious smell of golden syrup, when there was a loud knock on the door.

Jack had a moment of panic. What sort of idiot was he, coming here alone at night? The house had already been broken into, possibly by people intent on murder, and Jack hadn't exactly been discreet asking around town about Patrick.

Through the locked door, Jack said, 'Who is it?'

'I was going to ask you the same thing. I'm a neighbour and

saw the lights on. I thought I should check it out before calling the police.'

The voice sounded old and frail, and Jack could only wonder at the folly of such a plan, of confronting an intruder, but when he opened the door, he understood. The man was standing in brown-striped flannelette pyjamas and a tired pair of slippers, and although he looked friendly, the large German shepherd standing by his side looked anything but. The dog was seriously overweight, but Jack didn't doubt for a moment it could tear someone, like himself, to pieces if required.

'Hi, I'm Jack.' He extended his hand, but when a menacing growl emerged from the depths of the beast, Jack retreated. 'I worked with Patrick. His daughter, Caitlin, asked me to collect a few things.'

The old man relaxed but the dog didn't – its black eyes fixed on Jack's.

'It's a terrible business,' said the neighbour. 'We've lived next to Patrick since he moved here. He was a nice man. Such an awful way to die.' Now the old man took a step forward and they shook hands. 'I'm Bill. Please give our condolences to Caitlin. From me and Lynette.'

Jack expected the man to turn and leave, but he just stood there. Surely he wasn't wanting a chat at this hour. Jack said, 'That's very kind of you.'

Bill still didn't budge. It was getting awkward.

Jack gave in. 'Tea?'

'That'd be lovely.'

Jack looked warily at the dog, which was still baring its teeth and growling.

'Don't worry,' said Bill, 'Patrick was always happy to have Rex in the house.' This was not what Jack wanted reassurance about, more the reassurance of the dog tied to a veranda post with heavy-duty steel chain.

Having already combed through the kitchen inch by inch, it didn't take Jack long to find everything and make the tea. They sat at the kitchen table. Rex stood beside Bill, eyes fixed on the biscuits.

Bill took a sip from his steaming mug. 'This Barry's tea is the best. It's Irish. Patrick introduced me to it. I have no idea where he gets it.' He took another sip, this time with his eyes closed.

Jack asked, 'Did you spend much time with Patrick?'

'We'd sometimes have a Sunday cup of tea, when he wasn't in the garden, or busy in the shed – he loved that shed.'

Jack watched in dismay as Bill reached for a biscuit.

'Do you mind?' The old man took a generous bite and gave the rest to Rex.

The biscuit disappeared down the dog's gullet in one gulp.

Jack reached for the remaining biscuit, but Rex emitted a guttural growl and butted his shoulders against the table, saliva drooling from his vicious jaws. Jack's hand made a tactical withdrawal.

He asked, 'On the night Patrick went missing, did you notice anything unusual?'

'Rex's barking woke us a few times that night. I thought it was the possums on the roof, but the last time he barked, just before dawn, I heard a motorbike. I think it was going down Patrick's drive, but I couldn't be sure.'

'Did you see anything?'

Bill savoured another sip of tea. 'It was too dark.'

A phone cheeped with an incoming message. Bill's. He fumbled in one pocket of his dressing gown before finding it in the other. He read the message and rose to his feet. 'You'll have to excuse me, my wife's trapped in the bathroom by a green tree frog. She's not very good with critters.' He pulled on Rex's lead, but the dog wasn't going anywhere. Bill looked at Jack, shrugged, and took the last biscuit. The dog wolfed it down. He asked, 'Are you going to Patrick's ceremony in the morning?'

Jack nodded.

'We'll see you then.' As he turned to leave, Bill pointed to the half-empty box of Barry's tea bags on the kitchen bench. 'Do you think I could take those with me?'

Jack showed them out, both with their tails wagging – Rex because of the Anzac biscuits, Bill because of the tea.

Jack returned to the kitchen. Short of a chicken that needed defrosting, he found nothing else to fend off his hunger, but he did find a worthy consolation – a half-full bottle of Bushmills single malt whiskey. He poured a generous measure into a heavy Waterford crystal glass. Calories with benefits.

The hours and the whiskey flew past as Jack forensically searched bedrooms, the laundry, bathrooms and the linen press. Nothing. He'd run out of places to search.

He needed to think. He walked outside, stood on the front lawn and took some slow deep breaths. His eyes were drawn up to a dark sky full of stars and he found himself staring into the heart of the Milky Way – something he never saw in Melbourne. His thoughts were interrupted by a loud thunk, followed by the rapid patter of tiny feet on a tin roof. A possum had jumped from an overhead branch onto the roof of the garage. He looked in that direction, and remembered what Bill had said – that Patrick loved being in that shed.

Jack found the light switch and the fluoros flickered for twenty seconds or more until they caught and cast their cold, blue glow over a concrete floor large enough to comfortably accommodate two cars. A high bookshelf stood at one end of the back wall, and a workbench stretched the rest of the way. The bench was the only flat surface in the house that wasn't clean and uncluttered. Patrick's OCD must have stopped at the garage door. Candle wax of all colours had spattered and dripped and dried where it had fallen; a battered saucepan sat on an ancient plug-in hot plate; glass jars of coloured powders sat shoulder to shoulder with bottles of essential oils and large slabs of white shiny wax. Each to their own, thought Jack, as he remembered all the candles scattered around the house.

The workbench was chaotically overcrowded and yet the bookshelf was empty and unloved. It was all very un-Patrick – why not be more organised and use the shelves? Jack examined every item on the workbench to make sure Patrick hadn't secreted anything among the teeming array of bottles and jars. Nothing.

The set of shelves still bothered him. So empty. He ran a hand under each shelf – there was nothing taped underneath. He tapped each shelf. Solid. Then he noticed scuff marks scratching out a circular arc across the concrete. He smiled to himself – it didn't get much more John le Carré than this. Jack lifted one end of the bookshelf and it easily swung away from the wall, revealing a concealed door. The door had a lock, a standard residential front-door lock. Forty seconds, thought Jack. He had it open in twenty.

Jack walked into a narrow, windowless room about two metres wide, running the width of the garage. A row of antiquated, gun-metal grey filing cabinets stretched shoulder to shoulder across half the back wall. A work desk ran along the rest of the wall, on top of which sat a printer, a document scanner, a tumble of pens and reams of paper still sealed in their wrappers. So,

Patrick hadn't been paper free when it came to the crunch. Jack grinned – this must be where the secret squirrel stuff happened.

His joy didn't last. The first filing cabinet he opened was crammed with hanging files, every one of them empty. And the next. Jack threw open drawer after drawer. Not a single document to be had in any of the cabinets.

Jack looked under the bench, and found the missing documents. And a large black shredder. Confettied effluent had been packed into a row of bulging black garbage bags. Jack tore open a bag and scooped up a handful of the paper, the tiny fragments fluttering through his fingers – there would be no reassembling of these documents. Why would Patrick shred everything? Had he finished with all his source documents, because he'd finished the story? Or was he afraid to be found with them? Maybe it wasn't Patrick who had done this. Had the intruders found this room and, in addition to stealing Patrick's laptop, destroyed the physical evidence? More than ever, Jack needed to find Patrick's data backup.

Inside the house, whiskey tumbler refilled, he sat on a lounge tired, hungry and frustrated. And defeated. Perhaps the burglars had also found Patrick's data backup. He couldn't think of any hiding place he'd overlooked. He took a sip of Bushmills. What he needed was someone more devious than him. He needed Ricky.

One minute later, a sleepy Ricky Martinelli answered the phone. 'Jesus, Jacko, what time is it?'

Jack looked at his watch, it was 2 a.m. 'Oh, how times have changed, Ricky mate. Five years ago it would be you calling me at this hour, singing down the phone and telling me how much you loved me.'

'Yeah, well, I prefer sleep to booze now. What's so urgent at this hour of the morning in Byron Bay? Isn't the whole place tucked up in bed by eleven?'

'I'm in someone's house trying to find a laptop backup, some sort of external data drive. I've turned the joint upside down and found nothing.'

'Why don't you ask the owner?'

'He's dead, Ricky.'

There was a long silence on the other end. 'Jack, are you sure this is a conversation you want to have on your phone? I'm happy to help, but this should be burner to burner. I'll text you a number.'

'I appreciate your offer, Ricky, but it wasn't me that killed him.'

'Oh, right.'

'I'll walk you through.' Jack switched the call to video and panned around the room. 'This is the lounge room—'

Ricky cut him off. 'Jack, wait, are you telling me you were looking inside? Nobody keeps stuff inside, that's the first place everybody looks. Take me into the garden.'

At the back door, Jack switched on the outside lights and stepped into the yard, his eyes blinking as they adjusted to the searing brightness of Patrick's security lights.

He heard Ricky's scratchy voice. 'Just pan slowly from one side to the other.'

Jack started from the garden beds on the left, panned past the fishpond and had only reached the clothesline when Ricky stopped him. 'It's the birdbath.'

'What?'

'Sometimes I wonder about you, Jack. All that misspent youth for nothing. It's the birdbath. Why would you have a birdbath when you already have a pond the birds could drink from? Oh, and Jack, I'm sorry to hear about your father giving you your marching orders from Melbourne.'

'Thanks, Ricky.'

'Do you want me to take care of him?'

'Fuck, Ricky, no. I can look after myself.'

'Well, just say the word. And, Jack, get some sleep, you look shithouse.' Ricky, never one for long lingering farewells, hung up.

A cool breeze had sprung up and Jack shivered. One of the bats squabbling in the trees overhead broke away and he involuntarily ducked as its wings flapped close over his head.

The large stone bowl of the birdbath was full of cloudy water and liberally decorated with bird shit. It stank. Jack heaved the bowl up off its plinth and had only taken one step when his hand slipped, and the birdbath smashed to the ground in pieces. Jack hardly noticed as rancid water gushed down the front of his clothes, soaking him through to his Y-fronts – his attention was on a zip-lock bag poking up out of a hollow carved in the top of the plinth. Jack grabbed the bag. Inside was a small, blue USB memory stick. He smiled – everyone needs their very own Ricky.

Back inside, overwhelming weariness overcame his jubilation. He had no laptop with him to check the contents of the memory stick, and he'd promised Caitlin they would look at it together. After downing the last of his whiskey, he set his phone alarm, dismayed it would wake him in less than an hour.

Jack stripped out of his damp clothes. He couldn't bring himself to sleep in Patrick or Caitlin's bed, so made himself as comfortable as he could on the lounge. He closed his eyes and his thoughts drifted to Caitlin. She was different. He liked her wildness, her energy, her sharp edges. He liked that she showed him no respect, in contrast to the fake respect, even obsequiousness, of most people when they found out who he was and imagined how much money he might have. There was nothing fake about Caitlin.

In the few seconds before sleep consumed him, Jack wondered what it would be like to have Caitlin lying beside him.

Chapter Twenty-five
Thursday, 7th November

The alarm need not have bothered, Caitlin had been awake for hours, simultaneously dreading and looking forward to the dawn, and wondering how many people would turn up. She hoped for more than a handful. But when she arrived, she saw she needn't have worried, at least about the numbers. Hundreds gathered in the pre-dawn gloom on Tallows Beach at Cosy Corner, under the lea of the cape and its lighthouse. So many people had turned out to honour her father. Hopefully, she wouldn't find it too overwhelming, and wouldn't let her emotions spoil the moment.

Caitlin felt the chill of the water as she led them out, Zoe paddling by her side. Beyond the breakers, they formed a large circle. Most of the surfboards were covered with flowers or tied with ribbons, and some of the riders held red roses in their mouths. She felt Zoe take her hand. Then she noticed everybody had their hands linked, waiting silently for the first rays of the sun. Her throat and chest tightened, and she felt like shrivelling into her misery, to bow her head and gaze into the black depths, and yet, at the same time, wanted to experience the moment, of all these people paying respect to her father.

She forced herself to scan the profusion of faces – sun-battered, acned, wizened, pockmarked, pallid, grey hair, no hair, even the zinc-painted faces of young children – all staring at her, and she drew strength. There were familiar faces – some of them non-surfers on borrowed boards, like their neighbours Bill and Lynette. Old school friends. Her parents' friends. Even that policeman Kowalski perched wobbling on a mal.

Jack was nearby, wearing his boxers, and holding hands with two men. He sat deep in the water on a small pink board, Caitlin recognised it as one of Zoe's. He smiled at her and she nodded back – he could at least have put on some boardies out of respect.

When the sun rose and its first rays warmed the surfers, they each took a turn to call out 'Patrick O'Shaughnessy' and throw flowers into the water. A board adorned with handwritten messages was washed in the water, leaving the words to float away – 'Surf in peace, Patrick' and 'We love you'. Even some of the toughest old men had red-rimmed eyes, or wiped at their cheeks.

The surfer beside Jack raised a wrinkled, sun-speckled hand and said, 'Patrick was one of the kindest men I ever met, couldn't do enough for you. When some slime bag stole my board, Patrick turned up the next day and gave me one of his.'

Bill from next door raised his arm. A small wave almost capsized him as he told one of Patrick's favourite jokes. 'How can you spot a surfer at a wedding? He's the one not there.' More anecdotes followed, many of them funny. By the end, it was generally agreed that Patrick preferred to surf in the dark because he was such a shit surfer, which was only to be expected – he was Irish, after all.

With the stories and tributes done, there was a minute's silence. When Caitlin felt her resolve breaking and the first tear forming, she pinched her thigh until it hurt, and raised her chin.

After the silence, they all splashed water into the centre of the circle.

The non-surfers among them then headed back to shore. Caitlin patted cool water on her face, then paddled off to join the others, to catch a wave in memory of her father.

Chapter Twenty-six

After the paddle out, Jack queued with the multitudes for his turn at the outdoor shower in the carpark behind Tallows Beach. Caitlin was nowhere to be seen. Back at the Toyota, Jack had no choice but to change into yesterday's clothes again. He retrieved the memory stick from where he'd hidden it under the seat and walked back towards the crowd. He didn't find Caitlin, but someone had seen her driving off with Zoe as soon as they'd all come back to shore.

The memory stick was burning a hole in his pocket. He was so tempted to plug it into his laptop and look at what was on it, but it really belonged to Caitlin and she had said she wanted to be there for the big reveal. He tried her mobile over and over, but it went straight to voicemail.

A couple of hours later he still hadn't tracked her down. He sent multiple texts suggesting they meet at *The Beacon* but there was no response.

Jack was now highly suspicious that Patrick's death wasn't all that it seemed. So suspicious, that he felt the police needed to start investigating before more time was lost and the trail went even colder. He wanted justice for Patrick, and for Caitlin. So, as reluctant as Jack was to risk the wrath of Inspector Begley, he was soon pushing open the door of the police station.

When he presented to reception, Constable Anderson's eyes widened.

Jack leaned in and asked quietly, 'Is Begley in?'

'He's in a meeting, in his office.' The policeman glanced nervously at the door. 'With his wife. I have strict instructions he's not to be disturbed.'

'Good,' said Jack. 'Can I speak with Sergeant Kowalski, or is he with his wife too?'

Anderson looked perplexed. 'But Kowalski ... he's not married.'

After Jack pointed to the telephone, Anderson made the call.

Kowalski appeared and motioned Jack through the door to the inner sanctum. 'You're a brave man coming here, especially when Inspector Begley is in,' said a smiling Kowalski, 'but you've picked a good time, he's having morning tea with his wife, so you probably won't get your head kicked in.' Kowalski showed Jack down the corridor, and they entered his office. 'I'm told Mrs Begley's sponge cake is a winner, not that he ever shares any with me.'

As Kowalski closed the door, a booming voice made them both jump. Begley was leaning against the wall behind the door, waiting, his eyes hostile.

'I thought I could smell something.'

Kowalski stared at his feet, embarrassed.

Begley waved them to the seats on either side of the desk. 'Please carry on, I'm merely an observer. Pretend I'm not here.' And he remained exactly where he was, back to the wall, arms crossed.

After they sat down, Jack cleared his throat and looked at Kowalski. 'I'm here to report a crime.'

'What have you done this time?' asked Begley.

They both turned to the inspector.

It was Kowalski who spoke. 'Sir, I don't think—'

'You're right,' said Begley, 'I'm not in the room.'

Jack could sense Begley's intimidating presence behind him. 'It's about Patrick O'Shaughnessy,' he said.

Begley coughed, but said nothing.

'Patrick was investigating something that might have put his life in danger. He was scared. He upgraded the security at his house, took out a new life insurance policy, and went to extreme lengths to hide the documents he was working on. He also didn't think it was safe for Caitlin to stay at the house with him.'

Jack could hear Begley's breathing. The silence was worse than the interjections.

Kowalski nodded his encouragement. 'And the crime?'

'Someone is trying to shut down the story he was working on. Patrick's laptop was stolen the night he disappeared and was replaced with one that looks identical. His phone was also taken. Someone broke into his house and may have shredded all his documents. They also broke into *The Beacon*, there were new scratches on the lock.'

Kowalski opened a notebook and picked up a pen. 'How certain are you? You said, "may have shredded"?'

'Very.' But Jack felt Begley's hostile gaze boring into his back, and he suddenly felt a whole lot less confident. He risked a look at Begley, who was glaring at him and shaking his head.

Kowalski scribbled some notes, then asked, 'And are you thinking this is related to Patrick's death, given much of this happened on the same night?'

And that was it, Kowalski had lit the blue touch paper and Begley could control himself no longer. He walked over and placed both hands on the desk, leaning his face in so close Jack was suffocated by an overwhelming whiff of Old Spice.

There was a long pause before Begley asked, with barely contained fury, 'Tell me, Mr Harris, did you sleep well last night?'

Jack shook his head.

'Are you feeling anxious yourself?'

Jack didn't answer.

'Do you have scratches on your front-door lock? Have you ever bought a new laptop, or shredded a document?' Begley waited but there was no reply. 'And how much do you think, Mr Harris, these imaginary people in your mind, how much do you think they would have had to pay the shark to bite Patrick O'Shaughnessy's bloody leg off? Mighty smart shark to know which person to chew. Perhaps they blooded it, waved Patrick's underwear in front of its nose.'

Jack said nothing and the silence lingered.

'You're pretty fucking quiet for a so-called journalist.'

'We can't be certain it was a shark until we have the autopsy report.'

'Well, Sherlock, a good investigative journalist should get his facts right before he walks around sniffing other people's bums. The forensic pathologist gave me a verbal report this morning. Shark. A real one. Not an assassin dressed in an inflatable shark costume.'

Jack was shocked, but said nothing.

'Did you hear what I said?'

Jack nodded.

Begley continued. 'Have you discussed these lunatic conspiracy theories with Patrick O'Shaughnessy's daughter?'

Jack gave another small nod.

'Oh, well done you. So helpful in her time of need.'

Kowalski stared blankly at his notepad, avoiding the gaze of both men.

But then Begley re-directed his anger at him. 'I don't want you to waste a single minute more on this fantasy. Get him out of here. And if he ever puts so much as a toenail back in this police station, arrest him for public nuisance.'

With that, Begley was gone, leaving a large and welcome silence in his wake.

Chapter Twenty-seven

Zoe looked upset, the scissors tremulous in her hands. Jack leaned back in the chair, a little nervous himself as she grasped his hair in one hand and the scissors plunged towards him. Jack forced himself to relax, she'd probably done this a million times, but she nicked his left ear with the first cut.

He jumped and Zoe said, 'Sorry. I'm really sorry.'

'Zoe, we don't have to do this now.'

She took a few deep breaths to steady herself. 'I'm doing what everyone tells you not to do. I've booked a full afternoon so I can hide from my emotions. You're the second person I've cut today, so you can see what a crap plan it is.'

She resumed snipping jerkily at his hair and Jack changed the conversation to what he thought would be more calming territory – a large floral arrangement of natives that overflowed from a vase way too small for them. 'Nice flowers.'

Zoe abruptly stopped cutting and put down her scissors. She wiped her eyes on her sleeve. 'They're from Patrick. Every week he gave me a beautiful arrangement from his garden. And he brought me a new candle with a different scent, swapping it for the old one before it had even burned halfway.' She pointed to a huge candle alight in a glass jar. 'These will be the last ones.' She sniffed loudly and dabbed at her eyes, then sat on the bench against the wall.

'Let's do the haircut another time,' said Jack as he sat beside her. 'Coffee?'

She nodded, forcing a smile. 'Flat white.' He went to stand, but she stopped him. 'Eddie will bring them in. What do you want?'

'Same.'

She knocked loudly on the wall twice and then, after a pause, three more times.

They sat in silence for a while before Jack attempted another distraction. 'I wouldn't have picked Patrick as a candle maker.'

'Me neither. He caught the candle bug from his wife. It's one of his ways of remembering her.'

'Did you ever meet her?'

She dried her eyes on her T-shirt. 'I met them both soon after they first arrived. She was lovely. They were besotted with each other. It really was a match made in heaven.'

'What happened?'

She shrugged. 'They stopped inviting me around a few years before she died. Afterwards, I assumed she must have been depressed, but I really don't know. Even years later, when Patrick and I became very close, he would never discuss what happened.'

The door opened and Eddie and his bushy beard entered, a bright swathe of light cutting across the room. He put their coffees on the bench, briefly placed a sympathetic hand on Zoe's shoulder, then left.

They drank in silence for a few minutes, until Zoe said, 'I'm pleased there were so many people at the paddle out this morning. It helps.'

'And everyone had nothing but kind things to say about Patrick.'

Zoe raised her eyebrows in gentle admonishment. 'Those he pissed off are hardly likely to go to his memorial.'

'Were there many of those?'

'Seriously, you need to ask that? He was a journalist. Of course, there were. He had people he just irritated and others he annoyed the shit out of. Some of them might even have considered him an enemy.'

'Tell me.'

'The funniest was one of those self-help authors who wafted in for the Byron Writers Festival on a promotional tour for her new book. Glenda someone ... Glenda Davidson. Patrick published a book review before the festival, rightly savaging it. The book was called *Forgive, And Reclaim Your Life*.' She smiled at Jack. 'She has the record for the most threatening letters, twenty or more I'd say. He used to read them to me.'

'But harmless?'

'Harmlessly crazy, yes.'

'What about some of the more serious ones?'

'The anti-vaxxers, of course. And the greenies, and I'm talking the fringe radicals not the mainstream conservationists. Oh, and a nudist who got his knickers in a twist about some photos he said Patrick took of his wife. I could go on all day. Councillors were forever in his sights – he used to always say, "same shit, different politician". And then there's every developer who tried to screw over council – a long list in itself.'

When Zoe had finished her coffee, she looked at Jack and laughed. 'You can't go outside like that. It looks like you got stoned and tried to cut your own hair.'

Back in the chair, with Zoe's scissors still visibly trembling, he felt the same anxiety as when a dentist had him by the molars. He forced himself to breathe slowly.

She said, 'All the threatening letters and emails are at *The Beacon* somewhere. Patrick kept them all. Mostly for their entertainment value.' She stopped talking and focused on evening up his sideburns, which she did with only a small nick to his right ear.

Jack decided to bail out before she cut off his head. 'Let's do this another time.'

She nodded and put down her scissors.

Jack stood and removed the memory stick from his pocket. He showed it to her. 'I found Patrick's laptop backup. I'm waiting to meet Caitlin so we can see what's on it. Would you like to join us?'

She shook her head. 'I have a full afternoon. Hopefully there won't be any more blood. But please let me know what you find.' She checked her bookings. 'If you come back next Tuesday, I promise I'll give you a haircut, instead of blubbering.'

He smiled and turned to go.

She stopped him before he reached the door. 'Jack, Caitlin is very special to me, all I've got left of Patrick, really. I'm very fond of her. Be careful.'

'What do you mean?'

'I've seen the way you look at her. She's fragile around men.'

Jack wasn't sure 'fragile' was the right word. Defensive maybe. Hostile? He asked, 'Do you know why?'

Zoe shook her head, then showed him to the door.

Chapter Twenty-eight

Jack was feeling irritable. As he walked towards *The Beacon*, the pungent aroma of kebabs prodded and poked at his hunger, and he realised he hadn't eaten all day. Five minutes later, he let himself and his lamb and feta kebab into the office.

On his way to the kitchenette, Jack collected the latest edition of *The Beacon* from the box he'd left on the reception counter. Warren Parks's words at the impromptu wake the previous day had been swimming around in his head – that 'Patrick had no tolerance for the lunatic fringe', and that 'his last editorial was a cracker'.

Although the pathologist had told Begley that Patrick had died from a shark attack, Jack still had serious doubts. All the preceding events, like the swapping of the laptop, and the break-ins at Patrick's house and *The Beacon* suggested an intent to silence Patrick and cover something up. Could Patrick really have pissed someone off so much in an editorial that they came for him? Jack doubted it, but needed to check. And if someone had intended to kill Patrick, could a shark really have coincidentally beaten them to it?

Jack sat at the table in the kitchenette and opened the newspaper to Patrick's editorial. The kebab tasted surprisingly delicious, and not just because he was starving. Sauce trickled down his fingers, forming a mountain of congealed gloop on the paper as he read.

The earth is flat again. It is widely rumoured that Bill Gates straightened it out sometime after midnight last night. Henny Penny has put her helmet back on. The only moon Neil Armstrong saw was when Buzz Aldrin took a dump in the Lunar Module. There was no man in that moon. Oh, and 5G causes cancer.

Jack laughed out loud – Patrick must have had on his grumpy pants when he wrote that. And his grumpy socks.

The humorous introduction soon moved onto more serious matters, and Patrick showed his impressive craft as a journalist in giving a concise, but beautifully reasoned rebuttal of the anti-5G arguments. Until the last paragraph, when Jack's mouth fell open as he read:

To any of the anti-5G crowd that have read this far, congratulations. There were some big words there. Then again, all those words, big and small, are wasted because you will never change your mind. Yours not to reason why, yours but to do and die.

Jack wondered why such a fine journalist would veer off into something so unprofessional. Was there something personal hidden behind the words? Such a tirade might piss off the anti-5G community, but surely it wasn't enough motivation for murder – unless some of their number were extremists. Jack needed to find out, and he'd have to do it himself – the police clearly had no intention of helping, being as they were firmly in the shark-chews-man camp.

Jack enjoyed the flavours of the slow roasted lamb as he

flicked through rest of the newspaper. Justine, the court reporter, had filed the front-page story about a dog shot dead by a crossbow-wielding neighbour. Cassandra's horoscopes were full of foreboding. The lead back-page story was about a twelve-year-old rugby player who had survived a sixty-minute pounding on the football field, only to get his tongue stuck in a soft drink can at the end of the match, which required a trip to the local hospital to separate the can from the boy. Jack had hoped to spot a teaser for Patrick's self-proclaimed 'big story', but there was nothing. What had he been investigating?

The kebab was nearly history and Jack's fingers were almost stuck together when Caitlin pushed through the door and parked her skateboard. He felt a tingle of excitement when he saw her.

She wrinkled her nose. 'What is that smell?'

Jack held up the remnants of the kebab and she pulled a face.

'You might eat the next one outside.'

'Was that another one of your father's rules?'

'Yes, and I'm going to make up a whole lot more before we're done.' She fell into a chair. 'Why do you keep texting me to meet? What's so urgent?'

Jack hastily wiped his hands, but they were still sticky as he withdrew the memory stick from his pocket and held it up. 'I found it.'

She sat bolt upright, a sparkle returning to her eyes. 'Where?'

'Under the birdbath in your father's backyard.'

'Huh. He never let me feed the birds in case it changed their behaviour, then he installed a birdbath. I told him he was a bloody hypocrite.'

'Shall we?'

Jack went to wash his hands, accompanied by Caitlin

repeatedly telling him to hurry up. When he booted up his laptop and inserted the memory stick into the USB port, she moved her chair next to his.

'Dad encrypted everything,' she said. 'We'll need the password.'

Jack's excitement for all the secrets about to be divulged vanished. He'd spent most of the night looking for a memory stick they wouldn't be able to read. 'Well, that was a total waste of time.'

Caitlin looked puzzled. 'Why?'

'No password, no big reveal.'

'Oh, Dad told me the password.'

Jack's eyebrows shot up. 'Jesus, Caitlin, you nearly gave me a heart attack. Why didn't you say?'

'Sorry. It didn't even occur to me. A couple of years ago, Dad told me a password to remember, "just in case anything happened". I assumed it was for his password manager, so I could look after his affairs.'

Jack took some deep breaths and felt a flush of anticipation once more. He returned his attention to the laptop and opened a file explorer window. There was only one drive showing up, the local hard drive of the laptop. The memory stick wasn't on the list.

He said, 'That's strange.'

'What?'

'I can't see it.' Jack opened the device-manager window. The memory stick was listed as a 'USB mass storage device' and it was reported as working normally.

'Jack?'

He scratched his head for a while, as he considered. 'It's either empty and never been formatted, which is pretty unlikely given how much trouble your father took to hide it, or it's a file system not recognised by Windows.'

'How do we find out?'

He smiled at her. 'We ask Ricky Martinelli. There's not much he can't organise, or do, especially when it comes to IT. He's now a hacker.'

'Ricky?' asked Caitlin.

'Everybody needs a Ricky.'

Jack made the call but it went to voicemail. He hung up and sent a text.

'So now we just wait?'

Jack nodded. He felt as disappointed as she looked.

She reached for the newspaper sitting on the table. 'So, this is the last one.'

'It won't be the last,' said Jack, 'we'll keep it going.'

'That's not what I meant.'

'I know.'

'Is there another copy, one without your dinner smeared all over it?'

Jack pointed to the carton at reception. 'He wrote a no-holds-barred editorial on 5G.'

'Oh, not again.' She nodded towards the kitchenette. 'Luckily, there's a fridge magnet with the window guy's number – we're probably going to need it.'

'What?'

'You'll see.' She collected a clean newspaper and began reading.

There was a knock, and they both looked up as the door opened. It was Kowalski, out of uniform and carrying a large aluminium case.

Jack closed his laptop and slipped the memory stick into his pocket. 'Sergeant Kowalski, this is unexpected.'

Kowalski approached and shook Jack's hand. 'Steve, please.' The policeman then held out his hand for Caitlin, but, when she hesitated, he withdrew it. 'Again, I'm sorry for your loss,' he said to her. 'This morning's memorial was very moving. Your father was a good man.'

Caitlin's face began to crumple, and she looked away.

Kowalski said to Jack, 'I was thinking about what you said at the police station this morning. My parents grew up in a country where the press was under the total control of the regime. As were the people. Then we moved to Australia when I was sixteen. You have no idea what it is like to be able to say whatever you please if you haven't lived in a place like that.' Kowalski started unpacking the contents of the case onto the table. 'I want to find out if the laptop is your father's. If we find his fingerprints on it, there should be nothing to worry about.'

Jack pointed out which of the laptops was Patrick's and Kowalski set about retrieving the fingerprints from it. Caitlin handed Kowalski Patrick's coffee cup for comparison prints, and Jack and Caitlin provided their fingerprints too. Kowalski was meticulous.

At the end, he straightened up and stretched his neck. 'The only prints on the laptop belong to you two. Your father hasn't touched this machine.'

'And whoever swapped it, wiped it clean of theirs,' said Jack.

'Must have,' said Kowalski. 'But how did they swap the laptop? Your father had all that security in his house. And the laptop was in his car, which wasn't broken into.'

'They had the spare car key,' said Caitlin. 'That day you found us at Dad's house, I thought there was something out of place. The spare key was missing. Someone had been in there and stolen it.'

'But how did they get into the house? Did they have a door key? Those keys are hard to come by.'

Neither Jack nor Caitlin had an answer.

Kowalski packed away his equipment then pointed to the laptop. 'It might be better if I keep that in the evidence room.'

Caitlin nodded.

'When I get a chance, I'll try to track down the movements of your father's mobile phone, but I don't know when that will be. I'd need a warrant.'

Caitlin's colour rose. 'What do you mean, when you get a chance? My father may have been murdered. Jesus Christ—'

Jack cut in, 'Caitlin, he's trying to help.'

Kowalski said, 'Inspector Begley won't want to look foolish investigating what the pathologist told him was a shark attack.'

Caitlin jabbed a finger towards Kowalski. 'Well, you tell Begley that—'

Kowalski raised his hands, palms towards her. 'I'll speak with him.'

Soon after Kowalski had gone, Jack's phone pinged and he read the incoming message from Ricky: 'Fuck off, I'm very busy and important, I'll call later.'

Caitlin folded the newspaper and pushed it roughly aside, then stood and retrieved the most recent archive box from the shelf. 'I want to look through the most recent papers, see if something stands out.'

'According to Zoe,' Jack said, 'your father received threatening letters from time to time.'

'More than time to time. There were so many he didn't even bother reading them in the end.' She nodded towards the printer cabinet.

Jack opened the door and on the bottom shelf, pushed to the

back, was a large cardboard storage box. He was annoyed he'd missed it during his previous search – he'd make a shit detective.

Caitlin said, 'Dad called it the "box of doom".'

Jack hefted the carton onto the desk, then began rummaging through the vast array of letters. Patrick's penchant for orderliness had been deeply ingrained, even the abuse was filed in chronological order. Some letters were handwritten, some typed, others printed from emails. The most recent letter was printed in big bold letters.

BUTCHER'S ADS = BLOOD MONEY
WOULD YOU LIKE TO BE BUTCHERED?

Jack was shocked. He checked the envelope – not expecting, and not finding, a return address.

The next letter had been handwritten in beautiful cursive on paper reeking of lavender.

Dear Mr O'Shaughnessy,

I'm still waiting for you to publish the retraction I requested in my previous letters, the most recent of which are dated 3rd and 17th September, 17th, 24th, 26th, 28th, 29th, and 30th (twice) October. I am not one to hold a grudge, but consider this your final notice, after which I will advise my lawyers to seek financial redress arising from your inflammatory and unjust review of my book "Forgive, And Reclaim Your Life".

Yours faithfully,
Glenda Davidson

'There are hundreds of these,' said Jack, 'was your father worried about anybody in particular?'

Caitlin didn't answer, her nose still buried in the paper.

'Caitlin?'

She held up a hand. 'Wait. Look at this. An anonymous ad in the classifieds three weeks ago. "Anybody who worked in Northern Rivers Council administration in 1987, please call this number".'

'So?'

'It's one of Dad's mobile numbers.'

'He's got more than one?'

'The one provided by Harris, of course. But he has another one for secure communications. He made me remember the number. And told me to use the Signal app to call him, so our communications are encrypted.'

Jack was surprised. Harris had an embarrassing history of hacking into people's devices and knew how easy it could be. The company went to a lot of trouble to make sure the phones and laptops they provided to their journalists were secure. And yet Patrick must have felt that wasn't secure enough.

Caitlin took a photograph of the ad in the paper.

Jack asked, 'What was so special about 1987?'

'You tell me, old man, I wasn't even born until two years later.'

'Yeah well, I was only three, so I know about as much as you. Maybe we could check out the newspapers from back then?'

Caitlin scanned the shelves of *The Beacon* back issues. 'When did your father start *The Beacon*?' she asked.

'Some time in the late seventies. Why?'

She said, 'The oldest back issue here is 1988.'

'Maybe they just never kept them back then,' said Jack. 'I'll see if head office can send them.' He unfolded another letter from the box of doom. 'You cannot be serious?' He held it up to Caitlin. The author had cut letters from magazine headlines and stuck them on a page: 'Delete or die, you choose'.

'Yeah, right. I mean, he went to so much trouble, but Dad knew who it was. Some bloke called Bob Holmes. He calls sometimes too.'

'Does he just hurl abuse and hang up?'

'That's him. The note might look clichéd, but he was one of the scary ones and Dad was a bit worried about him. There had been a lot of press about the nudist beach, or should I say clothing-optional beach, at Tyagarah. There's been so many sexual offences occur there and so much anti-social behaviour, some people want to close it down. It's turned into open warfare in the letters column. Dad went out there to do a story and took his camera.' She pointed to the letter. 'The camera was a red rag to a bull. Bob Holmes went nuts. He thought Dad had taken nude photos of his wife.'

'Did your father report it to the police?'

'Yes, and the cops warned the guy, but it hasn't stopped him.'

A loud smashing sound made Jack jump out of his chair. Shattered glass from the front window sprayed all over the floor. Jack heard the roar of a motorbike racing away down the lane and he ran towards the door but, by the time he emerged, the bike had disappeared.

When Jack returned inside, Caitlin was still reading the paper. Unperturbed, she waved a hand vaguely towards the kitchen. 'The phone number's on the fridge.'

Jack picked up a house brick which had come to rest only a metre from where he'd been sitting. He unfurled the paper wrapping, and read its printed message: 'Suppress 5G, not the people'. Jack was surprised. Surely the brick thrower had heard

Patrick was dead? Or were they taking their anger out at *The Beacon* in general?

As Jack turned the brick in his hands, ideas turned in his head and assembled themselves into an action plan for the next day.

The office phone rang. Neither of them picked it up.

Chapter Twenty-nine
Friday, 8th November

Early next morning, Jack was reminded of the summer storms of his childhood as he and Caitlin drove through biblical rain, windscreen wipers slapping uselessly against the onslaught, and the wind howling like a demented banshee as it tried to hurl the car airborne. He couldn't see the potholes now lurking beneath a rampaging river, but they were still trying to demolish the suspension nonetheless. Frogs enthusiastically leaped from the verges to play Russian roulette between the whooshing wheels.

Jack could barely hear Caitlin above the rain drumming on the roof when she asked, 'Do you still think this is a good idea?'

Jack shrugged. He'd thought it a brilliant idea yesterday as he sat waiting for the glazier to replace the smashed window at *The Beacon*. The plan was to check out all the perpetrators of the more outrageous death threats. By virtue of their brick-hurling, the anti-5G crowd had reserved themselves a place high on Jack's list.

It had been years since Jack had been to Mullumbimby, with its quirky shops, on-trend cafés and historic pubs strewn along the main drag, accompanied by the occasional scent of marijuana emanating from hemp-clothed locals walking barefoot down the street. Mullum had always been given a bad rap as the anti-vax capital of Australia. Sure, there were anti-vaxxers here, but they were a noisy minority among a broader community of those who liked an alternate lifestyle or who just wanted to live in one of the most beautiful places on the planet. But it was that noisy minority Jack was wanting to find today, with the hope the anti-vaxxers could lead him to the anti-5G crowd and to the brick-hurlers themselves.

The best place to meet the Mullum locals was at the farmers' market. At least that was Jack's excuse to visit them. He'd always liked the markets although, admittedly, not when it was pissing down with rain.

They aquaplaned through the town centre and joined the flotilla of cars heading to the showground. Miraculously, as they parked the car in a minor tributary, the rain stopped so abruptly the silence was disconcerting – it was as though someone had pressed pause on the weather app. The storm clouds skidded away, replaced by coalescing patches of blue sky.

When Jack stepped from the car, both his feet disappeared deep into mud so squelchy it sucked at his legs and threatened to rip off his shoes whenever he tried to move.

Caitlin took one glance at the sludge oozing up his ankles and said, 'I'll mind the car.'

The demographic had changed since Jack was last at the markets. A new breed of customers had spent a great deal of money to look like they didn't have much money. Boho was in, no matter what it cost, and Jack's crisply cut, collared shirt was out.

The market was hectic despite the weather. Tables strained under mountains of fresh produce – mung beans and sprouts, honey, roasted coffee beans, sourdough bread and exotic fruits, some of which Jack had never seen before. He wandered from stall to stall, happy to be back in this buzzy, vibrant place. He was about to submit to the temptation of an apple and ginseng juice when he spied the anti-vaxxers. They had a stall hemmed in between organic cheeses on one side, and crystals of all sizes and hues on the other.

Two pairs of pale-blue eyes watched eagerly as Jack approached, their owners springing up from chairs in unison and smiling at him. Each had a single waist-length blonde plait, his intertwined with red, yellow and green ribbons. They could have been brother and sister. She wore a white T-shirt emblazoned with 'Freedom of choice is our birthright'. Whatever was written on the man's T-shirt was obscured beneath a woolly beard.

'Hi,' said the young woman, 'are you here to find out about the dangers of vaccines? If so you've come to the right place.'

'I'm interested in 5G,' said Jack.

Their smiles broadened further.

'That's great,' she said. 'I'm Jessica and this is my brother, Matty.'

'Jack.'

She leaned forward and whispered conspiratorially, 'They're trying to control us with our phones.'

A loud ringtone pierced the air, bringing the conversation to an abrupt halt. It was Jack's phone. As he took it from his pocket, Jessica and Matty both frowned and took giant steps backwards.

Jack shrugged apologetically and accepted the call. 'Ricky, can I call you back in a minute.'

'Don't bother. It'll be TAILS.'

'What?'

'Jack, have you been asleep for the last ten years? The memory stick, it's TAILS. Look it up.' Ricky hung up.

The siblings now kept plenty of distance from Jack, their enthusiasm rapidly waning.

'Sorry about that,' said Jack, and put the phone away. 'I'd really like to meet with the leader of your group. If you have one.'

Jessica looked hesitantly at Matty, who nodded. She said, 'That'll be Lars. He's kind of our local guru. He organises the meetings and manages the Facebook page, that kind of thing.'

'How do I find him?'

'You could make an appointment. He's a dentist in Byron. Lars Nielsen.' She picked up a leaflet from the table and offered it to Jack. 'If you join our anti-vax action group, he'll give you a discount. And he's holistic.'

Jack ignored the offer. 'Can I sign up online? Using my phone?'

Jessica shook her head, lips taut, her smile deep in cold storage.

Ten minutes later, as Jack sloshed back to the car carrying two juices so green they could only have been made by pushing The Hulk through a blender, Jack tried to remember where he'd heard the name Lars Nielsen before.

Chapter Thirty

The road remained a river, water gushing in high arcs from the car's wheels as Jack and Caitlin drove back along the motorway. With the clouds long gone, sunlight painted the freshly washed sugar cane bright green. Now that conditions had improved, and Jack didn't have to concentrate so hard on driving, he started noticing election posters staked along the side of the road. The first one was for a Greens candidate: a smiling Tabitha Frogmore above the tagline: 'We Only Have One Byron'. The next ten posters in a row were of Tom Bradshaw, the current mayor, pictured with his arms folded over a jacket and blue tie, laughing. His tagline: 'Developing A Better Byron'. Beyond the election signs, textured cane fields stretched all the way to the foothills of the distant mountain range.

Caitlin broke the silence. 'Dad loved this countryside. It reminded him of home, of the forty shades of green on the rolling Irish hillsides.' She watched out her side window as the cane fields slipped by and when she turned back, Jack could see she'd been crying.

'Are you okay?' asked Jack.

Caitlin nodded. She took out her phone and attached it to the loose end of a cable trailing from the car's radio. Through her sniffles she said, 'He used to play this all the time in the car.'

'Cattle and Cane' by the Go-Betweens came on. She cranked up the volume, but the speakers couldn't do justice to the driving base and crazy beats. It was an impossible song to sing along to, so they listened in silence. When it was over, Caitlin turned down the sound and returned her gaze to the cane fields. A few minutes later she looked at Jack's feet, then lowered her window all the way down.

'You know you stink?' she said.

He smiled at her. 'Thanks.'

'You're welcome. Did you learn anything back there?'

'The two at the anti-vax stall didn't look like brick-throwers, but I did find out who the conspirator-in-chief is. Some dentist called Lars Nielsen.'

'I can't remember Dad mentioning him,' said Caitlin. 'Have you heard from Ricky?'

'Yes, but I have no idea what he was talking about. He said it was tiles, or tails or something. I'll have to call him back and ask him to translate.'

'It's TAILS.' She must have seen the lack of comprehension in his face because she explained, 'Jack, you're a journalist, or at least pretending to be one. You're not exactly bringing a comprehensive knowledge of current affairs to the job. TAILS is what Edward Snowden used. It was all over the newspapers at the time, although not any of yours, obviously. Wait.' She fumbled for her phone and searched the term. 'Here. Wikipedia. "TAILS, or The Amnesic Incognito Live System, is a security-focused Linux distribution aimed at preserving privacy and anonymity. The system is designed to be booted as a live DVD or live USB, and will leave no digital footprint on the machine unless explicitly told to do so".'

He looked across at her. 'So, we're in?'

'There's a wiki with the instructions.' She smiled at him. 'How hard could it be?'

The song changed to 'Streets of Your Town' and this time they both sang along to the choruses. Caitlin's singing stopped when, instead of continuing down the motorway to Byron Bay, Jack took an earlier exit, to Tyagarah.

He said, 'I've organised for us to meet someone. A surprise.'

'No, Jack, I want to find out what's on the memory stick.'

'We'll only be a few minutes. He's one of the people who wrote threatening letters to your father.'

They pulled up outside a small, low-set, brick-and-tile house and climbed out. The red-brick front fence had such a precarious lean it would soon have to decide whether to stay up or fall down. A small aluminium motorboat sat on a trailer on a front lawn free of garden beds, but not of weeds. Crows heckled them from a dilapidated TV aerial, 'Fark, fark, fark.'

The front door opened before Jack had a chance to knock. 'You must be Jack.' The man who stood before them was moon-faced, mid-sixties and stark bollock naked. The only thing covering any of his darkly tanned, heavily wrinkled exterior was a slow-release nicotine patch buried in hair above his right nipple.

Caitlin turned her head away. 'I'll mind the car,' she said, and was gone.

'Bob Holmes.'

Jack hesitantly shook his extended hand.

The man looked down at Jack's muddy shoes. 'You'll have to take them off before you come inside.'

Jack slipped off his shoes and socks and left them beside the door. He was about to step inside when Bob stopped him.

'You'll also have to take the rest of your kit off. I'm a naturist, my wife is a naturist, this is a one-hundred-per-cent-naturist household. There are hangers here in the entrance. And a bowl to leave your mobile phone in, you can't bring that into the house.'

Jack stayed where he was. 'I don't think so.'

'I thought you wanted to ask some questions about that bastard Patrick O'Shaughnessy. But suit yourself, mate.' He shrugged and started closing the door.

'Wait,' said Jack. 'We could talk here.'

'The neighbours call the cops if I stand here naked too long, so it's inside or nothing.'

Jack still hesitated.

'Relax, mate. It's just me and my wife home, nothing to be ashamed about. It's natural.'

Jack stepped into the entry hall and stripped down to his boxers. 'That's as far as I go.'

Bob stood blocking the way with his arms folded, his penis seeming to point defiantly at Jack. 'Well, this is as far as you go then.'

Jack turned around, slipped out of his underwear, and covered himself with a hand. He reached into his trouser pocket and removed an envelope, then followed Bob into the house, determined his free hand was staying exactly where it was for the length of what would be a very brief interview.

He was shown into the lounge room. A woman sat reading a magazine. She, too, was completely naked.

'Jack, this is my wife, Barbara.'

She looked at least twenty years younger than Bob, her face obscured behind a thick layer of make-up, including rouge on her cheeks and bright-red lipstick. Bob was seriously punching above his considerable weight. Her large breasts jiggled as she stood up and reached out a hand to shake Jack's, who reluctantly freed his hand to take it. She kept hold of it and then bent towards him and planted a kiss on his cheek, an inappropriately long, lingering kiss.

'Nice to meet you, Jack,' she said in a surprisingly husky voice. 'But I'll have to leave you two alone, I have work to do.' She moved around Jack collecting things, her knees straight, bending from the waist as she picked up magazines and a coffee cup from the floor.

Jack, now feeling even more uncomfortable, looked away.

After Barbara left the room, Bob motioned to the lounge. 'How can I help?'

Jack looked carefully at the leather lounge chair before sitting in it, wondering how many naked bums had perched there before him. When he sat, it was so low he felt as if his arse was almost on the floor. Bob chose the chair directly opposite.

'Bob, what was your beef with Patrick O'Shaughnessy?'

'Who said I had any problem with him?'

Jack opened the envelope and placed one of the threatening letters, complete with its patchwork of pasted words, on the coffee table between them. Bob said nothing but Jack saw the flicker of recognition in his face.

'And I know it's you who makes the phone calls.'

A long silence followed, and Jack knew not to fill it. Bob broke first.

'You said you were a journalist working with Patrick, not the police.'

'Not the police, no.'

Bob sighed. 'Do you want a beer?'

Jack definitely didn't want a beer. He didn't want to prolong this more than he needed. His bum was starting to stick to the leather on the chair.

'Barbara and I moved here to Tyagarah because the nudist beach is just at the end of the lane. But over the last few years we've had a few undesirables hanging around, some with cameras, and others masturbating in front of my wife, or me. The police can't be out here all the time. Anyway, that bloody O'Shaughnessy came out a few months ago, to do a story, or so he said. He interviewed some people, including my wife, then disappeared up into the dunes, for some' – Bob gestured quotation marks with has fingers – 'location shots. But he had a big lens and spent a lot of time pointing it at my wife. I confronted him. He said it was a lens for wide angle shots, but I could tell it was a zoom. I got angry, pushed him and he fell over backwards. Some other blokes heard us arguing and pulled me off him. O'Shaughnessy refused to delete the photos, or even show them to me.'

Jack pointed to the letter. 'So, you threatened to kill him.'

'I never wanted to kill him. I just didn't want anybody perving at photos of my wife. Or putting them on the internet. My wife and I were both upset when we heard he'd been killed by a shark. Nobody deserves to go like that. Even a bastard like O'Shaughnessy.'

'Where were you on the night he died?'

'At the ANF.'

'What's that?'

'Australian Naturist Federation. It was our annual get together, in Cairns. Are you sure you don't want a beer?'

Jack shook his head then, using only one hand to push himself up from the low chair, stood. He had his answer, and he was getting out of here. Bob was a long way away when Patrick went missing, so he said. Jack could check the alibi if needed.

Bob followed him to the front door, and Jack dressed.

Jack said, 'I'd appreciate it if you stopped calling and sending threatening letters.'

Bob nodded. 'I'll stop. As soon as you find those photos O'Shaughnessy took and delete them.'

As Jack headed back to the car, he heard Bob call out, 'Why don't you come to the beach with us some time? And bring your girlfriend.'

When Jack returned to the car, he could see the amusement in Caitlin's eyes as she tried to suppress a grin.

'Don't say a word,' said Jack. 'Not one.'

She smiled and said, 'Now that you're done dicking around, I want to go back and have a crack at TAILS.'

Chapter Thirty-one

Jack's shoes stank, and Caitlin kept reminding him. As they walked towards *The Beacon*, he tossed them into a bin. They took a detour via a surf shop, where the sales assistant, with an almost incomprehensible French accent, sold him a pair of white canvas sneakers.

Back at *The Beacon*, Caitlin admired the newly replaced pane of glass. 'I was just getting used to the post-apocalyptic decor.'

Jack checked the lock, no new scratches. Inside, they sat side by side as he logged on to his laptop and inserted the memory stick into the USB port. Jack turned to Caitlin and said, 'White, no sugar. Thanks, honey.' He smiled as she gave him the death stare. He shrugged. 'I'm very busy and important. I have to get the tiles working.'

'TAILS.' She headed to the kitchenette. 'And I bet you won't last ten minutes without phoning Ricky.'

Jack returned his focus to the screen and the memory stick. Caitlin returned with the coffee cups and slammed one down in front of him, spilling much of its contents on the table.

'Oh, sorry,' she said, but sounding anything but. She took a seat and began tapping her fingernails loudly on the table, saying nothing.

The memory stick appeared to be empty, with no executable

file visible to launch TAILS. Jack just stared at the same error message they had seen before: 'You need to format the disk in drive D before you can use it. Format?'

He knew he was beaten, and he knew what was coming.

'Does it hurt?' she asked, as she kept tapping irritatingly on the table. 'Not being able to call him.'

'Okay, smart-arse, you win.'

Jack reached for his phone, but Caitlin had anticipated him. She grabbed it from the table and held it just out of his reach, taunting him.

'Have you tried turning the laptop off and turning it back on again?' she asked.

'Ha, fucking, ha,' said Jack.

'I'm serious. Leave the memory stick plugged in and reboot.'

Jack was sure she was still messing, but did as she asked.

She continued. 'When the screen goes blank, just keep hitting the F12 key.'

Now he was sure she was mucking around, but he hit the key over and over until a dialogue box appeared.

Caitlin continued speaking with authority. 'Choose USB boot.'

Jack was impressed. The TAILS boot sequence started, and messages appeared, followed by the TAILS logo on a dark screen.

She took the laptop from him. 'I kept busy in the car when you were playing nudist with your new boyfriend.'

A dialogue box said: 'Welcome to TAILS'. She was starting to get excited now, Jack noticed her hand trembling on the mouse. The dialogue box then asked for a 'passphrase' for the 'Encrypted Persistent Storage'.

'It's here, in a "persistence" directory, where Dad would have stored his documents.'

Jack said, 'And your father told you the password?'

'Yes and no.'

'What do you mean?'

'Well, he told me the first half of it. He said it wasn't safe for me to know all the password. My half is "Heroine". Dad specifically said it was the two "e" version, as I thought he meant the drug.'

'Okay, but if that's half the password, how do we find the other half?'

'Zoe has it.' She took out her phone and dialled. 'Zoe, I need your half of the password.' She listened, then said, 'Are you sure?' When the call finished, Caitlin frowned. 'That's weird. Her half of the password is exactly the same as mine.'

'What, heroine?'

She nodded, then returned her attention to the laptop and began typing. Two seconds later, the computer beeped, and an error message appeared: 'Cannot unlock encrypted storage with this passphrase'.

Jack asked, 'Did you enter your password and Zoe's?'

The death stare was back.

'Then would the "H" be upper case?' he suggested.

Jack watched as she tried multiple permutations, including 'HeroineHeroine', 'Heroine', 'heroine', 'Heroine&Heroine' and then, using one finger at a time to make sure she didn't make a mistake, retyped 'heroineheroine'. Beep, beep, beep, beep, beep.

Jack asked, 'Is there a limit to the number of tries before it locks you out or destroys the data?'

She shrugged. 'The website didn't mention it.'

Jack watched her mounting frustration. She was punching

the keys harder as she tried appending the digits of her birthday and her father's. Her eyebrows lowered and her lips formed an almost invisible line before she yelled at the computer, 'For Christ's sake, let me in!' Jack thought she would break the keyboard as she hammered out 'Password123' and, finally, 'fuckyou'.

The relentless beeps kept mocking them.

Jack leaned back in his chair, folded his arms, and grinned in anticipation. 'Ricky?'

'No, fuck Ricky.' She slammed the laptop closed. She only looked up when she heard him laughing.

'That was way too easy,' he said. 'I thought lawyers were trained to not bite back when your buttons are pushed.'

'Yeah, well, I just really want to know what Dad was up to.'

Jack phoned Ricky.

'Jacko, what's happening?'

'You know that TAILS memory stick we found? We don't know the password to access the files. Can you hack into it or something?'

'Jack. Seriously? You're giving me too much credit. Not even the CIA can crack TAILS file encryption. So, unless the password is written down somewhere, or they've told someone, you're screwed.' Ricky cut the call.

Caitlin looked at him expectantly.

Jack avoided her gaze. 'Computer says "no".'

'What do you mean? We have to get those files. You said Ricky was a master at this kind of thing. Can we send it to him?'

'He said it's impossible.'

'But we need to find out what Dad was working on.'

'We just need the correct password. Maybe if you sleep on it?'

Caitlin folder her arms across her chest. 'Yeah, right.'

Jack removed the memory stick from the laptop and returned it to his pocket. Then he took it back out again. 'This really belongs to you, not me,' he said. 'There may be some seriously bad people looking for it, but if you want to keep it ...'

She hesitated, then took it from him and pushed it deep into her pocket. 'I'll think about it and try some passwords tonight. Is there anything else we can be doing? Did head office have the missing issues of *The Beacon*?'

'No, so I've put a request in to the National Library. If they don't have them, short of pulling up lino in old houses, I think that's a dead end.'

'Remember the ad Dad placed in *The Beacon* trying to track down people who worked for Northern Rivers Council in 1987? We should visit the council chambers and look through their archives for that year.'

Jack agreed.

'And what about that dentist dude?'

As she spoke, Jack remembered where he'd seen the name he'd been given at the market that morning. He retrieved Patrick's box of doom from the printer cabinet and flicked through the letters until he found what he was looking for.

'Got you, Lars Nielsen.' He showed the letter to Caitlin. 'The Grand Poobah of the local anti-vaxxers was writing threatening letters to your father.' Jack read through the letter and handed it to Caitlin, then said, 'I might have to have a chat to Dr Nielsen, and ask him if he likes throwing bricks.'

Jack had completely forgotten about his coffee, which sat untouched. He took a sip, then pulled a face.

'What?'

'It's cold.'

'After all the trouble I went to. Talk about ungrateful.' She stood up. 'I'll make another.' She collected both cups and was about to take a step when she dropped one. It smashed to the floor in an explosion of liquid and shards of porcelain. Coffee trickled down Caitlin's legs, over her Ruth Bader Ginsburg tattoo and into her Doc Martens. The white canvas sneakers Jack had owned for less than an hour were now a dappled caramel colour.

Caitlin trembled. She dropped herself into chair and lowered her head into her hands. Jack placed a hand on her shoulder, but she jerked it away and yelled, 'Don't touch me!'

'Caitlin, it's just a cup of coffee. Cold coffee.'

She gave an involuntary shudder. 'I don't care about the fucking coffee.'

Jack couldn't blame her for being upset. He couldn't really imagine how she must be feeling. She'd now lost both her parents. He said, 'I know it's a really shit time. You miss him. Please, if I can help ... If you want to talk.'

She jumped up from the chair and glowered at him, her face flushed red. 'And this has nothing to do with my father.' She ran for the door, snatched up her skateboard, and was gone.

Chapter Thirty-two
Saturday, 9th November

The following morning was a hot one. Even the cicadas, normally quiet at this hour, buzzed loudly in anticipation as Jack stood at the front door of his father's house, waiting for Don to come around with his car to drive him to town. According to Don, Tony was 'unavailable'. He didn't elaborate, but when Jack pushed him, Don said he'd asked Tony to oil the deck around the pool. Jack was surprised – it was going to be too hot a day for that kind of work, and the deck didn't appear to need it.

Unlike Tony's trips, where they drove with the windows down and their elbows on the sills while some of Jack's favourite music blared out from the cassette player, in Don's car the windows were closed, the air conditioner on full blast, and Richard Clayderman tormented him from a CD.

Don wasn't very talkative today, which was unusual. He'd worked for his father for thirty years, but Jack had never really been as close to him as he had been to Tony during his childhood. Don was more formal, even aloof. Perhaps it was his military training. But he ran a tight operation while at the same time being considerate to the staff. Jack glanced at Don. He looked weary and, behind the wheel, he even seemed to be slumping slightly in contrast to his normal upright posture. Jack asked to be let out near a café, and Don drove off with a curt, 'Bye.'

Jack bought two coffees, hoping he could use one to bribe his way into a meeting with the author of some of the more intimidating threats Jack had found in Patrick's box of doom.

There was no mistaking the building he was looking for – a huge sign out the front announced, 'Lars Nielsen Holistic Dentistry'. Every letter 'i' had been painted as a tooth.

In the carpark, a little blue Nissan Leaf with personalised 'MO LARS' number plates was plugged into a charger.

Jack took the stairs two at a time, then entered a disarmingly all-white waiting room. A bowl of shiny red apples provided the only relief from white walls, white furniture, white floor tiles and even a vase of white roses. The blonde receptionist gave an impossibly broad smile, revealing a pristine row of large teeth perfectly matched to the colour of her over-starched white uniform. 'Welcome to Lars Nielsen Holistic Dentistry, how may I help you?'

'Jack Harris for Lars Nielsen.'

She checked through the bookings and drew a blank.

'It's a personal matter,' said Jack, before leaning forward conspiratorially and lowering his voice, 'very personal.'

'Ahm, why don't you take a seat and I'll tell Dr Lars you're here, but he is very busy this morning.'

Jack felt stiffness in his muscles as he sank into a white leather lounge. He'd swum eighty very irregular laps the previous night as he wondered what had precipitated Caitlin's over-reaction to the smashed coffee cup. He could only conclude that she was finding it difficult to cope with everything at the moment. There weren't many life stressors missing from the mountain of seriously shitty things she was trying to deal with – the death and possible murder of her father, potentially being struck off as a lawyer and losing her job, a court case on drug charges, perhaps even going to prison. Jack would be throwing coffee mugs, not dropping them. This morning he'd received a brief text from her – the council archivist had agreed to meet them – but Caitlin was otherwise incommunicado. He reached for his phone and tried calling her again. No answer.

Jack read the notice board, its messages pinned in perfect alignment, like a row of molars. Payment was to be made in advance. No drugs were kept on the premises (which meant there were). A meeting to discuss the 'harmful health effects of 5G' was to be held that night in the Byron Community Centre.

As Jack photographed the 5G notice, he heard a cough behind him and turned to see a tall man in a crisp uniform, its blinding whiteness broken only by 'Lars' emblazoned in blue over a pocket. The man's hands were behind his back, and he didn't look too pleased at being disturbed. He might even have been seriously frowning if not for an abundance of botox. The wrinkle-free visage made it difficult to determine his age, possibly early fifties, but he looked fit, tanned and muscular. He was solid enough to have passed for a bouncer if he ditched the white suit.

'You must be Lars Nielsen.'

'Do we know each other?'

'We do now, I'm Jack Harris.' He anticipated the crushing handshake and beat Nielsen to it. 'I have some questions about the anti-vax movement.'

'And you're asking because you're interested or for another reason?'

'I'm a reporter at *The Beacon*.'

Nielsen looked as if he was going to pick up Jack and throw him out, but still not a wrinkle in sight.

Jack continued. 'We're running a feature on holistic healing in a couple of weeks. I've a few questions.'

'I'm a busy man, you've ten minutes.'

Jack was led into an examination room. There was only one seat, and it wasn't offered to Jack, instead Nielsen motioned to the dental chair.

Nielsen accepted the coffee from Jack without thanks, then walked to a sink and poured it out. 'We holistic dentists oppose fluoride.'

'But Byron doesn't add fluoride to its drinking water.'

'So the council says. I don't take chances.'

'What's holistic dentistry?'

Lars depressed a button on the chair and Jack's head suddenly reclined.

'Open,' ordered Nielsen. The dentist's face hovered uncomfortably close and emitted increasing groans of disapproval as he examined Jack's teeth. 'Do you feel lethargic?'

'No,' said Jack.

'Do you sometimes have trouble concentrating?'

'No.'

Nielsen looked annoyed. Jack was starting to enjoy himself.

The dentist stared at Jack, menace in his eyes, then slowly selected a pick from the tray and stabbed it painfully into Jack's gum.

'Do you sometimes have trouble sleeping?'

Only if I'm partying and don't go to bed, thought Jack. But there was already enough blood in his mouth. Jack swallowed. 'All the time.'

'Your fillings are killing you. They're amalgam The mercury in them leaches out. You need to have them removed as soon as possible, before your hair falls out, you can't get erections and dementia sets in.'

Nielsen deftly swapped the pick for the drill, and its shrill whining filled the room. Nielsen yanked Jack's jaw open wider and Jack felt as if it would be ripped out of its sockets.

He swung up a hand and clamped it over his mouth. He spoke between his fingers. 'Perhaps I should make an appointment when we both have more time.'

Nielsen continued to glare, the drill buzzing loudly, until eventually he gave a reluctant nod and holstered the weapon.

Jack removed his protective hand. His forehead was covered in sweat. When he spoke, his voice was weak. 'And that's holistic dentistry?'

'Just the start. We also fix problems elsewhere in the body that arise from the teeth, and from bite imbalance.'

'Are you also anti-vaccine and anti-5G?'

'We have a holistic approach to health. We try to stop doctors harming us with vaccinations, and the government trying to control us with 5G. Why don't you come to the meeting tonight, and find out the truth?'

'Patrick O'Shaughnessy was very critical of you and the anti-5G crowd. You can't have liked him.'

Nielsen cleared his throat. 'Quite the contrary, I was very sorry to hear of his little run in with the, um, shark.'

'Then why did you send him this?' Jack removed Nielsen's letter from his pocket and held it up. 'You threatened him. You said if he published anything against the anti-vax movement you couldn't guarantee his safety from your so-called "disciples".'

Jack could smell peppermint, and feel the dentist's breath against his cheek as the man leaned in close and spoke. 'O'Shaughnessy was a denier. He ignored the science and blindly believed the lies peddled by global business interests; toothpaste manufacturers poisoning us with fluoride, and vaccine companies giving our children autism. He got what he deserved.' The dentist stabbed at a button and the chair whirred back upright.

'Do you know who threw a brick through our window at *The Beacon*?' asked Jack.

Nielsen smiled for the first time, but not enough to reveal any snow-white teeth. 'Like the letter says, some of my followers are passionate.' The smile disappeared. Furrows tried to form on his brow, battling the botox. 'So be very, very careful, Mr Harris. I can't control them. They'll stop at nothing.' He held Jack's gaze, trying to look fierce, but the botox prevented that too.

Chapter Thirty-three

Even though he knew it was childish, Jack unplugged the dentist's Nissan Leaf as he walked away. He promised himself he would brush his teeth twice a day from now on, and start flossing – anything to avoid ending up in the hands of Lars Nielsen.

Back in *The Beacon*'s Toyota, he checked his phone. Nothing from Caitlin. He searched through his photos and brought up the image of Patrick's surfboard. He was sure he was right, and the pathologist wrong – sharks don't untie leg-ropes before dining on surfers.

Jack started the car and drove to where it all began, at Tallows Beach, to take another look, and to think. In the carpark, the endless cycle of surfers coming and going was playing out, with boards of all shapes and sizes being pulled from the backs of vans, others being washed off and re-stowed. Wetsuits were squeezed into, others peeled off. A young couple sat on a blanket behind their campervan, she with eyes closed smoking a joint, he practising guitar.

Jack retraced what would have been Patrick's final steps down the soft sandy path through the casuarina trees to the beach beyond. For Jack, those last few steps where the closed forest suddenly opened to reveal the long sweep of sand and surf always took his breath away. He remembered the many parties he and his friends had here in the summer holidays. They'd sit around fires, laughing and messing until dawn. He smoked his first joint here, and that had also taken his breath away.

Two topless girls sunbaked close to where Patrick's body had been pulled up onto the sand. They draped arms across their chests as Jack walked past towards Cosy Corner, where Patrick would have launched his board on that last day. The surfers were having good luck with the waves, at the very place where Patrick's luck had run out almost a week before.

Jack returned to the carpark along the wider track to the south, just as an old man, hauling a large plastic water container, shuffled past and disappeared into the forest. Jack interrupted a couple of well-wizened surfers vigorously towelling themselves off. 'How was it?'

The older of the two snorted. 'Really shit. Mostly sitting around listening to him bore me to tears.'

His mate offered a lopsided smile to Jack. 'Don't listen to him. He's just a crap surfer. There were plenty out there all right, if you knew what you were doing.'

The older one rolled his eyes.

Jack asked, 'Were you here the morning of the shark attack?'

The younger one answered, 'Would have been. The best surf would have been here. But just as well, I guess.' He shook his head. 'Bloody awful way to go, poor bugger.'

Jack was puzzled by his answer. 'Why weren't you here if the surf was so good?'

'The gate was closed at the park entrance, so we all ended up at The Pass, bums on boards. I saw the ranger a few days later and he didn't know anything about it. Probably some prick messing around, trying to keep the best surf to himself, or landing some drugs.'

Jack left them to wriggle out of their wetsuits, and crossed the carpark to where he'd seen the old man vanish into the forest. There would only be one reason he was carrying water – he must be camping rough. Maybe he'd seen something.

A faintly worn path of flattened soil led Jack to a fire trail and on deeper into the forest until a tangle of fallen branches blocked the way. Jack climbed over and walked on, the waves sounding louder with each step. Out of nowhere, three tall white greyhounds were suddenly upon him. He stood still, wary, his heart pounding. The dogs raced towards him as a pack. They were sleek and swift and closed in on him quickly. When the first one jumped up he held his breath and expected to feel teeth, but it was attention it was seeking, not his throat.

When Jack recovered enough to resume walking, the dogs trotted beside him with their tails wagging. The path led to a makeshift camp where a tiny A-frame tent occupied one side of a small clearing. A tarpaulin stretched between trees, shading a small table, a gas stove, the water container and the old man. The man sat on a folding canvas chair, watching Jack. His clothes were tidy and clean, a green-checked flannelette shirt, shorts and thongs. His wide-brimmed straw hat was at least twenty years too late to prevent the sun-spots littering his face.

He looked at Jack warily. 'The track doesn't go anywhere; you can walk down and have a look yourself if you want to.'

'Actually, it's you that I've come to see.'

The man's eyebrows lowered, the wrinkles deepening in his brow. 'You're not from Social bloody Services are you?'

Jack laughed. 'No. Worse. I'm a journalist.'

The man's demeanour hardened. 'Oh, Jesus. Not another bloody do-gooder writing about the homeless. Well, you've got the wrong man. I like living here.' Then, more accusatory, 'And I like my own company.'

'Good for you. I'm not here to bother you. I just wanted to ask you if you saw anything the other night.'

'What night?'

'Sunday. A surfer was taken by a shark early last Monday morning.'

'What day is it today?'

'Saturday. So almost a week ago.'

The man thought about it. 'Was that the one with all the sirens? I thought someone might have been swept out, or one of those crazy hang-gliders might have crashed. A shark?'

One of the dogs ambled over and rolled onto his back in front of Jack, who reluctantly crouched down and started rubbing its belly. 'Do you remember anything at all?'

The man crossed his arms. 'I might be homeless, but I'm not stupid.'

'The man died.'

'From the shark attack?'

'So they say, but I'm not so sure. That's why I'm asking.'

He looked at Jack suspiciously. 'Are you gonna tell anyone I'm here?'

'As far as I'm concerned you can stay here as long as you like. Half your luck, it's a great spot.'

The man was quiet for a few moments, then nodded. 'I use the toilets at the carpark. That night I was caught short for a number two. There was a big black van and people moving around so I kept my distance. You never know what trouble you might get into. Sometimes drunks, or druggies.'

Jack stopped patting the dog, but it wriggled up against him until he started again. 'Were there any other cars?'

'Nah. It was early. The surfers don't arrive until around dawn. It was still dark when I got back here, but I heard a boat motor.'

'What makes you think it was a boat?'

'I walked back along the beach, to avoid whoever was in the carpark, and saw some lights just offshore. And next morning there was a new orange buoy floating off the beach. Probably a drug drop, or illegal fishing. Happens from time to time. I keep well out of their way.'

'Anything else?'

He thought for a while. 'Only the sirens later that day.'

The dog lost interest and loped off.

'Thanks, you've been a big help.' Jack held out his hand.

Without getting up, the old man took it. 'I'm Eric.'

'Jack. Nice to meet you, Eric. Do you need anything?'

'If you're offering, food for the dogs. It's bloody heavy, and a long way to carry.'

Jack turned to leave, but the old man stopped him.

'Aren't you going to ask me about the next night? They were back again.'

'The same people?'

'Either that or someone else pinched their orange buoy – it was gone the next day.' The man nodded towards the path. 'The track does go down to the beach, I just tell people it doesn't so they clear off. Why don't you have a look?'

The dogs kept Jack company as far as the beach before turning back. He walked across the warm sand and sat, staring out to sea. There was no orange buoy to be seen today; it was just him, the warm sun, a billion billion grains of sand and the mesmerising waves. And thoughts of murder.

Jack was now even more certain the pathologist was wrong. And yet he had nothing tangible, no proof, nothing that would stop Begley from throwing him out of the police station again and accusing him of time-wasting. And there was nothing Jack could write in *The Beacon* either – no amount of 'allegedlys' or 'sources close to the murderer' could give this story any credibility. So, for the moment, he would keep his own counsel. And keep turning over rocks to see what might lie beneath.

A sooty oystercatcher strutted along the shoreline. The bird inserted its long, lipsticked beak deep into the wet sand and pulled out a worm, distracting Jack long enough for a large wave to catch him by surprise, and soak his shorts.

'Shit.' He checked his watch. There was no time to dry off in the sun, he had an appointment with Caitlin, and he would only just make it in time.

Chapter Thirty-four

Jack was going to be late. He'd underestimated the traffic getting through Byron – he should have known better. Zoe, who was doing a hairdressing house-call for an elderly client, had agreed to drop off Caitlin, so hopefully she was already there. He raced along the pockmarked road out of town, hitting a pothole the size of a bomb crater, after which the car developed an ominous rattle that continued the whole drive along the motorway until he reached the council office in Mullumbimby.

Caitlin the chameleon was in professional mode today, her dreadlocks deftly assembled into a bun, and Betty Boop and Bader Ginsburg nowhere to be seen. She pointedly glanced at her watch when he arrived, looking as nonplussed as a lawyer waiting on time she couldn't charge out. She said, 'I'd be getting that prostate seen to.'

Jack was confused until she glanced towards the large wet patch on his shorts.

'It's nice to see you too, Caitlin.' And he was pleased to see her – he'd been worried when she hadn't answered his calls all day. 'Are you okay?'

She merely nodded, without offering an explanation as to what had upset her when she'd dropped the cup the previous day. 'C'mon, we're very late.'

The receptionist was unsmiling. She was even frostier when

she saw the wet patch on Jack's shorts. 'So your partner has finally arrived then?'

'Oh, he's not my partner,' replied Caitlin, 'he's my executive support officer. Or was.' She didn't look at Jack, but he saw a flicker of a smile. 'He's finishing up today; late once too often.'

A well-rehearsed 'whatever' look came over the receptionist's face. 'I'll let Marlene know you're here.'

A few minutes later they were led along narrow, low-ceilinged corridors. Packed offices opened higgledy-piggledy on each side. Printers and cabinets were packed into every available space.

A sign on the door announced: 'Marlene Jennings, Archivist'. Inside, her office was an oasis of order compared with the post-cyclonic decor they'd just walked through. Wall-to-wall shelves were heavy with an array of ring binders, archive boxes and manila folders. Marlene's welcoming face was framed by a bob cut of thick, dark hair, her matching eyebrows parallel lines beneath a sharp fringe. Two photos stood on her desk, one of an elderly man, presumably her husband, the other a dog. Both photos were the same size.

When she greeted them, she took Caitlin's hand, holding it in both of hers as she spoke. 'Caitlin O'Shaughnessy? You must be Patrick's daughter. I'm so sorry.'

Caitlin took a deep breath before she answered. 'Thank you.'

Marlene offered them chairs. 'Your father spent a lot of time here over the years, especially the last few months.'

'What was he doing?' asked Jack.

She laughed. 'You'd think I'd know, but I don't. Lately he was pretty cagey.'

Caitlin asked, 'Do you have a record of the documents he accessed?'

Marlene looked a little embarrassed and lowered her voice.

'I'm supposed to. But your father and I had a little arrangement. He brought in a bottle of red or one of his lovely, scented candles from time to time, and I didn't waste ratepayers' money recording everything he looked at. I just let him work quietly away at the other desk.' She pointed at a table at the side of the room, beneath the window.

Jack turned and looked at the masses of documents on the shelves and his heart sank. 'We're trying to find out what Patrick was investigating when he came here. Are we able to look through documents ourselves?'

She raised an eyebrow. 'Can you narrow it down to a particular time? Otherwise, you could be spending the rest of your lives in here.'

Caitlin replied, '1987.'

Marlene's eyes widened. 'Are you sure? 1987?'

They both nodded.

Marlene sat quietly and placed her palms face down on the desk, then seemed to make a decision. She walked to the door and quietly closed it before pointing out a large gap between a row of folders. 'See those missing documents? That's 1987.' Her voice was low, infused with anger. 'It was Tom Bradshaw himself who came down a few weeks ago and took them. He said he needed to do some research. Research, my foot. Now he's refusing to return them, but what am I supposed to do? He's the goddamned mayor.'

Jack and Caitlin looked at each other and their eyebrows rose simultaneously.

Caitlin recovered first. 'And online?'

The anger was still in Marlene's face. 'Digitising the older records hasn't been a priority for funding.'

Jack asked, 'Do you know what happened in that year?'

Marlene shook her head, her bob swaying backwards and forwards. 'Before my time. What are you looking for?'

'Something big or something controversial, a planning decision, corruption, major conflict of interest. We really don't know,' said Jack.

There was a very long silence before she spoke. 'Look, there might be a way. As long as you don't disclose the source of the information.'

Jack and Caitlin exchanged glances, and quickly agreed. Jack felt a little flutter of hope. He was sure everything was tied to whatever story Patrick had been chasing.

'Give me a few days,' Marlene said. She wrote out her personal mobile number and handed it to Jack. 'Don't call me at work.' She then opened the door, looked each way down the corridor, and walked them quickly out.

Chapter Thirty-five

Later that evening, Jack skirted around an animated throng of people as he made his way down Jonson Street to the anti-5G meeting. The crowd was keeping a respectful distance as they watched a busker juggling. They cheered as he hovered unsteadily on a unicycle and tossed roaring chain saws from hand to hand. Jack stopped to watch, transfixed, but when the busker dropped one of the buzzing monsters, scattering those in the front row, Jack moved on in case there was a blood bath.

Jack arrived at the Byron Bay Community Centre just as Warren Parks, *The Beacon*'s 'conspiracy theory' reporter, was leaving. He didn't look happy.

'Blacklisted, again,' he said to Jack. 'Take notes for me if you get in.'

The sentinel guarding the auditorium door was a young woman. Her T-shirt was printed with a large '5G' slashed through with red. She insisted Jack turn off his phone, before handing him a clipboard on which he scribbled a fake email address and phone number. He then headed straight to the bathroom, where he turned his phone back on, switched it to silent and reassured himself he had enough storage space and battery.

The auditorium was semicircular in shape. Jack chose a seat on the side. Among the audience of fifty or so, he recognised

Jessica and Matty from the previous day's market stall. A hard-core group in the front row waved placards: '5G – NO WAY, GO AWAY', or the '5G' slashed through in red.

Lars Nielsen arrived fifteen minutes late, still wearing his pristine dental uniform. To Jack's disbelief, most of the crowd stood and clapped as Nielsen bounded to the stage, waved, then flashed teeth so impossibly white they looked backlit.

Nielsen held up his hands and the crowd settled. 'Welcome, my fellow concerned citizens. Thank you for giving up your valuable time to help us fight for our rights, our right to say no to 5G and ensure a healthy future for our children.'

The first image of his presentation was projected on a big screen. 'I know many of you here are already aware of the dangers of 5G, but tonight is also an information session for those that haven't yet shaken off the shackles of the government's deliberate misinformation.' He turned and pointed to Jack. 'Like this man over here.'

The crowd turned to Jack in unison.

'My presentation will be followed by a Q&A session then, after the general meeting, there will be a closed session for the members of the 5G Action Committee.'

Nielsen was a charismatic speaker and had everybody, except Jack, spellbound. He spoke enthusiastically to a procession of slides expounding the dangers of 5G: the radiation was higher than 4G; there hadn't been adequate testing; mice who slept on 5G transmitters had shorter life expectancies; and on he went, accompanied by outbreaks of clapping and nodding.

The last slide thanked the event sponsor – Lars Nielsen Holistic Dentistry. During another standing ovation, Nielsen drank in the adoration, even bowing, before asking for questions.

Jack raised a hand. 'Does the group operate strictly on a code of non-violent action, or did someone throw a brick through the window of *The Beacon* two days ago?'

Everybody stared at Jack now, except one man in the front row more interested in examining his feet.

Nielsen's piano-key smile now looked almost sinister. 'It's polite to introduce yourself before asking a question, but let me do that for you. This is Jack Harris. Jack is a journalist for *The Beacon*, and I'm sure all of you who read last week's editorial will know what that means – he's no friend of ours.'

Heads whispered to each other. Boos emanated from the front row.

'I'm happy to humour you, Mr Harris. Did anybody throw a brick through the window of *The Beacon*?'

There was silence.

'You see, we are a completely law-abiding group.' He turned back to his acolytes. 'Would anybody here like to throw a brick at *The Beacon*?'

Hands quickly went up in the front row, followed by the remainder of the auditorium as the peer pressure mounted. Nielsen flashed most of his thirty-two teeth at Jack before taking more questions.

When the Q&A ended, Nielsen wished everybody strength in their fight against 5G, and reminded them to collect a discount card for his dentistry services on the way out. To avoid trouble with the crowd, Jack waited until only Nielsen and his small action committee remained before he left the auditorium.

Outside, needing to kill some time, Jack crossed the road and strolled through the leafy park to The Rails. This hotel had always been his favourite watering hole, even before his infamous eighteenth birthday party was held there. His father had paid for the bar for the night, and also for legal representation when Jack was charged with indecent exposure after having been found the following morning tied naked to a light pole at the railway station as the first train pulled into the platform.

The Rails was far enough from the main thoroughfares to be frequented mostly by locals rather than tourists and, being in the now decommissioned railway station, had character the other hotels in town couldn't match. Apart from a fresh coat of paint, the place didn't seemed to have changed – it still had the same friendly vibe. Best of all, the back bar retained the replica of an old single-engine plane, maybe a spitfire, dramatically crashing through the ceiling. It was an unusual sight, and an incongruity none of the locals or bar staff had ever been able to explain to Jack.

No sooner had he taken a seat in the beer garden than a policeman walked past wearing a pair of fishnet stockings. The officer was followed by two men in nappies, then a man-sized pink flamingo. Fred Flintstone arrived arm in arm with a bearded Princess Leia and soon Jack was surrounded by people – all in fancy dress, with the exception of a sheepish adolescent in jeans and T-shirt who must have missed the memo. A heavily rouged nun told Jack it was their soccer team's end of season party, then flashed Jack with an enormous pair of pendulous, knitted boobs.

Two schooners of pacific ale later, Jack ambled back through the park to wait. To avoid being seen, he kept back from the footpath, hovering between a tarot reader and a pair of clumsy fire jugglers until the 5G Action Committee filed out of the community centre. Nielsen was the last to leave, and Jack watched him fold himself into the little electric car and soundlessly depart.

Jack returned to the community centre, where he told the

attendant closing up that he'd left something behind. Inside the auditorium, Jack collected his phone from under his seat and ended the recording.

He returned to The Rails Hotel, where Princess Leia and the menagerie were cheering on the nun, now dancing topless on a table, his fake boobs flapping around his ears. Jack took his pint to the table furthest away so he could hear his bootleg recording above all the din.

When he started the playback, Jack's delight at outwitting Lars Nielsen soon turned to disappointment. The phone had been too far away and, even with the volume turned right up, he could only hear snippets of what the action committee had said. *The Beacon* may have been mentioned and he thought he heard Patrick O'Shaughnessy's name, but he couldn't make out the context. Some voices were louder than others and he clearly heard one person describing a plan to unfurl an anti-5G banner from the side of the Byron Bay water tower. This would happen the next night there was heavy rain – presumably so they weren't seen by insomniac dog walkers or nocturnal snoggers. At last, Jack would have some content for his first edition of *The Beacon*. It would be a good story, and if he could get a photo, it might even make the front page.

As he finished his beer, he watched security usher the nun and a penguin from the premises.

Chapter Thirty-six
Sunday, 10th November

'Fuck it,' said Jack, as he pounded his phone into silence at two the next morning. His irritation wasn't due to the alarm itself, but to the wakeful hours of tossing and turning in anticipation of being woken so early.

After a brief detour to the kitchen for coffee, Jack stood and stared at the red shiny monster. The Ferrari. His car of last resort. The drive to Newcastle was six hours and he didn't trust the death rattle of *The Beacon*'s old Toyota. Besides, it was motorway all the way and the Ferrari would eat the miles. For Jack, still somewhat pissed at his father for sending him to Byron Bay and swapping his stepbrother into his role at head office, there was an added bonus – the car was in showroom condition and the trip would add a shitload of kilometres to his father's odometer. Bad Jack, he thought, and smiled in anticipation.

He wasn't smiling four hours later when he pulled into a service centre to refuel both the car and himself. The Ferrari's impossibly low-slung roof line meant an almost semi-recumbent driving position, and his body was stiff with protest as he climbed out. Although the car effortlessly drank almost ninety litres of fuel, Jack struggled to drink the acrid coffee, only managing to do so by convincing himself it was medicinal, to keep him awake. He took one bite of his ham and cheese sandwich before binning it, his tastebuds overruling his hunger.

Jack shoehorned himself back into the beast, then, as the car growled towards motorway speed, he wondered what the hell he was doing. The closest forensic pathologist was in Newcastle, some six hundred kilometres to the south of Byron. Patrick's body would have been taken there, but Jack had no appointment, didn't know the name of the pathologist who performed the autopsy and didn't even know if they would be working on the weekend. But he figured if they weren't, at least if it was the hospital switchboard that connected him through, the pathologist might agree to talk to him on the phone. Begley had said the pathologist confirmed a shark attack as the cause of death, but Jack wanted to hear it directly from them, and to determine if there had been any doubt, because Jack was certain there was no shark.

A few hours later, Jack pulled into one of the last spaces in the carpark. Being only three stories high, but stretching almost half a kilometre long, John Hunter Hospital looked like a colossal builder's fuck-up. Jack wondered whether the architect had accidentally printed the construction drawings in landscape format instead of portrait. Whatever the cause, a cardiac arrest patient would have rigor mortis by the time the crash team arrived breathless from the other end of the hospital.

Inside the main entrance, Jack searched the signage for the mortuary. A lift took him to the floor below, where he picked up an internal wall phone, found the number he wanted on a card, and dialled.

It took forever for the operator to answer, 'Switch.'

'Hi,' said Jack, 'I'm one of the cardiology interns. I'm trying to track down the forensic pathologist who called me this morning about a post-mortem, but I didn't catch their name.'

'That will be Dr Fox. Would you like me to put you through?'

'Thanks.' He heard the ringtone. An internal phone directory hung from the wall and Jack frantically scanned it before the call answered.

'Nicola Fox.'

'Hi, Nicola. This is Dr Alex Andrews.' Jack checked back to the phone directory. 'One of the rheumatology consultants. I wonder if I can come and chat to you about one of the post-mortems you did?' There was a long pause at the other end. This was bad, thought Jack. 'Look, I'm sorry, I know you're really busy, it will only take a few minutes. I'll bring coffee.'

Again, the silence stretched interminably before she finally answered, 'Okay, but give me twenty minutes. C1 courtyard. A double-shot flat white.'

With a coffee in each hand, Jack found his way to ward C1, ignored the 'Staff Only' sign on the glass door, and entered the courtyard. The large open-air atrium was planted out with small trees and ferns, providing a peaceful retreat from the disinfectant smell permeating the hospital.

Jack waited anxiously on a bench, watching the door. So far, so good he thought. He'd dressed neatly, and none of the stethoscope-draped doctors he'd passed had been wearing white coats.

It was thirty minutes before a woman pushed through the glass door and approached him. Her oversize glasses had thin blue rims that matched the colour of her eyes and her scrubs. She exuded weariness and was unsmiling, and unwelcoming.

'Thanks for seeing me,' said Jack, offering her the coffee.

She hesitated before asking, 'Is it safe to drink?'

'Sorry?'

'The coffee. You're not a stalker? Or trying to poison me?'

The glass door opened. A burly security guard entered and took a position by the door, directing an intimidating stare at Jack.

Dr Fox said, 'Dr Alex Andrews happens to be a good friend of mine. She also happens to be female.'

Jack couldn't help but let out a laugh as his hastily formed plan crashed around him.

'I only came because I was intrigued.' She nodded towards the security guard. 'But if you're a journalist, I'll unleash the hounds.'

'I'm not trying to poison you. We can swap cups if you prefer?'

She shook her head and gave a tired smile.

'My real name is Jack Harris. But before you throw coffee over me, you don't have to say anything at all, just listen.'

She looked curious and gave a slight nod.

'Did you do the post-mortem on Patrick O'Shaughnessy?'

Dr Fox didn't answer. Out of the corner of his eye, Jack saw the security guard take a few steps towards them.

'He was supposedly taken by a shark at Byron Bay.'

She raised her eyebrows. 'Supposedly?'

'I'm a friend of Caitlin O'Shaughnessy, Patrick's daughter. Before he went missing, Patrick was in fear of his life. He was a journalist and it seems he wandered into some dangerous territory. He'd recently upgraded the security in his house and taken out a life insurance policy. On the night he died, his laptop and phone were stolen.'

The pathologist stared at him impassively. The security guard took a few more steps.

'But the thing that really concerns me is that Patrick's leg-rope hadn't snapped off as you'd expect with a shark attack.

It had been removed from his ankle, and the velcro strap closed up again.'

'Why are you telling me this?'

'I figured that if you knew there were suspicious circumstances you would be less likely to overlook something, well, suspicious. That you might arrive at a different conclusion.'

She looked at him for some time before she spoke. 'So you doubt my professional ability? You think I'm incompetent?'

'No, of course not. But I drove six hundred kilometres to see you because Inspector Begley told me you'd given him a verbal opinion that it was definitely a shark attack. I just wanted to be sure. I want to be sure for Patrick. And for Caitlin.'

The pathologist stood up without a word and walked over to the security guard. They spoke briefly and the guard left, but not before aiming another frosty glare at Jack.

Dr Fox returned to the seat. 'Ultimately, it is the coroner who decides the cause of death. All I can do is report my findings to them.' She sipped her coffee then looked at Jack. 'I'm prepared to say a few things off the record on the condition you don't quote me and, given you are a journalist, you promise to protect your source.'

'I never said I was a journalist.'

'Oh, c'mon. You knew Mr O'Shaughnessy, so the chances are … And you have journalist's balls waltzing in here pretending to be a doctor.' She took another sip of coffee, her eyes not leaving Jack's. 'Besides, my brother's a journalist; I can smell them a mile away. As a matter of fact, if my brother wasn't a journalist I would have told you to get lost.'

Jack laughed. 'It's a deal. I've never spoken with you. In fact, I have no recollection of ever meeting you.'

She leaned forward and spoke quietly, even though they

were alone in the courtyard. 'There were some unusual findings. His lungs were full of water. Victims of shark attacks usually bleed to death, they're not dragged under and drowned. And although sharks will sometimes bite right through the bone, that's unusual. Typically, they just tear off some flesh, decide they don't like the taste and leave. But none of that definitively rules out a shark.'

Jack felt sick. This wasn't just someone you read about in the paper, it was Caitlin's father.

Dr Fox must have seen the pallor in his face, and asked, 'Are you okay?'

Jack nodded.

She said, 'In the circumstances, it still seems most likely to be a shark attack; all I can do is raise some doubt. I told as much to Inspector Begley, but I don't think he wanted to listen.' She stood up and extended her hand.

Jack shook it. 'Thank you for your time, Dr Fox.'

She nodded. As she walked away, she said, 'Next time, don't buy me a hospital coffee. It tastes like poison.'

Chapter Thirty-seven

The return trip was another six hours of semi-recumbent driving and Jack wondered whether a paramedic would need a winch and a jar of lubricant to extract him from the Ferrari on his arrival back in Byron Bay. Black clouds full of spite tracked the car for long distances, dumping enough rain to give the wipers repetitive strain injury. Highway Patrol cars repeatedly sat on his tail, willing him to go faster, ticket books and smug smiles at the ready. He had to stop twice – one hundred and seventy litres of fuel, one litre of coffee, almost a litre of urine, two Violet Crumbles, and a twelve-pack of gourmet dog food cans.

Too much caffeine had made his brain feel twitchy and hyper alert, as though it was floating a few feet above his head, yet the rest of his body was bone tired. By the time he finally turned off the motorway, he desperately wanted to get out of the car, but had to resist the urge a little longer. He needed to take a small detour before meeting Caitlin at *The Beacon*.

As he headed into town, the side of the road was lined with election posters. For every poster of a Green or Labor candidate there seemed to be five or ten of Mayor Tom Bradshaw, still with arms crossed, still laughing. Developing a better Byron.

The Ferrari emitted sickening sounds of metal scraping over bitumen as Jack inched the car over the speed bumps on the road to Tallows Beach. The V8's throaty roar stopped the surfers waxing their boards and they stared as one as he pulled into a park. He grabbed the carton of dog food and climbed out of the car, accompanied by catcalls of 'wanker' and 'dickhead'.

Jack had an increasing sense of foreboding as he approached Eric's camp – no dogs intercepted him. When he reached the clearing, there was no Eric. The only indication he'd been there was a rectangular patch of flattened yellow grass. Jack was disappointed – he'd wanted to ask where exactly Eric had seen the orange buoy floating when it mysteriously appeared and disappeared around the time Patrick died. And now Eric himself had disappeared. Hopefully it was nothing sinister, and he'd simply decided to move on. Jack lugged the dog food back to the car, wondering what he would do with it.

Later, when Jack arrived out the front of *The Beacon*, he heard the click clack of wheels, and soon Caitlin dismounted her skateboard beside him. Her Doc Martens were back, with ripped black jeans, and a satchel draped over a white 'Ramones' T-shirt. They both stared up at the pane of glass, so expertly replaced the previous day, which now lay shattered around them on the footpath.

A sudden movement made Caitlin jump.

Angus Bain materialised in his tweed jacket and a cat-that-got-the-milk grin; his voice recorder extended towards Caitlin. 'Miss O'Shaughnessy, a shark attack would be a horrible way to die. How has it affected you?'

Caitlin clenched her jaw, and her fists, and looked as though she was intending to take Bain out.

Jack, resisting the urge to deck Bain himself, stepped between them. 'Fuck off, Angus.' But as soon as the words were out of

Jack's mouth, he knew they were wasted – being told to fuck off had always just encouraged him.

Bain continued without faltering. 'Any comment, Miss O'Shaughnessy, on your arrest for dealing in controlled substances? Do you think you'll receive a custodial—'

Bain's words were cut off by an apple ricocheting off his shoulder. Caitlin retrieved another missile from her satchel, this time an orange.

Bain raised his hands in mock surrender. 'Just doing my job, lady.' He turned to Jack. 'Which is more than I can say for you.' Bain backed away, keeping one eye on Caitlin, the other on the orange, then turned and scurried off down the lane.

Inside, Jack called the glazier and asked him to replace the window with plywood.

Caitlin sat at the table. 'You know you've missed the printer's deadline for next week's edition? It was this morning.'

'I vote we plead extenuating circumstances. Mind you, that won't stop my father lecturing me.'

Jack told Caitlin of his chance meeting in the forest with Eric, and of all the activity in the carpark the night her father disappeared. And of Eric's disappearance. He also told her of his meeting with the forensic pathologist, and the doctor's concerns regarding the drowned lungs and the atypical bone markings.

When he finished his account, Caitlin sat silently, head bowed. He probably shouldn't have been so insensitive telling her such graphic details. 'Caitlin?'

'But the pathologist couldn't be absolutely certain it wasn't a shark?'

'No.'

She sat motionless, staring at the table.

'Caitlin, are you okay?'

'No, of course I'm not, I'm raging.' For the most part, she appeared externally calm, but her eyes were restless, and her lips were compressed into a taut line. She looked at Jack. 'I, or we, are going to find out what Dad was up to and publish it. And we are going to find out what happened to him. Then I'll cry. Deal?'

'Deal.' Jack hoped when they did find the truth, it would provide some sort of consolation to Caitlin – but he wasn't sure it would. He sat next to her and reached out a hand, but she yanked hers away.

'I don't understand,' she said. 'If he was murdered, why go to so much trouble to make it look like an accident when they could have made the body disappear?'

'They didn't want any suspicion of murder. This was a highly planned operation specifically targeting your father, not a random, spur of the moment killing by some nut job.'

'Tell me what you think happened.'

He hesitated. 'Are you sure?'

She glared at him.

'They were probably waiting at Tallows, with a boat. Maybe divers too, who grabbed him off his board, drowned him and ...' He searched for the gentlest words. 'Made it look like a shark attack. Whoever it was must be pretty connected, they somehow had a copy of your father's special house key, a copy that shouldn't exist. They let themselves in, collected the spare car key, probably searched the house, and drove back to Tallows where they swapped the laptop and took your father's phone. Then they released the board, with a chunk gouged from it.'

'What about the orange buoy?'

'No idea.'

'And why wasn't Dad found until a day later?'

Jack shrugged.

'But why Dad?'

'Hopefully the answer is on the memory stick. When you think of the password.'

'Jesus, Jack, do you think I'm not trying? I want to find out what's on there as much as you. Probably more. I was up most of the night and would have stayed up all night if I hadn't fallen asleep at the keyboard. I must have tried thousands of combinations.' She took the memory stick out of her pocket and placed it on the table. 'Ricky Martinelli must be able to help. You said he was a hacker for Christ's sake.'

'You want me to call Ricky again?'

She nodded and he reached for his phone. After ten rings he heard Ricky's voicemail message: 'Fuck off, I'm busy.'

There was a knock at the door and the glazier's face appeared at the window. 'Is it okay to fix this now?' They watched for a while as he measured up the window and then went back outside. A circular saw started with such a racket there was no chance of conversation.

After it fell silent, there was a knock at the door and Kowalski entered. Caitlin surreptitiously pocketed the memory stick.

The policeman motioned to the broken window. 'Do you want to make a report?'

Caitlin shook her head. 'You haven't caught the people who broke the other three yet.'

Kowalski shrugged. 'May I?' He sat with them at the table. 'I'm here about the window, we didn't talk about anything else, okay?'

Caitlin and Jack stole a glance at each other.

'I didn't waste my time asking Inspector Begley for a warrant for your father's phone – he's still convinced it was a shark attack. But a friend of my father's works for a phone company. He may have accidentally looked at Patrick's phone records.'

Jack and Caitlin exchanged glances again.

'The phone was turned off early on the morning he went missing.'

Jack said, 'So, when they got into the car to swap the laptop, they took the phone. And then what, turned it off or destroyed it?'

'They didn't destroy it. The phone was turned on for a few minutes that same afternoon. But it hasn't reconnected to the network since.'

'Did you get a location?' asked Jack.

'The signal was weak. It was only picked up by one phone tower at Suffolk Park, so there was no triangulation. Caitlin, did your father need the phone to log on to his laptop?'

She nodded.

'Maybe they were trying to see what was on the laptop. Which means, unlike Inspector Begley, I'm not convinced there was a shark. So, tell me everything I need to know.'

Jack was relieved that, at last, someone in the police force was taking them seriously. He recounted everything Eric had told him, including about the vanishing orange buoy. Then he told them about the surfers reporting the gate on the road into Tallows Beach being closed the morning Patrick disappeared. He didn't mention visiting the pathologist.

'Can you convince Begley to open an investigation?' Caitlin asked.

Kowalski pondered before replying, 'I can hardly tell him I illegally accessed phone records. And, without any hard evidence, there's no way I could persuade him.' He stood up. 'I'll do what I can, which isn't much with Begley breathing down my neck. If you want to check out the buoy yourself, there's a crab fisherman who works the coast here. He operates out of Ballina. He might have seen something. In the evenings you'll find him in the Shaws Bay Hotel, trying to offload crabs for cash. Ask for Rosco and tell him I sent you.'

No sooner had Kowalski left than the circular saw buzzed back into life, making conversation useless until it fell silent.

Jack's phone rang and Ricky Martinelli's name scrolled across the screen.

'Ricky, mate.'

'Jacko, what's happening?'

'It's the TAILS folder. We really need to get into it.'

'Jesus, Jack, it's starting to sound like you're stuck on repeat. I'm assuming you're calling me because you still don't know the password.'

'Yep.'

'Like I said, without the password you're screwed.'

'By "screwed" do you mean completely totally, or probably maybe?'

'It depends how long the password is.'

'How am I supposed to tell you how long it is if I don't know the password?'

Ricky sighed and said, 'Jack, you need to stop writing shaggy-dog stories for your father's fish and chip wrappers and get with the program. Send the file to me and I'll see how long the hash is.'

'The hash?'

'Just send it to me.'

Jack downloaded the file from the memory stick to the laptop and sent it to Ricky. He offered the memory stick back to Caitlin. 'Do you still want to hang on to this? It worries me when you have it on you. They would do anything to get hold of it.'

She grabbed it, then clutched it to her chest. 'I'm going to keep trying.'

Chapter Thirty-eight

Jack opted for motoring discretion and took *The Beacon*'s car for the half-hour scenic coastal drive south to Ballina. He wasn't sure it was the best decision, the car's suspension sounded pre-terminal, but he arrived at the Shaws Bay Hotel without incident and parked next to a black Range Rover. The car had white plastic tubs in the back.

Jack heard Rosco even before the barman pointed to him, his thunderous laugh echoing around the room. He was leaning on the other end of the bar, his massive size eclipsing the man next to him. Jack ordered two pints and headed towards the fisherman.

Rosco interrupted his conversation and looked Jack up and down. 'What size are you after?'

'I'm not after crabs.'

'Are you police?'

'No, but Kowalski sent me.'

Rosco nodded, downed the rest of his pint and headed towards the back door. In the beer garden, they sat on benches at a hardwood timber table. Children chased each other around the broad expanse of grass. There was a fine view across the bay and a lone swimmer, far from either shore, seemed to be swimming to nowhere.

Jack introduced himself and handed Rosco one of the pints. 'I'm told you fish for crabs off Tallows.'

Rosco grunted in the affirmative.

Jack continued. 'Did you happen to notice an orange buoy off Tallows Beach last week?'

'Are you the guy from Fisheries?'

Jack shook his head.

Rosco swallowed half his pint then emitted a belch loud enough for the children to stop running and start giggling. 'Ah well, I guess that would have been wishful bloody thinking. I did see that buoy and thought it was someone doing some illegal fishing, or a drug drop. We tried to pull it up, but it was snagged. We didn't have our dive gear, so we left it. It was gone the next time I was there.'

'Can you remember exactly where it was?'

'I don't have to remember. I reported it. That's why I thought you were from bloody Fisheries.' Rosco hunted through his phone and showed the screen to Jack. 'GPS coordinates.'

A smile stretched across Jack's face.

Rosco remained serious. 'Hey, if it's drugs, I'm having nothing to do with it. Is Kowalski involved in this?'

Jack felt some trepidation at having to tell the man his suspicions. He didn't want too many people knowing he was investigating Patrick's death. Could he trust him? Kowalski had recommended him, if only for crabs, and there was no other way Jack was going to find out what, if anything, was hidden under the water. 'I think the buoy has something to do with Patrick O'Shaughnessy's death.'

Rosco's brow furrowed. 'Wasn't he taken by a shark?'

'Not if we find something under that buoy.'

'Patrick and I used to play golf together, for years. He was a shit golfer, but he was a whole lot of fun.' Rosco finished his pint. 'Will you need diving gear?'

Jack was embarrassed. 'I can't equalise. My ears hurt even if I put my head under in a bath.'

Rosco laughed and slapped Jack's shoulder with his hand. It felt like being king hit by a bear. 'No problem. Five tomorrow morning at the wharf. You can babysit the crabs.'

Chapter Thirty-nine
Monday, 11th November

Jack was half asleep as they motored out of Ballina Harbour before sunrise the following morning. He had expected a rickety wooden trawler, but Rosco and his brother Stefano's boat was white fibreglass, sleek and powerful. After clearing the heads, Stefano opened her out and, with a throaty roar, they skimmed across the water. Above them, only the brighter stars were yet to succumb to the lightening sky.

Jack regretted not bringing a jacket, the wind chill was surprising for November. It wasn't long before he also regretted not bringing sea-sickness tablets. Nausea nagged at his stomach and threatened to rise into his throat. He fixed his eyes firmly on the horizon to reduce the chance of embarrassing himself in front of two men who lived on the water. Stefano must have clocked his pallor, as he soon eased off the throttle.

They stopped at buoys along the way for Rosco to pull up traps and effortlessly extract the crabs, band their claws and drop them into tubs. Two hours and seventeen crabs later, they arrived off Tallows Beach, motored to Rosco's GPS coordinates and dropped anchor in ten metres of water.

The brothers gave Jack brief instructions on how to operate the boat and radio before they donned diving gear, dropped over the stern and disappeared into the depths.

Jack had walked Tallows Beach many times, even camped overnight as a boy, but he'd never looked back on it from offshore. The perfectly proportioned lighthouse standing sentinel high on the cape would have been a picture-postcard view if not for looming black rain clouds sneaking up behind it. A brahminy kite hovered in the updraught of the cliffs and, like a semaphore, its wings flashed white then rust and white again as it banked and turned before retreating to shelter ahead of the approaching rain.

Jack was returning a runaway crab to its incarcerated colleagues when one of the divers surfaced and called to Jack. It sounded like Rosco. 'Throw me the rope.'

Rosco caught the end and disappeared back under before Jack could ask him what he'd found.

The few minutes before both divers returned seemed to stretch out forever, and Jack felt his muscles tense in anticipation. He helped them onto the boat and asked them what they had found before they had even removed their masks.

Rosco dropped his tanks and regulator onto the deck and removed his flippers. 'Dunno yet. We'll have to pull it up.'

Whatever was on the end of the rope was heavy, and required their combined strength to drag it in. Vague shimmering shapes slowly solidified into three large, concrete Besser blocks which were hauled onto the deck. The blocks were bound together by a long chain whose loose end still hung in the water. Rosco deftly heaved on the chain and pulled two large packages onto the deck, each tightly wrapped with black plastic sheeting.

It began to rain.

'Drugs,' said Stefano. 'I bet you.'

'Should we call the police?' asked Jack.

Stefano said, 'Well, that depends. If it's a small amount of drugs we'll call the cops. If it's a shitload of drugs, we might drop you overboard attached to those blocks, and start planning our retirement in the Maldives.' He looked serious, but then a huge roar of laughter broke the tension.

Rosco winked and Jack smiled in return, but still weighed up jumping overboard and swimming to the beach, just in case the big man was serious.

Rosco kneeled by the larger parcel, slit through the plastic with a fishing knife and peeled it open. The men exchanged puzzled looks. Inside were a water-logged chainsaw and a pair of large secateurs.

Rosco took his knife to the other parcel. No sooner was the plastic penetrated than a rancid smell assaulted them, and Jack's nausea flooded back. They all moved upwind before Rosco peeled back the plastic.

'Oh, Christ,' said Rosco as he jumped back from the parcel.

Stefano beat Jack to the side of the boat, and they vomited together over the side. When there was nothing more to come, Jack lowered himself onto a seat. His eyes were drawn back to the contents of the parcel. It was a leg, a decaying human leg, hacked off below the knee. The leg was still wearing the tattered remnant of a wetsuit. The jagged stump of the shin bone protruded through the top of the swollen, decomposing flesh. A stainless-steel gaff hook pierced all the way through the calf muscle, its vicious barb protruding from the other side.

Even upwind, the smell was putrid, and Jack felt sick again. Seagulls arrived and began circling the boat. One landed on the water and began pecking away at the vomit.

Stefano was the first to recover. He crossed himself before re-wrapping the leg in its plastic and placing it in an unused tub.

The rain was heavy now, and Jack was soaked through, but he

hardly noticed. How was he going to break the news to Caitlin? His phone had signal, so he dialled Byron Bay Police Station and Anderson answered.

When Anderson realised it was Jack, he said, 'Inspector Begley said not to let you in the station, or take any calls from you.'

Before Jack could respond, Anderson cut the call.

It took Jack a few moments to collect his thoughts. He pushed aside visions of strangling the constable and called back, using an American accent. 'This is Inspector Graham Gadget, returning Inspector Begley's call.'

Seconds later Begley was on the line.

'It's Jack Harris.'

'Christ on a bike, I should have known – Inspector bloody Gadget. What do you want?'

'We found a severed leg.' When Jack finished providing the details, the ensuing silence was so long he thought the call may have cut out. 'Begley?'

'I'm sorry,' said Begley. 'The poor man.' The policeman soon recovered his composure and snapped back to professional mode. He ordered them to do the bleeding obvious – not to handle the leg, record the coordinates, and return immediately to the harbour.

Stefano weighed anchor. Rosco turned the boat south and opened the throttle to maximum; there was to be no consideration for sea-sick passengers on the return journey.

The rain had stopped and Jack was shivering in his wet clothes. But his discomfort was soon forgotten as his anger rose. The police had screwed up all the way along. Apart from Kowalski, they had ignored his concerns and had squandered every chance of collecting forensic evidence. He hoped their incompetence didn't mean Patrick's killers would escape justice.

Jack mulled over and over about calling Caitlin, but this wasn't news to impart by phone, especially if she was by herself somewhere. Then again, Caitlin would be rightly furious if he didn't tell her straight away. He also needed to tell Zoe. In the end he opted to call Zoe first.

She was very quiet when Jack told her what they had found. After a long silence, she said, 'I was expecting something like this. Doesn't make it any easier, but at least now we know for sure.'

'Can you find Caitlin and let her know?'

Zoe agreed, and they ended the call.

Jack's next call was to John Hunter Hospital. He told the switchboard operator he was a doctor calling from Lismore and asked for Dr Nicola Fox. When she answered, Jack had trouble hearing over the roaring wind and the waves crashing into the speeding hull. 'It's Jack Harris. Have you finished the post-mortem report on Patrick O'Shaughnessy?'

'I was hoping I'd heard the last from you.' When Jack didn't respond she said, 'I'm about to sign it off.'

'We've just found Patrick's amputated leg. It was chained to a concrete block offshore.'

'Oh God.'

'Can you examine his other leg for signs it may have had a rope or a chain around it?'

'Jack, you know I can't tell you anything. The report is confidential until released by the coroner.'

'Dr Fox, I've just saved you some serious embarrassment. And now, if you change the report before the news comes out, you'll look like a genius. Text me.'

'It would be contempt of court.'

'Then call, don't text. Use your private mobile. And if they ever check the phone records, I called to ask you out and you rang back after due consideration to tell me to get lost.' He gave her his mobile number and hung up.

Jack's nausea was coming in waves, irresistible waves, and he was soon back holding firmly to the side of the wildly tossing boat and throwing up.

Three police cars and a van waited for them at the dock. Begley stood on the edge of the wharf, arms crossed, watching them impassively. Kowalski waited by his side. There were other officers, some holding cameras and cases. The police boarded as soon as Stefano secured the boat.

Begley introduced himself to the two brothers and then nodded at Jack. Kowalski shook hands with Rosco and Stefano.

'Okay,' said Begley. 'Let's have it.'

Stefano pointed at one of the tubs and two officers in white coveralls and blue gloves carried their cases over, kneeled by the tub and slowly lifted the lid. The foetid smell was back clawing at Jack's nose, and he wondered whether he would ever be able to forget it. That, and the image of the rotting leg that seemed hard-wired into his memory.

The scene-of-crime officers briefly examined the contents of the tub then took photographs from all angles. They repeated their examination of the other parcel, the tools and the concrete Besser blocks, then everything was bagged and carried off.

The brothers were shown to a police car and driven away. Jack was put in the back seat of another car, with Begley at the wheel. Begley yelled out of the window and sounded the car horn impatiently until Kowalski hurried towards them carrying a fishing tub. He placed it on the back seat next to Jack and secured it with a seat belt.

Begley gunned the car away from the harbour and headed north along the coast road towards Byron Bay.

Jack lifted the lid of the tub. The beady black eyes of a spanner crab stared back at him.

Chapter Forty

At the police station, Jack was left alone in an interview room, and he settled himself on the uncomfortable plastic chair to wait. Begley and Kowalski were no doubt interviewing the fishermen in another room, and organising an ongoing supply of crustaceans.

Jack's phone rang – it was Nicola Fox. He answered, 'I'm in the police station.'

'I'll be quick. There are faint abrasions and pressure marks on the remaining ankle. No embedded rope fibres. The pattern may be from a chain. You didn't hear that.' She ended the call.

The abrasions were just what Jack was expecting. Whoever killed Patrick must have submerged the body for a day or so and released it when they removed the orange buoy. Perhaps they thought the prolonged immersion would make the body look less suspicious, or wash away any forensic evidence. It seemed a lot of trouble to go to, and yet Jack shouldn't have been surprised – everything had been so meticulously planned, the murderers had almost got away with the deception.

An hour passed before Begley and Kowalski entered and sat facing him across the table. Kowalski nodded acknowledgement. Begley just glowered.

Jack wasn't perturbed when Kowalski switched on the

equipment to record the interview, but was shocked when he began reciting the cautions Jack had heard so many times before. Surely he wasn't being considered a suspect?

Begley asked, 'Tell me why I shouldn't charge you with murder?'

'What?'

'You found a leg in the middle of the Pacific Ocean. You had the crab fishermen take you straight to the exact location. That implies you knew where it was in advance. Oldest trick in the book, of course, pretending to assist us with our enquiries to remove suspicion from yourself.'

Jack laughed. 'I thought you'd be offering me an honorary appointment at the station, given I'm the only one doing any policing around here. Or at least roll out some red carpet, even just a metre or two.'

Begley glared. 'You still haven't told me why I shouldn't charge you.'

Jack told him about finding Eric in the forest, the vanishing orange buoy, and the crab fisherman. He didn't mention it was Kowalski who suggested he speak with Rosco.

Begley leaned back in his chair, arms crossed. 'Okay, you got lucky. Someone saw the buoy and gave you the perfect cover story for going back for the leg and making yourself look innocent.'

Jack wasn't intimidated by the bluster. 'You're sore because I made you look foolish, and so you want to take me out. Go ahead, charge me. You'll just look even more incompetent.'

Begley looked at Kowalski then nodded to the recording equipment. Kowalski announced the termination of the interview and stopped the recording.

Begley said, 'Your account is corroborated by the fishermen.

I needed to be certain before the homicide detectives arrive from Sydney.'

Kowalski looked surprised. 'Sydney? What about our guys?'

Begley turned to Kowalski, an eyebrow raised as if to say his question wasn't appropriate in front of Jack. 'Overruled by the assistant commissioner. He's flying up Duffy and Maguire.'

'For God's sake,' said Kowalski. 'Not them.'

'I know. Two of the most useless detectives on the planet.' Begley turned to Jack. 'And that's off the record. In fact, this whole bloody thing is off the record.' He placed his hands on the desk, clearly thinking, before addressing Kowalski. 'Perhaps you'd fetch Mr Harris a cup of coffee?'

Kowalski's faced tensed and, with an almost imperceptible shake of his head, he stood abruptly and left – operating the coffee machine was apparently not in the sergeant's job description.

Jack wondered whether Begley intended to shirtfront him up against the wall again, but instead the policeman remained seated and spoke quietly.

'Something really stinks here. Skippy the fucking Kangaroo has solved more crimes than Duffy and Maguire combined. Which means, as bloody irritating as it is to team up with a journalist, especially a Harris journalist, we find ourselves on the same side. I want to know what the hell is going on. So, anything you tell the detectives, or choose not to tell the detectives, I want you to tell me. I don't trust them.'

Jack nodded, even though he wasn't really sure what he was signing up for.

Begley continued. 'And none of this is to go into your bloody shit-sheet, comprendez?'

Before Jack could respond, Kowalski re-entered and placed

a cup before Jack none too gently, some coffee splashing onto the plastic table.

'Now,' said Begley, 'tell me everything again, and I mean everything, or I'll charge you with obstructing a murder investigation.'

Jack's natural reaction was that if you were ever going to tell a policeman like Begley anything it would be to go fuck themself, but he knew he and Caitlin couldn't do this alone and that they would need help – police help – if Patrick's killers were to be caught. And it sounded like Begley and Kowalski would be better allies than the incoming detectives. He would have to trust them. Mostly. And so he started from the beginning: Patrick's fears for his personal safety, the new life insurance policy, the laptop exchange, the duplicate security key to Patrick's front door, *The Beacon* being searched, Eric's account of the black van and the boat and, finally, Jack's theory of the motive being to suppress the story Patrick was pursuing.

Begley was quiet as he digested what Jack had told them. 'And that's the lot?' He stabbed a threatening, nicotine-stained finger towards Jack. 'If you are holding anything back ...'

Jack shook his head. Although there was one thing he was definitely not going to tell them – if he did, it would be goodbye memory stick forever.

Begley stood and offered his hand to Jack before leaving. It could have been interpreted as a conciliatory gesture if Begley's face didn't look as if he'd just been forced into a deal with the devil.

Kowalski waited until Begley was gone. 'In the absence of anyone else, I'd like to thank you for your help.' They shook hands. 'Take care, Jack. These are dangerous people. I don't want you to be the forensic pathologist's next case.'

Chapter Forty-one

Caitlin wasn't sure how long she'd been standing there, up on the high lookout at The Pass, lost in her thoughts. Dark thoughts. She shivered as a gust of wind tore at her.

She felt drained. It had been another emotional afternoon. Zoe had come home with the news of the divers. Although Caitlin had made a pact with herself not to cry until after she'd published her father's work and the killers had been found, thoughts of what her father must have suffered in those final moments had been overwhelming. Tears had gone unwiped, tea undrunk. But there were hugs. How would she have coped without Zoe?

Caitlin hadn't wanted to believe in Jack's theory, that there was more to it than a shark attack, even though she knew he was probably right. Now she was so grateful for what he had done – if not for him they would never have known her father had been murdered, and there would never have been a chance of justice. She thought of the calm, cold justice she was so used to in court rooms. She didn't feel calm and collected at the moment. She wanted to catch the bastards and ... Caitlin pushed the vengeful thoughts out of her mind, but again and again they returned.

Constable Swift had arrived to tell Caitlin the news she already knew. Begley mustn't have had the balls to admit to

Caitlin in person he'd messed up completely. But Caitlin was glad it was Lucy, she was kind.

Another gust of chilly wind brought her back to the present and she shivered.

There was a creak on the decking. Caitlin's heart felt as if it was about to break out of her chest; instinctively she turned toward the noise, toward the threat. 'Jesus.' She placed a hand over her thumping heart. Jack. 'It's just you.'

'Sorry, I was worried about you, after what happened today. I wanted to check you were okay.'

'I was until you scared the bejesus out of me.' Caitlin turned back to the water and took some deep breaths to compose herself. She felt his presence beside her and drew comfort. She'd been hoping he would appear, but then chided herself – she mustn't lower her defences now, not when she was feeling so vulnerable. There should have been no more tears left, but a few stragglers appeared, and she left them untended, wet on her cheeks.

She lost track of time again. Was it five minutes, ten minutes, or more that they stood silently together?

To the west, the sky had turned orange and the wispy clouds skidding past high above were beginning their journey from pink to persimmon. As if she cared.

A cormorant landed in a tree branch next to the lookout and spread its large black wings to dry. Below her, a few surfers waited in vain for absent waves, her father not among them.

She said to Jack, 'When I was a little girl, I made Mum and Dad wake me up and bring me here when Dad surfed. I'd stand here and watch the sun come up. He'd wave to me from down there as he waited for waves. And then he'd be standing on his board, and I can remember jumping up and down with excitement. If he was wiped out, I would hold my breath until he came back up and waved to me again. I idolised him.'

In the receding light, they watched a woman effortlessly launch herself onto the last wave of the day and carve away towards the distant shore.

'Now I'm here standing where I always stood, but this time I'm watching the sun go down.'

She leaned in towards Jack and felt his arm placed around her shoulders. She rested her head against his chest, could hear his heart beating. He placed a single kiss on the top of her head, then they stood quietly and watched as the clouds transitioned from red to grey, and the light faded into night.

Chapter Forty-two
Tuesday, 12th November

Jack was looking forward to the day ahead, especially to seeing Caitlin. His session in the pool the previous night had been a big one, swimming clockwork lap after clockwork lap, all the while thinking of Caitlin. He'd put his arm around her to comfort her, but was it more than that? Thoughts of her, pleasant thoughts, seemed to bump into his consciousness unbidden all hours of the day and night. Was her attraction because she was so inaccessible? He'd never experienced that before. He'd only ever had the opposite. When a woman found out who he was or, more specifically, how much he might inherit, he couldn't keep them away. It took a court order to stop his last date, the pathologically persistent Coralee, from stalking him night and day. And so he'd resolved, for the moment at least, to distance himself from new relationships, especially romantic ones – there'd be plenty of time later. But was now later? Caitlin not only showed zero interest in him, but had impregnable defences keeping him away, at least until last night.

Later, as he'd slowly drifted towards sleep, he'd hoped those thoughts of holding Caitlin would keep him company, but dark thoughts of Patrick's killers pushed them aside and he tossed and turned restlessly until the early hours. It seemed as though he had only just drifted into deep sleep when the shrill of his ringtone woke him. He fumbled around the bedside table and found the phone.

'Yep.'

'Jacko, what's happening?'

'Ricky, mate. You woke me.'

'It's half past seven, you lazy bastard. That file you sent me – the hash is twenty-eight characters long. That is one serious password – that file is meant to stay secret.'

'But can you crack it?'

'Twenty-eight is pushing it. But it's doable, depending on how much computer time you're prepared to buy.'

'What's your guess?'

Jack heard an intake of breath. 'Half a mill, maybe more.'

'Fuck a duck. And how long?'

'Depending on how many processor cores you throw at it, I'd say weeks if you get lucky, but more likely months.'

'We haven't got that long.'

'Then you'll need the password. Look for a Post-it note on the keyboard. It'll be bright yellow.'

'Haha.'

Ricky hung up.

Jack dragged himself out of bed, dressed and headed downstairs, where the aroma of coffee announced somebody had beaten him to the kitchen. It was Tony, perched at the kitchen bench, reading one of the Harris newspapers, *The National*. He greeted Jack with a beaming smile. 'You've only been here a week and I'm still getting used to it. What would you like first, coffee or to read some very dodgy reporting?' Tony slid the paper towards Jack.

The headline was '*Shark Declared Innocent*'. Underneath was a colour photo of Rosco and Stefano Conte aboard their fishing boat, dressed in diving gear and grinning at the camera. Rosco was quoted as having had to dive in 'dangerous, shark-infested waters' to retrieve the leg from 'the depths of the ocean'. Jack was relieved his name wasn't mentioned but, even so, he still anticipated a thunderous reception from Begley when next he saw him. He checked the by-line – 'Angus Bain'. Of course it was.

Footsteps were heard heading their way. Tony glanced at Jack, his lips firmly pressed together. 'I'll see you at the car.' He promptly rose and slipped out of the kitchen through a side door just as Don entered the room.

He saw Jack, and simply nodded in greeting.

'Good morning, Don.'

Jack had noticed the brevity of Don's greeting. And he was walking perceptibly slower as he went to the fridge and removed a bottle.

'Okay, Don, what's up?'

'Nothing.' He removed a glass from a cupboard and looked as if he was going to leave the room, but changed his mind and sat opposite Jack.

'Yeah, right. If you'll excuse me for saying, I think aliens have abducted Don and replaced him with Mr Grumpy.'

Don poured himself a pinky-purple smoothie from the bottle, then just stared at the drink. 'I should be happy.' Don shot a glance at Jack, then his eyes returned to the gloop in his glass. 'I met someone.' There was a long pause that Jack didn't fill. Don took a drink from his glass and pulled a face. 'You know, for thirty years I've lived here, alone, and been very happy.' He gestured around him. 'What's not to like? Your father has always been very kind to me, and there are always interesting people coming through here. I've loved this job. But now I've met someone, and I don't want to be here anymore. He lives in Perth.'

'Don, I'm pleased for you. Not the grumpy bit, of course.'

The man shrugged. 'I think, after all this time, I'm going to have to leave.'

A car horn sounded loudly.

Don stood up. 'You'd better go.' He downed the rest of his smoothie and walked slowly from the room.

Tony drove Jack into town. Today the Kingswood served up the Choirboys' 'Run to Paradise' as they reminisced about the time a red-bellied black snake had found its way into Jack's bedroom in the old house, terrifying him, and Tony had to catch it in an old sack.

As they got closer to town, Tony said, 'After I've dropped you, I might take Millie for a spin up the coast.' He glanced across at Jack. 'Get a few hours break from Don. He's become a right pain in the arse.'

'Maybe he's got something on his mind.'

'Well, whatever it is, I'm too old for this shit.'

Chapter Forty-three

Because of the traffic, Tony dropped Jack a block away from *The Beacon*. As soon as Jack was out of the car he was caught by a sudden bucketing of rain. He quickened his pace and, spotting a shop awning on the other side of the street, stepped onto the road to cross. A car horn blasted his ear drums and he leaped back, heart pounding, as a shiny, snot-green VW Kombi glided past in complete silence – 'EV conversion' written in white letters along its side. Silent but deadly. If the anti-5G army wanted to finish him off, that could be a weapon of choice.

A klaxon sounded from his pocket, a ringtone Jack assigned to just one person, his father, Malcolm Harris. Jack ducked under shelter and took the call. 'Dad.'

He heard his father's gravelly voice and pictured him sitting sullen-faced behind the leather-topped desk in his citadel at Harris HQ. 'I understand Patrick O'Shaughnessy was murdered.' There were no civilities, no *Hi, Jack, how are you going?* Just straight down to business as always.

'Yes.' Jack automatically resorted to short answers with his father, preferably of one syllable. He wondered whether his father ever read the truth into that, or if he simply thought Jack was economical with words.

'That's bad news. Very bad.'

It was, and Jack immediately felt sympathy for Caitlin.

His father, however, didn't sound sympathetic when he continued – more self-interested. 'As you know, our supervising editor for the regionals normally keeps an eye on the servers, just to check what Patrick is working on, and signs off on the final edition of each paper. But O'Shaughnessy recently stopped uploading to the server. I tried to call him a few times, but he didn't answer. I was worried he might be in trouble. Or working on something sensitive. It seems I was right. Maybe it was something very dangerous and that's why he was murdered. We need to find out what the story was as soon as possible. And by "we", I mean "you". You are my eyes on the ground there, Jack. I want you to come straight to me as soon as you find anything.'

'Okay.'

'Angus Bain was on holidays up there when the shark attack, or rather murder, happened. You two should work together on finding out what story Patrick was chasing.'

Before Jack could reply, his father had cut the call. Jack would have liked to tell his father that Angus Bain would be the last person he would ever work with, but he also knew his courage would have, as always when speaking with his father, failed him.

When Jack arrived at *The Beacon*, he was angered to see a scrum of journalists gathered outside. And behind the seething horde of hacks, the newly installed plywood window hoarding had already been graffitied. '*YOU CAN'T UNVACCINATE*' it said. A large tombstone had been added in black.

Jack lowered his head and pushed through the journalists to the door, key in hand, but Angus Bain grabbed his arm. 'C'mon, Jack, say a few words and we'll go away.'

'Get lost, Angus.' Jack inserted the key in the lock, shook off Bain's hand, and hurried inside. He turned the lock and leaned back against the door, eyes closed. Not for the first time, he wondered whether he had it in him to be a journalist – he certainly couldn't be one of the coffin-chasing variety. He opened his eyes and was surprised to see Caitlin sitting at one of the desks, typing away at her laptop.

'Caitlin. How did you get in?'

She didn't look up. 'I climbed through the bathroom window. Only an idiot would use the front door with all those jackals outside.'

Last night, in the pool, Jack had anticipated a warm greeting from Caitlin this morning, perhaps even a hug. It wasn't to be. She was all business.

'Are you still trying the password?'

'What else?'

'So, no luck then?'

She shot him a frosty stare, then went back to typing.

Jack watched over her shoulder as she entered more passwords – 'heroinex2', '2xheroine', 'double heroine', 'heroine2', and 'heroine+heroine' – each attempt met with an incorrect password message, and an increasingly irritating beep. She then tried 'heroin', 'junk', 'smack', 'dope', 'Chinawhite' and 'skag'. Nothing. She slammed the laptop closed, removed the memory stick and pushed it into her pocket.

'Caitlin,' said Jack.

She didn't respond.

'Caitlin.'

She lowered her head. 'This is shit. I miss him.'

Jack once again reached out a hand to take one of hers, but as usual she yanked it away before there was any contact. Her reflexes were sharp, presumably from all that practice.

She said, 'I'm sorry about yesterday. I shouldn't have let you ...'

Jack felt as if she'd inserted a blade. 'Caitlin. The whole physical contact thing. I have to ask.'

She glared at him. Green, hostile eyes. 'Ask what?'

'Is it just me, or is it everyone?'

She looked down, and closed her eyes.

When she didn't answer, he took a deep breath and pressed on. 'Did you have a bad experience? A very bad experience?'

She slid her hands down her jeans, straightening out some non-existent wrinkles.

He was pushing into uncomfortable territory, for both of them. Private territory. But he wanted an answer, wanted to break down the barrier between them. 'Was there a violent relationship?'

She still didn't respond.

'Caitlin, these things can be worked out, but not if you don't talk about it.'

'Jesus, what are you, a pretend psychiatrist now?'

'I'm sorry.'

Her eyes returned to his. 'The thing is, no amount of talking can fix it.'

'Try me.'

Long seconds passed before she answered, 'If I did, you certainly wouldn't want to come anywhere near me, even if I did let you, which I won't.'

'Please.'

She fidgeted with her dreadlocks, nervously winding and unwinding them around her fingers. Jack let the silence linger, sure that if he said anything it might break the moment. But then the sound of laughter intruded – the journalists outside had found something amusing.

'Caitlin?'

She stared at Jack in silence, then abruptly stood up. 'Okay. But not here.'

Jack followed her into the bathroom, where she climbed onto the sink and was through the window before he could offer to help. He almost had to run to keep up with her as she hurried along Jonson Street. Shoppers ambling down the footpath had to dodge out of her way as she hurtled towards them. When she reached the Main Beach promenade, she turned north towards Belongil Beach, and it was only when she reached the sand that her pace finally slackened.

They walked on in silence. When the crowds, the frolicking dogs and the last of the beachside mansions were left well behind, she stopped, removed her boots and walked slowly down to the water, where she stood staring towards the horizon. Waves lapped at her ankles. He stood close beside her, anxious now about what she was going to say.

It was some time before she spoke.

'They say that daughters are naturally closer to their fathers, but I was always close to Mum. All my friends went through difficult times with their mothers, but not me. We were best friends. And then, all of a sudden, she was gone.'

Jack had to wait for her next words, and they were so quiet he almost missed them in the sound of the waves.

'She took her own life.'

She glanced momentarily at Jack, and he could see her trying to fight away her tears, as though it had happened yesterday.

'Oh, Caitlin.' He was surprised to feel dampness in his eyes too.

'She'd been unwell for a couple of years. At first, she hid it from me, but it soon became obvious. She took the easy way out, or the hard way, I've never been sure which.'

Minutes passed in silence until she turned and looked directly into his eyes. 'She had Huntington's disease.'

Jack felt as if his heart had stopped momentarily. He wasn't really sure what he'd been expecting. Cancer, maybe. Like his mum. But Huntington's? He knew it was a bad one. He felt a sense of panic beginning to course through him – here was Caitlin baring her soul, revisiting the most painful parts of her life, and yet as much as he scoured the deep recesses of his memory, he couldn't recall any details of Huntington's. Would he fail Caitlin in her moment of need?

He reached for her hand, but she slipped it away. 'I'm so sorry, Caitlin. I know what it's like. From when Mum died.'

She nodded in acknowledgement, then waited. When Jack said nothing further, she kicked angrily at the water, forcing spray up into the air, and Jack wasn't sure whether she was angry at him in particular, or the world in general for taking her mother.

She shook her head. 'Okay, so I have to do it the hard way. Like you, most people have heard of Huntington's but have no idea. It started with involuntary movements – the doctors said it would only get worse, that eventually Mum wouldn't be able to walk or feed herself, and she would be totally reliant on care. And as shitty as that sounds, that's not the worst part. She would forget where she'd left things, then she would forget she had things, then her past would slowly fade away. Cruelly, she would have remained completely aware as her world shrank to nothingness.'

Jack tried to comprehend the horror of it all, tried to imagine what it would be like to live with such a disease.

Caitlin continued. 'Most people die after about twenty years. Unless they kill themselves first, which is common. Like Mum, they do it while they still can.'

She stared at her feet as they sank into the sand, then flashed a forced smile at Jack, before walking away up the beach to sit down on a dune. He sat by her side as she drew circles in the sand with her fingers.

'You haven't worked it out, have you? The whole avoiding touch thing.'

Jack was so overwhelmed he'd forgotten he'd even asked the question. 'No.'

In one quick motion of her hand through the sand, she destroyed her drawings. 'Jack, not only is it an awful disease in its own right, it has a vicious twist in the tail. Any children you have are born before you develop symptoms. And it's hereditary. Each child has a one in two chance of inheriting the Huntington's gene. I have a one in two chance of ending up like Mum.'

His insides lurched, as though life's roller coaster had just catapulted him over the abyss. He looked at Caitlin. She was so young and beautiful and vibrant, and yet her life could be stolen away in such a dreadful way. It wasn't fair. How could she carry such a burden and manage to be so successful and accomplished? Then he was ashamed of himself, of his health, of his privileged life. He remembered how pissed off he'd been when his father banished him to *The Beacon* – how inconsequential that was compared with living with the prospect of such a disease.

She picked up a handful of sand and let it run between her fingers. 'I'm afraid,' she said.

'Can you get tested?'

'Would you get tested? Would you want to know for certain

that you had a nightmare future ahead of you? A miserable, early death. Or would you rather live with hope?'

Jack ran his own fingers through the sand as he thought. Would he? 'I don't know, Caitlin. I really don't know.'

'Well, I do. I haven't been tested. And it's why I'm trying to squeeze a normal life into half the time – just in case. Why I've thrown myself at my work. Why I am, or was, on track to be the youngest ever full partner at Bernstein. Why I've bungee jumped, smoked dope, got tattoos and read *Middlemarch*.'

'And why you're so upset when you drop something?'

'I was always clumsy, but that's how it started with Mum. And it's why I don't drive – I'm scared of killing someone.'

'And why you avoid relationships.'

'And there we go, you got there in the end.' She smiled at him. 'Not so dumb after all. That's my number-one rule. I couldn't do that to someone. So, I've built a wall around myself. So far it's worked really well.'

'But there's a fifty-fifty chance you don't have the disease. Think of what you might be missing out on.'

'I don't think I'm missing out. On the contrary, I have a fuller life than most people. Exhausting, but rewarding. You should try it.'

'You're right. Absolutely. I waste so much time.'

'Well, that ends now.' She stood up. 'Get your gear off. We're going for a swim. Just remember, rule number one still applies.' She threw off her clothes and ran.

Jack didn't move as she raced to the water, his gaze fixed on her naked back, her bum swaying gloriously with every stride. The spell was only broken when she dived under a wave, popped up on the other side and called to him, 'C'mon loser, your new life starts now.'

The water was still chilly for November, but he couldn't have cared if there was ice floating in it. They stayed in the water, playing among the waves and laughing until their skin wrinkled and they were shivering with cold. She raced him up the dune to collect their things and then they ran along the beach to dry off, only putting their clothes on when they saw people walking towards them.

They fell in step side by side, and Jack asked, 'Did your mother know she was going to get Huntington's?'

Caitlin splashed her feet in the water as she walked. 'No. She was adopted. Which was just as well for me, as she may have decided not to have children.' She smiled at Jack.

They walked a little further, watching the waves.

'And you won't get tested?' he asked.

'Nope.'

Jack's heart sank. Was he falling in love? For the first time, seriously in love? He'd only known her for just over a week, but that's what it felt like. He thought about her day and night. Dreams of her woke him when thoughts of her weren't keeping him pleasantly awake. But now? What of the future? Even if she would have him, which he doubted, did he want to commit to a relationship where he might have to watch her become increasingly incapacitated, and die young? Would Caitlin take her own life? Was he prepared to spend twenty years looking after her? He could walk away; he should walk away. And then he was overcome by shame and anger at himself for his self-pity. He might be able to walk away, but Caitlin couldn't. The beach lost focus. He blinked to clear the moisture from his eyes as they walked on in silence, a metre apart.

Chapter Forty-four

Begley sat at his desk, fuming. He swivelled from side to side in his chair. He played with his stapler. He hit the stapler's head over and over, spewing spent staples over his desk. He stood up, paced back and forth, then sat and swivelled some more.

He'd never met either of the homicide detectives Maguire and Duffy, but he'd heard of them. Everyone had. The two detectives had, allegedly, the lowest homicide clearance rate in the whole state. They were officially the worst detectives in the force, at least they would be if those participating in station gossip could bestow such an award. What worried Begley was why, after twenty years of not solving homicides, they hadn't been demoted to highway patrol or, better still, the bomb squad. He wondered whether they were the detectives you had to have if you didn't want a murder solved. So why were they being flown up here? Begley smelled a rat. He didn't know which species of rat, but he was determined to find out.

His desk phone rang, and he yanked the handset from its cradle. It was Anderson at reception. 'Detective Sergeant Matthew Maguire and Detective Graham Duffy have arrived, sir.'

'Send them through. And then make them both a cup of coffee.'

'No problem, sir.'

'And make sure you put some of your body fluids in the cups. You can decide which.'

'Sir?'

Begley slammed down the phone. He took some deep breaths to calm himself, as he'd been trained to do by the psychologist. He'd seen her so often they were on first-name terms – at least until he'd yelled at her during their last session. Anger management had featured in nine of his last twenty annual performance reviews. He reminded himself that number would have been a whole lot higher if the flat-bottomed bureaucrats had thought to introduce performance reviews in the nineties. He promised himself he'd keep a clean sheet for the one remaining review before he retired. He would be polite and cooperative. He took some deep breaths before pounding the stapler a few more times with his fist.

The detectives knocked on the door and Begley beckoned them in. Before he met them, Begley would have bet big money they were corrupt. But there was not a Rolex to be seen, not even cheap knock-offs, just cheap. And their suits had deep wrinkles radiating from their groins, having spent aeons crushed between arse and chair, or arse and police car. So, either they weren't corrupt, or they were very good at being corrupt.

The older one, Maguire, had a greyish complexion that matched the colour of his suit so closely they blended into each other. But his short-cropped hair was dyed black, 'bottle-black' as Begley liked to call it, and so dark it was like staring into a hole. The younger detective stood rigidly upright, all arms and legs, his long narrow head shaved bald. Neither of them smiled.

The older one stretched out a hand. 'Detective Sergeant Matthew Maguire. Matty.'

Begley arranged his face into the best smile he could muster, took Maguire's hand and crushed it. 'Inspector Begley.' He sure as hell wasn't going to be on first-name terms. He held the handshake just long enough to avoid being hit with Maguire's free hand. Duffy introduced himself and Begley shook his hand with an insipid, limp grip. That would mess with their heads during their tearoom debrief. Begley motioned them to sit, and he felt a warm glow when he spotted Maguire surreptitiously stretching the fingers of his right hand.

Begley reclined into his chair, smiling. 'Have you been to Byron before?'

They both shook their heads.

Begley leaned forward and stared at each of them in turn, his smile gone. In a low menacing voice he said, 'And what the fuck are you two doing here now?'

The two detectives glanced at each other before Duffy said, 'There's been a murder.'

Begley feigned surprise. 'Oh, has there? Has there?'

There was a knock at the door. Anderson entered and placed a steaming mug of coffee in front of each of the detectives. Snot. He'd hoped Anderson had chosen snot.

Begley continued. 'Gentlemen, you insult my intelligence. Actually, no, you insult your own. The question was not why we have homicide detectives here, but rather what the fuck you two homicide detectives in particular, are doing here?'

Begley heard a commotion at the door.

'Because I sent them,' said a strangely familiar voice. Assistant Commissioner Terry Mitchell strode into the room.

Begley jumped to his feet, and the two detectives smiled for the first time.

'At ease, Inspector.'

But Begley remained standing. Fuck, he thought, hoping at least they wouldn't send him back to the same psychologist.

The assistant commissioner continued. 'I see you've met two of our finest detectives.'

'Yes, sir,' said Begley, trying to sound normal through gritted teeth.

'I wasn't sure the local detectives were up to it, they only have a few murders a year on their patch, so I flew in Maguire and Duffy. I want the best. I want a result. In fact the Minister for Police wants a result. I'm sure you know this is his electorate.'

'Very good, sir.'

'And I'm expecting full cooperation.'

'Yes, sir. Of course. Who will they be reporting to, sir?'

'The officer in charge of the case, as usual. I believe that is currently you?'

Begley nodded, relieved. He'd be able to keep an eye on the useless wankers.

'Well, I'll be taking over,' said Mitchell. 'I'll also be taking over your office.'

'Of course, sir.'

The assistant commissioner picked up a photo of Begley's wife from the desk and stared at it before handing it to Begley. 'You've ten minutes to clear out anything you want, then we'd like a briefing on the case. And if you wouldn't mind making me a coffee, a flat white would do nicely.'

Chapter Forty-five

Caitlin and Jack were stuck behind a battered old Hillman Hunter doing forty kilometres an hour as it wound through the bends towards Bangalow. At least the view soothed some of Jack's irritation at being late as the car crawled over the range – lush rolling hills, macadamia farms and the distant sweep of the coastline. The election posters along the side of the road had become even more numerous – Mayor Tom Bradshaw's still outnumbering all the other candidates.

Bangalow hadn't changed since Jack was last there fifteen years before. It hadn't changed for the fifty years before that either, which gave the tiny town its charm. Historic terraced buildings lined the steep main street, many with upper-storey covered balconies. The cafés, boutiques and galleries were bustling with tourists.

They pulled up in front of a Queenslander-style house with large wrap-around verandas, its grandeur long lost to peeling paint, a rusty corrugated iron roof and neglected gardens. Marlene, the council archivist, had agreed to another meeting, insisting Jack and Caitlin come to her house.

It was Marlene who greeted them at the door but, rather than inviting them in, she led them along an overgrown path around the side of the house to a stand-alone weatherboard garage. Its windows were covered with black plastic and a rattling old air conditioner protruded through a wall.

After the heat outside, Jack welcomed the blast of cold air as they entered. When his eyes adjusted to the dim light, he saw there was barely room to park a scooter in the garage, never mind a car. Shelves lined every wall, stacked high with archive boxes, document trays and piles of newspapers.

In the centre, a man sat at a long desk that was covered in papers and all the paraphernalia of a modern office – printer, scanner, computer and dirty mugs. He rose awkwardly with the aid of a walking stick. Even though he must have been pushing seventy, he had a thick mane of silver hair.

'This is my husband, Brian,' said Marlene.

'Welcome to man-cave central,' said Brian. 'I don't normally let people in, Caitlin, but your father spent a bit of time here recently. I enjoyed his company. I'm sorry about what happened to him.'

Caitlin nodded in acknowledgement, her hands suddenly restless.

Brian motioned them towards a battered lounge chair whose wadding was attempting to escape through splits in the covering. The springs had gone, and Jack's bum sagged almost to the floor. It was like the Hotel California of lounges and Jack wondered how they were going to get back out.

Jack surveyed the crowded shelves. 'What is all this stuff?'

'I'm not very mobile now, so I'm keeping myself busy by writing a book. The definitive history of Byron Bay. A proper history, fully referenced to all the source documents I've collected. Marlene tells me you are interested in 1987.'

Before Caitlin could answer, Brian was wracked by a bout of coughing, loud and moist. His face turned red with the effort. Caitlin waited for him to stop.

'We think Dad was looking at something that happened that year. Did he tell you?'

'He said it was better I didn't know. And I'm only up to the seventies so far, but the documents are all here from eighty-seven. You're welcome to take a look. I have a rough chapter outline somewhere.' He woke the computer from its slumber.

It took Jack and Caitlin a couple of attempts to get up out of the lounge.

Marlene showed them the relevant shelves. 'There are some documents you can't copy. Or quote. Documents that aren't really here, if you know what I mean?'

Jack smiled. 'Council documents?'

Her grin was mischievous. 'They seem to copy themselves and climb into my handbag.' She handed Caitlin a box. 'Every issue of *The Beacon* from 1987.' She handed Jack another box. 'Council minutes. Boring as batshit, I'm afraid.' She grabbed a large folder for herself. 'I'll check the planning decisions.'

Brian read from his computer screen. 'January saw the high school open. In February there was a council election. Believe it or not they had another election later in the year, after the mayor did a Harold Holt.'

Caitlin asked, 'What do you mean he did a Harold Holt?'

Brian looked at them perplexed. 'Harold Holt. The Australian Prime Minister. He drowned swimming at a beach, in the late sixties.'

Caitlin said, 'I know who Harold Holt is. Are you saying the local mayor also drowned?'

'In April,' said Brian. He looked back at his spreadsheet. 'And *Crocodile Dundee* was released. Actually, I think that that was '86. But boy, did that change Byron Bay. Paul Hogan moved here, and half the world followed.'

Apart from the constant clatter of the air conditioner, the room was silent as they scoured their documents. It was also freezing cold. Jack's shorts and T-shirt weren't providing much insulation and, an hour in, Jack was shivering. 'It's bloody arctic in here, Brian.'

'It's to preserve the documents, not the people.' He winked at Jack. 'I'd have thought you'd be used to the cold, being from Melbourne. Do you want to borrow my dressing gown?'

Jack declined and returned to the task, trying to concentrate, and stop his teeth from chattering. Marlene was right, the council minutes were dreary. They seemed to have been recorded merely to satisfy a mandatory requirement rather than to provide any useful purpose. The agenda items were all listed, sealing gravel roads, a proposed kiosk in a caravan park and the like, but no details were recorded of any of the discussion. Jack laughed to himself the first time he read of a motion to increase the length of a councillor's speech by two minutes, passed with only one objection. It would have taken longer than two minutes to pass the motion, and yet there was no mention of a single word the councillor had said. Jack wasn't laughing after he'd read hundreds of similar entries.

Caitlin pushed a copy of *The Beacon* towards Jack and pointed to a front-page story. 'Your father must have had a good lawyer. You'd never be able to write stuff like that now. And not an "allegedly" in sight.'

Underneath the headline '*Would You Vote For This Man?*' was an unflattering photograph of a councillor, next to a photograph of his wife, likely taken without her knowledge as she sat at an outdoor café. Her arm was covered in bruises. Jack read:

Neighbours of Councillor David Naughton and his wife said they have heard noises coming from the house in the evenings. People familiar with the couple have said the marriage has sometimes had difficulties.

And then the kicker – a quotation from a social worker from the University of Melbourne:

Domestic violence is not acceptable at any time in our community and won't ever be satisfactorily addressed if women aren't brave enough to make complaints to the police.

At no stage did the newspaper article explicitly state the councillor had hit his wife. Jack could see the foundation stones of Harris Media's reporting style right there.

Brian referred to his computer. 'The councillor in that article, David Naughton, wasn't re-elected. He was replaced by some guy called Frank Cameron.'

That name sounded vaguely familiar to Jack, but he couldn't place it.

'Oh, my God,' said Caitlin, 'your father was at it again in the next week's edition.' She read out loud, '"A local veterinarian has reported several cats have been poisoned near where Mayor George Ferris resides in Browning Street. The vet, who declined to be named, suspects Panadol was hidden in cat food, causing a slow and horrible death for these much-loved family pets."' Caitlin held up the paper. A picture of a dead cat beside another of the mayor looking shifty. The headline was: *'Our Mayor: A Cat Killer?'*

'Mayor Ferris was re-elected,' said Brian, grinning. 'There must be a lot of people who hate cats. But then he drowned a few months later.'

Caitlin rifled through her pile of newspapers. 'Here it is.' She placed it on the table where they could both read it.

MAYOR FERRIS DROWNS. Locals reported seeing the mayor enter the water for his usual evening swim. Later that evening, after his wife reported him missing, his towel, clothes, and car keys were found on the beach.

Brian had another bout of coughing and they waited for him to recover. 'Like Harold, they never found his body, but nobody accused the Russians of abducting our mayor in a submarine.'

Marlene had been so quiet Jack had forgotten she was there until she suddenly laughed and started reading out loud. '"A Mrs Kentish of Suffolk Park successfully appealed her development application when she pointed out a typographical error made by council. She did not wish to enlarge her house to accommodate a brothel, she wished to accommodate a brother."' Marlene looked up at them. 'More seriously, there are a few interesting development applications. A fast-food chain was blocked unanimously after local protests. Rezoning of industrial land for the Jetty Hotel was approved in July. A residential subdivision was approved in Suffolk Park, and the applicant was our current mayor, Tom Bradshaw.'

Jack checked the minutes. 'The mayor elected to replace George Ferris after he drowned was Ian Bradshaw. Any relation?'

Marlene nodded. 'Ian Bradshaw was Tom's father. We had our own little property-development mafia at that time.'

Caitlin said, 'So the current mayor, Tom Bradshaw, is a property developer. Isn't that a conflict of interest?'

Marlene said, 'Bradshaw claims he is no longer an active developer, but of course his wife is still a director of all his old companies. Rumour has it he was one of the brown-paper-bag developers, wads of cash being handed out in return for planning decisions, but of course he was never caught or charged.' She turned to Jack. 'And I wouldn't put that in your paper. He's very litigious. Not to mention he's my boss. Hopefully he'll lose the election in a few weeks' time.'

'Isn't he the one whose election signs say, "Developing a better Byron"?' Caitlin asked.

'Yes,' said Marlene, 'and there's a photo of him laughing at us.'

Jack recalled Mark, the barman, saying he didn't know who owned the Jetty Hotel before him. Jack asked, 'Who was the applicant for the Jetty Hotel?'

Caitlin scanned her documents. 'It doesn't say.'

Brian was coughing again. It sounded like a whole lung was coming up this time.

Jack stood and walked around, flapping his arms, trying to warm up, but it was no good. He'd reached the end of the council minutes and his thermal tolerance. Time to leave before frostbite set in. 'Thanks for your help, Brian. And Marlene. You've given us lots to think about.'

Caitlin snapped a few more photographs of the last of the issues of *The Beacon*. She asked, 'Brian, are any of those people still around?'

'Tom Bradshaw's father passed away a long time ago. Plane crash in the Maldives. Frank Cameron and David Naughton are hanging in there against all the odds, the smokes and booze should have killed them a long time ago. They both pretty much live in the pub – different ones, of course, as they can't stand each other. As for Mrs Kentish, I'm not sure if she's still running her brothel.' He laughed at his joke and descended into a coughing fit so bad Marlene put her arm around his shoulders.

As Jack left, he worried Brian's magnum opus might never be finished before his lungs caught up with him.

Chapter Forty-six

On the return journey down the hill, given it was pushing two o'clock and both Jack and Caitlin were ravenous, they decided to head to the Jetty Hotel. They parked behind *The Beacon*, where things were looking up – the journalists had vanished and no new graffiti had been added to the hoarding, possibly because there was no room.

Inside, Jack returned the car keys to their drawer. Someone had slipped a brown envelope under the door and Caitlin picked it up. He heard her giggle and by the time he turned she was laughing uncontrollably.

She wiped a tear and said, 'I might keep this one myself.' She turned around a large glossy photo of Jack – side-on, and completely naked.

His heart jumped and he felt the hairs stand up on the back of his neck. 'Where did you get that?'

'Oh, there's more than one.'

She showed him another, a full frontal.

Jack's dread increased. He tried to snatch the photos from Caitlin, but she was too fast.

Caitlin held up another – Jack standing beside a striking woman, her large breasts in full view. It was Barbara, the wife of Bob Holmes, the naturist. Jack was so furious he couldn't speak.

'This one's my favourite.' She handed him a side-on shot of

Barbara bending over, pendulous boobs hanging, her rear end lining up perfectly with Jack's groin. They looked mid-shag.

Jack's face was burning, and he wasn't sure whether it was from embarrassment at Caitlin staring at the naked photos, or fury at having been set up.

'Oh, lovely, there's a letter.' Caitlin unfolded it. 'From your nudist friend.' She read aloud, '"Delete the photos of my wife, or you and your pathetic excuse for a penis will be uploaded for all to see."'

Jack's fury now out-gunned his embarrassment. 'What the hell? He wants the nude pictures of his wife erased, pictures that don't exist, or he'll upload pictures of me with his nude wife!'

'Wife?'

'Yes, that's his wife, Barbara. She was at the house.'

Caitlin laughed. 'That's not his wife. I went to school with this girl. And her name's not Barbara. It's Elanna. She's a sex worker.'

This time, Jack successfully yanked the photos from Caitlin's hands. He carried them straight to the shredder and fed them in.

Caitlin said, 'You didn't want to take them to the police? I'm sure Begley would be interested.'

Jack was still shaken as they walked towards the Jetty Hotel. And angry.

Caitlin broke the silence. 'Do you think he Photoshopped on the bigger willy? I remember it smaller, although the water was pretty cold.'

Jack snapped back, 'Ha, fucking, ha. And, anyway, I don't think someone of your stature is in a position to talk about size.'

She slapped him hard on the arm and at last he laughed.

She asked more seriously, 'What are you going to do?'

He didn't answer.

They sat at the bar. The comfy seat in the corner was again unoccupied, but this time a half-full pint was keeping the reserved sign company. Jack suddenly remembered the name Brian had mentioned that morning – Frank Cameron. He was the councillor who was elected in 1987, and the man the seat at the bar – 'Cameron's Corner' – was reserved for.

When Mark appeared behind the bar, they both ordered the beer-battered barramundi and Jack asked, 'What's Frank Cameron like?'

'You'll have the dubious pleasure of finding out yourself in a minute.' Mark leaned forward and lowered his voice. 'To tell you the truth, the whole thing is a right pain in the arse, he's a pain in the arse.'

'What thing?'

Mark put down the glass he was cleaning, and the tea towel. 'I bought this pub sixteen years ago. There was a weird covenant as part of the sale – so long as Cameron is still alive, that seat must be reserved for him, *and* he gets free drinks.'

Jack and Caitlin exchanged surprised glances.

'And the miserable old bastard just won't die,' said Mark. 'He's been knocking hard at the door for the last five years but I'm starting to think he's immortal. To tell you the truth, I'd run over him with my car given half a chance, but even that probably wouldn't kill him.'

Jack said, 'There was another councillor, David Naughton, who lost an election to your friend Cameron. He doesn't get free booze?'

Mark shook his head. 'David Naughton drinks at The Rails – he and Cameron hate each other's guts.'

Caitlin asked, 'Who did you buy the pub from?'

'You know, that's the other strange thing. I can't tell you. There was a non-disclosure clause in the contract, but the truth is I never knew. It was owned by some shelf company in Luxembourg. All very mysterious, but in the end, who cares? There haven't been any problems, and the place is now worth twenty times what I paid for it, so my retirement's sorted.' He looked at Caitlin and then at Jack, smiling. 'I don't suppose you want to buy a pub?' He resumed polishing the glasses. 'Here comes the bullet-proof bastard now.'

An emaciated old man in clothing too big for him was driving a mobility cart back from the bathroom. He crashed into a woman's leg on the way, and no apology was offered through the plastic oxygen mask covering his face. After dismounting, he slowly heaved an oxygen cylinder onto a wall hook. By the time he settled in his seat, he was severely short of breath. Jack let him recover enough to take his first sip of beer, before moving over and sitting beside him. Frank Cameron's eyes gazed unwaveringly at his pint.

'I'm Jack, Jack Harris.' He put out his hand.

Frank didn't move.

'I'm taking over from Patrick O'Shaughnessy at *The Beacon*.'

Frank ignored him. A minute ticked by, but Jack wasn't going anywhere. When Frank finally spoke, his oxygen mask fogged up.

'Bugger off.'

'I'm wondering how an ex-councillor gets free drinks for life. I reckon it could be a good story.'

There was no answer, but Jack noticed the man's eyes widen a little at the question and his oxygen mask fog up of its own accord. A scrawny arm extended and lifted the pint, while the other hand moved the mask aside as he took a sip.

'And a reserved seat in the pub?'

'I said, bugger off.' The effort of saying just four words made him gasp even harder for breath.

An acned adolescent appeared with their food and Jack returned to his seat. His growling stomach had outvoted his intense curiosity about how Frank Cameron slotted into the puzzle, if at all.

'That went well,' Caitlin said. 'Have you thought of a career in journalism?'

Jack was halfway through his fish and chips before he realised Cameron had disappeared. Jack spotted him perched on his buggy near the exit. He'd removed his oxygen mask and was speaking slowly, between gasps of air, into a phone. His eyes rose and caught Jack's before looking quickly away. After the call was over, he replaced his oxygen mask. He only crashed into one table as he drove out.

Jack had almost finished his food when he heard that voice behind him. It made his skin prickle. That faux poncy accent.

'Fancy meeting you here, old boy. And the elusive Caitlin O'Shaughnessy.'

They both turned, chips frozen in motion halfway to their mouths. Angus Bain was mutating into a local, having not only lost the tweed jacket but now wearing shorts and a white linen shirt.

Jack felt his knuckles clench involuntarily. He forced himself to relax, and turned to Caitlin. 'You've met Angus Bain. I presume you know he works for my father. Feel free to keep hurling oranges at him, just never tell him anything.'

Caitlin said, 'You don't need to warn me – we have history. He practically stalked me after my arrest in Sydney.'

Bain threw his head back and laughed. 'Oh, it's not you I'm

interested in my dear, way too late for heartfelt quotations about him being the best father in the world, etcetera.'

Caitlin's face reddened and she went to stand, but Jack put a brief restraining hand on her shoulder.

Bain continued. 'It's you I want to talk to, Jack.'

Mark was hovering at the end of the bar, watching warily. Caitlin's anger was palpable. Jack wondered which of them might toss Bain out on his arse first.

Bain charged on. 'I've heard there was history between you and this lovely girl's father. That you were in the process of firing him.' He extended a voice recorder towards Jack. 'Perhaps you could reassure our readers you had nothing to do with Mr O'Shaughnessy's murder. Why don't you start by telling us your alibi for that evening?'

Jack remembered the drunken night at his father's house. Actually, he couldn't remember it at all, only waking in the morning with the worst hangover in his life. Did Bain know? And where was this going? He was suddenly wracked with uncertainty and stared dumbly at the voice recorder.

It was pinot noir that broke the tension. Jack was impressed with Caitlin's restraint – the glass was still in her hand, but Bain and his formerly white shirt looked like the lone survivors of a chainsaw massacre. Bain was unfazed and his recorder remained pointing accusingly at Jack as security carried him away.

A cleaner appeared with a mop and Mark with replacement drinks. 'You two certainly seem to be shit magnets. It won't happen again – he's really barred this time.'

Caitlin's lips were taut.

'Don't worry,' said Jack. 'He's the type of journalist who doesn't think he's doing his job properly if he isn't assaulted. There's a YouTube video of Sean Penn decking Bain with a right hook. Most people watch it to see a movie star losing his shit. I watch it to see Bain being hit.'

'Why is Bain asking you for an alibi?'

'He's just stirring to see what reaction he gets. It'll be nothing.' But Jack was worried. Bain's enmity towards him knew no bounds and might even surpass Bain's loyalty to Jack's father. And Jack knew how devious Bain could be.

They finished their meals in silence, ruminating about Bain.

When they were done, Jack said, 'Let's head to The Rails and see if that other councillor is there, David Naughton.'

'I'm sorry, Jack, I'll have to leave you to it. The coroner has released Dad's body.' She shuddered as she spoke. 'The funeral is the day after tomorrow. I'm meeting with Zoe to finalise the arrangements.'

Jack's hand got halfway to hers, but at the last moment he changed his mind and pulled it back. 'Let me know if I can help.'

Chapter Forty-seven

As Jack walked towards The Rails Hotel, he called Begley for an update, only to be told the detectives from Sydney had done 'fuck-all', and seemed to be 'sitting around polishing their arses on chairs, hoping the fairy godmother would hand them the killer on a plate'. Jack felt as angry as Begley sounded at the lack of any progress, and even more so at what sounded like a lack of effort. Were the detectives really not investigating? Or was that merely typical Begley bluster?

Even at this hour of the afternoon, the sun was beating down and Jack was sweating by the time he reached The Rails. He made a beeline to the cooler back bar and paid his respects to the spitfire wreckage in the ceiling.

Jack asked the barman, 'Is David Naughton in?'

'You got lucky,' he said, and pointed him out. 'But then you would have got lucky any time you came.'

Jack bought two pints, including Naughton's usual, and carried them through to the outdoor beer garden, past a musician doing a sound check.

Naughton only had his drink for company. He sat well back from the table to make room for his ample beer gut. His hands, their rheumatic fingers intertwined, rested on the horizontal shelf made by his belly. Dappled black and grey hair was long and bushy and merged imperceptibly into his beard.

'Mind if I sit here?' asked Jack.

'Go right ahead, but you know it's the smoking section, right?' Naughton took out his cigarettes, lit one and offered the pack. When Jack shook his head, Naughton's brow furrowed. 'Oh, that's bad.'

'What do you mean?'

'You don't smoke and you're in the smoking section, and you've bought an extra beer. Which means you want to talk to me.'

Jack laughed and offered his hand. 'Jack Harris.'

Naughton hesitated, then shook it. 'I assume you know who I am if you want to talk to me.'

Jack handed him one of the glasses. 'I've just started at *The Beacon*. I came to work with Patrick O'Shaughnessy, but I guess I'm now taking over. I'm trying to run down a story he was working on and, to tell you the truth, I think it might have something to do with his murder.'

Naughton took an enormous drag on his cigarette, then blew the smoke out slowly. 'Go on.'

'I want to know what happened in 1987.'

Naughton took another very deep drag on his cigarette, but after an even slower expiration, didn't respond.

'I saw an unflattering newspaper article about you in *The Beacon* from that time.'

Naughton picked up his beer, chugged a lot of it down, then sat the glass on the table. 'What did you say your name was?'

'Jack Harris.'

'That's a bit of a coincidence, isn't it? Surname of Harris. Working at *The Beacon*.'

'Malcolm Harris is my father.'

The silence stretched on for some time before Naughton said, 'Will you do me a favour?'

Jack waited as the man took another drag so deep the smoke must have reached his ankles; it seemed to take forever to come back out. But, eventually, Naughton returned his gaze to Jack.

'Tell your father, from me, that he's a cunt.'

It wasn't the first time Jack had heard that description of his father, but it still shocked him.

Naughton became more animated. He leaned forward, his gut bumping the table and spilling their drinks, and he pointed his cigarette at Jack. 'Your father published a string of slanderous articles about me. Apparently, I was a drink driver, I fraudulently claimed travel allowances from council, and I was involved in tax evasion. But that article suggesting I beat my wife was the worst. I was spat at in the street and almost hounded out of town. It ended up costing me my marriage.'

'You're saying my father made it all up?'

The man's eyes were wide now, and the cigarette shaking so much a pile of ash was growing on the table. 'That photo was taken years earlier. We had been riding our bikes and were side-swiped by a car. My wife suffered severe bruising down her side where she landed. She was the lucky one. I broke my ankle and spent a week in hospital.'

'Why would my father do that?'

'Because he's a cunt.'

'Had you pissed him off somehow?'

Naughton shook his head. 'I'd never met him before.'

'Then why?'

'The same reason your father still does it. Only now he does it to prime ministers. It was all to do with the council elections that year. He wanted political influence, wanted his man on council. In order to do that he had to make sure one of the existing councillors wasn't re-elected, and I was the bunny.'

And there it was again – another reminder of Jack's increasing discomfort at the immense power his father held, and the abuse of it. The Harris surname was beginning to sit even more uncomfortably with him. He asked, 'Frank Cameron, was that my father's man?'

Naughton nodded. 'Saint Frank. He should have been beatified after the glowing things your father wrote about him.' He downed more of his pint, then lit another cigarette.

The first song burst from the PA. 'Bridge over Troubled Water'. Jack hated the song, even when it wasn't being sung out of key. He stood and shook the other man's hand. 'Thanks for your help. I'll send another pint out for you.'

Naughton took a long pull on his cigarette. Jack was halfway to the bar when Naughton called after him, 'Don't forget to tell your father he's a cunt.'

When Jack arrived back at *The Beacon*, he found a plain brown envelope slipped under the door. Jack felt the muscles in his neck and jaw tense. He ripped it open and slid out a large colour photo – Jack naked beside the equally naked woman who was not Bob Holmes' wife. How many photos did he have? It didn't really matter, only one would be enough if it was leaked. Jack turned the photo over. There was a message stuck to the back, the words cut from different magazines: *You have 3 days, or these photos will be going virile.*

Even with the typo, or 'cutto', the threat was clear. It was time for Jack to make a move.

Ten seconds later, the photo was in the shredder. A minute later Jack was in a surf shop around the corner, where he bought a pair of rubber soled sneakers, black jeans and a black hoodie. He added a pencil torch from an outdoor store, then stashed them in the boot of the Toyota.

He headed to Eddie's for coffee – he had a long night ahead of him. An enjoyable night, if all went well. He was fond of a little break and enter.

Chapter Forty-eight
Wednesday, 13th November

Jack didn't hear Caitlin arrive at *The Beacon* the next morning, his attention completely focused on a laptop in pieces on the table in front of him. He bent the motherboard backwards and forwards until the solder joints popped – he loved that sound. Only when she yelled his name, did he look up.

'Oh, hi.'

'What are you doing?'

'You don't want to know.'

'Jack?'

He unscrewed the solid-state drive from the motherboard and prized it off with a screwdriver. 'Making absolutely sure no naked photos of me go into circulation.'

Her eyes widened in horror. 'How did you get his laptop?'

Jack bent the storage drive until it snapped in two. It felt so good.

She shook her head. 'For Christ's sake, Jack, have you forgotten I'm on bail? Don't make me an accessory to your one-man crime wave.' Caitlin was still shaking her head when she walked to the kitchenette. She wet some paper towel and started dabbing away at fresh blood oozing from a scrape over her right elbow.

Jack watched her tend her injury. Late last night, after arriving home from his midnight laptop raid, he'd spent hours reading everything he could find about Huntington's disease. Thanks to Professor Google, Jack knew which chromosome the faulty gene was on (4), what went wrong with it (too many CAG repeats) and even what CAG stood for (cytosine, adenine, guanine). He knew the first name of the Dr Huntington who 'discovered' the disease (George) and his wife (Mary). He had even looked up autosomal dominant inheritance, because he and Ricky had paid no attention during science classes at school, or any classes for that matter. Jack also now knew everything about the symptoms of Huntington's and loss of coordination was an early sign. As he watched Caitlin throw the bloodied towel into the garbage and dab at the wound with a fresh sheet, he wondered whether he was reading too much into grazes on an elbow, grazes on an experienced skateboarder.

Caitlin, her bleeding stopped, sat beside Jack at the table. 'Begley called. Off the record. He's been taken off the case. But he said the DNA results are back ...' She stopped, unable to continue.

Jack waited, before filling the gap. 'The leg is your father's.'

She nodded, then took a deep, slow breath. 'It had been cut off with a chainsaw.'

'Oh, Caitlin.' Of course, Jack knew the leg had to be hacked off somehow, but it still sounded shocking when she said it. He realised how much more distressing it must have been for her – it would be impossible not to visualise the chainsaw screaming as it hacked through the bone.

She stood and walked back to the towel dispenser and patted her eyes.

'Did Begley say how the investigation was going?'

She took a big sniff. 'He said the useless detectives up from

Sydney couldn't solve a sudoku, never mind Dad's murder.'

'What the hell? It doesn't sound like they are ever going to find your father's killer. So, I guess that means it's over to us.'

Caitlin nodded. 'It's a long time since I studied criminal law, but in order to convict you need to prove means, motive and opportunity. The motive's on a memory stick we can't get into. And means is hardly our area of expertise. We don't exactly move in the circles of hired assassins.'

'Speak for yourself, although assassins were more Ricky's father's line.' Jack picked up a drill and started making random holes in the motherboard.

'We do know the planning was meticulous. Which I'd say rules out your nudist boyfriend. It's more in the line of organised crime, or government. Or zealots like Lars Nielsen's little army.'

Jack wasn't so keen to dismiss the doggedly determined naturist, Bob Holmes. And he wasn't so sure murder by shark was the modus operandi of foreign governments. Russia preferred slow death from exotic radioisotopes, the French limpet mines.

'Did your father ever mention ASIO?'

She shook her head. 'But then ASIO doesn't send email notifications that you are a person of interest.'

'Okay, so organised crime. Drugs? Byron's a big market.'

'No. Drugs are same old, same old. Dad wouldn't have bothered unless the Minister for Border Security was running a smuggling ring. My vote is corruption.'

'But corruption must be small fry in Byron, and hardly a shoo-in for a Walkley Award for excellence in journalism.'

'Then why was Dad combing through council archives, and putting notices in *The Beacon* looking for old council staff? Then there's the two Bradshaws, both mayors, one in '87 and one now.

The son's big residential development was approved when his father was mayor.'

Jack said, 'I thought the Jetty Hotel was stranger. Nobody seems to know who owned it.'

'Well, that's probably the one thing in this shitshow we can answer.' She slid her mobile from her pocket and dialled. 'I'll have my ESO at work do a property search.'

'Aren't you suspended?'

'She'll do it – we've worked together forever.' When the call answered, she said, 'Hi, it's me.' Caitlin listened for a while before she responded, 'Thanks. The funeral's tomorrow. And thanks for the card.' She listened some more, then asked, 'Can you do a sneaky search for me? I'm looking for the previous owner of the Jetty Hotel in Byron Bay. The sale was sixteen years ago.'

After a few minutes, Caitlin said, 'No, nothing in writing, just tell me.' When the call ended, she said, 'Metol Partners S.A. It's based in Luxembourg. What sort of company name is that?'

'Dodgy, I'd say. Did she know anything about them?'

'That info's not in the property records, but I can ask someone I know in our Paris office.'

Jack logged onto his laptop and googled 'Metol Luxembourg'. All that returned was a list of thrash-metal bands, like 'Stormthrone of Dripping Blood'. He tried searching the Harris Media archives for 'Metol Partners S.A.' but an error message popped up with a stop-sign icon – *Search term not available.* He tried 'Jetty Hotel' and saw the same error message.

Given the Bradshaws had featured so heavily in council affairs, Jack wondered whether they might have been involved in the Jetty Hotel development. He made a mental note to put that question to Mayor Tom Bradshaw himself. Then he recalled that back in the day his father and Tom Bradshaw's father, Ian, had been friends. A memory came back to him of the elder Bradshaw chain-smoking as he sat on the lounge in their old house – Jack couldn't remember ever seeing him smile.

Jack's thoughts were interrupted by the ring of the office phone. He picked it up and heard heavy breathing, then a deep voice said, 'Have you got my laptop?'

Jack switched the call to speaker. 'Bob Holmes, and good morning to you too.'

'You stole it, didn't you? I'm reporting you to the police.'

Jack smiled at Caitlin. 'I was thinking of calling them myself. They'd be very interested in some of the other photos you have on your hard drive.' Jack didn't think it worth mentioning he'd destroyed the laptop without searching it.

There was a long silence, then, 'You bucket of scum. I'll get you, Harris. Consider yourself toast.'

Chapter Forty-nine

After Caitlin left to finalise the next day's funeral arrangements, Jack wiped his prints off all the computer parts, placed them in a garbage bag, locked up the office, and headed off down the lane. He traversed the rear carpark to avoid any security cameras on Jonson Street, then slid the garbage bag into a bin a few blocks from *The Beacon* before doubling back towards Zoe's salon.

Outside the salon, workmen in fluoro jackets were in an animated discussion with Zoe as they collectively stared in through the door. Water gushed out around their wellies. After lots of pointing, the plumbers waded in with torches and ladders.

Zoe rolled her eyes when she saw Jack. 'The apartment upstairs has sprung a leak. Hopefully it's just water. Seems you're destined never to get this haircut.'

'Can't we do it out here?'

She nodded. 'Al fresco. Why not?' She waded inside and returned with stool, comb and scissors and set up on a dry section of pavement. The queue at Eddie's turned to watch, glad for the entertainment.

'Now, no distractions today. Don't even talk to me until I'm finished. Can't have you looking scruffy at the funeral.'

She had only made a few cuts when Jack's phone rang. She gave him a tired look. The ringtone was the warning klaxon assigned to his father. The sound always made his muscles clench. He motioned for Zoe to continue cutting. Jack put the phone to his ear and Zoe started back in.

'Dad,' said Jack.

Zoe raised an eyebrow.

'I expected to hear from you by now, son. Have you found out what Patrick O'Shaughnessy was investigating?'

'Not yet.'

It was a while before his father spoke, as silent judgement was passed and Jack found guilty of not giving his father what he wanted. 'And you missed your first edition as editor of *The Beacon*, the only time it hasn't been published in forty years. You've let me down, son. How can I be confident you won't fail me on the next edition? You've only got a few days.'

Jack didn't answer.

'Jack?'

'I'm on it.'

'If you don't have Patrick's story, what are you working on?'

Jack hesitated. He was never good at spontaneous lying, especially to his father, but he wanted to reassure him he wouldn't miss another edition of the paper, even though the deadline for publication was impossibly close. 'I was thinking business as usual for my first issue. Council approved a building in town that's a metre over height. Endangered frogs.'

'Then why were you searching for a company in Luxembourg?'

Jesus, would his father ever leave him to do his own thing? Jack hesitated. He needed to be careful – his father would definitely not approve of him investigating a shelf company in Luxembourg if it turned out to belong Ian Bradshaw, one of his old friends.

Eventually, after too long a pause, Jack said, 'It was nothing.

One of our political contributors was thinking of writing a story on tax havens, and so he used my logon to check our archive. I've talked him out of the piece.' The long silence that followed was telling, and Jack could visualise the well-used, disapproving look that would be at the other end of the line as his father realised he was lying.

Zoe tapped him on the head a few times and he looked up. He was so engrossed in the phone call he forgot she was cutting his hair. She mimed swapping the phone to the other ear.

'I'm very disappointed in you, Jack. You're my eyes on the ground there. You're my son. I expect you to tell me the truth. And, for goodness sake, do something useful for once and find out what O'Shaughnessy was up to.' His father ended the call.

Zoe had stopped cutting, waiting for the debrief, but Jack remained silent. She said, 'That didn't sound very warm and fuzzy. Trouble?'

He nodded, but didn't elaborate, so she resumed cutting.

'Have you heard how the police are going with the investigation?' she asked.

'Badly, apparently.'

She looked disappointed and stopped cutting momentarily.

'So, Caitlin and I are going to keep digging,' said Jack. Perhaps you can help.'

'Of course, if I can. As long as it doesn't involve client secrets.' She combed up hair on the top of his head and started thinning.

'We still haven't been able to access the memory stick.'

'Then I'm not sure I can help. Patrick wouldn't tell me what it was all about. He was scared not only for himself, but also for me.'

'Did he pump you for information about anything lately?'

She shook her head.

'Then was there anything he recently stopped talking about?'

'He became quieter about everything. He was distracted. But he still sometimes spoke about that loopy nudist that was threatening him. And that dentist.'

'Lars Nielsen?'

'Especially Nielsen. Nothing irritated him more than conspiracy theorists.' Zoe stopped cutting and looked at Jack, then seemed to make up her mind. 'Nielsen is a fake. One of my client's sisters is a kindergarten teacher in Tamborine Mountain, a small village over the border about two hours away. Nielsen's family lives there in a palatial house perched on the escarpment with views to the Gold Coast. He goes home for the weekends. Nielsen is a randy one, that's for sure; he's got five children – all of them vaccinated. And if he's ever there for the school run, he ditches that little electric car for a Porsche Cayenne.'

Jack said, 'But I don't understand.'

'This area is the anti-vax capital of Australia. It's brilliant marketing. He gathers as many disciples around him as he can, then offers them a discount at his holistic dental practice, which charges twice as much as a normal dentist. He's cornered the anti-5G crowd, anti-fluoride, the anti-vaxxers. He's their hero.'

Jack relished the thought of having dirt on Nielsen. 'Now that is some story. Did you tell Patrick?'

She shook her head. 'But that doesn't mean he wasn't on to it some other way.'

'Would Nielsen kill Patrick for that?'

Zoe shrugged. 'If word got out, his clients would disappear overnight. There'd be no more private schools for Lars's kids. He might even have to sell the Porsche. I think Patrick might have visited him recently – I noticed he had some of those dental hygiene packs his practice hands out.'

Jack heard loud music approaching and two shirtless backpackers shimmied past, one carrying a speaker blaring from his shoulder. The other called out to Jack, 'Bellissimo,' then blew him a kiss.

'I know this is hard to believe,' said Zoe, 'but you're done.'

Jack stood up and the queue waiting for lattes at Eddie's burst into applause.

She refused to take payment. 'It's the least I can do, I've messed you around so much. Besides, the cash drawer is full of water.'

Jack lowered his voice and turned his back on the crowd. 'Zoe, there's one more thing we'd like your help with. We're trying to identify a black van behaving suspiciously around the time Patrick disappeared. We don't have much of a description, just that it was like a delivery van, with no windows in the back. One of your clients might have seen something.'

Zoe nodded. 'Leave it with me.'

They hugged.

Jack held her and said, 'Big day tomorrow.'

She squeezed him tighter and buried her head in his shoulder.

He asked, 'Would you like me to collect you and Caitlin? We can go together.'

They separated, and she nodded her head. 'That's very kind.'

As she carried the stool back to the door, the plumbers emerged from the salon, soaking wet, but victorious. The deluge had stopped.

Chapter Fifty

The restaurant was full, but Begley and his wife were seated at the best table, one of the perks of booking under the name of Inspector. Their view extended across the glittering bay where kayakers and stand-up paddleboarders were revelling in the calm conditions.

Begley was happy. The grilled king prawns had been swimming in garlic, and the dry-aged rib-eye had stretched from one side of his plate to the other. And now the waiter stood before them, tempting him with the dessert menu. Veronica wouldn't rebuke him today, no matter how much he overate, so he opted for the salted caramel chocolate fondant.

The maître d' appeared, smiling. 'Would you like a dessert wine, or coffee? We also have a vintage port that would be the perfect accompaniment.'

They both agreed on the port.

Begley took his wife's hand in his and they smiled at each other. He had been so incredibly lucky to marry this woman. It was only because of her love and support that he was still in the police force – and able to deal with the stress of the job most of the time. She'd followed him without complaint every time he'd been transferred from one shitty police station to another. He was pleased that, finally, here in Byron Bay, they had a posting that made her happy.

A shadow fell across the table. When Begley looked up, his happy mood vanished. Assistant Commissioner Terry Mitchell stood before them in full uniform. Every eye in the restaurant was trained on them.

'Out of uniform, Inspector Begley?' asked the assistant commissioner.

Begley saw the consternation in his wife's face, and he fought to suppress his anger at the intrusion. 'I'm off duty, sir. It's our anniversary.'

'Well, congratulations. Do you mind if I join you?' Before waiting for an answer, he called for the maître d' to bring him a chair.

Before separating hands, Begley squeezed his wife's reassuringly and she squeezed back. Begley said, 'Thirty-nine years today.' Having heard rumours the assistant commissioner's wife had recently left him, Begley asked, 'How long have you been married, sir?'

The assistant commissioner was saved from replying by the arrival of his chair, the chocolate fondant, and the glasses of port.

'I might have a port myself,' the assistant commissioner said to the waiter, 'and a spoon.'

Begley felt his anger mounting. The knuckles of his clenched fists were white, so he hid them under the table.

'Anderson told me you were here,' said the assistant commissioner. 'You were overheard, Inspector, talking to the victim's daughter about details of the case. How do you know she is not a suspect?'

'His daughter? Sir, there's no way—'

'Disclosing evidence to a suspect is misconduct. Serious misconduct.'

This was ludicrous. Begley tried to remember the key points

from his anger management sessions, but his mind went blank. 'I really don't think—'

'Stop,' interrupted the assistant commissioner loudly, before leaning forward and speaking with quieter menace. 'I don't want you to think. I want you to keep clear of the investigation, and Harris Media in particular.' The assistant commissioner picked up his spoon, carved off half of Begley's chocolate fondant and placed it in his mouth.

Begley took slow deliberate breaths. His wife stared at her hands.

'The victim was a journalist, a Harris journalist. Why would the investigation—'

The assistant commissioner's spoon stopped mid-flight towards the remaining fondant. 'Really?' He rolled his eyes. 'Because Harris is a major donor to the minister's election fund. And the minister tells us what to do.' The spoon continued its trajectory and the remaining fondant disappeared.

Begley was breathing faster now. 'I assume any such direction would be unofficial, sir.'

The assistant commissioner swallowed, wiped his face with Begley's napkin and turned to Veronica. 'Mrs Begley.'

Her eyes were wide with trepidation as she slowly looked up. 'Hmmm?'

'How do you feel about getting out of this backwater? Perhaps a transfer to Sydney? Somewhere like, say, Blacktown.' The assistant commissioner reached out a hand and placed it on her shoulder. 'It's very multicultural, with lots of good restaurants for your next anniversary. Or, better still, Broken Hill. Yes, that would be perfect.'

Begley saw the tears forming in his wife's eyes. He was breathing way too fast, and feeling dizzy. Stars danced across his vision. His fingernails were digging into his palms. He knew he could deck the fat fucker with one punch. He forced his voice to be steady as it fought its way out through his clenched teeth. 'I'll keep away from the investigation. And Harris.'

The assistant commissioner removed his hand from Veronica Begley's shoulder, then drained his glass of port. He smiled at Begley, stood up and placed his hat on his head. 'Happy anniversary. You make such a lovely couple.' He turned and was gone.

Begley took a huge breath and let out a long sigh. He reached for his wife's hand. 'Don't worry about him. Shit like that always floats to the top.'

She nodded.

He said, 'I love you.'

She smiled at him, like she'd done for over forty years, that beautiful smile, and said, 'I love you too.'

The maître d' appeared and cheerily wished them a happy anniversary before depositing the bill. Begley was shocked. The port was thirty-nine dollars. Each! He felt his anger returning. He hated being taken advantage of. Christ on a bloody bike, he thought, you can buy a whole bottle of port, a nice one, for twenty bucks.

As he paid, Begley took pains to get the full name of the smiling maître d'.

'How was everything today?'

'Couldn't be better,' said Begley, proud his anger management training had finally surfaced. Later, back at the station, he would look up the maître d' in the database and when he pulled the thieving scoundrel's car over, the fine would make this bill look like small change.

He smiled at his wife, took her hand, and they strolled out.

Chapter Fifty-one

That same afternoon, Jack started the car and drove out of the carpark. As soon as he'd driven beyond sight of the police station, he picked up his phone and made a call, keeping a wary eye out for rogue potholes as he dialled.

'Northern Rivers Shire Council, this is Megan, how can I help you?'

'Mayor Bradshaw, please.'

He was connected to a tired-sounding female voice. 'Mayor's office.'

'I'd like an appointment to see the mayor this afternoon.'

After a cluck, clucking of disapproval, she said, 'I'm afraid he's only here until four, and he's fully booked. The next available time is tomorrow at three. Who's calling?'

'I'm an auditor from the Australian Tax Office. It's personal. Tomorrow at three suits perfectly. Have a good afternoon.' Jack ended the call. That should cause a few sleepless nights for Bradshaw if he's bent, he thought.

The drive to Mullumbimby was magical: sunflowers bobbing in the breeze, iridescent-green cane fields, the perfectly pyramidal peak of Mount Chincogan, Hilltop Hoods on the radio, and a dodgy property developer shitting himself about a tax audit. Occasionally, all the planets did line up.

He parked the car in a quiet street and phoned Caitlin. When she answered, he said, 'I need you to do something for me. Can you stay on the line? You can talk if you want, but I won't be listening. Just don't hang up. I'll explain later.'

'Jack?'

As he slid the phone under the driver's seat, he could still hear Caitlin talking, 'Jack. Jack. What the hell? JACK.'

He pulled on a plain grey hoody before setting off, head down, towards the council office. He approached from behind and came to a stop with his back to the rear wall of the building. The staff carpark was full, but he didn't need the 'Reserved Mayor' sign to identify the car he was looking for. How many council employees could afford a racing-green Aston Martin?

A single security camera watched over the carpark from low on a wall. Jack checked there was nobody in sight, removed his hoody and, after a few swings, managed to loop the hood over the lens of the camera.

Ricky Martinelli had shown him how to break into most cars, but Aston Martins hadn't been part of the syllabus. To be fair to Ricky, they were hard to get hold of. It took Jack longer than he'd hoped, but eventually, after wiping his fingerprints from the door, he found himself comfortably seated on soft leather in the rear seat. The window tinting was so dark, he didn't bother crouching down to hide.

Bradshaw was recognisable from his election posters. He emerged from the building right on cue at four o'clock, a hand energetically gesticulating as he spoke into his phone. Big jowls gave his head a distinctive pear-shape, jowls that wobbled in sync with his equally pear-shaped torso as he waddled towards the car. In contrast to all those posters, he wasn't smiling. Jack remained silent in the back seat as Bradshaw, still on the phone, opened the door and sat behind the steering wheel.

'Pick the kids up later. I want you to take the laptop and as much paperwork as you can to your sister's, in case they arrive with a warrant. I'll warn the accountants. I'm on my way.' The mayor ended the call and said to himself, 'Jesus H Christ.'

The motor sprang to life with its trademark eight-cylinder roar and Jack could breathe again. Bradshaw turned the car out onto the road, drove past the council building and was approaching a roundabout when Jack leaned forward, close to his ear, and said, 'You must be Tom.'

Even minor accidents seem much worse when you're sitting in a half-million-dollar car. In retrospect, Jack thought, he might have waited until after the car had safely negotiated the roundabout, particularly a roundabout with a dozen or so small ornamental trees in its centre. As it was, at the sound of Jack's voice, Tom Bradshaw yanked his head around in fright and the car, in the absence of any other guidance, ignored the give-way sign and careered straight through the centre of the roundabout, scraping the length of the driver's side along one of the sturdier saplings, all accompanied by a very expensive sound of screeching metal. The car bucked and bounced out the other side of the roundabout and Bradshaw jerked his eyes back to the front, yelled, 'Shiiiiiiit!' and snatched the steering wheel to the right just in time to avoid crashing into a drainage culvert.

Bradshaw stomped on the brakes and the car jolted to a halt in the middle of the road. His head spun around. He was breathing heavily, eyes wide. 'What the hell are you doing in my car?'

'I want to ask you a few questions about your tax.'

'What?' Bradshaw shook his head as if trying to untangle

a confusion of irreconcilable thoughts. 'Are you from the ATO?'

'No. I'm not interested in your Australian tax affairs.'

'Then what the hell do you want?'

'I'm interested in your Luxembourg tax affairs.' And there it was. Jack saw the flicker in Bradshaw's eyes, and the brief hesitation before he recovered, and Jack knew he was right, knew who had been the beneficial owner of the Jetty Hotel.

'I don't know what you're talking about. I'm calling the police.' Bradshaw reached for his phone.

'Suit yourself. I'd say you'll get done for dangerous driving and damage to public property.' Jack opened his door a fraction, in case Bradshaw tried to lock him in.

A car sounded its horn behind them.

Bradshaw put down his phone. 'You broke into my car.'

'Why did you block access to all council documents from 1987?'

'Who the hell are you?'

'I'm a journalist at *The Beacon*.'

Jack could see Bradshaw trying to make sense of it.

'So, you must be Malcolm Harris's son?'

'Uh huh.'

Bradshaw visibly relaxed. 'Why didn't you say so? Your father was a very good friend of my late father, Ian.'

'Are you the owner of a company called Metol?'

The rage returned to Bradshaw's face, his jowls tremulous. Too late, he screamed, 'Get out of my car!' but Jack was already gone, a cacophony of horns from backed up cars accompanying him as he set off to reclaim his hoody.

Back at the Toyota, his phone was still connected with Caitlin's, but she wasn't listening. He ended the call, locked the car and walked to the supermarket on the main street, where he used his credit card to buy provisions from the deli.

The tree had been shaken hard, now all he had to do was wait and see what fell out. He didn't have to wait long.

Chapter Fifty-two
Thursday, 14th November

Zoe lived in one of the new trendy developments on the fringes of the Arts and Industrial Estate. Jack felt conscious of his appearance as he walked past busy designer shops and climbed the stairs to her apartment. Among all the boho devotees with their flowing linen, flower garlands and sandals, his charcoal-grey suit seemed out of place. The suit also seemed out of place on him. Had he acclimatised so much in the two weeks since he'd left the boardroom?

He knocked. Approaching high heels clacked over a timber floor. The door opened to reveal Zoe in a sombre black pants suit. She looked surprised to see him.

'Jack! What are you doing here?'

'I'm driving you both.' He checked his watch. 'And for once I'm on time.'

Zoe stared at him for a moment, then said, 'You haven't seen it have you?'

'Seen what?'

'You'd better come in.'

She ushered him into the kitchen. An enormous bouquet of white roses lay on the table, still wrapped in cellophane. Jack kicked himself for being so insensitive as to arrive empty handed.

Caitlin stood with her back to him, leaning against the kitchen bench, staring out the window. Her dreadlocks were tied at the back and fell over a simple midnight-blue dress that flowed uninterrupted from her shoulders to her knees. High heels had replaced the Doc Martens.

'Hello, Caitlin.'

She turned to him, and his heart jumped. She wore no jewellery, and her freckles had been painted out. She looked beautiful. And vulnerable, her moist eyes betraying her sadness. She simply nodded in reply, with no change of expression.

'Here,' said Zoe, as she threw a thick newspaper onto the table.

Big black letters. *JACK HARRIS: PERSON OF INTEREST IN MURDER INVESTIGATION.*' Shocked, Jack grabbed the paper and read.

One of Australia's most eligible and secretive bachelors, Jack Harris, the son of the publisher of this newspaper, Malcolm Harris, is allegedly a person of interest in the brutal murder of Patrick O'Shaughnessy in Byron Bay eleven days ago. Police are said to be keen to interview Mr Harris about his whereabouts on the night of the murder. Sources close to the investigation stated there was a troubled history between the two men, and that Mr Harris has been unable to produce an alibi for the night the murder was committed.

Jack could feel his fury rising, knowing whose name he would find on the by-line. And there it was, the man who'd been seeking revenge on him for all those years, Angus fucking Bain.

'You know this is rubbish, don't you?' said Jack.

'Of course,' said Zoe, 'but it's pretty insensitive timing.'

Caitlin turned back to stare out the window and Zoe placed an arm around her shoulders.

Jack turned the newspaper to page two and saw what he was dreading. The photograph was deliberately chosen to make him look guilty, but at least the large sunglasses, low hat and bowed head meant he was virtually unrecognisable.

There was a knock at the door and Zoe said, 'I've asked a friend to drive us. It would be better if you went separately.' She turned to Caitlin. 'Ready?'

Caitlin nodded, collected her clutch bag from the table and said softly to Jack, 'I'll see you there.' She reached out and touched the rose petals. 'It was very kind of your father.'

'What?'

She turned and followed Zoe down the hall.

Jack snatched the card from its ribbon.

Please accept my deepest commiserations at your loss. Your father was a great man, and one of our best journalists. You should be very proud of his legacy. Malcolm Harris.

Jack wondered whether he would ever be free from his father's shadow. He resisted the temptation to tear up the card, then walked to the door.

Chapter Fifty-three

Jack could feel the sweat trickling down his back as he hurried towards St Finbarr's Catholic Church. Following the 'exclusive allegations' published in that morning's newspaper, Jack knew he'd become the money shot. All the camera crews and reporters would be looking for him, to capture the alleged 'person of interest' attending his victim's funeral. Jack burrowed his way into the centre of a large group of mourners walking to the church, and kept his head down.

Inside, an electronic organ filled the space with sombre chords. The pews were overflowing. Jack recognised some of *The Beacon*'s freelancers scattered through the congregation, including Cassandra, today in a black head scarf rather than red. He wondered if her horoscopes this week would be all doom and gloom. Caitlin sat in the front row, Zoe's arm around her shoulders.

The coffin was draped in navy velvet and adorned with an abundance of white lilies. Patrick smiled at the mourners from a large photograph beside the coffin.

Jack avoided funerals whenever he could. When he did go, involuntary tears would flow even if it was for someone he never knew. But today he chose to sit in the back row not so much to avoid the embarrassment, but rather to avoid scrutiny.

A young woman next to him stared at her phone, long false

fingernails clacking away on the screen. She was reading a news site, and Jack's photograph scrolled past, then reappeared, then scrolled away again. He turned aside and buried his head in the order of service.

As the organist finished, Jack felt a nudge on his shoulder. It was Begley, his old navy suit too small for his expanding girth. Jack made space for him.

The priest began: 'Friends, family and loved ones, we are gathered here today, not to mourn a life sadly taken from us, but to celebrate a life, to celebrate Patrick O'Shaughnessy. He—'

Begley leaned in uncomfortably close to Jack's ear and whispered, 'Detectives Humpty and Dumpty have been buzzing around like blue-arsed flies this morning. Maybe today's newspaper woke them from their slumber.'

Jack tried to ignore him.

The priest continued, 'Those who knew Patrick will remember his great fondness for—'

The annoying whisper was back in Jack's ear. 'The assistant commissioner tried to stop me from coming.'

Jack could hear the priest again. 'Patrick loved this community, and the people loved him. Warm-hearted and generous seem to be common descriptions, and—'

This time the whisper was accompanied by a light spray of saliva. 'I told him to fuck off, that this was a private matter.'

The woman next to Jack shot them a frosty glare.

Begley continued. 'This is your last chance to tell me straight. Are you involved in this?'

Jack shook his head. 'It was a revenge piece from a disgruntled employer.'

The woman beside Jack reprimanded them with an angry, 'Shhhhh.'

Begley looked at her and nodded.

The woman stared at Jack longer than she should have. A few seconds later she was checking her phone and scrolling to Jack's photo. She glanced back at Jack, then quickly away, and a few moments later started angling her phone camera towards him.

'Christ on a bloody bike,' said Begley, too loudly. The woman looked at Begley and he flashed his warrant card, then, with two fingers, pointed at his eyes and then hers. She quickly put down her phone.

The eulogies were moving, none more than Caitlin's. She stood straight, without notes and, after a long silence, began. 'My mother, whom I loved more than anybody else except my father, and now my father, have been cruelly taken from me and I stand here, surrounded by friends and family, but feeling totally alone ...' By the time she'd finished, Caitlin's were the only dry eyes in the congregation – even the priest wiped a tear. Paparazzi girl next to Jack was trying to reattach one of her false eyelashes. Jack blinked in a futile attempt to try to clear his eyes. Begley sniffed.

Caitlin leaned forward, head bowed, and rested her hands on the coffin. She stayed there, motionless, until eventually Zoe guided her back to her seat.

After closing words from the priest, the mourners stood. The pallbearers lifted the coffin and set off slowly down the aisle, as the organist played 'Amazing Grace'. Jack wished he could offer some support to Caitlin, however small. Perhaps to squeeze her hand as she walked by, or even catch her eye, but he was lost in the crowd.

The church was slow to empty. Through the doors, Jack saw Caitlin swamped by well-wishers. He also saw reporters and camera crews searching the crowd, searching for him. He sat, to wait it out. After twenty minutes, all was quiet outside and Jack was about to chance it when he heard footsteps entering. Two sets. Two men. Jack knew they were detectives, even before he saw the bulge of their guns. Begley's Humpty and Dumpty, thought Jack. He stood and moved into the aisle before they reached him.

The older of the two asked, 'Jack Harris?'

'Yes.'

'I'm Detective Sergeant Maguire and this is Detective Duffy.' The detective looked around the empty room. 'You seem to be hiding in here. All alone. Like a criminal. Are you a criminal?'

'No more than you,' said Jack.

Neither detective reacted.

Maguire said, 'We need to question you about the murder of Patrick O'Shaughnessy.'

Inside, Jack's anger was boiling away furiously, threatening to break loose, but he was determined to appear outwardly calm. 'What, in here, a church, at the man's funeral?'

Duffy replied, 'At the station.'

'You want me to walk out that door, with you?'

Maguire shrugged. 'Unless you'd prefer to do it wearing handcuffs?'

'And the camera crews are still there?'

A malicious grin spread across Duffy's face. 'Unfortunately, someone seems to have given them a tip off.'

Jack laughed, shrugged in resignation, then feinted leaving with them. Instead, he leaped onto the closest pew, jumped over a few more and then ran across to the central aisle. He sprinted to the sacristy door, pursued by loud shouts and fast footsteps.

A corridor took him to some stairs. He bounded down and burst through a door to find himself outside. He ran across the rectory lawn, scattering garden furniture as he went, until his way was blocked by a high cyclone fence topped with barbed wire. Jack didn't hesitate. He climbed the fence where it joined a garage. At the top, he leaned as much weight as he could on the garage roof, then gingerly stepped over the barbed wire. As he jumped, his trouser leg snagged, and he felt barbs slice into his thigh before he fell heavily to the ground.

Jack grimaced in pain and looked at his trousers. Blood was seeping into the torn cloth.

The detectives appeared on the other side of the fence, running towards him and screaming at him to stop. As if. Without looking to see if their guns were drawn, Jack picked himself up and limped as quickly as he could towards Jonson Street, where he disappeared into the holiday crowds.

He hobbled on, trying to ignore the pain. Progress was easier with his left hand applying pressure to the wound. Behind The Rails Hotel, he limped north along the old tracks as fast as he could, heart pounding, covered in sweat, and trying to ignore the stinging pain in his thigh. He felt moisture under his hand and saw that a red patch was spreading on his trousers.

A few minutes later he burst through the doors of the police station, startling Anderson at reception.

Jack yelled at him, 'Begley. Now!'

Anderson, too shocked to protest, picked up the phone and dialled.

For the first time in his life, Jack was pleased to see Begley, who was already back in uniform. On seeing the state of Jack, the policeman quickly showed him inside. After checking the staff tearoom was empty, they entered, closing the door behind them.

'You look like shit,' said Begley, as he tore off long lengths of paper towel and handed them over.

Jack patted them on his face and neck to soak up the sweat. 'I met Humpty and Dumpty.'

A lopsided grin spread across Begley's face. 'Oh, this is going to be good.'

'They tried to drag me through the press cordon after the funeral.'

Begley looked shocked. 'Christ on a bloody bike.'

'I might have slipped out the back door.'

Begley frowned, then said, 'I have no doubt you did that to get to the police station in the most expeditious manner, to assist with our enquiries.'

'Exactly.'

Begley looked at Jack's leg. 'Do you need anything for that?'

Jack separated the slash in his trousers. The gash in his skin was a few centimetres long, and not too deep. He was expecting worse given the pain, and a blood stain increasingly looking like the aftermath of a massacre.

'Amputation, I'd say,' said Begley as he handed Jack more paper towel.

As Jack dabbed at his wound, they heard a commotion outside. Begley opened the door just far enough for them to hear the two detectives arguing as they walked past.

'You know he's going to lose his shit.'

'Well, if you weren't such a slow fuck, he wouldn't have got away.'

The footsteps receded and Begley turned to Jack. 'Ready?'

Jack nodded and followed Begley to the increasingly familiar interview room. He then watched from the door as Begley walked along the corridor towards the source of the shouting.

The assistant commissioner didn't sound happy. 'What do you mean you lost him?'

'He escaped, sir.'

'You two clowns couldn't find your own dicks with your hands down your trousers.'

Jack heard Begley knock and say, 'Sir.'

'Not now, Inspector,' and then, 'I don't know why I brought you useless specimens up from Sydney.'

Another knock.

'Inspector, I said not now. Are you deaf as well as stupid?'

Begley's voice, 'Sorry, sir, but he's in the interview room.'

The shouting stopped.

'Harris. In the interview room, sir. Mr Harris said detectives Duffy and Maguire asked him to meet them here at the station fifteen minutes ago. He's been waiting for a while. Shall I tell him they're on the way, sir? Or make him a cup of coffee?'

Jack just had time sit in the chair before Duffy and Maguire burst through the door, their faces like thunder. Duffy shook his finger at him, 'You little ...'

The assistant commissioner entered the room, followed by Begley.

Jack, still seething inside, smiled calmly back at them. 'I understand you have some questions for me, gentlemen?'

The assistant commissioner turned an angry face to his men. 'You two, my office.'

They left, Duffy giving Jack the evil eye as he backed out of the room.

When they'd gone, Begley said, 'I've just remembered why I love this job so much. I'll bring you a coffee.'

Chapter Fifty-four

It took more than an hour for the detectives to return, but Jack enjoyed the wait. The interview room was cool, and he stopped sweating. Begley had sent out for real coffee and Anderson delivered it with a tandoori chicken and avocado wrap, and a first-aid kit. Never before had Jack been treated like a VIP in a police station.

The pampering wasn't to last. Duffy and Maguire's smiles, when they re-entered the room, could best be described as malicious. No doubt they were looking forward to making the next few hours as unpleasant as possible.

The detectives were accompanied by a well-groomed, middle-aged man in a sharp, charcoal suit and crimson tie. Jack smelled lawyer. His watch was a Patek Philippe. Expensive lawyer.

'This,' said Maguire, 'is Rajiv Chowdhury, he's here to represent you.'

Chowdhury shook Jack's hand overenthusiastically. 'Your father sent me. Just in case. I'm very pleased to meet you.'

After his initial surprise, Jack's mind flooded with questions. How had his father even known he was being brought in for questioning? Why had he organised a lawyer? Was it some sort of atonement following the false allegations made in his own newspapers?

He and Chowdhury sat facing Duffy and Maguire across the
table. Duffy opened a notebook and removed a pen from his
pocket. Jack couldn't decide whether the detectives' expressions
were malevolent or smug. Perhaps one of each.

Maguire kicked off the hostilities. 'We'd like to ask you a few
questions.'

Jack said, 'Am I under caution?'

'Not yet.'

'Good,' said Jack, and smiled at the detectives. 'I can say what
I like.'

Maguire tried again. 'Like I said, we'd just like to ask you a
few questions.'

Jack interrupted, 'Jack William Harris. Fourth of April, 1984.
Currently residing at Seven Mile Beach Road. Would you like
me to spell "seven" for you, Detective Duffy?'

Duffy glared back at him.

'We've a couple of matters to discuss,' said Maguire. 'I believe
you are familiar with Tom Bradshaw.'

'Oh, yes,' said Jack. 'Very. Unfortunately. It's definitely the
worst terminal at Los Angeles Airport. Why do you ask? Did I
forget to pay for a bagel?'

Jack felt a hand on his arm – Chowdhury's. 'That's Tom
Bradley not Bradshaw.'

'Ah, my mistake,' said Jack. 'It is a shit terminal, though.
Luckily, QANTAS has changed to—'

Maguire shouted, 'Enough! We've received a complaint from
Mayor Tom Bradshaw.'

'The mayor?'

Maguire nodded.

Jack scratched his head. 'Nope, I don't know that I've ever
met him.'

Duffy's pen stopped writing and the detectives exchanged glances.

Maguire asked, 'Were you in Mullumbimby yesterday afternoon?'

'Yes.'

'Near the council chambers?'

'Yes.'

'What were you doing there?'

'Buying cheese.'

Maguire's eyebrows shot up. 'Cheese?'

'The IGA supermarket in the main street has an awesome deli. You guys should head out and take a look. If you like blue vein, then—'

'Harris!' yelled Maguire. 'What time did you buy this cheese?'

Jack pulled out his phone, navigated to his bank transactions and showed the detectives. '4:53'

'And what were you doing before you bought the cheese? In particular' – he checked Duffy's notes – 'between 4 and 4.30 p.m.?'

'Sitting in my car.'

'Were you with anyone?'

'No'.

'So, nobody saw you sitting in the car?'

'No.'

The detectives both leaned back in their chairs, looking pleased with themselves.

'But I was on the phone. To Caitlin O'Shaughnessy. From ...' Jack checked his calls records, '... nineteen minutes to four. The call lasted fifty-eight minutes.' He showed his phone to the detectives, who resumed glancing at each other again, uncertainly.

Maguire said, 'To Caitlin O'Shaughnessy, for fifty-eight minutes?'

Jack said to Duffy, 'You don't have to write that down twice. Would you like me to spell O'Shaughnessy? It's a tough one.'

A redness was creeping up Duffy's neck, spreading towards increasingly hostile eyes. Jack was enjoying himself – not long now before Duffy went thermonuclear.

Maguire asked, 'What did you and Ms O'Shaughnessy speak about for almost an hour?'

'Are you sure you don't want to record this?'

Maguire was losing patience. 'Just answer the question, Mr Harris.'

'We talked about the incompetent investigation into her father's death. How the police wouldn't recognise a murder if it bit them on the arse. How they wasted the first few critical days, contaminated the crime scene, lost the opportunity for fingerprint and DNA evidence—'

'Shut the fuck up,' said Duffy, his face now red with anger.

'Objection,' said Chowdhury. 'You are insulting my client, who is fully cooperating with your enquiries by answering your question.'

Jack looked back at the detectives. 'Would you like me to continue cooperating?'

Maguire's lips had disappeared into a tight slit, but he nodded.

'We also spoke at length about two useless detectives from Sydney who have made zero progress. I think we used the word "zero", although it could have been "fuck-all".'

Duffy slammed his pen onto the desk at the same time Maguire jumped up from his chair.

'And then I bought some Jarlsberg.'

Duffy leaned over the table and grabbed a fistful of Jack's shirt. 'I am going to—'

'Gentlemen.' Chowdhury was firm, but calm. 'I would very much like to suggest you stop assaulting my client and that we all take a break and calm down.'

Duffy slowly, and reluctantly, released Jack's shirt, snatched the notepad from the desk and followed Maguire to the door.

Jack called after them, 'White with no sugar, thanks.'

After Duffy had slammed the door, Chowdhury raised a quizzical eyebrow.

Jack shrugged. 'What?'

'Well, as your lawyer—'

'Are you my lawyer? Or are you my father's lawyer?'

Chowdhury didn't blink. 'As your lawyer, I would very much like to advise you not to try to make them angry.'

'I'm the one who's angry. Those detectives wanted my face on every TV in the country, looking like I'd been arrested. You can't recover a reputation after that. Worse, a man has been murdered and they really have done fuck-all. So I'm seriously pissed off. The difference is, Mr Chowdhury, that I don't show my anger, because if you do that you lose. Unfortunately, you stopped him from hitting me, because then it would have been game over.'

'But, as your lawyer, Mr Harris, I advise you—'

'Advise all you like. I'm just making sure they don't mess with me again.'

They made small talk as they waited for the detectives to return. But it wasn't Chowdhury's interest in medieval jousting, or that all his five children were lawyers that interested Jack. Rather, it was how a Melbourne-based lawyer had travelled over fifteen hundred kilometres to Byron Bay before midday. Jack had only been brought in for questioning a couple of hours ago.

Duffy and Maguire were calmer when they returned to their seats. They didn't skip into the room holding hands, but the threat of physical violence seemed to have dissipated.

'Mr Harris,' said Maguire, 'I presume you've seen the newspaper allegations implying you are a person of interest in the investigation of the murder of Patrick O'Shaughnessy?'

Jack nodded.

'Obviously, it would be remiss of us if we didn't question you after such an allegation.'

Jack nodded again.

'Did you murder Patrick O'Shaughnessy?'

He felt Chowdhury's hand on his arm again. 'As your lawyer, I would very much like to advise you not to answer that question, Mr Harris.'

Jack turned to Chowdhury in surprise. 'What? Of course I didn't murder Patrick.'

Maguire continued. 'Could you tell us your whereabouts during the night of Sunday the third of November this year?'

He felt the hand on his arm again. 'Mr Harris, as your—'

Jack ignored him. 'I was in my father's house at Seven Mile Beach Road. There is a ring of video cameras around the property. Nobody can get in, or out, without being seen.'

'We checked,' said Maguire. 'The video cameras were not functioning on the evening in question.'

An alarm bell started ringing quietly in Jack's head. He said, 'I was drinking with my father's assistant, Don Hargreaves, until very late in the evening.'

Maguire pressed on. 'Well, according to Mr Hargreaves, he last saw you heading off to bed before midnight and didn't see you again until after nine the next morning. Did you murder

Patrick O'Shaughnessy sometime between those hours?'

The hand was back. 'Mr Harris, I advise you—'

'I repeat, I didn't murder Patrick. I was so pissed that night I could barely make it to the bathroom, never mind drive ten kilometres along a winding gravel road in the dark. I'd like to remind you that you didn't even know this was a murder until I found the leg.'

Maguire pushed on regardless. 'Some criminals want to be caught. Is that you, Mr Harris?'

Jack turned to Chowdhury. 'Don't even think about it.' He looked back at Maguire. 'Next question.'

Maguire just shrugged. 'You said Mr O'Shaughnessy's laptop was stolen. Do you know what Mr O'Shaughnessy was investigating at the time of his death?'

'As your lawyer, I advise you to answer the question as truthfully as possible.'

The alarm sounding in Jack's head became a cacophony. He turned to the lawyer in disbelief. 'You advise me to answer that question?'

'Yes, please,' said Chowdhury. 'It doesn't incriminate you, and may help solve this dreadful murder.'

Jack was still staring at his lawyer when the alarm bells switched off, their job done. His father wasn't paying Chowdhury to be Jack's lawyer, he was paying him to gather information. Which made sense. As his father had already said to Jack, if Patrick was murdered because of a story he was working on for *The Beacon*, Harris could be liable. That would be one big compensation payout. Chowdhury was defending Harris Media, not Jack. He was annoyed it took him so long to realise, given his father had always put his own interests first, including before Jack's.

He turned back to the detectives. 'Do you intend to charge me?'

Maguire couldn't hide the disappointment in his voice. 'No. Not yet.'

'In that case, I believe we've finished.' Jack turned to Duffy. 'I was disappointed not to see you two doing the good cop, bad cop routine, but I guess that's difficult when you're both bad cops.' He stood, shook Chowdhury's hand and said, 'I very much hope you have a pleasant flight back to Melbourne.'

Chowdhury tried to say something in protest, but Jack turned and was gone.

He stopped outside the front door of the police station, distracted by the pain throbbing in his leg. It was getting worse. He needed the wound attended to. And a tetanus shot. He searched on his phone for the nearest GP practice and made an appointment. Then he tried to gather his thoughts. Why was the video surveillance not working that night? Why didn't Don back up his alibi on the night of the murder? And what was his father up to?

Chapter Fifty-five

As Jack walked towards the doctor's surgery, he saw a man sitting against a wall, his dog lying immobile by his side as though glued to the footpath. The man held a handwritten sign, that said: 'Piss poor advice by donation'. Jack threw a five-dollar note into his hat and the man looked up at him with rheumy eyes. Just when Jack was about to give up and walk on, the raspy voice said, 'Beware the Ides of November.'

Jack laughed, and went on his way.

The medical centre had the lushness of a hotel reception foyer – leather chairs, pot plants, bad muzak. A stack of last week's copies of *The Beacon* sat on a table, taunting him. They should have been this week's edition. Somehow, in his spare time between hunting a murderer and uncovering Patrick's story – one that may have cost him his life – Jack was supposed to be publishing a newspaper, but had failed to do so.

The doctor was running late, so Jack amused himself reading the notices (no, he didn't have scabies), and flicking through pamphlets (no, he didn't want a Mirena implant). Twenty minutes later, an elderly woman limped down the corridor towards the exit, calling to the receptionists as she went past, 'Bye, girls.'

One of the receptionists called after her, 'Doctor Bannerman, you have another patient. Sorry, last minute add on.'

When the weary doctor turned and stared at Jack, her shoulders slumped. Without smiling, she introduced herself as Belinda and motioned him to her room. Jack couldn't decide whether she was exhausted just by this day, or life in general.

When he dropped his trousers and she saw the gash on his thigh, her mood changed from grumpy to outright morose. She glanced at her watch, and the frown lines on her forehead deepened. 'You were lucky. A bit higher and you would have bled to death from your femoral artery. Follow me.'

Daphne, the practice nurse, joined them in the treatment room. She was bubbly, perhaps overcompensating for the glum countenance of the doctor. Jack removed his trousers and lay down. Daphne pin-balled from shelf to shelf, collecting the instruments of torture, then glanced at the gash and winced. 'Ooooh, nice job.'

'Barbed wire.'

'Ouch. I hope there's an interesting story. You wouldn't believe some of the wild tales I hear, especially the Insta injuries.'

'I was trying to outrun armed police officers.'

Daphne stopped pouring saline solution into a kidney dish and looked at him hopefully. 'Really?'

Jack shook his head and, disappointed, she resumed her preparation.

Belinda approached Jack with a loaded syringe. 'Tetanus shot. This is going to be very painful.' She jabbed the needle into his shoulder and depressed the plunger.

Jack was pleasantly surprised. 'I didn't feel a thing.'

'I don't mean now,' said the doctor. 'Tomorrow, it'll hurt like hell.' She inspected the gaping gash in his thigh. 'I'm going to clean and stitch the wound. It'll sting. I could give you a local anaesthetic, but then you'll have to put in your own stitches.

It's an extra five minutes I don't have because I'll be playing croquet. It's our semi-final.'

Jack opted out of DIY and Daphne took his hand unbidden. The doctor doused the wound with a copious amount of clear solution that looked innocuous, but it felt as if the gash was being washed out with chilli sauce. The stitches were worse. Belinda grabbed the skin at the wound's edges with forceps and stabbed the suture needle in. Jack flinched involuntarily and was ordered to keep still. Daphne stared at the wall and hummed throughout the entire procedure, squeezing Jack's hand so tightly it hurt.

Job completed, pain inflicted, Belinda stripped off her gloves. 'Stitches out in ten days. Either take them out yourself or Daphne here can do it. Make sure you keep the wound dry, we don't want your leg to fall off.' She gave the barest hint of a smile for the first time.

'Good luck with the croquet,' Jack called after her, but she just limped out the door without answering.

Chapter Fifty-six

When Jack walked out of the medical centre it was much darker than it should have been for 6 p.m. on a November evening. He looked to the sky. The sun had prematurely retired for the day behind a threatening bank of black clouds. Jack reached for his phone and, with increasing dismay, scrolled through the evening's weather forecast. One-hundred-per-cent chance of rain. Thirty to fifty millimetres. Flood warnings. Perfect weather for ducks. And for Lars Nielsen's anti-5G army. In Jack's covert recording of the anti-5G meeting, Nielsen could be clearly heard saying they would unfurl protest banners from the water tower at midnight the next time they could do it under cover of rain. Jack let out a long, low groan.

He was sorely tempted to ignore Lars Nielsen's nocturnal antics, but Jack desperately needed more stories for his first edition of *The Beacon*. Although the freelancers had already filed some articles for the next edition, as things stood it promised to be the slimmest ever issue and an inglorious start to his career as a newspaper editor. On the other hand, what better front cover photograph than Lars Nielsen, holistic dentist, respected member of the community, caught red-handed breaking the law.

Jack collected the Toyota from behind *The Beacon* and

drove towards his father's house to fill in the hours before midnight, pain stabbing at his thigh whenever he used the brake.

After changing out of his blood-stained suit, Jack joined Tony for dinner. He found him in an uncharacteristically gloomy mood. According to Tony, Don was becoming even more unbearable. It upset Jack to see Tony feeling down, he'd always been so happy here in what was effectively his home. After a long chat, they parted on a double espresso and a hug.

The drive back to town was perilous. The heavy rain had transformed the gravel road into a rapidly flowing brown torrent and the car threatened to head off into the bushes whenever he touched the brakes.

He parked a hundred metres from his destination, transferred the camera into a waterproof bag, grabbed the tripod and stepped out into the beating rain. He wanted to be in position well before the protesters arrived for their planned midnight rendezvous. It was going to be a miserable, wet wait.

Perched on the highest hill overlooking the town, and with mobile-phone masts bolted around its top, the cylindrical water tower was the perfect place for the Anti-5G Action Committee to hang their protest banners.

Jack had fond memories of the water tower. Its six-metre-high walls were completely covered in graffiti. Jack and his mates had hung around here as kids, spray painting their tags which would, in turn, be covered over in short order. His first rebellious cigarette had been smoked here, a habit long gone. A brief cask-wine era had also started eagerly and ended, badly, here. Perhaps most memorably, this was the place where he'd put his hand inside the bra of his first girlfriend.

Jack's torch picked out the track leading up and away from

the water tower to a lookout popular at sunset, where wooden benches offered views spanning the coastline. There were no such views on offer tonight. Even the powerful beam of the lighthouse was a feeble flicker in the distance every fifteen seconds, barely able to penetrate its rainy shroud. The water tower itself was scarcely visible in the infinite void of soggy blackness.

Jack set up the tripod and took a few test photographs, struggling all the while to keep the camera dry and water drops off the lens. Even though his naked eye could perceive nothing, with a ten-second exposure the camera showed a passable image of the water tower.

He sat on a bench and waited. A nearby sound made him instantly alert. He kept dead still and peered into the darkness, seeing nothing. Then a wallaby startled him by leaping out of the gloom and hopping away down the track. Jack started breathing again.

The minutes felt like hours. He'd brought an umbrella, but that was for the camera, and by the time cars began arriving at the water tower, he was soaked through to his jocks.

A flash of lightning tore through the sky and the image of people gathered at the base of the tower's maintenance ladder was burned onto Jack's retina. He took a photograph. The exposure took ten seconds and when the image appeared on the screen, it was perfect. A bit gothic, the figures blurry, but definitely a cover shot.

Jack hoped the lightning hadn't given away his position to the protesters. He didn't have to wait long to find out. As he bent to take his next photograph, there was a firm tap on his shoulder. He spun around in shock, bumped the tripod and sent the camera crashing to the ground.

A blinding light shot into his eyes, then a vice-like grip twisted his arms up behind him. Pain tore at his shoulders. Jack struggled against the powerful hands, only succeeding in making the pain worse.

The torch was lowered from his eyes and, as his retinas slowly recovered, the face of Lars Nielsen materialised, smiling calmly at him. 'Jack Harris, well, well, well. Taking a few sunset snaps perhaps? Although, to be honest, it could be getting a little dark for that. Or perhaps you knew we were going to be here?'

Jack was being crushed between two beefy men. Someone's hand slid into his pocket, removed his mobile phone and handed it to Nielsen.

'Did you ever wonder why your recording at the action committee meeting became clear when we discussed our plans for this evening?' Nielsen held up Jack's phone. 'This was sitting next to me on the table.'

Nielsen appeared to be enjoying himself. He dropped the phone to the ground, picked up a rock and smashed the phone to pieces. He then turned his attention to the camera, still attached to the tripod, but now semi-submerged in a stream of water. He removed the memory card, placed it on a rock, and repeated the demolition job. He smiled at Jack. 'Wouldn't want a journalist getting hold of these now, would we?'

The torch beam slammed back into his retinas and Jack screwed his eyes closed. His arms were yanked tighter. His toes were now barely touching the ground, and the searing pain in both shoulders was overwhelming.

Nielsen shouted over the rain, 'I couldn't get your predecessor, O'Shaughnessy, to listen, but I'm sure you're a much more reasonable man. In fact, I think you and I will get along just fine, assuming, of course, we get plenty of positive anti-vax and anti-5G coverage in *The Beacon* from now on. Maybe we could even be friends.'

Nielsen nodded to one of the thugs, who started tormenting one of Jack's fingers, bending it impossibly backwards until it felt as if it was about to snap.

Nielsen moved his face in close to Jack's. 'On the other hand, if you don't cooperate, I might not be able to stop my overenthusiastic friends from getting, let's just say, a little over-enthusiastic.'

Jack was thrown sprawling, face-first into the mud. By the time he dragged himself to his feet, the torch beam was bouncing away down the track. He wriggled his aching shoulders to try to restore some circulation, then massaged his throbbing finger. As the rain started beating down again with renewed fury, he felt a sharp stinging in his thigh and remembered the doctor's warning not to get his stitches wet.

The first part of his half-hour drive home in the early hours was filled with rage at Lars Nielsen and his two henchmen, but this gave way to fatigue as the car snaked through the forest and, exhausted, his mind wandered. He fell asleep at the wheel and the last thought he had on earth might have been of various types of revenge on Lars Nielsen if he hadn't been jolted instantly awake a short time later when one of the car's wheels smashed into a pothole that felt deep enough to be an open-cut mine. Suddenly, charged with adrenaline, Jack saw a massive tree trunk heading towards the windscreen and just managed to steer to safety on the slippery gravel. He slowed to a stop, his heart walloping wildly in his chest. He had no trouble staying awake for the rest of the journey, nor remembering the not-so-piss-poor advice he'd been given the day before: *Beware the Ides of November.*

Jack mistakenly assumed the warning referred to the events that had just happened. But things were about to get much worse.

Chapter Fifty-seven
Friday, 15th November

In the morning, bacon and eggs waited under the silver dome in the kitchen, but Don was nowhere to be seen. Jack felt better with a full stomach, clean clothes and the warm sun beating down on his face as he crossed the white flagstones to the Toyota. He was going to meet Caitlin. The next edition of the paper was due at the printer in two days. It was a near impossible task, but Caitlin had offered to help him try to pull it together.

Jack passed the water tower as he drove down Paterson Street. A giant banner flapped in the breeze: 'SAVE THE BEES – BAN 5G'. His anger rose as he remembered his treatment at the hands of Lars Nielsen's acolytes the night before.

The traffic in town was diabolical so he parked a couple of hundred metres away from the office and walked. At the front door of *The Beacon*, a tradie in an orange fluoro jacket was working on the lock. When Jack asked him what he was doing, the man gave Jack his best oh-here-we-go-what-does-it-look-like-I'm-doing expression.

Jack persisted. 'I didn't ask you to change the lock.'

'No, but he did.' He jabbed a thumb over his shoulder towards the office before begrudgingly stepping aside to let Jack pass.

Inside, everything was as it always was, except for Angus Bain sitting in Jack's chair, his feet up on the desk. Bain had changed. Not only was he wearing a blue Hawaiian shirt patterned with palm trees, he wore a huge smile, a genuine one.

'Morning, Jack.' His contrived bonhomie was also gone, and Jack apparently was no longer an 'old boy'.

'What are you doing here?'

'I was going to ask you the same thing. Don't you read your emails or texts?'

Jack felt his muscles tensing. He didn't answer.

Bain rubbed his hands together with glee. 'You've been released to explore other opportunities at your leisure.' He smiled even wider. 'I'm not one to give career advice, but I reckon lollipop man could be your calling.'

'What?'

'Lollipop man, you know, the ones that hold the stop–go signs at school crossings.'

'Angus, cut the crap.'

'You, Jack, have been fired. Again. Properly this time. You are no longer the editor of this newspaper.'

'Says who?'

'Management.'

'What do you mean, "management"?'

'Jack, I always took you for an idiot, but even I didn't think you were this stupid.'

'My father?'

'He wants someone he can trust to look after Harris interests. Me. Your father was pretty annoyed when *The Beacon* wasn't published for the first time in its history. But what really kicked him over the edge was when I told him you weren't working on the next week's paper at all, and that you could be found most days alternating between lying on top of a surfboard and a Brazilian backpacker called Rosita.'

Jack's jaw clenched, along with his knuckles. He forced his breathing to slow down, to stop himself from hitting out at Bain. He kept reminding himself, *if you show anger you lose*, but it felt like he had already lost.

'Smug' didn't begin to describe the look on Bain's face. He held out his hand. 'Keys to the car.'

Jack threw them onto the desk, never more glad he'd parked so far away in a little used side street – it would take Bain days to find it.

'I also need all your documents – paper and electronic. And any O'Shaughnessy was working on before he ...' Bain paused, '... handed over to you. They remain the property of Harris Media.'

'I don't have any.'

'Bullshit.'

When Jack didn't elaborate, Bain waved him away. 'Shouldn't you be studying for your lollipop-man exam?'

Fortunately, the tradie wasn't behind the door as Jack threw it open on his way out. He hurried to the street. He needed to buy a phone. Thirty minutes later he had one, but the experience hadn't restored his mood. The heavily encrusted adolescent had given him the third degree, and only reluctantly recorded the name of Jack's first teacher as 'Jesus Christ' and his favourite pet as 'For Fuck's Sake'. The SIM card, he was told, would take ten minutes to activate.

It was hot and humid outside, the sea breeze strangely absent, and Jack felt damp circles of sweat forming under his arms by the time the phone came to life. He punched in his father's number and listened to it ring and ring until it cut out. Like God, Malcolm Harris didn't have voicemail.

As Jack walked to the taxi rank, he entered his Harris email details into the phone. He stared as the wheel of fortune went around and around as servers connected to servers. An error message appeared: 'Access denied'.

The only taxi Jack could find was a maxi-taxi. They doubled as mini-buses and mobile vomitoriums after the nightclubs closed. This particular taxi had duct tape covering gaping wounds in the seats. The air conditioning wasn't working, and Jack wound down the window to dilute the pervasive smell of partially digested kebab. The driver was all courtesy, and seemed impervious to the heat and the pungent aromas as they drove towards Zoe's apartment.

On his third attempt, Jack recalled the correct phone number for Irina Markov at Harris HQ and she answered the call.

'Irina, it's Jack.'

'Well, well, well, if it's not my long-lost boyfriend. Probably ex-boyfriend now. And no caller ID. Have you gone dark, Jack?'

'Irina, what the hell is going on?'

'You are the water-cooler topic du jour. And the tearoom's. You've even made it into the women's toilets. "Leper" and "fucked" seems to be the general consensus. What was it? Lines of white powder? Teenage pregnancy? I'm told Byron can do that to you.'

'Why can't I access my emails?'

'Orders from on high, Jack. Don't blame me, I'm just doing my shitty job.'

'From whom?'

'The bear. The one you've pissed off.'

Jack was silent.

'Jack, you of all people should know how things work around here. If you're not prepared to grovel to your father and give him whatever he wants, go and set up a florist shop. And then you can send me tulips every day, preferably yellow.' She ended the call.

Jack stabbed hard at each number as he called his father again. No answer.

Chapter Fifty-eight

Caitlin opened the door. 'Jack, where have you been? You weren't answering my calls. I was scared something had happened to you.' He looked terrible, dark shadows under swollen, bloodshot eyes, a nasty graze on his left cheek. 'Jesus Jack, you look like shit.'

'Sorry, Caitlin, I had a rough night. And now I'm melting.'

There were only a few small dry patches of light blue on his shirt, between the areas soggy with sweat. More sweat ran down his forehead.

She ushered him into the lounge, then filled a large glass with ice cubes and water and watched him gulp it down. 'How about you have a cool shower? I'll throw your clothes in for a quick wash and dry.'

Jack hesitated.

'So you'd rather whine about the heat and drip sweat all over my apartment. Or are you allergic to taking showers?'

He smiled. 'Thanks.'

She fetched him a towel and showed him to the bathroom. He passed his clothes out through a narrow gap in the door and she carried them to the laundry where soon they were doing somersaults in the washing machine. Back in the lounge, she turned down the air conditioner a few degrees and cranked up the fan.

Ten minutes later he returned from the bathroom, naked, apart from a towel wrapped around his waist. Caitlin was pleased she'd been able to find such a small one.

He moved over and stood under the cool blast of the air conditioner. His hair was wet and tousled and he looked a little embarrassed to be semi-naked in front of her. Caitlin enjoyed his discomfort. And the view. He was fit. When they'd swum together in the ocean he'd run towards her naked, but she hadn't paid any attention, hadn't been interested at the time. But now she was. He had always been kind to her, and thoughtful. And he'd managed to give her hope – had even made her laugh during such a horrible time. Not to mention those moist abs.

She dragged her attention away from him. 'I went to *The Beacon* first thing.'

'Angus Bain?'

'I almost decked him with my skatie. It wasn't so much the disrespect for Dad, or being told to piss off, it was the smug look on his face.'

Jack laughed, then turned around so his front faced the arctic wind.

When the washing machine played its cheesy tune to announce it had finished, Caitlin threw his clothes into the dryer. Soon they were clinking around on the rapid-dry setting. On her return to the lounge room, Jack hadn't moved, and she decided the rear view of him was as equally impressive as the front.

She enjoyed the moment for a few seconds before asking, 'Bain said you'd been sacked as editor. Was that your father?'

'Bain told him I wasn't going to make the deadline for the next issue of *The Beacon*. And Dad's not answering my calls.'

'Like father, like son. I tried to call and warn you about Bain, but you weren't answering.'

'Lars Nielsen destroyed my phone last night.'

'What?'

As Jack recounted his run in with Lars at the water tower, she became increasingly concerned. She'd been right to be worried when he wasn't returning her calls.

Caitlin sat down on a lounge chair, choosing the one with the best view. Jack glanced over his shoulder at her. She turned her eyes away from him and then remembered the other news she was trying to phone him about. 'My friend called from Paris.'

Jack turned to face her. 'And?'

'You'll never guess who owns the Luxembourg company, Metol.'

'Tom Bradshaw.'

'You knew?'

'I guessed. I had a meeting with him, and he looked shifty when I mentioned Metol.'

'Can you believe it? Tom Bradshaw's father was mayor at the time the Jetty Hotel was approved by council. And all the while his son secretly owned the hotel. I bet he didn't declare that conflict of interest.'

Jack began pacing. 'Frank Cameron was a councillor then too, and he has free drinks for life at the Jetty Hotel. That smells like a pay-off.' Jack stopped pacing, and re-tightened the towel around his waist. 'Would this be a story your father would go after?'

'Sure, corruption always got him fired up. But it seems pretty small fry, and a long time ago. Hardly something that would put him in any journalism hall of fame.'

'I presume it's not illegal for Bradshaw to own a pub through a shelf company, but surely you'd only go to all that trouble if you wanted to do something shady.'

'Like hide the money from someone, or avoid tax?'

Jack shivered. 'Do you think my clothes are dry yet?'

The clothes dryer had gone quiet, so she went and fetched them.

Jack dressed in the bathroom. On his return, he asked, 'Do you think it's a bit coincidental George Ferris disappeared about the same time all this was happening?'

She shrugged.

Jack retrieved his phone from the kitchen bench, selected a number and placed the call on speaker. It was answered quickly.

'Constable Anderson.'

'It's Jack Harris. Can you put me through to Inspector Begley?'

There was a long pause. 'I can't. He's on gardening leave.'

'Likes a bit of gardening, does he?'

'He hates gardening, so I thought it was strange—'

Jack rolled his eyes at Caitlin and she smiled back. He interrupted Anderson. 'Can you give me his mobile number?'

The silence may have gone on forever if Jack didn't end it.

'I had his number, but lost my phone. Begley and I are friends, we go to the same gardening club.'

Anderson didn't respond.

'Why don't you ask him to call me?'

Anderson seemed relieved to be given a way out. 'Good idea. I'll let him know.'

'By the way,' said Caitlin when Jack had hung up. 'Bernstein sacked me.'

'What?'

'My boss called. Orders from on high. Basically they say it's a bad look for them to continue having an accused drug dealer on their staff. And there's fine print in my contract about not bringing the firm into disrepute, blah, blah, blah.'

Jack looked shocked. 'That's appalling. You should sue.'

'Assuming the charges are dropped, I could. But then I'd never get work again.'

'What will you do?'

She shrugged. 'I'll worry about it after we find out what happened with Dad.'

She longed for a time when thoughts of her father, murder, and *The Beacon*, didn't occupy most of her waking hours, but there would be no reprieve yet. She grabbed her laptop and the memory stick from the kitchen table and walked towards the door. 'I need to try some more passwords. And eat.'

Chapter Fifty-nine

Downstairs, they passed a shop selling everything from haircuts to boys' adventure books, food smokers, solar eskies and uber cool clothing. There was no polyester in sight. The café was large and the lunch crowd were in. No polyester here either, instead there was an abundance of beads, bangles and the ever-present linen. Part-poodle dogs of various sizes lay bored beside bare and sandalled feet.

Jack noticed the sea breeze had finally put in an appearance, so it was cool enough to sit at an outdoor table. Kombucha arrived for Caitlin. His own pacific ale was made by Stone & Wood, a brewery so close Jack reckoned they could have plumbed in a direct line to the café rather than deliver the beer in barrels.

Jack looked at Caitlin across the table. Apart from the usual family and work suspects, he couldn't remember ever spending so much time with another person. He was enjoying her company, if not the circumstances that had brought them together. He raised his glass. 'Cheers.'

'Sláinte,' replied Caitlin. 'That's Irish.'

'Do you speak Irish?'

'No.'

Jack took a sip of cold beer. 'I thought Irish was just a form of English, with more swear words.'

'Feck off.' Caitlin's phone beeped and she read the incoming message. 'Zoe's on her way. She's something to show us.'

As they waited for their food, Caitlin opened the laptop and booted it into TAILS. She started guessing passwords.

Jack interrupted her. 'Ricky worked out it's twenty-eight characters long. And your father was so security conscious he never would have written it down, would he?'

She shook her head.

'Nobody can remember a string of twenty-eight random characters. So it must be a long phrase or a group of memorable words.'

'But he told me "heroine".'

'I reckon it's a clue, not the password. It'll be a sentence, or a song title or the names of all the streets he ever lived in joined together.'

Jack's phone rang and he took the call.

'It's Begley. What do you want?'

'How are the petunias?'

'What?'

'Anderson told me you were on gardening leave. I didn't know you had a green thumb?'

'Listen, Harris, if you rang just to get on my tits, I'm getting enough of that here already. The bloody assistant commissioner sent me home and, after just two days, my wife wants me to go back to work.'

'I was hoping you could check a police file for us. It might have something to do with the case.'

'What part of gardening leave do you not understand? Not only do I have orders not to have anything to do with the investigation of Patrick O'Shaughnessy's murder, I've been sent home, "just in case I feel any temptation to get involved".'

'In that case, I'm sure it's got nothing to do with Patrick's murder.'

There were a few seconds of silence. 'Go on.'

'George Ferris was the Northern Rivers mayor in 1987. He was seen entering the water for a swim, but never reappeared, presumed drowned.'

'And what makes that suspicious?'

'The timing. We think there was council corruption at the time and that some people may have profited from his disappearance. Patrick may have been on to it.'

Begley took a while to answer. 'I'll see what I can do. But it won't be until I can get back into the station.'

'Thanks.'

'Hey, don't get bloody tickets on yourself. I'm not doing this for you, I just fucking hate petunias.' The call went dead.

A vegetable platter and lamb kebabs arrived. The food was so good the conversation all but ceased. Halfway through, Caitlin bumped her glass and spilled kombucha onto the remaining kebabs. Yet another clumsy spill. They looked at each other, but said nothing.

Jack finished his beer, then tapped the memory stick on the table. 'I think we've got this, Caitlin. What are some of your father's favourite things? Holiday destinations, food, music?'

She tapped her fingers on the table as she thought. 'He loved Bowie, and his favourite album was *Heroes*.' She looked up at Jack excitedly. My clue was "heroine". That's just like Dad, he wouldn't want it to be too obvious. Could it be the song lyrics?'

'I suppose so. Easy to remember.'

Caitlin started counting on her fingers as she sang a song in her head. Her excitement turned to disappointment. 'Only twenty-six.'

Jack said, 'What if you swap "heroines" for "heroes"?'

Her eyes lit up and she started bouncing in her chair with excitement. She reopened the laptop.

Jack dared to hope at last. He moved his chair beside her. The TAILS boot sequence seemed to take forever. When the password dialogue box popped up, Caitlin smiled at Jack, then, using one finger to ensure she didn't make a mistake, typed: 'Wecanbeheroinesjustforoneday'.

They watched eagerly as the ants chased each other around the circle. Seconds ticked by and the ants kept circling. Just when Jack thought the program must have locked up, the computer beeped and a message box appeared: 'Incorrect password'.

'Fuck,' said Caitlin loudly. Heads turned in their direction. 'Fuck, fuck, fuck.' She slammed the laptop closed, ripped out the memory stick and threw it onto the table where it bounced onto one of the plates and buried itself in mint sauce.

Chapter Sixty

Caitlin was pleased to see Zoe had already arrived when they returned to the apartment. It would have been so difficult to get through the last couple of weeks without her. They hugged long and hard, burying their heads in each other's shoulders.

Zoe gave a shorter hug to Jack. When they separated, Zoe said, 'One of my clients owns the servo at Suffolk Park. Jack, was it a black van seen in the carpark on the night Patrick went missing?'

Jack nodded.

'She said they have a few black vans fill up every day and so she copied me the camera footage. It could be nothing, but worth a look.' Zoe held up a memory stick.

Caitlin let out an involuntary groan. 'I hope that's not password protected.'

They copied across the surveillance footage to each of their laptops. It was a slow process.

'These are huge files," said Caitlin.

'It's open twenty-four hours,' said Zoe.

'Of course it is,' said Caitlin. It was going to be a long afternoon.

The footage stretched over three days, and they took a day each, agreeing to quickly scan through and record the time any black vans appeared, after which they would review each sighting together.

Caitlin opened her file, and her screen filled with the video from four cameras – one positioned inside behind the counter, another facing outwards across the forecourt to the road beyond, the others positioned on each side facing towards the petrol pumps. Impressive. And the resolution was good.

The video app allowed her to speed up the footage and soon cars were zooming in and out. It was easy to spot vans, but they were mostly white. The work was strangely mesmerising. After half an hour, she'd scrubbed through eight hours. No black vans.

Caitlin pulled herself out of her trance and stood and stretched. She put on the kettle and soon they were all back at the mind-numbing work, each with a steaming cup of tea untouched and growing cold beside them. An hour later she was done, her bum sore from sitting. She rubbed her weary eyes. 'I saw five,' she said.

In total, they had twelve.

They gathered around Caitlin's laptop and started working through Jack's list. The first hit was a large black van with no side windows. It pulled up to the petrol pump and a male driver in his thirties wearing nothing but board shorts climbed out and filled the tank. The inside camera provided a clear view of his face. He approached the counter, smiled at the attendant as he paid, walked back to his van and drove away.

'Shit,' said Caitlin. 'How do we identify a murdering bastard?'

Jack shrugged. 'Dark sunnies, black clothes, looking shifty. Just like in the movies.'

Zoe said, 'So we're looking for Chopper Read?'

'Yes,' said Jack, 'although our man probably won't have his ears cut off.'

They moved methodically through each sighting. They quickly crossed off the first six – their drivers were wearing thongs, had a dog or were hobbling on crutches. The first female driver had caused an argument. Jack wanted to cross her off, Caitlin accused him of being sexist, and the argument was only settled when the driver collected her baby before going inside to pay. That left one possible suspect on the basis of nothing particularly scientific. Caitlin was losing hope; the van they were looking for could have stopped at any of the petrol stations in town, or none at all.

She loaded her footage and skipped to her first van. The driver was a big unit in black jeans, black T-shirt and dark sunglasses.

Zoe whacked Caitlin on the arm. 'Here comes Chopper now.'

As the man walked inside to pay, Caitlin felt an ice-cold constriction around her chest. Her breath seemed to be trapped inside her. She said, 'I recognise that man.'

'Who is he?' asked Zoe.

'I do too,' said Jack. He grabbed the laptop and rewound the footage for another look.

Zoe asked again. 'Who, Caitlin? Who is it?'

Caitlin said, 'Jack, Jack.' She shook his arm and he looked at her. 'He's the man that was hanging around outside my apartment in Sydney before the police raid.'

Jack's face blanched. 'Jesus. Fuck.'

Zoe was more insistent this time. 'Who is he?' she said loudly.

Jack just stared straight at Caitlin. He didn't answer.

'Jack?' Caitlin prodded.

'His name is Fidel.'

'And?'

He couldn't hold her gaze, and looked at his hands. 'He used to be my father's head of security.'

'What?'

'He's bad news. Very bad.'

Caitlin's mind raced. She thought of the tumultuous last couple of months, the drug raid on her house, of her arrest and dismissal from her job. But mostly she thought about her father. Were all of these things linked? This man was at her apartment and then here when her father died – and he used to work for Malcolm Harris.

He killed her father. He must have.

All her suppressed rage erupted. She let out a howl and jumped to her feet, grabbed her teacup from the table and hurled it at Jack. He ducked, but it struck him on the shoulder, cold tea spraying everywhere. She threw Zoe's cup and it collected him on the elbow. She charged at him. Jack backed away, tripped over a chair and fell heavily.

Zoe yelled, 'Caitlin!'

Caitlin leaped onto Jack and screamed, 'You bastard!' She punched him in the cheek and he put his hands up to cover his face. 'Your father killed my father.' She pummelled her fists into his chest and abdomen until Zoe dragged her onto the floor where she curled up into a ball, sobbing.

She felt Jack's hand on her shoulder. He spoke quietly to her. 'Fidel doesn't work for my father anymore.'

Caitlin called out through her hands, 'Why didn't you stop him?'

She felt Zoe lie on the floor behind her and wrap an arm around her shoulders. They lay together until her tears eventually dried up and her breathing settled. When at last Zoe helped her up from the floor, Jack was nowhere to be seen. She couldn't blame him.

Zoe helped Caitlin onto the lounge and fetched her a blanket, then sat and held her hand.

Jack returned from the bathroom, a large red mark on his cheek.

'I'm so sorry, Jack,' said Caitlin. She could feel burning in her hands where she'd struck him.

'I would have lost it too,' said Jack. 'Although I'm not sure I could have punched as hard as you.' He tried to smile, winced and put his hand to his face.

Zoe asked, 'Should we call Begley?'

'Fidel could just say he was holidaying in the area,' said Jack. 'We need some evidence he was involved.'

'And holidaying out the front of my house in Sydney?'

Jack returned to the table and the laptop. He centred the image of Fidel and the black van on the laptop screen, then took photos with his phone. He then reloaded a different video and started searching again.

Caitlin said, 'So the drugs in my freezer were a warning to Dad, from whoever hired Fidel to kill him? Who does Fidel work for now?'

'I don't know,' said Jack. 'It could be anyone – he sells himself to the highest bidder.' He returned his attention to the computer screen. After a few more minutes he said, 'There it is.' He turned the laptop to Caitlin and replayed a video for her. 'This was around dawn on the morning of the murder.'

A black van could be seen driving along the road past the service station.

'But it could be any van,' she said.

'Maybe. But as we've seen, they're uncommon. And it's heading south.'

'And?' asked Caitlin.

'I think they were using our old house as a base. I normally stay there, but I was told some guests were using it. And Fidel sometimes stayed there when he worked for Dad. Maybe he still has a key.' Jack stood up from the table. His clothes were covered in tea stains, his cheek growing redder all the time. 'I'm going to take a look. And find Don – he knows everything that comes and goes at the house. I want to know if Fidel really was staying there.' He headed to the door.

Caitlin called after him, 'Jack, be careful.'

He nodded at her, and was gone.

Caitlin felt remorse creeping in. Why had she hit out at Jack? A few hours earlier she was admiring his abs, then she was hitting them. Maybe the stress was getting to her, making her irrational.

'Tea?' asked Zoe.

Chapter Sixty-one

Back at Jack's father's house, Don was nowhere to be seen. Jack went to his own room to change out of his tea-stained clothes, after which he intended searching the old house for any hint of his father's fixer having been there, or for any link to Patrick's murder. Then he'd call Begley.

His reflection in the bathroom mirror shocked him – bloodshot eyes, a swollen cheek, and hair looking like it was a prop from *The Muppet Show*.

After changing into fresh clothes, he hurried out of the bedroom door and collided with a wall that hadn't been there a few minutes before. A wall of a man. Jack bounced off him like a table-tennis ball.

The man looked Polynesian, and could well have made the Samoan rugby team, the whole rugby team. He was about the same height as Jack, but twice as wide, twice as thick and more than twice as heavy. The man stood there, completely impassive.

'Who are you?' Jack asked.

A rumbling voice came forth, so low it might have come from the basement. 'I'm Bruce.' He stepped aside to reveal an even larger man mountain that could have been his younger brother. 'And this is also Bruce.' Bruce Two looked as though he lived on a diet consisting exclusively of anabolic steroids.

Bruce One said, 'We're your personal security detail, bro.' As though choreographed, both Bruces widened their stance and crossed their arms over their chests.

'I don't need security.'

'They're worried about you, bro. They think you might be in danger.'

'Who's they?'

No answer from either Bruce.

'I'm not in danger.'

Both Bruces remained silent.

Jack yelled out for Don but there was no response. There was no way he could get around the two men. He took out his phone but Bruce One extended a hand the size of a pizza.

'Phones are dangerous. People can track you.'

Jack reluctantly relinquished the phone. Without taking his eyes off Jack, Bruce One passed the phone to Bruce Two and instructed him to turn it off. Jack heard glass smash and saw Bruce Two grinding the phone into the polished concrete with what looked like a size seventeen boot.

'You'll be safer in your room, bro. We'll make sure nobody gets in.'

Jack considered the options, decided there were none, and returned to his room. The door was closed firmly behind him.

He lay on his bed fuming for ten minutes then returned to the bedroom door and opened it. Bruce Two's enormous bulk sat in a chair seriously under-engineered for the task. The chair faced Jack's door.

The guard glanced up from his phone. 'Relax, man, we've got this.'

His clothes were all black, with the exception of 'SECURITY' emblazoned in white letters across his shirt. A chest harness held a body cam pointed directly at Jack, and an assortment of kit hung from a webbing belt around his massive waist, including a walkie talkie and a truncheon.

Jack retreated inside and closed the door. The landline phone had disappeared from his bedside table. He retrieved his laptop from the desk and powered it up. There was no internet signal.

He lay back on his bed, angry and confused, and attempted to tie all the threads together. Trying to understand why he was a prisoner in his father's house.

Chapter Sixty-two

Jack was woken by a bladder the size of a small planet. He dragged himself to the bathroom. How long had he been asleep? He checked his watch – four in the afternoon. Then he remembered he was a prisoner in his own house. He stormed to the bedroom door and threw it open, ready to have it out with the security guard, but the chair was empty. Not a Bruce in sight. Bathroom break? Shift change? Jack didn't care.

He flew quickly and quietly along the hall and down the stairs, avoiding the kitchen in case Bruce had gone for food or a glass of water to swallow his roids, then threaded his way through the house to the back door. He was, as far as he could tell, unseen. He sprinted across the expansive lawn, then cut through the forest until he intersected with the narrow track leading down to the old house. He stopped and listened. Apart from the frenzied buzzing of the cicadas, all was quiet. Then he heard the rustling of dried leaves. He spun around, ready for combat. A bush turkey stared back quizzically, then resumed scraping leaves onto its nest mound.

Jack pushed through the forest, then stayed under the cover of the trees when he reached the old house. Nothing appeared amiss.

He needed a plan. First, he should make sure there was nobody in the old house so that he wasn't caught by surprise.

Then he'd search the house for signs that the crew who murdered Patrick had been staying in the house. If that drew a blank, he'd check the grounds.

The lock box near the front door surrendered the key to the same old code. Jack silently opened the door. The house felt empty. He moved cautiously from room to room. Nobody. He started over, this time with a meticulous search. There was no evidence of the previous occupants – not a toothbrush, not an errant hair in a drain. The house had never been so clean.

The search outside was equally unproductive. No sign of a boat or van. No tyre tracks on the gravel. The garden shed held only Tony's tools, along with Jack's tiny childhood footprints pressed into the concrete slab of the floor, preserved for eternity. The garage, too, was cleaner than he could ever remember – not even a grease mark on the floor. They'd been good. Or they hadn't been here at all.

Jack couldn't suppress his feeling of frustration. He was sure he was right – somebody would only be this meticulous tidying up if they had tracks to cover. But it was hardly something that could be used in court for a conviction. *Your honour, the house was much cleaner than usual.* This had been a complete waste of time.

He stood in the middle of the lawn and took a last look around, willing something to appear. And then he saw a strip of freshly turned earth where the grass met the rear wall of the garage. Jack scooped away soft, moist soil until his fingers felt something firm. He dug more urgently, and a small square of plastic came into view. Black plastic. When his excavations were complete, he kneeled and stared at a two-metre-wide roll of thick plastic, knowing this would be a match for the black plastic shroud that had wrapped Patrick's amputated leg. Got you, thought Jack. Their first mistake. They should have taken it with them. Although perhaps they didn't want to risk being caught with something that would clearly tie them to the murder.

Jack used his keys to hack off a sample of the plastic, then re-buried the roll so that if Fidel reappeared, he wouldn't know it had been discovered.

He reached for his phone to call Begley before remembering the Bruces had smashed it. Tony would have one. He set off towards Tony's lodgings next to the big house.

As Jack crept through the bush beside Tony's cottage, a whipbird let rip one of its pistol-shot calls, causing Jack to jump. He tried to calm himself with deep breaths. He emerged from cover and ran quickly down the side of Tony's. He rounded the corner towards the front door and was brought to an abrupt halt by a collision into the very beefy Bruce Two.

'Jesus,' said Jack, in both fright and pain, his ribs sore from the bruising impact.

Bruce Two stared at him impassively.

Jack turned to flee, but Bruce One had materialised close behind him.

Bruce Two said, 'Put your arms up slowly, and keep still.'

Bruce One patted him down. Jack felt a huge hand slide into his pocket and pull out the black plastic. Jack put down his arms.

Bruce Two said, 'Mr Harris, is there anything at all I can get for you? A cup of tea?'

'What the hell?' said Jack, totally confused.

Bruce Two smiled. 'Have I told you what I'm going to do with that tiny girlfriend of yours when I get hold of her? First, I'm going to pin her down and then I'm going to—'

Before he could even think, Jack lashed out at Bruce Two

with a left–right to the stomach, then put his head down and charged into the guard's midriff. Bruce Two wasn't quick enough to brace and tumbled backwards with Jack on top of him. Jack rolled away as Bruce One's hands clutched at his shirt.

There were angry shouts behind Jack as he ran away, but he was confident he could outrun such big men, their bodies built for strength not speed. Yet when he reached the driveway, the sound of pursuing footsteps remained alarmingly close. Jack gave a burst of maximum speed and, by the time he reached the front gate, his stitches were tearing painfully at his thigh and he was gasping for breath. He risked a glance over his shoulder, the Bruces were ten metres away and closing.

He launched himself out onto the road. Jack hadn't heard the car, and looked up as it hurtled towards him. The driver hit the brakes and the car skidded to a halt, almost touching Jack's knees. He stood transfixed with shock as a cloud of dust enveloped him. One of the Bruces yelled at him, breaking the spell, and Jack sprinted around the car to the passenger door. He scrabbled at the door handle. It was locked. He knocked hard on the window and, when the driver released the door, threw himself into the passenger seat and slammed the door closed.

'Jacko, what's happening?'

Jack knew that voice.

Ricky Martinelli smiled at him, then floored the accelerator as the Bruces started pounding on the door. With stones scattering everywhere, the car lurched forward and away.

Jack was breathless and incredulous at the same time. He grinned wildly and slapped Ricky on the shoulder. 'What the hell are you doing here?'

'I was overdue for a holiday.'

Jack laughed between gasps of air. Ricky never did holidays. Ricky never left Melbourne. 'How did you know?'

Having left the pursuers well behind, Ricky slowed the car to a safer speed. 'You've called four times in two weeks, you're trying to hack into someone's data, your father turfed you out of your job, and you're not answering your phone. I thought you might need reinforcements.'

Jack patted him on the shoulder again, so grateful to see his old friend.

Ricky looked at him. 'So, why weren't you picking up?'

'Every time I get a new phone somebody smashes it.'

'Do you want a burner?' Ricky pointed to the glove compartment.

Jack opened it and half a dozen phones spilled out.

'Why,' asked Ricky, 'were those two brick shithouses chasing you?'

As Ricky wound through the forest back towards town, Jack told him what he knew about Patrick's disappearance, and what he didn't, like who had murdered him. When he finished, he said, 'I'm hoping the answer is on the memory stick. If we can find the password.'

'I'll try a dictionary attack using Hashcat. We might get lucky.'

'Patrick provided a clue, if that helps.' Jack told him about Caitlin and Zoe.

'Then we won't need Hashcat,' said Ricky.

When they got back on the bitumen, Jack called the police station with one of the burner phones. Constable Anderson answered.

'It's Jack Harris. I need to speak with Inspector Begley.'

'He's on gardening leave.'

'It's urgent.'

'I still can't put you through. He said if I called him at home he would break my balls.'

Jack couldn't help but laugh. 'Did he say anything about text messages?'

There was a pause. 'No.'

'Then message him to call me.' Jack could almost feel the policeman's relief at having his dilemma solved, gonads intact.

'Okay,' said Anderson.

Jack ended the call and turned to look at his friend, happy that he was there. 'Nice rental,' said Jack.

'I had a choice of a Beamer or a Barina.'

As evening settled over the town, Ricky put his foot down, expertly evading the potholes. Not to mention the potheads cycling towards him, without helmets, on the wrong side of the road.

Chapter Sixty-three

Jack still felt jittery as he knocked on the door of Zoe's apartment; he still hadn't calmed down from his narrow escape from the Bruces. At the same time, he was looking forward to seeing Caitlin, and introducing her to Ricky.

It was Caitlin who opened the door. 'Jack, where the hell have you been? Maybe just once in your life you could answer your phone when I call – I was worried about you.'

'I was taken hostage in my father's house. I escaped and they tried to beat me to a pulp ...'

Caitlin wasn't paying attention, just staring at the stranger standing behind Jack.

'Caitlin, did you hear what I said? Two massive thugs tried to attack me.'

There was a pause before Caitlin looked back to Jack. 'Are you going to introduce us?'

'Oh, Jesus,' said Jack. 'I'm sorry. Caitlin, this is Ricky Martinelli.'

Caitlin's eyes widened and there was a flicker of a smile. She seemed lost for words, even awestruck. Jack knew it wasn't because of his friend's good looks. Ricky was pasty and suffering from a resurgence of puppy fat – side effects of too much time in front of a computer. Then again, Ricky did constantly wear an infectious grin and an impish look in his eye. But Caitlin's awe was more likely because she was meeting a Martinelli; the family had occupied a large part of her criminal law curriculum.

Caitlin had never been in awe of Jack as far as he could tell. Maybe that's because she wanted to stab him when they first met. And maybe that was one of the reasons why he liked her so much. She didn't give a rats that he was a Harris.

'Come in,' said Caitlin.

They followed her into the living area where Zoe sat at a small dining table covered with empty pizza boxes.

'Hi, Zoe,' said Jack, 'this is Ricky.'

She rose and they shook hands, both recognising each other – one famous, one infamous.

'I'm very sorry about your father, Caitlin,' said Ricky, who knew what it felt like to lose a parent – he'd seen his father shot dead in front of him on the driveway to their house. 'If the police don't deliver, I'm happy to offer my family's assistance to settle it privately.'

'Thanks, but I'm a lawyer.'

'A straight one?'

Caitlin nodded.

Ricky looked at Jack. 'I can see why you've got the hots for her.'

Jack replied, 'I never said that.'

'You don't have to, mate.'

Caitlin flushed a little and looked at her hands.

'And,' Ricky continued, 'don't believe Jack's stories about massive thugs chasing him. They were pussycats. He's always been a big sook.'

Jack shook his head. Then the doughy aroma of the pizza caught up with him, and his hunger. He stared at the empty boxes. 'Is there any more food?'

Zoe collected the empty boxes. 'I'll get them to send some more up from downstairs.'

Ricky said to Caitlin, 'I believe you're having a little trouble with a memory stick. Shall we have a crack at it?'

Caitlin nodded and slid it across to him, along with her laptop. In no time, Ricky had started the TAILS boot sequence.

For the first time, with his old friend Ricky by his side again, Jack felt confident they would find the answers that had eluded them to date.

When the password dialogue popped up, Ricky asked, 'So, the password you were given doesn't work?'

'Patrick gave each of us half the password,' said Zoe.

'The problem is,' said Caitlin, 'he gave us both the same password, "heroine".'

'As in smack or as in superhero?' asked Ricky.

'The "e" on the end version,' said Caitlin. 'We've tried every possibly combination of "heroineheroine" with upper case, lower case, abbreviations. Nothing works.'

'That's because "heroine" isn't the password,' said Ricky. 'We're looking for a password twenty-eight characters long. If you'll excuse the pun, "heroine" doesn't cut it. What were the exact words your father said?'

They both stared at each other, trying to recollect.

Zoe broke the impasse. 'He said something like, "I'm telling the first half of the password to Caitlin and the second half to you. You're 'heroine'."'

Ricky turned to Caitlin. 'And to you?'

'Pretty much the same.'

Ricky looked at Jack. 'I'd stick to your day job, Jacko. Oh, yeah – you don't have one now, do you?' He smiled then turned back to Caitlin. 'What if he didn't mean "you're heroine" as in "you are heroine", but "your – y-o-u-r" heroine, as in the person you look up to and admire.'

Caitlin blanched and lowered her head into her hands. 'Jesus, I can't believe how stupid I am.'

Jack looked down at the tattoo staring back at him over the top of Caitlin's Doc Martens, and also couldn't believe he'd missed it. 'Ruth Bader Ginsburg.'

Caitlin grinned. 'Pretty much every female lawyer's heroine.'

'Mine,' Zoe said, 'is Evonne Goolagong Cawley. I took up tennis the day after she won Wimbledon.'

They counted out the letters: 'BaderGinsburgGoolagong Cawley'. Twenty-eight.

There was absolute silence, apart from the sound of Ricky's fingers flying across the keyboard. Until the laptop beeped and the ever so familiar error message popped up. They let out a collective groan.

Ricky made another attempt, and this time there was no beep, no error message. 'We're in,' he said, 'it was the other way around – GoolagongCawleyBaderGinsburg.'

Caitlin jumped up and down in her eagerness, then grabbed the laptop from Ricky and sat down to finally discover what secretive project her father had been up to, the one that had cost him his life. The others gathered around.

She scrolled through lists and lists of documents, then looked up at Jack and smiled. She returned her attention to the laptop and navigated to a folder called 'Bank statements' and randomly opened one. It was headed 'Banque de Luxembourg' and dated January 1990. The account was in the name of Tom Bradshaw.

Caitlin beamed at Jack. 'We've done it. Ricky's done it. It's Tom Bradshaw. Not Lars Nielsen. And not your nudist friend.'

She stood up, danced a little jig and then turned to Jack.

To his surprise, she stepped towards him and extended her arms, but the hug he had long waited for was never delivered. There was a knock at the door. Caitlin lowered her arms. 'That'll be the food.' She disappeared off to the front door.

Jack returned his attention to the screen. True to form, Patrick's file structure was impeccably organised. One directory was called 'Jetty Hotel', another 'Tom Bradshaw'. But it was a different directory that really caught his attention – 'Malcolm Harris'. Jack was shocked. Surely his father wasn't involved. Perhaps Patrick made a mistake. Or, during the initial investigation, was casting his net widely. Maybe his father had been assisting Patrick.

Jack was so focused he didn't notice Maguire and Duffy burst into the room until they shouted, 'Police!'

Caitlin quickly followed them, her face reddening with anger. 'You have no right to enter private property. I did not give you permission.'

The detectives ignored her, both staring intently at Jack.

Caitlin continued. 'I demand you both leave at once.'

Duffy turned to glare at her, placed his hand on his gun in its holster and stayed where he was.

Maguire shouted, 'Everybody stand slowly, and move away from the table.'

Zoe had lost all her colour. She stood abruptly and stepped away. Jack and Ricky didn't move.

Instead, Ricky smiled and said, 'I assume you have a warrant?'

The open documents on the laptop made Jack feel uneasy. He remembered how the detectives had shown an inordinate interest in what Patrick had been investigating, as did Chowdhury, his father's lawyer. Worse, the memory stick protruding from the laptop seemed to be shouting for attention.

'We don't need a warrant,' Maguire replied. 'Jack Harris, we arrest you for the assault today on Bruce Smith. You don't have to say anything if you do not want to. Do you understand?'

Caitlin's eyes widened, her voice full of concern. 'Jack?'

Ricky turned to Jack. 'Who's Bruce Smith?'

Jack shrugged. 'The security guards were called Bruce.'

'Both of them?'

'Uh huh.'

Ricky laughed. 'So these detectives are charging you with assaulting those two thugs who chased you through the jungle this afternoon wanting to beat the shit out of you?'

Jack just shrugged.

'That's like a toy poodle attacking a Great Dane.' Ricky patted Jack on the shoulder. 'Proud of you, Jacko.'

Maguire had lost patience. He yelled, 'Jack Harris, stand up and turn around slowly!'

Jack didn't move.

Ricky was still smiling. 'I'm sorry, Constable, his English is very poor. You may need an interpreter.'

As Duffy took out his handcuffs and walked towards Jack, Maguire asked, 'Whose laptop is that?'

Jack and Ricky glanced at each other. Both knew what they had to do. Ricky grabbed the laptop and started punching keys. Jack ripped out the memory stick just before Duffy's hand grabbed his and slapped it in a handcuff.

Maguire lunged for the laptop, but it was already shutting down when he yanked it from Ricky's grasp. Duffy roughly twisted Jack's other arm behind him and locked it into the handcuffs.

Maguire looked furious. 'Whose laptop is this?' There was no answer, so he shook his head, pulled an evidence bag from his jacket and placed the laptop inside. To Jack's dismay, Maguire prised the memory stick out of his hand and also placed it in the bag.

Duffy looked at Jack, satisfaction written across his face in big letters.

Jack said, 'Seems like he does all the thinking, and you do all the manual labour, Duffy. Does he make you iron his shirts and fold his underwear?'

Duffy scowled back.

Maguire barked, 'Okay, let's move.'

Jack looked around. Caitlin, seething with anger, stared with hostility at Maguire. Zoe, sickly white, was as still as a statue.

Ricky peeled off his white T-shirt as Duffy shoved Jack forwards. When they reached the door and Maguire turned the handle, Jack's vision was whited-out by something coming over his head and then he was blinded through the cloth by dozens of camera flashes. As Jack was manhandled down the stairs, one of the detectives was trying to pull off the T-shirt while someone else, presumably Ricky, was following behind holding it on.

The circus somehow made it to the ground with everybody still on their feet and Jack was jostled the short distance to the paddy wagon. He was bundled into the prisoner pod on the back and the door was slammed and locked.

Ricky called to him through the grate. 'Jacko, it's so awesome having the band back together.'

The pod only had a smooth shelf to sit on. Against the rules, Duffy had deliberately left Jack with his hands cuffed behind him, which could only mean one thing. He separated his feet, planted them firmly on the floor and pressed his back hard against the wall. The detectives would be repeatedly stomping hard on the brakes to avoid hitting black dogs crossing the road in the dark.

Chapter Sixty-four

For the second time, the police truck slammed to a halt so abruptly Jack was thrown to the floor. The back of his head struck the wall with a sickening crack. He used his feet to turn himself around and then thrust himself back up onto the shelf as though nothing had happened – he wasn't going to give Duffy and Maguire any satisfaction.

The pod door opened. Hands grabbed him firmly and hauled him out. The white T-shirt was pulled off his head. They were taking him in via the front door of the police station. Grinning down at him from the top of the steps was Angus Bain. And a photographer. Jack ducked his head just before the flash fired.

Duffy and Maguire waited until the photographer was done, then shoved Jack up the stairs.

Bain held out a voice recorder. 'Jack Harris, any comment about the alleged brutal attack on your personal security guard.'

Jack knew better than to respond.

Bain tried again. 'Do you think you are a fit and proper person—'

Jack lurched towards the door, dragging Duffy behind him, and Bain jumped out of the way to avoid being shoulder charged.

Inside, Jack was taken straight to the charge room. Three separate prisoner docks stretched along the back wall, each secured by padlocked perspex doors. The only concession to comfort in the docks was a cold, stainless-steel bench – no reclining leather armchairs, no flat-screen TV, not even a drinks cabinet.

A charge sergeant sat behind a desk strategically placed to provide a clear view into each dock. The old policeman looked like he was part of the furniture, except that he moved, albeit slowly. He looked nonplussed about life in general, and having his peace disturbed by a newcomer in particular. He folded his newspaper, slid it aside and poked a finger at a keyboard to wake his computer. 'Name?'

After Jack was signed in, his wallet, watch, shoelaces and belt were removed. The burner phone Ricky had just given him was inserted into a brown-paper evidence bag. His fingerprints were scanned and then he was locked into one of the docks.

The policeman returned to his chair, placed his feet on the desk and opened his newspaper.

'I'll have the beef Wellington, with potato gratin and fresh field mushrooms,' said Jack, 'and a glass of the pinot.'

The sergeant's lengthy stare dripped with derision. That done, he removed a bluetooth speaker from his drawer and placed it on the desk. He smiled mischievously at Jack as he pressed play. The room soon filled with Paul Kelly's 'How to Make Gravy'. On first recognising the song, Jack laughed, but by the seventh repeat it was seriously giving him the shits.

Hours passed. There was a shift change, and the replacement charge sergeant must have been cut from the same cloth – feet up on the desk, same arsenal of hostile stares, but he'd swapped the newspaper for a MotoGP magazine and, in what Jack considered a significant downgrade, he farted and burped like clockwork, each burp finishing with a flourish. The only consolation was that he turned off the music and Paul Kelly could finally stop making gravy.

Just when Jack thought time must be running out, and the detectives would either have to charge him or release him, his dock was unbolted, and the charge sergeant walked Jack through to an interview room where Maguire and Duffy were waiting. A laptop and document folder sat on the table. And a large white paper bag.

Maguire set up the recording equipment. Duffy inserted his hand into the paper bag and withdrew a long, orange jelly snake and started chewing. Duffy offered Maguire a snake; he took a red one.

Duffy asked, 'Hungry?'

Jack nodded, his mouth moistening in anticipation. He'd had nothing to eat since breakfast and was ravenous – it was nearly 1 a.m.

'Good,' said Duffy, without offering him anything.

Maguire switched on the recorder. After the usual IDs and time check, Maguire kicked off. 'Jack Harris, I'm going to ask you some questions in relation to the assault of Bruce Smith. You don't have to say or do anything if you do not want to. I will record what you say or do, and I can use this recording in court. Do you understand?'

'Yes, but I'm not sure your colleague here will. Perhaps you should speak more slowly.'

Duffy scowled. He was well practised.

Maguire continued. 'Would you like a lawyer to be present?'

'No.' Jack knew a duty lawyer would probably be some junior graduate with less experience of the process than Jack. And if he had to conjure up his own lawyer, they would keep him in the dock overnight. Besides, the charge was ludicrous.

There was rustling as Duffy fished in the paper bag for another snake.

Maguire placed a security-photo-ID card of Bruce Two on the table in front of Jack and asked, 'Do you know this man?'

'Yes.'

'Why did you beat his face to a pulp this afternoon?'

'I didn't.'

Maguire placed a colour photograph on the table. It was Bruce Two, sporting two severely bruised eyes. Dried blood was caked under his nose above a split lip.

It was a few seconds before Jack realised he was staring with his mouth wide open. Then he laughed as he thought about how they must have staged it – Bruce One must have hit Bruce Two, more than once. 'He didn't look like that when I left him. Perhaps he's been chasing parked cars.'

Maguire opened his laptop and turned it to Jack. It was the body-cam footage from Bruce Two. The quality was very good.

Jack could clearly see himself looking at the camera and he heard the guard ask, 'Mr Harris, is there anything at all I can get for you? A cup of tea?' The video then showed Jack throw a punch. Bruce Two's lewd reference to raping Caitlin had been edited out. The footage became blurry, and it looked as though fists were repeatedly striking the guard.

Externally, Jack remained calm, but inside his mind was in turmoil. Someone had gone to a lot of effort to properly stitch him up. He said, 'The video is a fake. Parts of the footage have been cut out. The camera angle is wrong – the body cam was on his chest. Under provocation I lashed out once at his abdomen, bowled him over and ran away.'

Maguire took back the laptop. 'A jury won't see it that way.'

'And I suppose you're going to tell me the external security cameras at the house weren't working,' said Jack.

'It seems they have a recurrent fault.'

Duffy smiled at Jack, then lowered a green snake into his mouth.

Jack ignored him and concentrated on the alarming turn of events. This happened at his father's house. Was his father in on it? His name was among Patrick's documents. Was it Tom Bradshaw covering the tracks of his shelf company and bank accounts in Luxembourg? Would Tom Bradshaw set him up, without conferring with Jack's father?

Jack provided a detailed account of his version of events to be typed up as a statement.

When he finished, Maguire said, 'Jack Harris, I am charging you with the aggravated assault of Bruce Smith.' Then he reached over and paused the tape.

Jack wasn't happy, but he knew even if the charges did stick, at worst he would probably be sentenced to 'good behaviour'.

'Are we done?' asked Jack.

'In your dreams.' Maguire smiled maliciously at Jack. 'We're just starting. I thought we'd stop for a little stretch before we get into the serious stuff.'

'What serious stuff?'

The detectives stood and walked over to lean by the door, taking the bag of lollies with them.

Duffy said, 'I think I like the yellow ones best.'

'Nah, you can't. Nobody likes the yellow ones.'

They ate a couple of snakes each in silence, all the while staring at Jack, before returning to the table. Duffy arched into a back stretch, then cracked all his knuckles one by one.

'Okay,' said Maguire, 'let's go.' He pressed the start button on the recorder. 'I'd like to ask you some questions about the murder of Patrick O'Shaughnessy. You understand you are still under caution, and what you say may be used in a court of law?'

'Yes.'

Maguire opened his folder again and took out a black square of plastic inside a clear evidence bag.

Jack looked warily at the two detectives.

'Do you know where this piece of plastic is from?'

'My pocket.'

Maguire raised an eyebrow. 'What do you mean your pocket?'

'One of the security guards removed it from my pocket.'

'No, Mr Harris. After we arrested you this afternoon, we received an anonymous tip off. The scene-of-crime team dug up a roll of black plastic from the ground behind your father's garage. This piece of plastic is a sample we took from that roll. We lifted fingerprints from the plastic. Yours, Mr Harris. Nobody else's, just yours. Can you explain how they may have got there?'

Jack now knew he was in serious trouble. Someone had done a really good job on him. He forced himself to stay calm. 'I went there this afternoon looking for evidence that men involved in Patrick's murder stayed at our old house. I found that roll of black plastic behind the shed.'

'And you buried it back where it was, rather than call the police?'

'I attempted to call Inspector Begley, but I couldn't get through.'

'And your visit to the old house down the hill was this afternoon?'

'Yes.'

Maguire tapped a few keys on the laptop and turned it

343

towards Jack. A video showed Jack walking into his bedroom. It was more footage from Bruce Two's body cam. Apart from when Jack briefly opened the door to check he was still captive, the video continued to point at Jack's closed bedroom door. A time stamp on the bottom right corner of the video counted away.

Maguire said, 'The security guards, including the one you assaulted, said you were in your room all afternoon and that you did not leave the house at any time under their watch. This video footage would seem to confirm that. You didn't come out again until the evening when you assaulted Mr Smith. Although I'm guessing you're going to tell me this video has also been faked.'

'Only because it has. I was at the old house today.'

'Or,' Maguire said, 'the fingerprints could still be there from the night you murdered Patrick O'Shaughnessy. A night for which you have no alibi.'

'I did not murder Patrick.'

'You really didn't like him, did you?' asked Maguire. 'What was it about Mr O'Shaughnessy that riled you so much? Angered you to the point you wanted to kill him?'

'You can confabulate all you like to suit your wild theory, but you're completely wrong.'

In a well-rehearsed manoeuvre, Maguire reclined in his chair, crossed his arms, raised a disbelieving eyebrow and said nothing.

'I never met him,' said Jack.

'But he worked for your company.'

'As do twenty thousand other employees.'

Maguire removed a document from his folder and slid it across the table. 'Then why did you try and sack him from your paper?'

Jack stomach was churning and, for the first time during one of his many police interviews, sweat was forming on his brow. He needed to get out of there. He needed to find Patrick's killers before they finished framing him for murder. He looked at the two smirking detectives. It was time to stop proceedings. 'I'd like a lawyer before answering any further questions.'

Maguire couldn't hide his disappointment, and let out a long breath before announcing the end of the interview and turning off the recorder.

Duffy leaned forward in his chair and in the best menacing voice he could conjure said, 'We're going to nail your arse for this, Harris, it's just a matter of time. A win-win-win. You're in the slammer, the minister is off our backs, and we're covered in glory.'

Jack said incredulously, 'Are you charging me for the murder of Patrick?'

'As soon as we get a match for this plastic and the plastic wrapped around Mr O'Shaughnessy's leg,' said Duffy. 'The lab will have that to us within twenty-four hours. But I'm feeling pretty confident.'

'So, I'm free to go then?'

Maguire said, 'No way. You've committed a violent assault. We can't have the community put in danger, can we?'

Duffy offered Jack the bag of lollies. Jack eagerly placed his hand inside, only to find it empty. He couldn't believe he had been duped so easily – it must have been his hunger and fatigue.

They handed Jack back to the sergeant in the charge room, who placed him back in a dock and slammed the bolt home with unnecessary vigour.

'Sweet dreams,' said Duffy, as the two detectives left.

Jack sat on the steel bench. He tried to think his way through the puzzle, but he was so exhausted his thoughts weren't coming clearly and, instead, the same question circled endlessly in his head – would his father really do this to him? He struggled to keep his eyes open. When his head started bobbing, he lay back on the hard, cold bench and immediately fell into a deep, long-overdue sleep.

He was awoken against his will by someone roughly shaking his shoulder. Jack's head was foggy, his back cold and aching. He opened his eyes into the searing fluorescent glare and closed them again. Then he opened one eye slowly. Kowalski was bending over him.

Jack sat up and rubbed his eyes. The charge sergeant wasn't at his desk. 'Where's the commandant?'

'Shhh,' said Kowalski, looking nervously at the door, 'he's taking a slash. Begley asked me to pull the file on that missing politician from the eighties – George Ferris.' Kowalski showed Jack a battered document folder. 'Took me forever to find it. Thing is, you were right to be suspicious. He disappeared in 1987.' Kowalski checked in the file. 'April 2nd. It was a Thursday. The coroner's finding was "missing presumed dead". But, get this, no witnesses. Nobody saw him go in the water. His clothes were found later on the beach.'

Jack sat up, his mental functioning trying to find focus. 'But the papers said he was swimming with friends.'

Kowalski nodded. 'Even Wikipedia.'

Jack thought about the implications.

Kowalski said, 'I need to go, before he comes back.'

'You know I'm being set up.'

'I know. And I'm sorry, Jack. There's nothing I can do. This is all happening way above my pay grade.'

When Kowalski had gone, Jack lay back down, wriggled around unsuccessfully in an attempt to get less uncomfortable, then gave up. Something about the date George Ferris disappeared seemed familiar, but the more he forced himself to concentrate, the more blurry his mind became.

The sergeant returned to his seat. Just as Jack was drifting back into uncomfortable sleep, he remembered what it was about that date. He sat up and forced himself to stay awake, so he would still remember it in the morning.

Chapter Sixty-five
Saturday, 16th November

It was impossible to have any sense of time in the enclosed room, with the constant flickering of fluorescent light. At some stage, Constable Lucy Swift replaced the overnight charge officer. In the morning she opened his door. In contrast to her predecessors, she didn't seem irritated to see him.

'Morning, love. I hope you found the room to your liking and the bed comfortable.' She placed a tray on the bench beside him. A plastic tray, with plastic plates and plastic cutlery. There was a bowl, a small cardboard box containing cornflakes, a tiny carton of long-life milk, and two slices of cold toast. 'I'm expecting five out of five on Tripadvisor.' She smiled at him and handed him a cardboard cup. He wrapped his hands around its warm sides then took a sip – police-station coffee had never tasted so good.

'Thanks,' said Jack. 'The coffee makes it a six.'

The phone rang on Lucy's desk. She took the call. As she listened, she turned to look at Jack, nodded a few times and hung up.

Jack's door opened. He hadn't even had time to eat the cornflakes.

'Follow me,' she said, and walked him down the corridor. 'I don't know what you have over those two detectives, but I hope it's good. That letch, Duffy, ran his hand down my bum in the tearoom.' She looked embarrassed. 'Sorry, I shouldn't be sharing, I'm just so furious.'

'Jesus,' said Jack, 'have we gone back to the eighties?'

'I don't think Duffy ever left them.'

Lucy took him into an office and said, 'The charge against you concerning the assault has been dropped, love. I am to inform you that you are still being considered a person of interest in the murder of Patrick O'Shaughnessy, and that you are required to remain within Northern Rivers Shire until notified otherwise.' A tray on the desk contained his wallet, watch, shoelaces and belt.

'And my phone?' asked Jack.

'Duffy and Maguire have kept it to assist with their enquiries. They've probably kept all the money in your wallet too, to assist with their bar tab.'

She buzzed him out the door, into the waiting room.

Tony rushed towards him, grinning. 'Jack, you're out.' He gave him a big hug.

Anderson, at the front desk, looked away in embarrassment.

'What happened?' Jack asked. 'One minute they were going to throw away the key, and then I'm out the door.'

'You're the lead story on breakfast TV. I saw that footage of you beating up a security guard and knew you would never do that. Don had told me to switch off the security video yesterday afternoon. That's the second time now, and I didn't like it. So, I just switched off the feed to the monitors, but still recorded the stream. I showed it to your detective chums. They were seriously pissed off.' He patted Jack on the shoulder. 'C'mon, I'll drive you home.'

'Why would Don do that?'

'I don't know. But I'll be giving him a piece of my mind as soon as I find him.'

'What do you mean?'

'He's missing in action. Something's going on there.'

As they drove home in the Kingswood, Skyhooks' 'Horror Movie' blasted from the speakers, but Jack was asleep before Shirley Strachan could sing the first chorus.

Chapter Sixty-six

After a couple of hours of desperately needed sleep, Jack was woken by pain. He was in his own bed and could only vaguely recall Tony helping him up the stairs to his room. The stitches in his thigh were burning, his back felt as though it was still lying on the steel bench in the police station, and even the soft pillow was tormenting the growing bruise on his head. He carefully ran his fingers along his throbbing right hand and wondered if he had a punch fracture from hitting Bruce Two.

He padded across the cold concrete floor to the shower where he let icy water distract him from his battered body. As the water hammered on his head, he tried to piece together the events of the day before. Was his father trying to frame him for murder? He shivered. There were lots of pointers to at least some involvement by his father, including the documents on Patrick's memory stick. Should he go to Begley? If he gave the police the password for Patrick's files, would the detectives selectively choose information to suit their preferred theory, and just delete 'unsuitable' files so that they could still charge Jack with the murder and close the investigation?

He towelled dry. His leg wound was now not only red, but oozing. He needed to get that seen to.

There was a knock on his door and a voice called out, 'Hi,

Jack. I'm serving lunch if you'd like to come down.' It was Sophie, his father's long-time housekeeper and chef. She must be back from leave.

The glass wall of the dining room had been fully retracted, revealing an uninterrupted view across the travertine of the courtyard, the infinity-edged pool, the lawn, the forest and, ultimately, the ocean beyond. No wonder this room was a favourite of the design magazines. And the gossip mags – although they liked to position his overdressed father in shot, gazing pensively at the view, wife du jour beside him, her hand on his shoulder.

Sophie shuffled in with platters and placed them on the table. There was a lot more food than Jack could eat. 'So nice to have you here, Jack.'

'Sophie, you're back.'

'Yes. I've been settling Mum into a nursing home. We finally found her a bed.'

'Oh, Sophie, I'm sorry.'

'Don't be, Mum's much better there. She doesn't know where she is anyway, but she's happy and that's all that matters.' She started for the kitchen. 'I'll bring the rest.'

Jack sat facing the view. There were two unoccupied place settings on the other side of the table.

'Sophie,' he called, but she'd gone. He loaded his plate with steaming-hot spanner crab spaghetti – Sophie's signature dish. He could smell the garlic and parsley. He twirled the spaghetti around his fork then put it in his mouth. He closed his eyes and enjoyed the moment – food at last. Glorious, delicious food. He savoured the salty taste of the crab on his tongue.

'Hello, Jack.'

His eyes shot open, and he choked on his pasta. His father

stood on the other side of the table. Jack coughed to clear his throat and swallowed, no longer noticing the divine taste. 'You're here.'

'This morning.' Jack must have slept through the sound of the chopper. 'I thought we should have a chat in person. Some things are best not spoken over the phone.'

Malcolm Harris sat opposite Jack. His father was in his ever-present navy suit, starched white shirt and yellow silk tie – a statement of status and power he felt the need to display even in his home. Although he was approaching sixty, he looked younger, and exuded confidence and authority.

Sophie returned carrying an ice bucket in one hand and, in the other, a board covered with sliced bread that smelled freshly baked. Jack's stomach resumed growling audibly. They didn't speak until Sophie had poured the wine and left the room.

Malcolm took a sip from his glass and swished it around his mouth. Jack knew this performance only too well, his father would be concentrating on the flavour, and after swallowing, concentrating on the finish. Then he did it all again. Malcolm always liked to control the room, even for an audience of one. Jack was bursting with questions, including – if he was brave enough to ask it – whether his father had ordered his previous head of security, Fidel, to kill Patrick, but he knew he would have to wait. His father wouldn't be diverted from what he intended to say, in his own house, in his own time.

Malcolm put down his glass, filled his plate with spaghetti and took a mouthful. He nodded his head a few times in appreciation. At last, he was ready. 'Why,' asked Malcolm, 'do you think I sent you to Byron Bay?'

'I assumed that because you started your journalism career here, you thought it would be a good place for me to start, to learn about journalism and about the business from the basics.'

'That's not the reason.'

'Then was it because I spoke out about Harris needing to pay more credence to its social contract?'

His father laughed. 'You were correct. We do need to start making noises about being a model corporate citizen, so we can continue business as usual.' There was a long pause as Malcolm took a large forkful of spaghetti. Then he sipped some wine. 'Jack, there are some things I need to tell you.'

Jack said nothing. The divine smell of the bread was goading him to eat, but his appetite had vanished.

'Have you seen Don?'

Jack shook his head.

Malcolm took his time over more spaghetti, then put down his cutlery. 'There are some things I did a long time ago that I'm not proud of.'

Jack was in two minds – he wanted to hear and he didn't.

'I'll come back to that. It's relevant.'

Jack heard the splash of someone jumping into the swimming pool.

Malcolm said, 'Don was blackmailing Tom Bradshaw.'

'What?'

'I needed my own eyes and ears on the ground. Your ears. Family ears. That's the real reason I wanted you here.'

'Don? Why?'

Over his father's shoulder, Jack saw a woman come into view as she swam a length of the pool. Jack fleetingly wondered who she was before his attention returned to his father's shocking revelation.

'Don wants to retire. He's lived here most of his working life, doesn't own his own home. I promised I'd look after him, but I think he saw his opportunity to be independent. Very independent, and very wealthy.'

The woman swam back the other way, long dark hair streaming behind her. Slim. Tanned.

Jack asked, 'Do you know what he was blackmailing Tom Bradshaw about?'

Jack's father nodded as he buttered a chunk of bread and took a bite, washing it down with a pensive sip. Another lap was swum.

'It was presented to him on a plate. Patrick O'Shaughnessy had heard rumours Tom Bradshaw was shonky, so he was doing a deep dive into Tom's affairs.'

'Patrick?'

'Patrick was bloody good. Once he put his mind to something he was absolutely forensic. One of the best investigative journalists we have.' He paused, then corrected himself. 'We had. More than once I tried hard to coax him to Melbourne, offered him whichever portfolio he chose, but he liked it here. He had a daughter at school. The usual. And then he complained he never received recognition for his work at *The Beacon*.'

More wine. Another fast lap of the pool.

'Patrick approached Don looking for information. He wondered whether I was involved with Tom Bradshaw, given I had been friends with his father, Ian. Instead of telling Patrick to get nicked, like a loyal employee should have, Don saw an opportunity. He provided the proof Patrick was looking for, in the form of documents Don himself had forged. Old bank statements, that kind of thing. Don traded those documents for information from Patrick. And that information was gold. Like I said, Patrick was good. He'd tracked down Bradshaw's overseas holding accounts and trust funds, a trail of shelf companies. It was complicated. Tax avoidance, of course. Millions. The ATO has been after Tom Bradshaw for years, but had no evidence. Patrick had the evidence.'

The conversation paused as Sophie entered the room and collected the leftovers. Jack was reminded how hungry he was as he watched the food depart to the kitchen, and his stomach growled again in protest.

The swimmer showed no sign of slowing down.

His father continued. 'Don demanded money from Tom Bradshaw.'

'How much?'

'You know, I didn't ask.' Malcolm took out his phone, turned it to speaker and dialled. He made a silence gesture to Jack as it rang.

'Hello, Malcolm.' Jack recognised the mayor's voice. It sounded as if he was in his car, which brought back happy memories of Jack's recent encounter.

'Listen, how much is Don demanding?'

'Too bloody much.' Malcolm waited. A turn indicator clicked away in the background. 'Fifty per cent of what I owe the tax office. Excluding interest.'

'Bloody hell. Are you going to pay?'

'No bloody choice. At least I've screwed him down from fifty to ten per cent.'

'Which is what?'

'None of your bloody business. Unless you're volunteering to pay. He's your man, after all.'

'I just wanted to let you know he's not here in the house. I've got feelers out.' Malcolm hung up, then smiled at Jack. 'I believe you had an interesting meeting with Tom Bradshaw recently. You scared the living daylights out of him. He nearly shat himself when you mentioned Metol. He thought you must have found Patrick's documents.' Malcolm was twirling a wine glass between his fingers as he stared intently at Jack. 'Did you find the documents?'

Not trusting his voice, Jack shook his head.

Sophie re-entered with another tray amassed with food. The pasta had been an appetiser. Grilled whole snapper and a mango salad. She swapped the glasses, and the wine for a Chablis, then left for the kitchen. The smell of the food was now making Jack nauseous.

'But Don had the obvious problem. Patrick was going to publish the whole shooting match. Probably thought he was going to win a bloody Walkley.'

Jack's mouth was dry. He swallowed a mouthful of the wine without tasting it. 'And you think Don murdered Patrick?'

'You were here on the night. Did you see anything?'

'Don got me blind drunk. On your whisky stash.'

Malcolm laughed. 'I should have hidden the bloody key to that cabinet.' He transferred food to his plate. 'Of course, Don wouldn't have been able to do the deed himself. But he had contacts. All sorts of people have been through this house over the years. Not all of them good law-abiding citizens. It would only take a few phone calls.'

Malcolm helped himself to salad. Then a large piece of fish. Then wine. Jack stared at his own empty plate as his brain tried to process all he was being told.

Malcolm said, 'And now Don is trying to frame you. Calling in those security guards, staging the beating, all to get your fingerprints on the plastic. I assure you, Jack, I'm pulling out every stop to find him. To think I trusted him for all those years.'

357

Jack's internal radar cheeped. 'How did you know about the plastic?'

His father stopped eating and looked at him. 'I went to school with Terry Mitchell. Talk about punching above his weight, I never thought he'd make Police Assistant Commissioner. I personally asked the minister to send Terry up to oversee the murder investigation.'

'And yet they're going to arrest me tomorrow for a murder I didn't do. He can't be much of a friend.'

'He's a good friend, but I don't own him. And you can't blame Terry. You got yourself into this, poking around when you should have left it to the police.'

'Well the police don't seem to care too much who did it, as long as they have a half plausible suspect, and I seem to be the bunny.'

'Relax. I'll chat to Terry. He should be able to sort things out.'

'Should?'

'Yes, should. All I can do.'

That wasn't very reassuring. More questions were piling up in Jack's mind. He asked, 'Why did you publish the story about me being a person of interest in Patrick's murder? And the assault on the security guards?'

'We had to. I wasn't happy, of course. It was Angus Bain's fault. He's still seriously pissed at you for reporting him to the Press Council, so he leaked the story to all the rival networks. We had to publish, so at least we look as if we're unbiased. Same with the security-guard incident. When the other networks went with it, we had to follow. I gave him a serious shellacking and told him family was completely off limits. If he does it again, he's gone.'

'Why don't you go to the police if you think Don murdered Patrick?'

Malcolm's fork stopped halfway to his mouth. 'Jack, really? You think Tom Bradshaw can go to the police? And I might have a few little tax irregularities myself from back then. I told you, I'm not proud of some of the things I did when I was young.'

'But this is murder.'

Malcolm looked at Jack, annoyed. 'And what evidence do I have he murdered Patrick? It's circumstantial. And, bloody hell, if I'm wrong? You don't ever want to piss off a personal assistant of thirty years. With all the stuff he's seen and heard, he could write a book. Jesus.' Malcolm stuck his fork in a potato and then pointed the fork at Jack. 'And you're not going to the police either. What's been said in this room stays in this room.'

The swimmer had vanished, the clouds again reflected in the pool as though in a mirror.

Jack was burning with questions. Big ones. But should he poke the bear? He said, 'You wrote a series of derogatory pieces in *The Beacon* about councillors back in '87, lots of false allegations.'

His father stopped chewing. 'Says who?'

'I saw them. In a private archive.' Jack could see the anger in his eyes.

His father's cutlery clattered loudly as he put them down. 'I was an inexperienced, naive journalist back then. I was fed those stories. I'd never publish stuff like that now without independent verification.'

'It almost seemed like you were trying to swing the election.'

'I *was* trying to swing an election. That's why I own newspapers. I was just lousy at it back then.'

'And then George Ferris drowned. You reported that people saw him go in the water, which, according to the police report, wasn't true.'

Malcolm was very slow to answer. When he spoke, his voice was full of suppressed rage. 'Is my own son accusing me of a cover up? Of being involved in the murder of George Ferris?'

'The concrete slab in the old shed was poured the day after Ferris disappeared. The date is written next to my footprints.'

'That, son, is a coincidence. Go and dig it up. I bet Tony has a bloody jackhammer. You won't find anything in that slab. Conversation over.'

Malcolm and Jack stared at each other. The woman from the pool entered the room, wrapped in a white gown. She walked over to Malcolm's father and kissed him on the cheek. Jack had never seen her before, except in her movies.

She spoke in such a thick, high-pitched American accent it sounded fake. 'Hiya honey. What's for dinner?' She sat down at the empty place setting, helped herself to a small serving of salad and picked up a lettuce leaf. She looked at Jack, smiled that famous smile and said, 'And which son are you?'

Chapter Sixty-seven

Jack had excused himself from lunch with his father as soon as he judged it to be merely impolite rather than outright rude, which was about sixty seconds later. He found Tony admiring his handiwork – he'd just finished polishing the Kingswood. It looked like new.

'Tony, any chance of a lift into town?'

'Sure, where are we going?'

Jack realised he didn't know. He wanted to find Caitlin and tell her everything his father had told him not to tell anyone. But Jack had no way of contacting her. He'd lost three phones in a week, and apart from a few old numbers he could still remember, all his contacts had disappeared with them. 'I'm trying to find Caitlin. I'm hoping she's at Zoe's.'

As they set off, Tony pointed to a shoebox on the bench seat between them. 'I found some more.'

Jack was amazed to find the box was full of cassettes. He closed his eyes, picked one at random and inserted it. By the time the car turned onto the road, 'Into My Arms' was being sung inside the car – in three different keys.

As they drove towards the Arts and Industrial Estate, a Harley Davidson roared past them at high speed, its rider dressed as Animal from *The Muppets*. A motorised skateboarder with a death wish swerved within millimetres of the Kingswood at a roundabout, its rider raising a two-fingered peace sign when Tony honked the horn.

At Zoe's, Jack took the stairs two at a time. Nobody answered his knock. He had no idea how to find Caitlin now.

Then someone called his name. He turned to find Ricky and Caitlin walking up the stairs behind him. Ricky hugged Jack. Caitlin didn't.

'You escaped Alcatraz,' said Ricky.

Caitlin said, 'We went to the station to find out what was happening. The detectives wouldn't tell us anything because we weren't your next of kin.'

'They wouldn't believe you and I were married,' said Ricky, and blew Jack a kiss.

Upstairs in the apartment, Caitlin put on the kettle and took some Panadol. She looked exhausted.

'How are you going, Caitlin?' asked Jack.

'How do you think? We've lost all Dad's work. I was hoping it would be a tribute to him. Some sort of memorial.'

Ricky raised both eyebrows, in surprise. 'What makes you think it's lost?'

'I know how these things work. The police will have Dad's memory stick locked away in evidence hell for ever.'

'Trust me, anybody using a twenty-eight-character password has more than one backup,' said Ricky. 'You just need to find it.'

The kettle started whistling and was ignored.

Caitlin and Jack exchanged glances, then simultaneously asked, 'Where?'

'It won't be at his house – he wouldn't keep all the backups in the same location. Did he walk somewhere regularly where he could hide something? Is there a holiday house? Did he have any hobbies? What about a Post Office box? Nobody thinks to look there.'

They continued to ignore the increasingly insistent squeal of the kettle.

Jack suddenly slapped his thigh and his infected stitches retaliated with a sharp stab of pain. 'It's been right in front of us all along.'

'Where?' asked Caitlin.

Jack stood up and headed for the door. 'C'mon.'

Caitlin's clomping Doc Martens followed him. Ricky put the kettle out of its misery and went after them.

The Beamer made good time to Zoe's salon. No more Muppet costumes. No grey nomads driving caravans at half the speed limit. But Jack did notice Ricky spent an inordinate amount of time looking in the rear-vision mirror, yet whenever Jack looked over his shoulder, he saw nothing unusual – just cars.

Ricky parked illegally out the front of the salon. A 'Closed' sign dangled in the doorway. Jack cupped his eyes and peered through the glass and saw Zoe was still inside, cleaning up. Jack rapped hard on the door, and she let them in. Before even saying hello to Zoe, Jack went straight to the candle and picked it up.

'I'm sorry, Zoe, Patrick hid something inside.'

Zoe looked puzzled. 'And I thought, for all those years, he was being romantic.'

Jack ran hot water from the basin onto the outside of the porcelain jar until it released the candle. He hacked away at the wax with Zoe's scissors until a corner of plastic appeared, and soon he held a small bag in his hand. Inside was a memory stick identical to the one the police had confiscated.

Caitlin was jumping up and down in uncontrolled excitement. 'Can I hold it?' she asked.

When Jack handed it to her, she wrapped both hands around it so tightly it looked as if she would never let it go. She gave Jack a huge smile. 'Let's go and see what's on it.'

'Whoa,' said Ricky. 'Before we do anything else, we need to back that baby up – that might really be the last one.'

But nobody had brought a laptop. Their nearest one was back at Zoe's apartment. Jack and Caitlin rushed out the door together, and barrelled into two huge men standing outside. Jack's elation evaporated. It was the Bruce brothers.

Bruce One extended an enormous paw out to Caitlin. 'Give me that.'

Caitlin screamed and doubled over, clasping the memory stick to her midriff.

Jack swung a punch in the direction of Bruce One's head, but his fist glanced off harmlessly.

Bruce Two, who looked like an overweight raccoon with his two black eyes, wrapped a massive hand around Jack's neck and squeezed. Jack could hardly breathe. Bruce's other hand curled into a fist in front of Jack's face, preparing to strike.

Behind him, Jack heard Ricky shout, 'Vincent, don't even think about it!'

Both Bruces looked at Ricky. The fist in front of Jack's face unfurled.

'Oh, fuck me,' said Bruce Two, and Jack's neck was released. Both man-monsters turned and legged it along the lane without looking back.

Jack was overcome with relief – it had been a close call. He rubbed his neck and looked at Ricky, once again so grateful his friend was by his side. 'You know them?'

'Sure,' said Ricky. 'The Parata brothers. Everyone knows them. Small-time goons for hire.' He grinned. 'They're shit-scared of the Martinellis.'

As they walked to the car, Caitlin said to Jack, 'You were right.'

'Yes, but it was so obvious, I should have thought of the candle before.'

'Not about that.' Her smile was back. 'Everybody needs a Ricky.'

Zoe sat in the front of the Beamer with Ricky as he gunned it out of town. Caitlin couldn't sit still in the back. Ruth Bader Ginsburg danced up and down in time with the Doc Martens, Betty Boop smiled seductively at Jack from Caitlin's shoulder. Jack felt happy – the two people whose company he most desired in the whole world were here together, by his side.

Ricky pointed the Beamer into the carpark in front of Zoe's apartment and then drove straight through and out the other side without stopping. 'Change of plan,' he said.

'Why?' asked Jack.

'Man, have you forgotten everything I taught you? Didn't you see that white Commodore with an extra aerial? The apartment is being watched.'

Ricky drove back around and parked as far from the unmarked police car as he could. He turned to Zoe. 'Can you get the laptop while I distract them? Jack, you're driving.'

Zoe set off to blend in with the shoppers.

Ricky climbed onto a ute parked in front of the police car and started moon-walking on its roof. A crowd of onlookers gathered, including the ute's owner who started arguing with Ricky and then ran around and around his car trying to grab Ricky's legs. Ricky jumped off and climbed onto the bonnet of the police car. It was Duffy who got out and started yelling at Ricky, who was now running backwards and forwards from bonnet to boot. When Ricky jumped off and ran down the road, Duffy only had about twenty metres of chase in him.

Zoe returned with her laptop and Jack drove off. They found Ricky leaning against a lamp post a hundred metres down the road and as he stepped into the car, he was grinning like a child in a toy shop.

'Jack, why didn't you tell me Byron was this much fun?'

Jack pulled off the road into a carpark surrounded by industrial units. Caitlin handed Ricky the memory stick and he copied all Patrick's data across to the laptop, then uploaded it to two different cloud-storage services and emailed Caitlin their links. He closed the laptop, gave the memory stick back to Caitlin and said, 'Where to?'

'Somewhere safe where we can look at the documents,' said Caitlin. 'And we need a printer, we can't all gather around a laptop.'

Jack started the Beamer. 'I know the perfect spot. The last place the police would be looking for us.'

Chapter Sixty-eight

It was dark by the time they arrived back in town.

Caitlin's mind was brimming with competing emotions. There was the buzz of anticipation, even elation. In her mind, she'd built her father up into a top-rate journalist; she hoped she wouldn't be disappointed. In addition to her excitement, there was trepidation – even fear – needling at her. Somebody had a lot at stake, and had stopped at nothing to conceal the story she held in her hand, even the murder of her darling dad. She felt the tightly clasped memory stick poking into her flesh. Justice for her father was literally in her hands.

Caitlin's anxiety was heightened by Jack parking the car only a couple of hundred metres from the police station, but then she realised the police wouldn't be looking for Ricky's rental.

There were no lights on in *The Beacon*. Ricky picked the lock in quick time and smiled at Jack when it clicked open. The graffitied temporary hoarding over the side window had at last been replaced with glass, and it had already been smashed. They all stepped over the shards as they filed inside. The lights flickered to life.

A few minutes later, as Ricky sent file after file, the printer began spewing out paper. When one ream ran out, they loaded another. Her father would have been upset to see his paperless office so messy. Zoe and Caitlin sorted the documents into piles.

Jack supervised from the kitchen, leaning back in a chair, feet up on the table, eating the last of the arrowroot biscuits. Caitlin gave Jack a huge smile and he smiled back, crumbs spilling down the front of his shirt to join those already parked there.

There was no time to read the documents as they sorted them, but to Caitlin the nature of the documents was clear. Bank statements, trust deeds, money transfers, lawyers' letters, title deeds. As the pile grew larger, the pride she had for her father swelled in her chest and she had to hold back tears. At one stage, she stopped and pinched her thigh hard or she would have burst out crying. How did he gather all this information, some of it decades old, some from overseas banks? Some of the files were photographs. One of the photos had a face she recognised, and she beckoned Jack.

'That's my father,' said Jack. 'And a young Tom Bradshaw, I'd say.'

A loud, insistent knocking made them all jump. Worried faces snapped towards the door in unison. Caitlin dared not breathe.

A head appeared at the smashed window. Kowalski.

Jack unlocked the door and the policeman rushed in, breathing heavily. He paused long enough to stare in surprise at the piles and piles of paper. 'I've just run from the station. You need to leave, now.' He sucked in more air. 'They've triangulated you to a nearby phone tower. I guessed you'd be here. They might too.'

'Shit,' said Ricky. 'I forgot some of you were civilians. Who has a phone on?' Zoe and Caitlin, like schoolchildren in trouble, both hesitantly raised their hands.

'Turn them off,' said Kowalski. 'I'll take you somewhere they won't find you. And, Jack, they're going to arrest you in the morning when some lab report comes in.'

They frantically gathered the piles of documents and lugged them to the Beamer.

Kowalski said, 'Go south. Meet me at the Suffolk Park Hotel and I'll show you the way to a safe house. I'll be in a green Astra.'

Twenty minutes later they were tailing Kowalski's car through the back streets of the nearby seaside suburb of Suffolk Park. They stopped outside an ordinary-looking suburban brick-and-tile house perched on a fiendishly steep block of land. They followed Kowalski like ducklings up the precipitous path and the steps to the door. There were no lights in any of the windows. Caitlin checked her phone for the time, forgetting it was turned off. She guessed it must have been after midnight.

Kowalski knocked on the door. Then again. After a long wait, a gruff voice bellowed, 'Who the fuck is it?'

'Kowalski.'

The door opened. Begley stood there naked, apart from a towel around his waist. He held his service revolver down by his side. A poodle yapped maniacally at his feet. He took one look at the crowd assembled on his doorstep and said, 'Christ on a fucking bike.'

Chapter Sixty-nine
Sunday, 17th November

Half an hour later they sat on rickety camp chairs around a table-tennis table in the garage under Begley's house. He had refused to let what he described as 'riff-raff' into his home at one o'clock in the morning when his wife and dogs were trying to sleep. The garage smelled of motor oil and mildew. A fluorescent light flickered. Mosquitoes buzzed Jack's ears and feasted on his ankles. Geckos ran across the ceiling and occasionally shat from high above. Dogs started yapping upstairs. Nice.

Jack was weary, and his body was at him from all directions. Over the last few days he'd been battered, bruised, stitched, squeezed and grazed. He pushed all of that aside, so caught up as he was in the excitement of the imminent reveal. At the same time, he was anxious. How would they make sense of the thousands of source documents Patrick had gathered? Patrick would have had months or even years to pull all this together and find the truth.

They divided the monumental task. Jack had Northern Rivers Shire Council, Caitlin everything legal, Zoe the money trail and Kowalski the Jetty Hotel. Ricky had carte blanche with the laptop and was on a deep dive through all the files they hadn't had time to print.

Begley wasn't assigned any task but seemed on a mission to

make himself as irritating as possible. Not for the first time, Jack wanted to deck him. Begley had swapped his towel for a brown dressing gown, tied loosely at the waist and threatening to reveal all every time he moved. He moaned constantly about losing sleep as he wandered around the table, licking his thumb to flick through random documents, which he abandoned anywhere but where he found them. His mood was infectious. Two hours later they were all exhausted and demoralised.

Begley's wife came downstairs, wrapped tightly in a fluffy pink dressing gown, her lips pursed. 'Ken, are you ever coming to bed?' Her sleepy eyes slowly focused on the small crowd not normally found among all the usual junk in the garage. 'Who are all these people?'

'Honey, this motley bunch are trying to save us from being transferred to Broken Hill.'

Without a word, she walked out. Ten minutes later, she returned with a steaming coffee plunger, a pot of tea, and two packets of Tim Tams, one of which was devoured before the coffee was poured.

Between sips of tea, Zoe said, 'It's so confusing. There are hundreds of bank statements for six different account holders. Five of them Bradshaws, including Tom and his wife, Julie. The others are in the names of ...' Zoe paused for effect. 'Benji, Bilbo and Bandit.'

'So,' said Begley, as he scratched at his groin through his dressing gown, 'even his fucking dogs were avoiding tax.'

'Ken. Language.' Veronica Begley had pulled up a chair and was drinking tea.

'The accounts are in Deutsche Marks,' said Zoe. 'For years there were regular monthly deposits of ten grand into each account.'

Ricky's fingers skimmed over the keyboard in a blur. 'That's about three million dollars a year in today's money.'

Jack asked, 'And whose was the sixth account, Zoe?'

She hesitated before answering, and so Jack answered for her. 'My father?'

She nodded. 'Twenty thousand every month.'

Jack was the only one in the room who knew Don had provided some forged documents to Patrick. Jack assumed, and hoped, those account statements in his father's name were some of them. After all, Patrick had approached Don for evidence of his father's involvement. But for Caitlin's sake he also hoped that Don's forgeries weren't so extensive as to undermine all of Patrick's work and render it useless.

Caitlin said, 'My pile is impossible. Lots of interlinked shelf companies with obscure ownerships. I'm not even sure the ATO and its forensic accountants could work it out, but I guess that's the whole point.'

Jack felt frustrated that he hadn't turned up anything useful. He stood, stretched and took a few steps, standing on a ping-pong ball. He looked at Caitlin. 'Your father had years to make sense of all this. How can we possibly do it in a few hours? It's hopeless. Perhaps we should all get some sleep and start fresh in the daylight?' Although as soon as he said it, Jack remembered he'd be a wanted man in the morning.

Caitlin shot up from her chair so quickly it toppled backwards and clattered to the floor. When she spoke, her face was flushed. 'Why don't you just do that, Jack? Go and get your beauty sleep, it's not as though you don't need it. I'll go through your documents as well.'

'I'm with Jack,' said Ricky. 'You're wasting your time reading all that shit.'

Caitlin turned her withering look on Ricky.

Ricky smiled at her. 'Why don't you just read what your father wrote?' He turned the laptop towards them. 'The missing edition of *The Beacon* is here, ready for the printers.'

Caitlin almost knocked Zoe over in her rush to get to laptop. She tore it from Ricky's hands. On the screen was a fully laid-out copy of *The Beacon: Special Corruption Edition.* Caitlin grinned wildly. She put down the laptop dashed over to Ricky and smacked him with a high five.

Jack was caught up in her elation. But the thought of her deflation when he told her about the forgeries was like a growing constriction in his throat. He should tell her now. He scanned the headlines as Caitlin scrolled through the newspaper. *'Mayor Bradshaw, Tax Cheat', 'Corruption in Council', 'Bradshaw Hides Money Offshore to Avoid Tax', 'Malcolm Harris, Silent Partner in Jetty Hotel',* and *'Harris and Bradshaw Interfere with Election'.* Images of bank statements and deeds were dotted through the pages. Jack wondered how much of it was true.

Caitlin returned to the front page. *'Bradshaw and Harris: Did they kill Mayor Ferris?'* A photo of George Ferris, adorned in mayoral regalia, smiled at them.

'Oh my God,' said Caitlin. 'I can't believe Dad did all this by himself.' She took a wavering breath and her eyes teared up again.

'Read that out,' said Jack.

Ricky pulled the laptop closer. 'It's long.'

'Then just tell us the most important parts.'

'"The Mayor of Northern Rivers Shire in 1987, George Ferris, allegedly drowned while swimming off Main Beach on April 2nd that year. His body was never found and the coroner's finding was 'missing, presumed drowned'."'

There was a pause as Ricky scrolled down.

"'This newspaper has no incontrovertible evidence that Malcolm Harris and the current mayor Tom Bradshaw did murder George Ferris. But we do have evidence they interfered with an election, were involved in corrupt conduct with councillors, that they materially benefited from George Ferris's death by millions of dollars, and that they were involved in widespread tax evasion ...'"

Jack felt the constriction in his throat tightening. Was his father really involved? Or did Don stitch him up in exchange for information that he later used to blackmail Tom Bradshaw?

Ricky continued reading. "'This newspaper, then under the editorship of Malcolm Harris, falsely reported multiple witnesses as having seen the mayor enter the water, whereas the official police report states there were no such witnesses.'"

Caitlin glanced at Jack, and he could see the pride in those green eyes.

Ricky kept reading. "'In 1987, Council rejected, by two votes, a rezoning application that would have allowed the development of the Jetty Hotel. Mayor Ferris and another councillor, David Naughton, voted against. Before a council election three months later, this newspaper slandered both these councillors. Naughton was not re-elected following false accusations of domestic violence. He was replaced by Frank Cameron, later to be the beneficiary of free drinks for life at the Jetty Hotel. Mayor Ferris was surprisingly re-elected, despite fictitious claims of animal cruelty.'"

Ricky clicked to the next page. There was total silence in the room. Except from Mrs Begley, her head resting on the table, snoring.

"'After the election, Ferris again voted against the rezoning application. He disappeared a few days later. Ian Bradshaw was later elected to replace Ferris as mayor and the rezoning was approved at the next meeting.'"

Caitlin reached for the laptop and scanned through the remaining pages of the special edition. She looked up at Jack, her faced determined. 'If they killed the mayor, then they killed Dad to cover it up. We need to publish this as soon as we can. And before more bad things happen.'

Kowalski asked, 'When's the deadline for *The Beacon*?'

Caitlin paused for thought. 'Oh, Jesus, it's today at 9 a.m. I can upload it.'

Jack felt his constriction continuing to tighten.

Caitlin was busy at the laptop keyboard. 'Shit, Angus Bain must have changed the password.' She slammed the laptop closed and shoved it away.

'Who's Angus Bain?' asked Ricky.

Jack said, 'My father's go-to shit-stirring journalist. Not my favourite human. He's the new editor of *The Beacon*.'

Caitlin said, 'We have to find a way to publish Dad's special edition. He died for it. It's his legacy.'

Jack couldn't put it off any longer. 'We're not publishing anything.'

Caitlin frowned. 'What the hell do you mean?'

'We need to do some more due diligence before we publish.'

'Why? It's all here, ready to go.'

There was an uncomfortable silence as Jack steeled himself to break the bad news. 'I'm sorry, Caitlin. Some of the documents your father based his story on are forgeries.'

'What?'

They listened in shocked silence as Jack detailed everything his father had made him promise not to disclose – about Don providing fake bank documents to extract information from Patrick, which was then used to blackmail Tom Bradshaw.

Nobody spoke for a long time.

Caitlin broke the silence. 'Bullshit. Dad was meticulous and would have verified everything. He wouldn't have been murdered if it wasn't true. You have to publish, or Dad would have died for nothing. And the bastards will get away with it.'

She glared at Jack, and it was he who broke their gaze.

Only one of their fathers was telling the truth. Jack's father's version seemed the most credible. Don *had* disappeared. Tom Bradshaw *had* confirmed on the phone he was being blackmailed. It was hard to conceive how Patrick could have got access to hundreds of ancient overseas bank statements – unless they were forged.

And yet Patrick was accusing Jack's father of being a murderer. If that was true, his father would want to keep that hidden. And Patrick was a seriously good journalist. The Harris Media empire did seem to have grown impossibly quickly from its roots in a tiny regional newspaper. If his father was lying about everything, he might also be lying about the concrete slab.

Jack said, 'Without any evidence, my father's lawyers will tear us apart. If we publish, I'll never work in newspapers again and my father will make sure that you, Caitlin, will never work as a lawyer. We can't publish until we have hard evidence that Tom Bradshaw and my father did murder Mayor Ferris.'

Caitlin was livid. He'd seen her angry, but her face had never been this red.

'And how, Mr Morally-up-himself Journalist, are we supposed to find hard evidence? George Ferris died in 1987,' she said.

'By finding his body.'

'C'mon Jack, be serious,' said Caitlin. 'How are we supposed to find his body when it was so long ago?'

'Because,' said Jack, 'if my father killed him, I know where he's buried.'

Ricky stopped typing. Veronica Begley's snoring stopped with a snort, and she lifted her head from the table. Begley raised his eyebrows and his dressing gown gaped threateningly.

Jack could clearly conjure in his mind the impressions of his tiny three-year-old feet preserved for posterity in the slab of the garden shed, and the date gouged into the concrete: 03.04.87.

He said, 'My father laid a concrete slab at our house the day after George Ferris disappeared. It might be a coincidence, a very big coincidence, but if the body of Ferris is in the slab, we can publish with impunity.'

Everybody was staring at him wide-eyed.

Jack was insistent. 'But we can't publish before we know.'

Caitlin said, 'But then we'll miss the deadline.'

A rustling broke the silence as Ricky took the last Tim Tam. He looked at Jack. There was chocolate on his teeth when he spoke. 'I do hope you were using a condom, Jack.'

'What?'

'Angus Bain's new password was easy to crack. He's already uploaded this week's edition of *The Beacon* to the printer. His edition. And he's doing a proper hatchet job on you, Jacko. Oooh, yeh.'

Ricky turned the laptop around. Bain was running a full-size colour photograph on the front page of *The Beacon* – an image Jack had been certain he'd seen the last of. He groaned and closed his eyes – even then he couldn't erase the image from his mind. He was standing completely naked in Bob Holmes' house, appearing to be entering Elanna the sex worker from behind. Her face and breasts had been obscured with black rectangles, but Jack had not been given the same courtesy. The headline shouted: '*Jack Harris: Criminal Casanova?*' Page two was almost frivolous in comparison – a photograph of Jack using a coat hanger to break into *The Beacon*'s Toyota. The two large black eyes of Bruce Two stared at them from page three.

Jack dropped his head into his hands. Angus fucking Bain.

'So,' said Ricky. 'As I see it, Jacko, you've two options. I can replace Bain's edition of *The Beacon* now with Patrick's cracking exposé edition, but if you don't find George Ferris's body, you're screwed. Or we can let Bain publish his edition, and you're still screwed. It all comes down to whether there is a body ...'

Jack could feel blood vessels throbbing at his temple as he weighed up which of the shitty choices was the least calamitous. He stood and, as he started pacing, another ping-pong ball died beneath his feet.

'Jack, you can trust Dad,' said Caitlin.

Ricky smiled at Jack and repeatedly pretended to push a key on the laptop. 'No pressure or anything. Besides, if you publish and you're wrong, you can blame the current editor of *The Beacon*. Angus Bain. Sweet.'

Light was seeping around the garage door. Mrs Begley rubbed her eyes. Jack was hungry, tired, emotionally overwrought and his bladder was bursting. He was in no fit state to make such a consequential decision.

He nodded to Ricky. 'We go with Patrick's version.'

Caitlin beamed at him. Then, to Jack's surprise, she hurried over and wrapped her arms around him. He held her tightly and surrendered himself into the embrace. He drank in the smell of her, felt her dreadlocks against his arms, the warmth of her body pressed up against his. He would have held her forever, but she broke away.

'Wait!' yelled Caitlin. She grabbed the laptop back.

Jack watched her insert 'By Patrick O'Shaughnessy' as a by-line under every article.

'How long have I got?' she then asked.

Ricky checked his watch. 'Half an hour.'

Caitlin deleted the entire back-page story about the Bangalow Rebels flogging Byron Bay Rugby Club, then typed the headline: *'Patrick O'Shaughnessy. 1965–2019. RIP.'* She inserted a photo of Patrick grinning mischievously, then furiously typed an obituary as tears flowed freely down both her face and Zoe's.

After she finished, Ricky replaced Angus Bain's edition with theirs. It was ten minutes to nine.

Chapter Seventy

Dogs barked. Caitlin hugged Zoe. Ricky hugged Jack. Begley hugged his wife. When they separated, Begley's dressing gown slipped open to reveal the hairiest torso Jack had ever seen. And other things he would like to unsee. Kowalski studied his boots until his boss's modesty was restored.

They made plans. Ricky was to email a digital copy of *The Beacon* to 'everybody, including God'. Zoe and Caitlin were to drive to *The Beacon*'s printers to make sure they printed the correct edition – theirs not Bain's. They were also to double the print run and return with the first copies off the press.

Kowalski said, 'I'll go to the station to put out a watch for the black van and start the search for Don Hargreaves.'

Begley, Ricky and Jack were to go to the old house and break up the concrete slab in the hope of finding George Ferris's body.

Jack took another burner phone from Ricky, called Tony and arranged to meet him with a jackhammer at the old garden shed.

Begley refused to let Jack upstairs to use the bathroom, but went himself for a shower. Veronica Begley, still in her fluffy pink gown, looked the brightest of them all; she'd had a good six hours' sleep, even though her pillow had been a ping-pong table.

Given no choice, Jack stepped outside and pissed on the Begleys' petunias. It felt fabulous.

As soon as he climbed into the Land Rover, Jack regretted

Begley's insistence they travel together. The car reeked of fish, a smell so ingrained it didn't diminish even as they drove at speed to Seven Mile Beach with the windows wound down and Begley smoking a cigarette.

'So,' said Jack. 'A promotion eh? Broken Hill?'

Begley's face flamed red. The thousands of hairs on his neck stood to attention. 'Don't fucking start me. The assistant commissioner caught Kowalski returning the George Ferris file you bloody asked for and Kowalski had no choice but to finger me. I start there next week. One more year and I could have retired here. Just one year. Veronica is refusing to come. And she wants to keep Gizmo and Toto with her. And where are you supposed to fish in Broken Hill? The frozen fucking foods section, that's where.' He slammed the Land Rover into another gear. 'I'm hoping you can pull a fucking rabbit out of a hat here, or at least a body out of concrete. If I can solve an old case, maybe they'll let me stay.'

'I don't think we'll need the rabbit.'

'What do you mean?'

'Did you know my father asked for Assistant Commissioner Mitchell to oversee the investigation?'

Begley spun his head towards Jack. 'What?'

'And did you also know that the assistant commissioner and my father were at school together?'

Begley returned his attention to the road and resumed swerving around the larger potholes. 'So, if there's a body in the slab, the assistant commissioner is conspiring to interfere with an investigation?' Begley's whole face slowly transformed into a smile. 'Perhaps we could go fishing together sometime?'

Tony was waiting for them when Begley drove up onto the lawn behind the old house. He had already dismantled the garden shed, its wrinkly tin panels resting up against the wall of the garage and the gardening equipment it once held now scattered across the lawn. Ricky pulled up behind them in the Beamer. Dark storm clouds stretched from horizon to horizon in the south, pushing back the remnants of blue sky as they advanced with menace.

Jack stared at the exposed concrete. So much depended on whether they found poor George Ferris's body concealed inside. He felt sick with trepidation. That slab marked a fork in Jack's life that led in two completely different directions – both bad. Down one, his father was a murderer. His own father. The fallout would be massive, including for Jack himself. The other path was equally grim. His life as he knew it would be shut off to him: his father would disown and disinherit him. The endless court proceedings would stop only when his reputation was trashed, and he was bankrupt.

Jack's thoughts were dragged back to the present by Tony's voice. 'I'll do the first shift. Let's hope we can beat that rain.' He pulled on work gloves.

'Shouldn't the police do this?' asked Jack.

'Me?' asked Begley. 'No bloody way.' He grinned at Jack. 'I'll supervise.'

Tony donned a respirator, goggles and ear protection. When he started the jackhammer, the cacophony of noise assaulting their ears was so painful they all backed away. Clouds of dust drifted up from the slab and blanketed Tony in a ghostly grey. A few minutes later, he'd only removed a small corner section of the slab and he silenced the machine and lifted his respirator.

'We're going to be here for a while, Jack. The slab is four hundred mill thick. For a garden shed. It's ridiculous.'

Jack allowed himself a tiny sliver of hope. He'd heard of the mafia disposing of bodies like this, and there could be no other reason for a slab that thick.

Progress was slow. When Tony took a break forty minutes later, only the first quarter of the slab had been reduced to rubble.

Tony showed Jack how to use the tool. When he started it up, it felt as if his teeth were being shaken out of their sockets. As he smashed off chunk after chunk of concrete, he was willing a body to appear and yet at the same time hoping it wouldn't, hoping his father wasn't a murderer. As the slab progressively disintegrated, he moved closer to those tiny impressions of his feet made so long ago. He paused when he reached them. Was this symbolic? Was he about to destroy his past? And his future? He took a deep breath, and pulverised his footprints to dust.

By the time half the slab was gone, the barbed-wire laceration on Jack's thigh burned with pain. Concrete dust caked the wound and the stitches. That can't be good, he thought. If he didn't need antibiotics before, he definitely would now.

Jack was grateful to return the jackhammer to Tony who effortlessly resumed his next shift. Ricky had retreated to the Beamer, where he was taking a nap, his feet up on the dash. Begley sat in his Land Rover, working his way through a packet of cigarettes. By the time Tony stopped half an hour later, only a small portion of the slab remained. The rain was starting to fall now, pissing on Jack's parade. But he now knew there would be no parade. It really was a coincidence the slab happened to be poured when George Ferris disappeared. His father hadn't killed Patrick O'Shaughnessy to stop him revealing Ferris's murder. Which only left Don. A man who Jack had known since he was a child. Don must have killed Patrick so he could blackmail Tom Bradshaw.

Jack knew his father, after reading the 'Special Corruption Edition' of *The Beacon*, would tear him to pieces, in person and in court. And he deserved it. He had broken the fundamental principle of journalism: verify, verify and verify again before publishing. And where did this leave Patrick O'Shaughnessy? In disgrace. Pariah, not Walkley – he'd been duped, and got the story wrong.

Time seemed to slow down as Jack broke up the remainder of the slab. The rain pelted his skin and turned the powdered concrete to grey sludge as the jackhammer bucked and twisted and slipped in his hands. At the end, there was no body in the slab. Just a pile of concrete and tangled reo. Jack dropped the jackhammer, threw his gloves and respirator to the ground and stood staring at the mess. He turned his face up into the pounding rain to wash away the dust, and his troubling thoughts, but those thoughts weren't going anywhere.

He wiped his eyes clean with his sleeve and opened them. A sodden silhouette traipsed slowly towards them from the old house; head bowed against the sheets of rain. The figure stopped a few metres in front of Jack and raised its head. Don. He looked terrible – one of his eyes was partially closed over by dark-red bruising that was already starting to turn black. Blood had congealed on a split lip. Don's usual confident demeanour had abandoned him, his eyes darting nervously.

'Have they gone?'

Jack watched him warily. 'Don, what the hell is going on?'

'Those two security thugs. They tried to lock me in a room, but I got away.' He glanced towards the old house. 'I've been hiding in there. Have they gone?'

Jack nodded, still guarded. 'Was it Tom Bradshaw who sent them?'

Don looked confused. 'Why?'

'Was Bradshaw trying to warn you off?'

'I have no idea what you are talking about.'

'My father told me that you murdered Patrick O'Shaughnessy so that you could blackmail Tom Bradshaw.'

There was a long silence before Don replied. 'It was your father who told me to get you drunk with whisky that night. And to tell Tony to switch off the video surveillance. It was your father's men, including that brute Fidel, staying down here at the old house the night Patrick died. And those two boofy security guards were your father's work. They beat me up. I wasn't blackmailing anybody.'

If Don was putting on a performance, it was a good one – which perhaps shouldn't be surprising given he had so much at stake. Jack's thoughts pursued each other in ever tightening circles. If Don was telling the truth, it must be his father who was lying. But if his father had organised Patrick's murder, it was surely to cover up dark deeds in the past – in particular the murder of George Ferris. And yet, there was no body in the slab. Jack wondered whether he had been watching too many mafia movies. The body had to be somewhere else. Jack stared at the pile of debris in front of him and realised his mistake.

Ricky had left the comfort of the Beamer and ran through the rain to join them. He looked perplexed. 'Why have you stopped?'

Jack pointed to the pile of rubble. 'We didn't find a body in the slab. I think it might be under it.'

Ricky said, 'My father always said, "Bury them once and bury them deep."'

Jack grabbed a shovel from the lawn and started digging, at first slowly and then faster and faster. When he paused to rest and take a few breaths, a feeling of unease crept over him – a sense of being watched. He looked around. A lone figure stood in the distance, watching him from where the path from the new house emerged out of the forest. His unease turned to dread, clawing at his stomach. His father. He must have heard the jackhammer. For many long seconds, they stared at each other across the lawn, until Jack found himself walking, slowly – his ever powerful father seeming to reel him in.

His father met him with a stony face. There was a long silence until Malcolm said in his gravelly voice, 'I told you there was nothing buried in that slab. And you didn't believe me.'

Jack couldn't look his father in the eye.

'I always hoped you would be the son to take over from me. But you've let me down. Family loyalty, Jack, was that too much to ask?'

Jack could feel the shovel, heavy in his hand.

'The world would have been yours, but you've thrown it away. I'm so disappointed in you, Jack. As would your mother be if she was still here.'

Jack bristled at the mention of his mother – his father had hardly been honourable in that regard, leaving her after a string of not-so-covert affairs. And where had been *his* family loyalty been? He hadn't even visited her on her death bed. Jack stared at his father, his rage rising, his grip tightening around the handle of the shovel. He coughed to clear his throat, and found his voice. 'You did say there was no body in the slab, but you didn't say anything about *under* the slab.'

His father's neck and face flamed red with anger, and he turned and strode quickly back along the path towards the new house.

Jack ran to the others and soon, fuelled by his rage and

a growing certainty, lumps of concrete were flying in all directions, some smashing through the asbestos wall of the garage. Tony and Ricky joined him and, when they'd cleared the slab debris, they started on the exposed mud. The muscles of Jack's shoulders and arms were burning with fatigue by the time their excavations were knee-deep. He stabbed the shovel into the soil for what felt like the thousandth time, only for it to strike something hard. The others heard the noise and stopped to watch. Jack involuntarily held his breath as he scraped back the mud. A bone of some sort. More scraping. A wrist joint. Skeletal fingers.

They stood together silently in the rain as they contemplated the grisly find.

Begley joined them from the Land Rover and stared into the hole. 'Shit.' He looked at Jack, and nodded in acknowledgement, before taking out his phone.

For Jack, there was no feeling of satisfaction at being right. Instead, he felt wretched and nauseous. His father was a killer.

Ricky placed a hand on his shoulder. 'I'm sorry.'

Jack knew his friend understood how he was feeling – it seemed both their fathers had been cut from the same murderous cloth.

The silence was interrupted by a slow thwack, thwack sound that became increasingly insistent. His father's helicopter. Jack threw down the shovel and ran for the path up to the new house, the sound of the chopper blades urging him on.

He was gasping for breath as he emerged from the forest onto the large expanse of lawn. The chopper was still on the helipad, its blades a blur. And there he was, his father, walking quickly across the lawn.

Jack knew if his father made it onto that helicopter, he would get away with murder. Two murders. Gold Coast Airport was a short, fifteen-minute ride and, once there, his father could wait at his leisure for the next international flight, or for his private plane to arrive and whisk him away to safety. There was no way Begley, or anyone, could organise an arrest warrant in time – the airport was in a different state, beyond the jurisdiction of the New South Wales Police.

Jack put his head down and raced toward the helicopter.

His father opened the door, climbed into the passenger seat and slammed the door closed. Then he saw Jack.

Jack still ran towards him, the sound of the rotor deafening. Malcolm Harris made a hurried gesture to the pilot to take off and the screeching cacophony over Jack's head became even louder.

Just before Jack reached it, the chopper started lifting slowly off the ground. He flung out his arm and grabbed for the cockpit's door handle, his father glaring at him from the other side of the plexiglass, lips taut, red-faced, furious. Jack reefed at the handle, but the door held fast as the chopper lifted away, Jack falling heavily to the ground in its wake.

He lay where he landed on the grass, his heart hammering in his chest. He closed his eyes and screamed in frustration, but the sound was lost in the roar of the helicopter overhead.

As the smell of the avgas faded, Jack sat where he had landed and watched in dismay as the chopper receded into the distance until it became a black dot, and then disappeared. He dragged himself to his feet, turned and trudged, head down, back along the path through the forest.

By the time Jack arrived back at the old house, two police squad cars had arrived. Constable Swift was cordoning off the area with crime-scene tape as another constable was speaking with Don. Kowalski snapped photos. Begley looked earnest, pacing backwards and forwards as he spoke into his phone.

Ricky and Tony looked at Jack expectantly when he joined them.

Jack shook his head. 'Gold Coast, I reckon, then the first flight overseas. He's going to get away with it.'

Ricky shook his head. 'Nobody is above the law, Jacko.' He smiled. 'Except perhaps my father.' With that, Ricky took out his phone, strolled away from them, and punched in a number.

Chapter Seventy-one

Jack, Caitlin, Ricky and Zoe were perched at the bar in the Jetty Hotel that evening as the low sun cast soft light over the pine trees, the beautiful people sitting in the park eating tofu, and the waves gently breaking. They'd all had a long day – waiting at the old house until the scene-of-crime officers arrived and exhumed the body and then spending hours being interviewed at the police station. At one point, as Kowalski was taking his statement, Jack heard Begley shouting and swearing in his office, then watched the assistant commissioner stride briskly along the corridor towards the exit. Humpty and Dumpty were in close pursuit. Jack guessed Begley would no longer have to eat frozen fish, alone and dogless, in Broken Hill, and was glad the inspector could retire in Byron Bay with his wife in peace.

Kowalski had told them the burned-out remains of the black van had been found a week ago in bushland on the northern outskirts of Sydney. He was confident the police would catch Fidel and his known accomplices.

As Jack and Caitlin were leaving the police station, Tom Bradshaw was brought in through a barrage of camera flashes. Jack couldn't catch his eye, but saw the fury in Caitlin's. If the press weren't there, Jack may have had to hold her back. As it was, she had to settle for spitting 'You bastard' at Bradshaw as he stumbled past, head down, a policewoman at each shoulder.

Jack wasn't sure if Tom Bradshaw was directly involved in Patrick's death, or George Ferris's, but it seemed highly likely. He was at least involved in the chain of events that led to those murders – including instigating the tax-avoidance scheme shared with Malcolm Harris. But there was one thing Jack was sure of, Tom Bradshaw wouldn't be re-elected as mayor of Northern Rivers Shire in a few weeks' time, his plan to 'develop a better Byron', and further enrich his pockets, in tatters.

Now, in the bar, the mood was mixed. Their drinks sat before them, untouched. Caitlin played with her straw. The adrenaline of the chase had subsided, and any satisfaction they may have had from solving two murders, and publishing Patrick's exposé, was tempered by their grief. Caitlin and Zoe had both lost Patrick. Jack's father was responsible for two murders – and for bringing shame on the Harris name, Jack's name.

Jack was jolted out of those first stirrings of self-pity when his eyes were drawn to a wall-mounted TV behind the bar showing a match replay of the Roosters flogging the Bunnies. He would normally have had no interest, but a breaking-news banner flashed red at the bottom of the screen: *Media magnate, Malcolm Harris, wanted for questioning over murders, flees to Singapore.* Before he could draw it to the attention of the others, he heard a loud, cheery voice behind him.

'Hello, old boy.'

Jack turned around to find Angus Bain, smiling, smugger than ever, glee oozing from his every pore.

For the first time in his life, Jack was able to say, 'I'm very pleased to see you, Angus.'

'Oh, believe me, the pleasure is mine. All mine. I'm expecting the first copies of this week's *Beacon* any minute. I think you'll find it interesting reading. It took a while, but revenge, old boy, really is as sweet as they say.'

The others had fallen quiet, and Jack could sense their eager anticipation. With a ceremonial flourish, Caitlin handed Jack a folded copy of *The Beacon*. The newspaper was so hot off the press that the cloying chemical smell of the drying ink wafted through the air.

'This,' Jack said, 'is a very impressive piece of journalism. You should be very proud of your first edition as editor.' Jack handed him the paper.

Bain looked confused as he unfolded it, read the headline, and began frantically flicking through the pages. His eyes widened as they flitted from story to story. 'This is complete bloody bullshit. You made this up.'

Jack pointed towards the TV screen. As Bain's eyes widened, Jack said, 'I'm not one to give careers advice, but I reckon lollipop man could be your calling. Although you're probably underqualified.'

Bain's mouth opened and closed but, for once in his life, no words came out. After one furious glance at Jack, he turned and rushed towards the exit.

Mark appeared with a tray of drinks. 'These puppies are on the house. And anything else you want.' He was beaming as he nodded towards the end of the bar. 'The grumpy old bastard hasn't been back.'

The 'Reserved' sign was gone, as was the hook for the oxygen cylinder, and Frank Cameron was nowhere to be seen. In his place sat the other ex-councillor, David Naughton, who for once had abandoned The Rails Hotel and was sitting in his nemesis's seat, looking delighted with himself.

On seeing Jack, Naughton raised a glass in salute and called out, 'I told you your father was a cunt.'

Mark pointed a remote control at the large TV mounted above the bar and said, 'There's something you should see.'

Channels flicked past, then stopped on ABC News 24. The screen was filled with the front page of the 'Special Corruption Edition' of *The Beacon*. The large photo of George Ferris in his mayoral regalia smiled at them from below the headline: '*Bradshaw and Harris: Did they kill Mayor Ferris?*' A succession of screenshots from the newspaper followed, interspersed with copies of bank statements and highlighted excerpts from legal papers. Ricky must have sent Patrick's whole document trove to the networks. Talking heads appeared, looking serious and pronouncing judgements.

Ricky gave Jack the thumbs up. 'We did it, mate.'

Zoe gave Caitlin a long hug. When Caitlin turned to Jack, she was smiling, even though her eyes were moist with tears. They really had done it.

Jack felt the elation of the others, but this was soon tempered by a deepening anger. Although his father had been outed, Jack knew justice would never be served. His father had escaped. Singapore had no extradition treaty with Australia. In the unlikely event the Singaporeans did choose to cooperate, his father's lawyers would tie up the process for years, making it impossible to get him back to Australia to stand trial. And Singapore might only be a stopover for his father en route to somewhere that never plays nice, happily harbouring double-murderers. And even if his father was deemed not to be a fit and proper person to be a company director, he would simply appoint Jack's stepbrother, the heir du jour, as Chairman and CEO and become a shadow director from some safe, extradition-free haven in Bahrain or Uruguay or Cape Verde. Business as usual, but without the skiing trips to Aspen.

His thoughts were interrupted by Caitlin calling him. 'Jack, Jack.' She shoved him on the shoulder and pointed to the TV.

A red banner stretched across the bottom of the screen: *Breaking news: Business magnate Malcolm Harris detained in Singapore*. The image showed a private jet parked on a runway, surrounded by vehicles with flashing blue and red lights. The TV was muted, but a white caption informed them: *Cocaine found in the personal luggage of Mr Harris*.

Jack's initial response was confusion. As far as he knew, his father had no need for drugs – he got all the kicks he needed wielding the immense power bestowed by his media empire. Then Jack realised. He glanced at his friend, whose face was giving nothing away as he watched the unfolding events on the screen. Jack smiled to himself – everybody needs a Ricky.

The TV feed cut to the inside of a police station where a man fleetingly looked towards the camera. Jack froze. It was his father – on display for the world's press. No navy suit. No silk tie. His usual commanding presence replaced by a shrunken-looking man in handcuffs and an orange jump suit.

Although he had rarely felt any fondness for his father, Jack was shocked and even felt sorry for the man. But his pity was fleeting as he remembered Patrick O'Shaughnessy and George Ferris. His father might have escaped punishment for a lot of the things he'd done, but at least he would go to prison in Singapore.

When the news item finished, Ricky turned to Jack, who raised his glass towards his friend. Ricky returned an almost imperceptible nod of acknowledgement.

Caitlin asked, 'Doesn't Singapore still execute people for drug offences?'

'Not for such a small amount,' Ricky responded. 'He mightn't even go to jail. But they will deport him.'

Caitlin smiled. 'Back to Australia?'

Ricky nodded.

She took a sip of her drink and then turned to Ricky, thoughtful. 'How do you know it was only a small amount of cocaine?'

Ricky didn't answer. An uncomfortable silence ensued until Jack interrupted it by suggesting they all move away from the bar and the TV, which was starting to recycle the same feeds.

They settled at a quiet table. Caitlin lifted her glass. 'To Patrick Liam O'Shaughnessy, my father.'

They all responded, 'To Patrick.'

And it was on. They ordered food, followed by a succession of drinks, and soon they had a mini wake.

Although they hadn't ordered dessert, Mark brought everyone a slice of the chef's special, fig and pistachio tart. Jack watched in surprise as Caitlin took a huge spoonful and swallowed.

She saw him staring at her and said, 'What?'

'You told me you were allergic to nuts.'

She smiled. 'Only because I was really annoyed with you at the time.'

'And are you still annoyed with me?'

She didn't answer, but her smile broadened as she reached for another mouthful.

Hours later, with Caitlin and Zoe having gone to their beds and the pub long closed, Jack and Ricky sat on a park bench in front of the hotel and stared out to sea, savouring the smell of the salt spray and of dope being smoked nearby. They each had a beer in hand, and a half-empty case at their feet. An 'Alcohol Prohibited' sign glared down at them disapprovingly.

Jack put an arm around his old friend. 'Thanks for coming up.'

Ricky tried to wave away the gratitude with an uncoordinated hand. 'What,' he asked, 'are you going to do now?'

'I think I'll probably take a piss.'

'No, no, no, not that. Are you going to stay here or come back to Melbourne and play with me? Jacko, I haven't had so much fun since we were at school.' His speech was interrupted by a large swig of beer. 'You, you know what I mean? Apart from the whole dead-body thing.'

Jack put down his empty bottle and started on a new one. 'It is awesome having the band back together, Ricky.'

'Well, it's your decision. But if you stay here, I might move up. My life is just so boring now.'

They drank in silence, listening to the rhythmic sounds of waves breaking onto sand and of a couple making out somewhere behind them.

Chapter Seventy-two
Monday, 18th November

Three hours later, the sun rose and proceeded to baste Jack through the front window of the Beamer. When he finally forced his eyes open and they adjusted to the blazing sunlight, he saw the seat beside him was empty. Then he heard what sounded like a chainsaw coming from the back seat, and found Ricky looking perfectly content, untroubled by his own snoring.

Jack went for the piss he should have had hours ago, followed by a long session at a water fountain. Neither his throbbing head nor his stiffness were helped by the sight of lycra-clad joggers energetically bounding past in all directions. He walked slowly down to the beach. It was a glorious morning. Surfers queued for waves; seagulls queued for scraps.

As he watched the wispy white clouds drifting across the sky, Jack wondered what his future might hold now that his father was a murderer. Then his thoughts drifted to Caitlin. It had been a tumultuous fortnight for both of them, especially for her. But during those horrible days he'd also met the first woman he felt completely at ease with. A woman who had absolutely no interest in the fortune he would no longer inherit. A woman who lived life to the full just in case Huntington's disease prevented a long life. And so he decided he didn't really care what his future held as long as his future, in some way, maybe a big way, included Caitlin.

Jack returned to the Beamer and interrupted the sleep of the dead just long enough to say goodbye to his old friend. Then he made plans for the day. They were fairly simple. Go home. Get changed. Find Caitlin. The first two went smoothly, the third not so much.

Two hours later, thanks to Tony and the Kingswood, Jack was knocking on Zoe's door showered, shaved and in fresh clothes. Nobody answered.

He couldn't call Caitlin; the burner phone Ricky had given him had none of his contacts. Nor did it have his Uber account, so Jack had to fall back on a maxi-taxi vomitorium to check her known haunts: her father's house, the Jetty Hotel (way too early) and *The Beacon* (Bain missing in action). No Caitlin.

He stopped by the GP surgery. Dr Belinda was still grumpy – even though she'd won the croquet final. She gave him a prescription for antibiotics. He went to the chemist.

Then it was another vomitorium: Zoe's apartment, Caitlin's father's house, Jetty Hotel (a bit early), a florist to buy flowers for Zoe, and finally Zoe's salon. No Caitlin – and she didn't answer Zoe's call. A big hug from Zoe.

He went back to the Jetty Hotel and enjoyed a few free drinks.

He found Caitlin just before sunset at The Pass lookout. He sensed her presence as he climbed the stairs, his anticipation increasing with each step. She was leaning on the rail and staring down at the surfers. The last of the sun's warm light accentuated the red of the dreadlocks draped over her shoulders. Betty Boop, basking in the last of the sunlight, smiled at him from beneath the sleeve of Caitlin's green top.

He fought the urge to wrap his arms around her and, instead, stood close by her side.

'Hi, Jack.'

'Are you okay?'

She nodded. 'Just talking to Dad.'

They stood together for a long time and watched the surfers bob in the water, her closeness like an electric charge.

'Bernstein called,' she said. 'They've offered me a partnership – presumably conditional upon me indemnifying them against any legal action, and signing a gag clause.'

'Caitlin, that's great, just what you wanted.'

'Yes. That was what I wanted. But now I'm not so sure.'

They watched in silence as the sun slid behind the distant range.

'It's a strange feeling now my parents are both no longer here,' she said. 'A feeling of being alone in the world. But I feel less alone here in Byron. I feel their presence in the house, and Dad's here. That's something.' She smiled weakly at him. 'And what about you? Will the great white knight gallop back to Melbourne to save the empire?'

'I think that depends on you.' He reached out and took her hand, and she didn't resist. It was warm and soft, and a shiver of excitement ran through him.

She turned to him. Her emerald eyes stared into his. Then she bowed her head. 'Jack, I couldn't do it to you. It's the Huntington's. I accept it is what it is – God knows I can't do anything about it, but I won't inflict it on you. I'm sorry.' She leaned forward and kissed him, slowly wrapping her arms around him.

Jack's world stopped.

And then she was gone, walking towards the stairs and away from him.

'Caitlin.'

Without turning, she said, 'Goodbye, Jack.'

'Caitlin. Tell Mr Huntington to go fuck himself. I'm willing to take the chance.'

She turned slowly and looked at him for what seemed an age. Then smiled. 'You're very sweet, Jack. But I couldn't ask that of anyone, even you.' She began moving away again.

'We can just take it slowly,' called Jack. 'Kick the can down the road and see what happens.'

She stopped, but didn't look back to him.

Jack held his breath.

She said nothing, but Jack saw her shoulders tremble. He went quickly to her, and rested a hand gently on her shoulder.

Without turning, she placed a hand on his, then said, 'You'll enjoy being back home in Melbourne. And you'll forget all about me.' This time there was no hesitation. She let go of his hand and set off down the stairs, and away.

He watched her go, even though every fibre of his body wanted to run after her. He remained at the lookout, never in his life feeling so alone, hoping Caitlin would change her mind and return to him.

He watched in vain as the silhouette of the distant range faded away and the stars began, one by one, to puncture the vast black sky.

He shook himself from his gloomy thoughts and made a promise to himself. With or without Caitlin, from now on, he would live his life to the full.

He ran down the stairs to the beach and stripped off his clothes. Then he ran into the sea, dived under a wave and felt the calming cool of the water. He turned over and floated on his back, then looked up, waiting. And there it was. The beam of the lighthouse sliced silently through the darkness high over his head.

Acknowledgements

I am particularly indebted to all the members of my writing group, The Dead Darlings Society: Deanna Antoniolli, Mary Chang, Dan Fallon, Karen Hollands, Kaja Holzheimer, Nikki Mottram, Nicky Peelgrane, Isabel Prior, Fiona Reilly, Fiona Robertson and Warren Ward. Thank you for teaching me to write, for your friendship, and for the joy of being in your company. I could never have written this book without you. I'd especially like to acknowledge Deanna Antoniolli for your transformational structural edit – your talent leaves me in awe.

The Byron Writers Festival has long supported up-and-coming writers and I was fortunate to be a recipient of a BWF Residential Mentorship in the Byron Hinterland. What's not to love about spending a week with other writers in a beautiful setting under the expert mentorship of Marele Day? There may even have been some writing between the Jameson and the Jarlsberg. The mentorship was a gift that keeps on giving, having spawned my other writing group, The Poncy Pricks: Lee Adendorff, Vivienne Pearson and John Stevens. I have enormous gratitude for your contribution to and enthusiasm for *The Beacon*. I do, however, owe you an apology – although we all committed to including the words 'lamb roast' in our novels, those words only managed to sneak into this acknowledgement. I promise I'll do better in the sequel.

Many subject matter experts generously endured repeated interrogations to ensure there was some semblance of fact as a basis to this fiction and I am grateful to all of you, including those who wished to remain anonymous.

I'd like to thank:

The wonderful volunteers at Marine Rescue Byron Bay and the lifesavers at Byron Bay Surf Life Saving Club for their advice and for their dedication to keeping everybody safe on the water.

Simon, for your comprehensive advice on correct police procedures. The many deviations from the actual I have included for fictional purposes are my doing alone. Your advice on incorrect police procedures was so entertaining some of it also found its way into these pages.

Oscar Dougherty for linguistic advice (the term 'tighty whities' will stay with me forever).

Yolunda Walker for advice on all things aquatic.

Catherine O'Donovan for always having a warm welcome when venturing north.

Justine Dwyer for your faith, encouragement and love.

Lauren Finger, this book is so much better thanks to your remarkable editing expertise. Who knew punctuation could be so much fun?

Lisa White, cover designer to the Gods.

Martin Shaw, my agent, for finding my book such a perfect home, and for your advice and support.

Special thanks to Juliet Rogers, Diana Hill and all at Echo Publishing. A small, wonderfully talented team who just love good books. Thanks for showering so much care and attention on *The Beacon*.

To my mother Judi, my brother Stuart and the rest of my

Australian and Irish families and friends for your love and for making this wild ride so enjoyable.

Joanne and Brenda, may you find a heavenly library that has this book.

To my darling daughters Rhiannon Evans and Louise Dougherty for your critical contributions to this novel. But mostly for being you, and the amazing, talented women you have become.

Finally, Miriam, not only for your immense contribution to the book, but for the limitless joy and love we share.